NEVER A GREATER NEED

She lay back on the bed, her golden hair fanned out against his pillows. "I should sleep in the hammock," she said. "I'm much smaller than you."

"I don't want you falling out of there and bumping your pretty head," he said. "Besides . . ."

He came to her and embraced her with strong arms, pulling her close to his bare chest. "Oh, Princess," he murmured. "You do not belong in a hammock. You belong here, in my arms, where I can hold you all night long."

She felt her face burn, but she reached up and flung her arms about his neck; when he held her like this, she felt safe, secure. And something else, too. A new feeling that was nearly overwhelming . . .

She closed her eyes and felt his lips meet hers, then descend to seek the hollow of her throat. His long, slender fingers slipped aside the fragile, silken straps of her gown so he could explore her satiny flesh.

"Princess," he whispered, and she could feel his warm breath against her shoulder. Her arms tightened around him.

They needed no more words . . . and the hammock swung behind them, empty . . .

TODAY'S HOTTEST READS
ARE TOMORROW'S SUPERSTARS

VICTORY'S WOMAN (4484, $4.50)
by Gretchen Genet
Andrew—the carefree soldier who sought glory on the battlefield
and returned a shattered man . . . Niall—the legandary frontiers-
man and a former Shawnee captive, tormented by his past . . .
Roger—the troubled youth, who would rise up to claim a shock-
ing legacy . . . and Clarice—the passionate beauty bound by one
man, and hopelessly in love with another. Set against the back-
drop of the American revolution, three men fight for their
heritage—and one woman is destined to change all their lives forever!

FORBIDDEN (4488, $4.99)
by Jo Beverley
While fleeing from her brothers, who are attempting to sell her
into a loveless marriage, Serena Riverton accepts a carriage ride
from a stranger—who is the handsomest man she has ever seen.
Lord Middlethorpe, himself, is actually contemplating marriage
to a dull daughter of the aristocracy, when he encounters the
breathtaking Serena. She arouses him as no woman ever has. And
after a night of thrilling intimacy—a forbidden liaison—Serena
must choose between a lady's place and a woman's passion!

WINDS OF DESTINY (4489, $4.99)
by Victoria Thompson
Becky Tate is a half-breed outcast—branded by her Comanche
heritage. Then she meets a rugged stranger who awakens her
heart to the magic and mystery of passion. Hiding a desperate
past, Texas Ranger Clint Masterson has ridden into cattle country
to bring peace to a divided land. But a greater battle rages inside
him when he dares to desire the beautiful Becky!

WILDEST HEART (4456, $4.99)
by Virginia Brown
Maggie Malone had come to cattle country to forge her future as
a healer. Now she was faced by Devon Conrad, an outlaw
wounded body and soul by his shadowy past . . . whose eyes
blazed with fury even as his burning caress sent her spiraling with
desire. They came together in a Texas town about to explode in sin
and scandal. Danger was their destiny—and there was nothing
they wouldn't dare for love!

*Available wherever paperbacks are sold, or order direct from the
Publisher. Send cover price plus 50¢ per copy for mailing and
handling to Penguin USA, P.O. Box 999, c/o Dept. 17109,
Bergenfield, NJ 07621. Residents of New York and Tennessee
must include sales tax. DO NOT SEND CASH.*

Wanda Owen

Sea Princess

ZEBRA BOOKS
KENSINGTON PUBLISHING CORP.

ZEBRA BOOKS are published by

Kensington Publishing Corp.
850 Third Avenue
New York, NY 10022

First Printing: August, 1995

Printed in the United States of America

This book is dedicated to Angelina, my little black-haired, dark-eyed granddaughter who has the free spirit and loving, generous heart of many of the heroines in my novels. I love you, Angie!

Part One

Stormy Monihan

One

Springtime was evident everywhere around the English countryside. The rolling hills were turning green and the first colorful flowers had burst forth.

A mild breeze blew from the coast; the long, harsh winter was over. No one was happier about that than Jason Hamilton—he'd been bored lingering on land for the last several weeks. Jason's passions were the sea and his ship.

In fact, he'd been readying his slick-lined schooner, the *Sea Princess,* for departure. He'd hired the last of the crew he needed to cross the Atlantic, and he'd been assigned a hefty cargo to deliver to the East Coast of the United States.

When he left the wharf at sunset that evening, he figured he might as well tell his parents about his plans to leave within a week.

He could expect his mother, Lady Sheila Hamilton, to be very upset when she heard the news. She was always admonishing him about his "vagabond ways," urging him to settle down with a pretty young wife like his friend, Bart, had done over a year ago.

"Jason, love, I'll be so old by the time you make me a grandmother I won't be able to enjoy the child," she'd say.

"Oh, Mother, you'll never grow old. There's still far

too much mischief in those black eyes," he'd reply playfully.

It was impossible for Sheila Hamilton to remain riled at Jason—he was such a happy-go-lucky young man. He had always said it was his mother's black Irish heritage that made him the way he was; his English father was the serious one of the family.

Sheila had to agree that Jason was nothing like her husband, Addison. Her black eyes and hair had been passed on to him, unlike her daughters. They had inherited Addison's fair hair and blue eyes.

When Jason arrived at their country estate just outside London, he went directly to his mother's sitting room. He decided he'd tell her first; his father would pose no problem.

With all his sisters married, the spacious house was very quiet in the afternoons. He'd expected that his mother would become very depressed and lonely but she surprised him.

She spent hours in her sitting room, attending to her greenery or reading books. She would soon spend hours in the lush gardens surrounding the gray-stoned mansion.

With a pleased smile, she put her needlepoint aside as she looked up to see Jason. "Well, I was just sitting here thinking about you and here you are."

"I hope they were good thoughts, Mother." He smiled as he sauntered over to the settee. Bending down, he planted an affectionate kiss on her cheek.

"Ah, Jason, love, thoughts of you are always very dear, as you well know. Come, sit down by your mother," she urged.

Jason did as she requested, glancing at the pillow cover she was fashioning. "And which of the girls will receive this?"

"Angela. I don't know what else to get her for her

birthday. Her husband showers her with so much. I decided to make her four pillows for the matching settees in her parlor."

"Well, I'm sure she'll be pleased. The colors arc beautiful," he said.

The very perceptive Sheila Hamilton immediately sensed that her son was attempting to prepare her for something. She'd played this scene with Jason all too often over the years. Her wandering son was about to tell her he was taking off in that schooner again. There were times when she wished that Addison's brother had not left the schooner to Jason.

Since then he had been constantly traveling to some faraway place. Always, in the back of her mind, there was a terrible dread that one day he wouldn't return; one day he'd be caught up in a storm that he couldn't survive.

Her black eyes pierced him with the look he knew so well. She was the one person Jason had never been able to lie to—she always saw right through him. "Where are you off to now, son? With spring right around the corner, I should have known you'd be getting in that boat."

"Can't fool you, can I?" He laughed as he reached over to give her a hug. "Well, I might as well be truthful. I'm leaving in about a week for Charleston, South Carolina, on the eastern coast of the States."

Sheila leaped up. "Oh, Lord, Jason! Your father and Sir Henry Burgley were having quite a discussion the other evening about what a powder keg it was over there right now. Oh, Jason, of all places!" She began to pace around the room.

"I've heard rumors of a war, Mother, but I'm not staying in Charleston that long," he said, trying to soothe her ruffled feathers.

"You don't have to be there long to get caught up in a ruckus, Jason."

"Well, I know this won't make you feel any better but I don't think it's due to happen for a while. I, too, have heard the rumors father has heard. I do think there will be a war but I'll be long gone before it starts."

Sheila knew that nothing she could say would sway Jason—for he was as stubborn and headstrong as she'd always been.

She sank down on the settee beside him and took his tanned hand in hers. "Oh, Jason—I wish you'd find a pretty little thing like Bart did and stay in England."

He patted her hand, his dark eyes glowing with warmth, "I just may do that someday. But Mother, you of all people know that girls like Tawny Blair don't come along too often. Bart was always the luckiest rascal."

Sheila nodded. She knew what he was trying to say. It was still a big disappointment that Tawny had not chosen Jason over Lord Bart Montgomery.

But Tawny had followed her heart and Sheila admired her for that. Long ago, Jason had come to terms with the fact that his best friend had won out where Tawny was concerned.

Later when he was in his bedroom preparing to bathe after working all day on his schooner, Jason thought about the time when he and Bart were vying for the heart of the beautiful Tawny. It had almost destroyed their lifelong friendship.

In the end, Bart was destined to win her. He was a man of the land, raising fine thoroughbreds. Jason knew that he would always be a man of the sea. Tawny hated his ship and his love of the sea so they never had a chance together. Jason was glad he hadn't tried to fool himself; a man could be beguiled by a young beauty like Tawny Blair.

He knew he was right when he visited Bart and Tawny and saw them with their two children. Jason was honored that they had named their firstborn son for him.

* * *

Some people might not have thought Kip Monihan a rich man but Kip thought he was very wealthy, considering his humble beginnings. He'd first arrived on the East Coast from Ireland at the age of eighteen with one worn valise and a few coins tucked in his pocket.

After he'd settled near Savannah, Georgia, he'd worked hard for seven years for Tim Clancy, the owner of a little steamboat that carried lumber to the port cities along the Georgia and South Carolina coastline. Georgia's forests were thick with timber, and young Kip Monihan proved to be a good worker.

Kip had always loved the sea and ships so he found the constant runs up and down the coast a pleasant way to make a living. He lived simply and after he'd saved his salary for four years, he bought a small plot of land in a little cove off Cape Fear. The little shanty seemed like a grand castle to Kip. He took great pride in fixing it up as often as his funds would allow.

He planted flowers and a large vegetable garden in the back of the little cottage. At twenty-four, he was a robust figure; the young ladies found the Irishman quite handsome.

A young miss named Molly attracted Kip and it was not long before he took her to his little cottage in the cove. They had been married only a month when Clancy was stricken by an ailment which forced him to move in with his son. He offered Kip the *East Wind* at an affordable price.

Kip was elated to find himself the owner of the *East Wind*—life could not have been better. He was the owner of a steamer doing a thriving business and he had a pretty, fair-haired wife with eyes as green as emeralds. His husky six-foot frame towered over her, making him feel very protective.

He was delighted that she liked to make the runs with him instead of staying back in the cottage where she could have been more comfortable.

"I'm lonely when you're not there, Kip," she confessed. That was all he had to hear to invite her to accompany him.

Kip's crew knew that they were to treat his wife with the utmost respect if they didn't want to find themselves tossed into the churning waters.

There were times when the couple enjoyed leisure time in their little cottage. They loved to work around the yard and the garden. Molly was just like Kip—it took very little to make her happy. Kip couldn't have been more delighted when, six months into the marriage, she told him she was expecting a baby.

"Molly, you've made me the happiest man in the world! I don't deserve you," he said as he took her in his arms and swung her around.

"You're the dearest, sweetest man in the world, Kip Monihan. I won't allow you to talk that way about yourself."

"Ah, Molly, my love—I'd be lost without you." He gently lowered her back to the ground as he remembered her condition.

Molly stayed at the cottage as Kip made a couple of runs—she was suffering spells of morning sickness. But that passed and to her husband's delight she joined him on the *East Wind* on his next jaunt.

The time went by swiftly and Kip had mixed emotions as her pregnancy advanced.

But she quickly soothed his apprehensions. "I'd be alone in that cottage, Kip. Far better that I'm on the *East Wind* with you here to help me."

He could not argue. Their cottage was isolated and she would be utterly helpless.

So he allowed her to go with him whenever she

wished. The night their baby decided to arrive, a sudden, fierce storm hit the coast of Georgia and Kip's boat was tossed about by the churning waters and furious winds.

Molly lay in the bunk, trying desperately to bring their baby into the world. She was glad she was with Kip, for the same storm would have been assaulting Cape Fear.

Kip Monihan was torn between trying to help his poor wife and keeping his boat afloat.

Kip's huge hands awkwardly helped him play the role of midwife at the midnight hour to bring his daughter into the world. Molly fell into an exhausted sleep and he gently pulled the covers over her as he secured the newborn babe in a makeshift bed he made out of a wooden drawer.

"Molly, I got to leave for a minute. You all right?"

Weakly, she urged him to attend to his boat. It was two hours before he was able to return, for two of his crew had been tossed overboard. Though they searched for hours, the men were never found.

The storm was subsiding, but when he opened the door to his cabin he found his daughter was screaming. He had only to look at Molly to know she was no longer with him or her newborn babe. Kip sank down by the bunk and gave way to deep sobs. His Molly was gone.

It was only when he'd shed all his tears that he left the cabin and headed for the galley to see about some milk.

Old Paddy was as overwhelmed as Kip when he heard what had happened. He concocted a primitive nursing bottle for the baby and accompanied Kip back to the cabin, where he took charge of the situation.

The screaming little cherub started sucking ravenously at the bottle Paddy held to her small mouth.

"Molly sure gave you an angel of a daughter, Kip. She looks like a little doll lying there," Paddy said as he looked down adoringly at Kip's baby.

"That she certainly did, Paddy, and I don't even know what she would have wished me to name her," he confessed. They'd spoken only of a boy's name, because Molly was so sure she was carrying a son.

"Well, you don't have to worry about that tonight, Kip, but under the circumstances had we better not pull into the harbor here in Savannah?"

"Yeah, guess so," Kip said aimlessly.

The next day Kip decided he would name his daughter Savannah. It had a pretty sound to it and it was right off the coast of Savannah that she'd decided to make her entrance.

"Think I'll call my little angel Savannah, Paddy. What do you think?"

"It's really pretty, Kip," Paddy replied. "Think Molly would like that, too."

17

Two

The pretty little blond-haired Savannah was never lacking for care aboard the *East Wind*. Kip became both father and mother and Paddy was her doting uncle. By the time she was toddling, all the hands kept an eagle eye on her for there were times when she would slip out of the cabin.

When she was four years old she was dubbed "Stormy" and Kip wasn't quite sure who had first called her that during one of her fierce temper tantrums. Somehow, it stuck and Kip found that he was also calling her Stormy instead of Savannah. She was truly a little firebrand.

Stormy didn't wear fancy, frilly dresses like other little girls. Her usual attire was little blue pants and shirts. By four, she had a generous head of blond ringlets that fell all the way to her shoulders.

She roamed around the boat, feeling quite at home. Once in awhile Kip left her with Marcie Warren, one of his men's wives, to make his runs up the coastline but Stormy didn't like being left behind and let Marcie know.

Thereafter, Kip didn't impose on Marcie too often unless there was a possibility of foul weather. Then, even Stormy's tantrums wouldn't cause him to relent. She was too precious to him. She was all he had left of Molly.

When he was faced with leaving Stormy the next

time, he took her into town; he had a few things to buy before he left port. While they were in the store, he told her to look around to see if there was something she might like. She turned down his offer of a pretty little doll. She loved the teddy bear that Paddy had given her when she was two, but fancy dolls didn't interest her.

By now her teddy was worn. Kip had mended the thing two or three times but she still slept with it every night.

When he had offered to buy her a wide-brimmed straw hat, she shook her curly head, declaring she wanted a cap like his.

"Stormy, that straw hat would shade your pretty face from the sun when we're out on the boat."

"But I like the sun, Pa. I want a hat like yours," she insisted stubbornly.

"Come on then," he said as he led her over to the young boys' clothes. He had grave doubts that he would find a hat small enough to fit her.

He checked several and found them all too big but his daughter just happened to pick one up that fit her perfectly. Giggling, she called out, "Look, Pa—I found one!"

Kip looked down at her with a broad grin—she already had it sitting saucily to the side of her head. Her green eyes were shining brightly and there was a smug look on her pert little face.

"Well, missy—let's you and me go pay for your cap, eh?"

She nodded and followed him over to the counter. Some little girls could not have dressed like Stormy and looked as cute; people were always telling Kip what a pretty child she was.

One day, he knew he was going to have to persuade

her to let him buy her a dress. Every little girl should have some pretty dresses, he thought.

Kip had done well during the four years since Molly had died. He gave all his energy to his daughter and his boat.

Some men no older than he might have considered taking themselves a wife to help raise a young daughter. That never entered Kip's mind. Besides, he had no time for courting. His little fair-haired Stormy was more than enough to handle.

Kip often thought about how different she was from his sweet, easygoing Molly. He mentioned that to Paddy late one night when Stormy was sleeping soundly in her bunk. The two of them were drinking a couple of whiskeys before they retired.

Paddy threw his head back and roared with laughter. "And you can't figure out where she gets her hot temper and stubborn ways, eh?"

"That's what I said, Paddy."

"Look in the mirror, bucko." Paddy grinned deviously as he took a last gulp.

A slow, crooked grin crossed Kip's bronzed face. "Forgot how long you'd known me, Paddy. You could be right after all. Guess I'll have to take the blame for that."

"As much like you as two peas in a pod, Kip. Well, since we've settled that I think I'll turn in and let you do the same. We'll be getting into Charleston tomorrow, I guess."

"I'm planning on it," he said as the two of them called it a night.

There were many talks Kip and Paddy would have about Stormy over the next years. Kip was apprehensive about failing Stormy as a father. She wasn't having a normal childhood and never saw children her own age.

But Paddy always seemed to have an answer that

eased Kip's uncertainty. He pointed out, and Kip knew it was true, that some kids' parents didn't love them as much as Stormy was loved.

"Stormy is surrounded by love constantly," Paddy said. "Maybe that's better than a so-called normal life."

"Hell, I guess you're right. I had a ma and a pa and lived in a house with sisters and brothers but I got the living daylights whipped out of me. My pa was a bully. That sure wasn't love."

"Yeah, and you left home at fifteen, didn't you?"

"And never went back."

"Then I think that answers that," Paddy grinned.

At ten, Stormy's body was trim and firm and she had long, golden tresses. She often wore her hair in braids to keep it from flying into her face.

She still refused the wide-brimmed hat that Kip wanted her to wear. And she still resented it when Kip left her at Marcie's to sail the hundred miles up the coast.

But she was now a little kinder to Marcie. She could not be hateful to a lady who was so nice to her. She never ate as well as when she was at Marcie's. She slept in the little back bedroom which Marcie always had ready for her arrival. There were always fresh, clean sheets on the bed. It was so wide she could sprawl out, unlike her narrow little bunk on the boat. The pink floral spread matched the ruffled curtains. Pink was Stormy's favorite color, as it had been her mother's.

There was always a platter piled with cookies when she was at Marcie's. To have Stormy at the house was a wonderful treat for Marcie since she and her husband had been married ten years and couldn't have children.

Marcie enjoyed Stormy immensely. They took walks and picked wildflowers, sometimes eating a picnic lunch in a shady spot. They would sit and enjoy Marcie's fried chicken—Stormy's favorite. During these outings, Stormy saw squirrels playfully scampering up and down the trees or she'd watch as the beautiful orange and black butterflies fluttered down to take nectar from wildflower blossoms. She was utterly fascinated by the colorful little hummingbirds also taking their fill.

"Aren't they darling, Marcie?" Stormy asked excitedly.

"I could watch them for hours," Marcie confessed. "But they'll be leaving soon, Stormy, to go back to Central America."

"Oh, no. But they will return?"

"Yes—come springtime they'll return," Marcie told her.

"Oh, good—I'll be looking for them. It's—it's been such fun, Marcie."

"I'm glad you've enjoyed it, Stormy. I always look forward to the time you spend with me. I get very lonely when Tom's away so I know how you feel."

Stormy felt compelled to tell Marcie she was sorry she'd been such a brat in the past. "I don't know how you put up with me—honestly!" she said.

"Oh, Stormy—you were never a brat. I always knew you weren't angry with me. You were just unhappy. We all express ourselves differently when we're unhappy," Marcie said.

On impulse, Stormy leaned forward and asked Marcie, "How old are you, Marcie?"

"I'm twenty-six."

"I hope I'm as smart as you are when I'm twenty-six," the ten-year-old declared.

"Oh, you'll probably be much smarter, Stormy."

Over the next five years, Marcie Warren finally got Stormy to dress up in a simple gathered skirt and a soft batiste blouse with a drawstring neckline. Marcie had picked out a pale pink material for the blouse, making the skirt from a brightly colored floral pattern.

Once Stormy had seen how fetching she looked in the two-piece outfit, she asked Kip to take her to the store to get some clothes.

Kip was delighted to see the miracle that Marcie had brought about and thanked her privately.

There were so many things to be grateful to Marcie Warren for over the next few years. It was to Marcie that a frantic Stormy came running, her green eyes filled with fear, to exclaim, "Marcie, I'm bleeding down here." She quickly went on to say that she hadn't fallen or otherwise injured herself.

Marcie was glad that Stormy was staying with her. "It's all right, Stormy. Don't worry, nothing is wrong." She sat Stormy down and explained exactly what was taking place in her young body. She also explained what it meant. "Once a month this will happen, Stormy. It's just a normal, natural thing that happens to all young ladies when they grow up."

"Doesn't seem fair that young men don't have to put up with it," Stormy grumbled.

As she taught Stormy how to attend to herself, Marcie tried to hide her amused smile.

She could see that Stormy was dazed. "Lord, I had no idea about all this, Marcie."

"I had wondered if Kip had spoken to you. Mothers usually handle the situation. I'm just glad it happened here instead of out on your pa's boat. It's a time when you need another woman."

Stormy had the stack of little pads in her hand and was ready to go to her bedroom. "Marcie, I don't know what I would have done without you over the years."

Her words almost brought tears to Marcie's eyes. "Thank you for saying that, Stormy. Now, you better get in there and attend to yourself so you won't soil that skirt, honey."

Stormy nodded and dashed into her room.

When the men returned to Cape Fear after their run, Stormy gave Marcie an affectionate hug goodbye. Kip was relieved that Stormy no longer resisted when he'd leave her with Marcie.

Marcie told Tom what had happened with Stormy. "She's no longer a child, Tom. Kip should be aware of this since she's constantly around men when she makes those runs."

"Don't fret, Marcie. I'll tell Kip," Tom assured his wife.

Stormy had not mentioned anything to Kip and he was unprepared for what Tom told him. "Well, you thank Marcie for me, Tom. I don't know what Stormy or I would have done without her."

"Kip—Marcie loves Stormy as she would a daughter if she'd been blessed with one. God knows if ever a woman should have had a child, Marcie should have. I've—I've always felt sad about the fact that I couldn't help that dream come true," he told Kip.

Kip found himself far more selective in hiring men for his boat than he had been.

From the day Tom told him about Stormy, Kip began to observe certain changes in his little daughter—who was not so little anymore. If it was obvious to him, it had to be noticeable to his men. The faded blue shirt had a different shape than it had had before. And she now had firm, well rounded hips.

Kip knew that the sight of her was enough to stir up a fever in any man. He seriously wondered if he should bring her on his boat anymore when there was no way he could watch her all the time.

For once Paddy couldn't give him any sage advice. He too was aware of the changes taking place in Stormy. It amazed him how she had changed so suddenly from that ten-year-old into a blossoming beauty. She had that same feisty walk she'd had as a toddler when she sashayed around the boat, but her sensuous movements began to have a different effect on the men. After all, they were only human. He saw how their eyes followed her every move and understood why Kip was troubled.

Stormy could always stay with Marcie part of the time; Kip's other option was to leave her at his cottage but that could prove dangerous for a pretty fifteen-year-old.

His friend Kip had a problem on his hands! A young lady as beautiful as Stormy could cause a father a lot of sleepless nights, and Paddy figured Kip was having a few lately!

Three

When Kip caught a glimpse of his daughter in the pretty dress Marcie had made for her as a gift for her fifteenth birthday. He didn't want to think about the sensation she would create aboard his boat wearing that instead of her usual garb.

Paddy considered his friend's dilemma. Kip could sell his boat and father and daughter could live out on Cape Fear. Then she would not be around a crew all the time, but Kip was realistic enough to know that to bring enough money in, he had to keep making his runs with the *East Wind*.

Also, Kip had known no other way of life for over twenty years and was getting a little too old to change careers. He had a daughter to support. There was no question about it—he had to work a few more years. He had to face the fact that if something happened to him, Stormy would have no one to turn to.

Kip and Stormy had spent a pleasant ten days in the cottage while he waited to make his next run. He had already made up his mind that when he left he would ask Marcie to look after her.

The night before he was due to leave, he waited until after dinner to say, "Gather up what you'll need for a few days, Stormy. I'm taking you to Marcie's in the morning. We're sailing at midday for Virginia. I'm not taking you this time 'cause there's a hurricane churning up the ocean."

To his relief, she put up no fuss at all. Maybe growing up was calming his Stormy or perhaps Marcie's quiet, refined ways were rubbing off on her. If that was so, Kip was glad. Marcie Warren was a fine young lady whom he greatly admired. He put her in the same class as his Molly.

Kip often saw brassy, bold women in port cities up and down the coast. They might attract the fellows who worked with him but he had no time for that sort. Molly had spoiled him long ago.

He was sure Tom Warren felt the same way with a sweet wife like Marcie. Tom always seemed completely devoted to her. Kip had never seen him playing around when he'd gone into any of the taverns to have a drink with his buddies.

He had lied to Stormy about the hurricane. He recalled the words of one of the seamen who'd just landed in Savannah whose ship had gone through a fierce storm in the Caribbean: "Could be hittin' you here in a few days or a week. Ain't goin' to be no hurricane, though."

Kip didn't worry about it. Many storms never made it to their coastline. They often fizzled or veered off to the west toward the Texas coastline.

The next morning, Kip and Tom left to join the rest of the crew in the Savannah harbor. Marcie and Stormy stood on the bank and waved goodbye to the two men.

When they arrived aboard the *East Wind,* Kip was greeted by a stranger who had obviously been waiting for him. The young, dark-haired man wasted no time introducing himself. "The name's Patrick Dorsey, sir, but everyone calls me Pat. I'm here to see you 'cause I was told you could use an able-bodied man."

There was a cockiness about him and a sparkle in

his bright blue eyes. He had an infectious smile and Kip found it impossible to dismiss the young man.

"And I wonder who told you I could use another man?" Kip inquired. He would wager it was Paddy. Pat had probably met him at some tavern in the city and Paddy had told him to come to the boat this morning.

"Ah, his name was Paddy and a nice fellow he is. I told him I was a man needing a job and I also wasn't afraid of hard work and long hours."

The young man had a way about him that Kip liked. He respected his straightforward manner and was honest with him. "I don't pay much until I know a man is worth his salt, Pat."

"I'm willing to go along with that and prove I'm worth your wages," Pat Dorsey shot back.

"Then if you want to go with me you better get your gear because we're leaving Southport in another hour."

Pat gave him a broad smile as he admitted he had all his belongings in the old valise he had with him. "I'm ready to go, sir, whenever you are."

"Well, Pat, I'll take you to the galley where my old friend Paddy will get you settled in while I attend to some things," Kip said.

A sly grin crept across Kip's face as he ushered Pat into Paddy's galley. "I'm leaving him in your good hands to get settled."

Kip went about his business smiling. Paddy always tried to run his life but Kip had to admit he wouldn't know what to do without the wiry little Irishman. They had shared deep heartaches and great joys throughout their friendship.

An hour later, the *East Wind* was plowing through the waters taking its northern route up the coastline toward Charleston and Wilmington. It was a longer run this time as they were going all the way to Norfolk, Virginia.

Kip went to the galley to chat with Paddy, who was already puttering around with his pots and pans to prepare the evening meal. Kip sauntered over to one of the old oak chairs and sat down. "Get young Pat settled in?"

"Did just that—I imagine you'd find him with the men. He's not a shy one—he likes to talk. The friendly sort, if you know what I mean."

"I've already gathered that, Paddy," Kip said as he got up to get a cup of coffee.

"He's sharp, Kip, sharp as a whip. Knew it after we'd talked a while last night. He's a young man who could take charge if he had to."

"We'll see, Paddy. I'll know by the time we get to Norfolk and back to Southport."

"You leave Stormy with Marcie?"

"Yes, she's with Marcie and, believe it or not, she didn't put up a fuss at all this time," Kip said with a grin.

"Are you trying to say that our little Stormy is calming down?"

"I wouldn't swear to that, Paddy, but I think she has changed a bit," Kip said as he prepared to leave the galley.

There was no question in Kip Monihan's mind about the likable young man he'd hired. Kip knew Pat was well worth his salt by the time they had made the run to Norfolk and were heading back. Old Paddy's instincts had been right on target.

Kip came to the conclusion that the bad storm he'd heard about was not coming in their direction. They had had very calm waters all the way to the Virginia coast city; pleasant weather was still with them as they headed south.

A brisk breeze blew in—the *East Wind* was moving at a fast pace, which pleased Kip whenever he was homeward bound. By the time darkness settled in, he went to his quarters to take a rest. Everything seemed to be going smoothly.

It was the sharp-eyed Pat Dorsey who sensed something he didn't quite like. The stars had suddenly disappeared from the night sky and the air had become oppressive.

Pat knew he was overstepping his bounds when he knocked on Captain Monihan's door but he had a gut feeling he couldn't shrug off.

He would have to take a dressing-down if he was wrong, but Pat would rather have faced that than not do what he felt he should.

"Sir, our weather is changing fast. I felt you should know. I smell a storm brewing—a big one."

Kip could not shrug Pat's words off but he found it hard to believe that things had changed so drastically since he'd come to his quarters earlier in the evening.

But young Pat was exactly right—Kip had only to walk around the deck and look up at the sky to know it. He was grateful to the young man for alerting him and he told him so.

"You see what I mean about the air, sir?"

"I do and I don't like it." What also troubled Kip was that they were fairly close to Wilmington, which meant that Southport was quite a bit farther south.

Pat's sharp eyes caught the first flashing streaks of lightning to the south. With every few minutes, it became closer and more fierce.

Kip did the only thing he could do: guide his boat closer to the coastline and keep heading southward in hopes of moving out of the path of the storm.

Some of the other captains of the much larger schooners must have been taking the same precautions as they gathered closer to the docks along with Kip's *East Wind.*

With a suddenness that even Kip and Pat had not expected, an angry wind came out of the blackness with such fury that they were both stunned for a second before they could react.

The larger schooners could take the assault much better than the *East Wind,* which was hit so hard it was rendered utterly helpless. The churning sea caused two of Kip's men to be thrown over the side. He heard yelling and rushed to that end of the boat.

"Who went overboard?" he asked the men frantically searching the waters.

"It was Mick and Tom," said one of his men.

Kip moaned when he heard that one of the men was Tom Warren. Then another furious wind smashed into his boat and he found himself slammed against something hard. The sharp pain in his back was enough to make him black out.

There was nothing left for Pat Dorsey except to take charge and he did just that as he screamed orders to two of the men to get Kip to his quarters. He was hurt bad and Pat knew it—he had seen Kip's huge body being flung to the deck.

Pat saw there was no hope of rescuing Mick or Tom. The winds began to subside, and he guided the *East Wind* toward the small docks in Southport.

It was well past midnight when Pat was finally able to see how Kip was. He just hoped he had done what Kip Monihan would have wanted him to do.

Paddy had scurried out of his galley as the fury was breaking, following the two fellows carrying Kip to his quarters.

Kip was coming out of his stupor as the men lowered him into his bunk. He was trying to assure his men that he was all right. He heard Paddy's familiar voice in the background saying, "Sure, you're all right, Kip. I'm here to make sure of that." He urged the two men to leave Kip's care to him.

"Lie still, Kip, while I check you over," Paddy said. He noticed Kip was trying to lie on his right side instead of his back. He had not seen how Kip got hurt so he asked him what happened.

"The boat lurched wildly and I landed on my left side," Kip said. Paddy started examining Kip's neck and shoulder, asking him what hurt.

"Go easy, Paddy," Kip cautioned.

It wasn't long before Paddy said, "Think you've probably broke the upper part of your arm, Kip. I'll whip up a sling until we can get you to the doctor. Good thing we're here in Southport."

Kip moaned from the pain in his left arm as well as the pain in his heart; he had to face dear Marcie with the news that her husband wasn't coming home.

God, he dreaded having to tell her that!

Four

When Paddy had Kip's arm resting in the sling he asked his friend, "You think you can be good and rest while I get my galley fired up? I know some fellows who'll need some hot coffee. I'll bring you a cup as soon as it's brewed."

"I'll be good, Paddy, if you'll add a touch of that brandy over there in the cabinet," Kip said, managing a weak grin.

A broad smile lit Paddy's face. "I had every intention of doing that without you telling me, bucko. Sorta planned to help myself to a wee bit, too."

With a chuckle, Paddy shuffled out the door. Kip lay there smiling. There was no one on the face of the earth like old Paddy.

Kip knew they'd made port somewhere—the boat was no longer in motion. The vicious storm had left the area. He thanked God for that. Now he had to worry about the damage to his boat. It had already cost two lives and was possibly laying him low for a while, so there could be others injured, too.

About the same time Paddy was entering his quarters with two steaming hot cups of brandy-laced coffee, there was a knock on the door. It was Pat Dorsey.

"How are you feeling, sir?"

"Not too bad, I guess. Paddy's coffee will make me feel much better. Help yourself to a cup and tell the men to do the same." Then Kip asked Pat if anyone else was injured.

"I'm happy to tell you the few injured have only minor injuries, sir. Since it's still dark, it's a little hard to give the boat a thorough going over. When daylight comes we'll be able to tell more about that but at least we're still afloat."

"Thank you for taking over and doing such a fine job. Looks like I might have to be letting you take charge for a few days until I find out about my left arm."

"I'll do it, sir. You think it's broken?"

"Paddy thinks so. I'll have to see what the doctor says."

"Well, we're in Southport, so thank God for that," Pat declared as he prepared to make his exit. "Think I'll go get me a cup of Paddy's coffee—the men will welcome the news that coffee's waiting for them."

After Pat had left, Paddy took a sip of his coffee. "He's a nice lad, I'm thinking, Kip. Glad to hear you tell him he might have to be taking over—you may have to let someone do just that."

Paddy was watching Kip's eyes—they seemed to be getting heavy. He asked Paddy what time it was and Paddy told him it was almost one-thirty.

"What about me dimming your lamp and you trying to get some sleep so we can get you to the doctor first thing in the morning, Kip?"

"Yeah, I'll try to do that. You go on to your galley, Paddy. Get some sleep yourself."

Paddy took his cup and left the cabin. He'd purposely put a generous dose of the brandy in Kip's coffee in hopes it would dull the pain so he could get some sleep. It seemed to have done just that.

It was almost two hours later that Paddy was finally able to close his galley. The men drank an awful lot of coffee that night.

The next morning the tall, lanky Dorsey went up to the livery to hire a buggy so they could get Kip Monihan to the doctor. An hour later as they were returning to the *East Wind* Kip told Paddy he'd missed his calling—he should have been a doctor. "You were right, Paddy. I'm going to be laid up for a while."

It had been Kip's plan to find out the extent of damage to the boat and see just how long it would be before he could sail on to his own home down on Cape Fear. Then there was the trip he had to make out to the Warrens' place to get Stormy and tell Marcie the sad news about Tom. He figured he would bring Stormy back to the *East Wind*—there was no reason they couldn't stay aboard while the repairs were being made. It was almost four in the afternoon by the time the men had carefully scrutinized the entire boat. It had stood up well in the storm and he was assured that the *East Wind* would be ready to travel southward in a week.

Young Dorsey took him in the buggy to the little cottage where Tom and Marcie Warren had lived since the day they'd been married.

Kip confessed to Dorsey, "Damn, this is going to be one of the hardest things I've ever done, Pat. Tom had been with me for over a dozen years and his dear wife has taken care of my daughter through the years. Don't know what I'd have done without Marcie."

"Don't envy you, sir. Didn't know him that long, as you know, but he seemed to be a real swell fellow." He had also noticed as they'd left town that the coastline had had a taste of the strong winds. He saw several trees blown down.

Kip seemed so preoccupied with his thoughts about facing Marcie Warren that Dorsey figured he hadn't noticed the damage, but it had not gone unnoticed by Kip. He was sending up a constant prayer that there had been no damage at Marcie's cottage where his beloved Stormy was last night.

It was a welcome sight when Kip saw that the little cottage looked as serene and peaceful as usual.

As their buggy pulled up at the little picket fence and stopped at the gate, Marcie and Stormy came ambling around the side of the house. Kip could see the radiant smile light up Stormy's face as she recognized him. But her expression changed when she saw a strange young man leap out of the buggy and rush around to assist him out of the buggy.

With a look of consternation, she dashed toward the gate to meet him. "Oh, Pa—Pa, what happened to you?"

Kip hugged her with his right arm and assured her he was all right. "I just broke my arm, honey, but that will heal before long."

It was the first time Stormy had ever seen her big, husky father injured. She could never recall him even being sick.

"I'll tell you all about it when we get inside, Stormy honey. In the meanwhile, I'd like you to meet Pat Dorsey. Pat, this is my daughter, Stormy."

It was a most unusual name for such a beautiful young lady, Pat thought as he looked down at her golden hair and flashing green eyes. God, she was so beautiful she took his breath away! The glib-tongued Dorsey rarely found himself at a loss for words but it took him a second to gather his wits and respond. "Nice to meet you, Stormy."

By now, Marcie Warren had joined them at the gate. Instinctively, she knew something was wrong for Kip to be coming here without Tom.

She saw the pained compassion in Kip's eyes as he introduced her to Pat Dorsey and suggested they go into the house.

She knew that the fierce, howling winds they'd had last night were surely more severe out in the waters.

Kip had known her too long to try to prolong the agony. He saw the look in her eyes—she was a very perceptive woman. He moved toward her so his one good arm could embrace her. "Oh, Marcie—we lost Tom and Mick last night."

He held her close as she looked up at him, saying nothing as the tears formed in her eyes. Strong though he was, there were tears in Kip Monihan's eyes, too. They moved over to her settee. For two people who loved Tom Warren as much as they did, there was no need for words.

Pat Dorsey sank down in a nearby chair but Stormy stood in stunned silence. She found it hard to believe that Tom was gone and would never return to his cottage.

It was the first time she'd been faced with the death of someone she really cared for. Since her own mother had died when she was born, she didn't even have a memory of her. But Tom Warren was someone she'd known all her life, so it was a stunning blow to hear that he was dead.

Finally Marcie picked up her apron and wiped her eyes. "Kip, let me get us a cup of coffee and then I want you to tell me what happened." Kip gave her a nod and looked over at Stormy to suggest that she help Marcie. Stormy immediately got up and followed Marcie into the kitchen.

An hour later, Kip had told Marcie about the night before and how very swiftly the storm had hit. "It will take about a week for the *East Wind* to be repaired but Stormy and I can stay aboard until we can get back to Cape Fear."

"Why don't you and Stormy stay here with me until you're ready to go on to Cape Fear. I—I would like your company," she said softly.

"Marcie, you don't need us barging in on you at a time like this," he replied.

"That's where you're wrong, Kip. I need you two very much right now. I'd like you to be here with me—really."

"Well, if you really want us to, Marcie," he said.

So Kip changed his plans and told Dorsey he could go back to the docks and take charge. "Marcie's got a buggy, so I'll have her bring me to the dock a week from today. Tell Paddy I'm going to be here for the next few days. Go ahead and turn the buggy back into the livery when you get back to town."

Dorsey rose out of the chair, said his goodbyes, and left to go back to Southport. All the way into town and to the livery, he thought about the gorgeous fair-haired girl he'd just met.

Every chance he got over the next three or four days, Pat Dorsey quizzed old Paddy about Stormy. Paddy laughed, "So you find that a strange name for a pretty colleen. Perhaps it is, but it fits her perfectly. Actually, her name is Savannah." He told Dorsey she was born just off the coast of Savannah one stormy night as the *East Wind* was returning from a run up the coast.

"Kip's wife died giving birth to Stormy that night and that little imp grew up right here on this boat making the runs with Kip from the day she was born. She was always a little spitfire. One of the fellows started calling her Stormy after she'd kicked him in the shin in a burst of temper. The name stuck after that."

Dorsey smiled, "But she's so tiny—she looks delicate."

Paddy threw back his head and laughed, "Oh, bucko—don't you ever figure Stormy to be delicate. Would you be in for a rude awakening. Don't put her to the test."

All the things Paddy said only whetted his interest all the more about Miss Stormy Monihan. It spurred him on to do everything he felt Kip was expecting when he put him in charge.

None of the men worked any longer hours than Pat did. As a result, the boat was in fine shape in five days instead of seven. That's the way Pat had planned it.

The men liked Pat Dorsey—he easily won their respect during those five days as he pitched in with his shirt removed and sweat running off his body just like the rest of them.

Paddy observed the fine camaraderie between Pat and the rest of the crew. Yet, there was never any doubt about who was in charge.

Paddy was convinced Kip had himself a good man in Pat Dorsey.

Kip Monihan was spoiled by the time he left Marcie Warren's cottage. Her good home cooking and pampering was enough to make him begin to wonder if it might not be nice to have a woman in his life again. It had been a long time since he'd had this kind of care and it had been a very pleasant time despite his arm, which gave him a lot of pain.

Marcie's cottage had a relaxed atmosphere he hadn't had around the boat. Paddy was a good enough cook but he didn't began to compare with Marcie Warren.

He was almost sorry to have to get in Marcie's buggy with Stormy to return to Southport and the *East Wind*. When they reached the wharf and were preparing to get out of the buggy, Stormy reached over to hug Marcie.

Kip also gave her a warm embrace. "Marcie, all you got to do is let me know if you need anything and I'll be there."

"I know, Kip, and that's a good feeling. I'll be all right—really I will. But that doesn't mean I don't want you and Stormy coming by as often as you can. Stormy, that back bedroom is yours as long and as often as you wish."

When they boarded the *East Wind,* Kip was delighted. Damn if the deck wasn't almost as clean as Marcie's kitchen floor!

Stormy made quite a sight as she strolled along with her father. She didn't have on her usual garb—she wore one of her full flowing skirts and a soft cotton blouse. She was wearing soft leather slippers instead of padding around as she often did in her bare feet.

Her hair flowed around her shoulders framing her lovely face, giving her a completely different look.

Kip would have had to be blind not to have noticed how all the men had stopped what they were doing to stare at his beautiful daughter.

Like the rest of the fellows, Pat Dorsey was savoring the sight of her but he lingered for a minute at the corner before he moved forward.

Finally he advanced to greet Kip and Stormy. "Good to have you back, sir."

"Good to be back, Pat. I'll be back to talk with you as soon as I get Stormy to the cabin," Kip replied. Kip gave his daughter a gentle nudge so he could get her to the cabin as soon as possible, but she lingered a moment to return Pat's friendly greeting.

He was observing the way the two of them were looking at one another. Pat was very good-looking, with his thick black hair and devilish eyes. Stormy seemed to think so, too.

The reaction from his men was enough to convince Kip that from now on he should leave Stormy with Marcie when he went out on his runs.

Five

Kip Monihan realized that all fathers with beautiful daughters had to experience what he was feeling. She'd been a handful when she was a baby and there were diapers to change and bottles to warm. Later, he'd had to help her in and out of her clothes. It had been quite a responsibility to have a child—more than he'd realized, he'd often said to Paddy.

Paddy had just laughed. "Well, you expected to have a wife to take care of all that. But you wait, bucko—you haven't seen anything yet. When our little golden-haired princess reaches about fourteen, you're going to lose sleep."

How right Paddy had been! Marcie Warren had been a godsend the last two years.

The next morning he was glad to see Stormy dressed in her old faded pants and loose shirt. She didn't look quite as fetching as she had in that fitted bodice.

As she usually did when she was aboard the boat, she gathered up the dishes to take them to the galley. She gave Paddy a warm embrace, saying, "Oh, Paddy— I'm glad you weren't injured and grateful Pa wasn't hurt any worse than he was. The time at Marcie's was good for him. She took very good care of him."

"How's she doing, honey?"

"She's doing fine, Paddy. Marcie's a strong woman. She's cried her tears and now she's ready to go on with her life. No, she'll be fine. I intend to spend time with her when Pa goes on his runs, Paddy. She helped me when I needed her so I'll be there to help her," Stormy declared.

"Well, she and Tom were always fine people to my way of thinking," Paddy said.

In her usual direct way, Stormy began to quiz Paddy about Pat Dorsey. "How come Pa hired him on? I thought he had a full crew."

"Good thing Kip did hire him on. He was just an extra man on this last run, but we could have used two or three Pat Dorseys, Stormy. When your pa got hurt, Dorsey took charge and did a damned good job."

"So it's lucky this Dorsey was there then," she said.

"Unless I've misjudged the young man, he's going to make a good, hardworking crewman on the *East Wind.*"

Her green eyes searched his wizened face. "So you like him?"

"Up to now, I sure do, honey."

She bounced abruptly out of the chair to announce she had to go shopping before they took off for Cape Fear. "Don't know when Pa will want to go down that way so I want to get some things before we head out. Marcie taught me how to sew, so I'm going to make me some pretty clothes while we're at Cape Fear."

"Has she now? You mean you're finally ready to shed those pants?" He grinned at her.

"I already have, Paddy, and I rather like dressing like a girl instead of a boy," she confessed.

There was a twinkle in Paddy's eyes as he told her, "Well, it was bound to happen sooner or later, young lady."

She laughed softly as she bade him farewell and left to tell her father what she planned to do.

She sashayed across the deck to where Kip was talking to Pat Dorsey.

"Morning, Pat," she said to Dorsey.

"Morning, Stormy," he replied.

When Stormy announced that she was going into town to do some shopping, Kip attempted to protest her going alone. Pat saw the green fire begin to flash in her lovely eyes and understood why they started calling her Stormy. She was a very independent little lady!

She told her father indignantly, "Pa, Marcie has been letting me take the buggy into Southport for over a year. I'm not a baby anymore! I know every store and the clerks even know me by now."

Kip had no inkling that Stormy had been given those liberties by Marcie for no one had mentioned it. He realized he still saw her as his baby daughter but she was certainly not that anymore. He was well aware of that!

"All right, Stormy, but be careful," he cautioned.

She smiled and started to walk away, hesitating to ask if there was anything he wanted her to pick up for him.

"Now that you've mentioned it, I could use some pipe tobacco, honey." Stormy gave him a nod as she prepared to leave the boat.

The first place she headed for was Gooden's General Store where Marcie bought all her material and sewing needs. She browsed around for over a half hour before she finally purchased some lovely challis to make herself a bottle green skirt and enough brown plaid to make a second one.

She couldn't resist buying one of the soft woollen shawls in a cream color—the only wrap she owned was an old blue jacket. That old jacket would look rather strange with a nice challis skirt.

But the thing that really held her attention was a lovely

dress in a brilliant shade of green with delicate lace edging around the scooped neckline and a long, flowing skirt. The fitted sleeves were also edged with lace. For the longest time Stormy stood there staring at it, then counted the money in the little leather pouch in her pants pocket.

The price was too high. Her practical side won out; she could have two skirts and a woolen shawl for what she would have had to pay for the dress.

So she paid for her purchases and left the store for the tobacco shop to buy tobacco for her father.

The tobacco shop was down the street from the general store, next door to a tavern. Had Kip remembered this, he would probably not have asked her to pick up the tobacco. In little port cities or towns like Southport, it didn't matter whether it was late at night, late afternoon, or late morning—there were always men roaming in and out of Tucker's Tavern.

Once Stormy had purchased the tobacco, she headed for the wharf. Just as she was about to emerge from the tobacco shop, she paused long enough to slip out of her leather slippers so she could walk back to the wharf in her bare feet.

She had taken only a couple of steps when she heard the sound of men's voices and laughter behind her. They had just come out of the tavern.

Just as quickly, she turned away from them—they were obviously drunk. She heard one of them say in a lusty voice, "Well now, isn't that the prettiest little thing you've ever seen? Think I got to steal myself a kiss from those lovely lips."

Before Stormy knew what was happening, she felt a vise-like grip around her waist as he whirled her around so he could kiss her as the two others laughed.

Three other men just happened to be ambling up the opposite end of the street and saw the bullies attacking Stormy.

"You take care of the two laughing baboons and I'll take on the one grabbing the little lady," the tall, black-haired man told his companions.

One mighty blow was enough to lay the two drunks low. Stormy suddenly found herself released as the ruffian was yanked away from her.

She had dropped her packages as she tried to fight him off. Everything happened so swiftly that Stormy found herself released from one man's arms only to find herself held in another's. She was looking up into the blackest eyes she had ever seen and a very handsome face.

The strange effect he had on her was enough to make her feel a sort of panic. The searing warmth of his arms stirred her in a way she'd never experienced before. As he kept holding her securely in his arms, he introduced himself but by now Stormy was agitated and confused. She yanked herself out of his encircling arms and threw her arm back to slam a mighty blow to his face. "I can fight my own battles, sir!"

A stunned Jason Hamilton stared into the most beautiful green eyes he'd ever seen. He'd hardly expected this reaction.

His black eyes scrutinized every inch of her as she picked up her packages.

An amused grin came slowly to his handsome face. "Surely I have the right to know the name of the pretty lady who just slapped me so hard that my ears are ringing."

"Good. I'll gladly tell you my name so you won't interfere with me again. The name is Stormy Monihan!"

She turned around quickly and moved at a feisty pace down the street. Jason watched her go as her bare feet took the fast-paced steps. He was taken back to yesteryear when he'd lost his heart to another girl—a barefoot girl from Virginia.

He'd taken his best friend to Virginia to buy a prized Arabian for his stables in England and it was on the Virginia farm that he'd first seen the barefoot Tawny Blair. But Bart had won her heart and married her

Jason's first mate and another member of his crew had witnessed the slapping their captain received from the little lady. They felt free to break into laughter when Jason turned around and began to laugh himself. "That was a little hellcat if I ever saw one."

His first mate voiced Jason's sentiments. "Ah, but the loveliest little spitfire, with those flashing green eyes."

All the way back to the wharf, Stormy felt a crazy kind of giddiness. The handsome face and black eyes kept flashing back as she walked along. She could not dismiss the way his arms felt for that brief moment. His name had etched itself in Stormy's mind—she found herself repeating it over and over as she walked on down the wharf.

Kip was a nervous wreck—she'd been gone for over two hours. In the meanwhile, he'd hired another man to replace Mick; there was no need to try to replace Tom—Pat Dorsey more than filled that void.

As he fretted in his cabin waiting for Stormy he saw no reason to delay the *East Wind* any longer. Pat could get them to his cottage out in the cove of Cape Fear and head for Savannah. There was a shipment of lumber waiting for the *East Wind* to take it up the coast.

A couple of times he'd paced to the galley to get a cup of coffee and talk with Paddy, who knew that his old friend was going to have to get over his overprotective attitude about his daughter. Things were changing quickly where Stormy was concerned.

Kip had wandered back on the deck of the boat about the time Stormy was approaching the wharf. He felt like a heavy load was lifted off his chest when he saw her.

An hour later, the *East Wind* was leaving Southport. It was only when they were on their way to Cape Fear that Kip realized that their little cottage could have suffered damage from the storm.

Kip's little cottage was spared any damage. Not one tree had been downed and for that he was glad—he was hardly in a position to tackle a downed tree.

It was a strange feeling to be turning his boat over to a young man he hadn't even known for two months, but he was doing it. He and Stormy said their goodbyes to Paddy as Dorsey saw them safely inside the cottage before he left to return to the boat.

He told Kip, "I'll do the very best I can, sir." He turned to go, taking the time to glance back at Stormy before he went on down the pathway.

Kip enjoyed the next week at the cottage with his daughter. More and more, he had to give Marcie credit for the young lady Stormy had become. He could not have done it alone. It amazed him all the things he learned about his daughter. She could read and write, so Marcie had been her tutor as well. She had also learned to sew and had stitched herself a lovely skirt to wear in the cold winter months.

Kip was ready to take charge of the *East Wind* by the time he'd stayed at his cottage for a week. Stormy could tell that he was itching for Dorsey to return by the time the weekend came around.

Two weeks away from the *East Wind* must have seemed like an eternity to him, Stormy realized. She never remembered him being away from his boat for that long.

So his announcement at dinner didn't come as any surprise when he told her he would be able to make the next run. He couldn't have been more pleased when she said, "Well, I'm going over to stay with Marcie while you make your run, Pa."

"Ah, honey, she'll welcome your company," he said with a smile. Having her at Marcie's took a big load off Kip's mind.

For the next few days, Stormy did a lot of cooking so she could use up the fresh vegetables they'd brought with them. She knew they'd be gone a week to ten days.

Along with teaching his daughter how to sew and read and write, Marcie had obviously given her lessons in cooking—Stormy had become much better at it.

Kip complimented her on the apple pie she'd baked that evening. "Between you and Marcie, a man can sure get spoiled. Paddy can't bake a pie like this."

"You better not tell him that."

"And don't you dare tell him I said that, you little imp!" he cautioned playfully.

Six

Kip couldn't believe the enormous meals his daughter was cooking for the two of them every night but she explained she was trying to use up the things in the pantry. "Two weeks from now they'd be spoiled, Pa."

"Lord, I didn't know we had so much," he admitted.

Stormy had her valise packed and had included the two long challis skirts she'd made for Marcie to look over to see if she'd done a good job.

Tonight she would slice up the last of the big shank of ham. Tomorrow she would use the ham bones for a pot of soup if they didn't leave.

Life out on the cove moved at a slow, leisurely pace. It didn't take much time for Stormy to put the cottage in order and cook their meals so she had plenty of time on her hands. Many afternoons, Kip sought the comfort of the hammock as he'd bask in the sun.

Stormy spent her leisure time daydreaming about two young men. She could not deny that she was attracted to Pat Dorsey and she knew he was definitely attracted to her. She was grateful to young Dorsey for helping her father—and Paddy seemed to have a high opinion of him, too.

But another handsome man haunted her dreams. She could not forget the look in his eyes or the feel of his arms. She liked being near him but her fierce Monihan pride forced her to put him in his place.

She'd never seen such a handsome man, but something told her that Jason Hamilton was only passing through. His manner and speech indicated that he was not from this part of the country, so she told herself she would probably never see him again.

She and Marcie had talked about everything and Marcie had told her how she felt the first time she met Tom. "My heart started pounding and I stammered and blushed. But Tom told me later that he was feeling the same way," Marcie confessed.

"So that's how it feels, Marcie?" the wide-eyed Stormy had asked.

Marcie had laughed, "Well, that's how it was when that old lovebug bit me."

"Well, I guess I haven't been bitten yet but at least I'll know the symptoms."

"I'm thinking you'll know them and very soon," Marcie said with a smile. She'd seen the changes taking place in Stormy in the last year and it amazed her how utterly beautiful she'd become. Stormy was always a pretty child but she had really blossomed now.

She shared Kip's apprehension about how wise it was for him to allow her on the *East Wind*. All men are human and Marcie knew Stormy was enough to tempt the soul of any man. Kip surely had to know that, too.

The sun was beginning to sink in the western sky. Kip always enjoyed taking a stroll at this time—with its churning waters and dense groves of trees, the cove was a serene setting. As he roamed out on the wooden dock, he was thinking about the time when he would grow old and Stormy would no longer be with him. This would be the ideal place for a man to enjoy the latter part of his life. He was also thinking how perfect it could be if Molly were only with him to share those days.

What happened next so startled Kip Monihan that he would never have told anyone, not even Paddy, but he knew it happened. He hadn't had one drop of his favorite whiskey.

A gentle breeze suddenly stirred through the branches of the tall pine and cypress trees. As he stood there he heard a soft, drawling whisper: "Mar-r-cie, Mar-r-cie."

What did it mean? Kip had never thought about Marcie Warren as anyone but Tom's wife and yet, she was everything he admired in a woman. She was very attractive, that he could not deny. So what was this strange thing? Being Irish, he couldn't just shrug it off—he sincerely believed it was a sort of prophecy.

He forgot about all that when he saw his boat coming into view—it was a wonderful sight. Stormy had been right—she had said Pat just might get here this evening.

Only Pat Dorsey and old Paddy were aboard—Pat had given the other men a couple of free days so he and Paddy could sail down to Cape Fear.

"Paddy told me you often did this after a run," Pat said to Kip.

"Hey, that's fine, Pat. You two come on up to the cottage. Stormy's got a fine meal cooking. I'll tell you, Paddy, she's become one hell of a cook. She's going to put you to shame," Kip teased his old friend.

The three of them laughed as they walked up the pathway to the house. Pat gave Kip the leather pouch filled with the money made from the run. "I paid off the men before we left, sir."

"That's just how I would have done it, Pat. I'll settle with you after we have ourselves a drink."

When they entered the neat little cottage and Stormy came dashing out of the kitchen to fling herself into

Paddy's outstretched arms, Pat Dorsey envied him. He wished it was his arms she was rushing into.

He stood with Kip and smiled until the two of them finally broke their embrace. She turned to greet Pat and her warm, friendly smile was a sort of reward. "I knew you'd arrive this evening," she said.

"Now how did you know that, Stormy?" Pat grinned.

"I just felt it in here," she said as she gestured to her heart.

Pat's blue eyes danced over her lovely face. He saw her as the enchantress all men dream about but never expect to meet. It's at night lying in the dark when a man can have wild fantasies about a little goddess with long, golden tresses.

Kip invited them to have a drink and Stormy left to tend to her supper.

An hour later they all congregated around the Monihan table enjoying Stormy's ham, sweet potatoes, and corn. By the time they'd all downed a generous serving of peach cobbler, they were feeling like they'd truly had a feast.

Pat Dorsey insisted on helping Stormy with the dishes and she accepted his offer. Paddy and Kip left the two young people in the kitchen and went into the small parlor to chat.

As Stormy washed the dishes, Pat dried them. He welcomed the brief time alone with her. "Stormy Monihan, you're not only beautiful but a magnificent cook," he said cheerfully.

"I wasn't always this good. Ask Pa. I tried making biscuits and they were so hard the birds wouldn't even eat them."

"Well, let's just say you've learned a lot since then."

"Marcie Warren can take credit for that. I've spent a lot of time with her over the years," Stormy said.

"Paddy told me. I didn't get to know Tom very well before all that happened."

When the dishes were all done and put away, Pat asked her if she'd like to go for a walk. "Looks like a nice night."

The two of them walked right through the parlor. Paddy and Kip were so engrossed in their conversation, they didn't even notice them.

Pat and Stormy exchanged glances and smiled. He said he had no doubt Kip would be leaving with them in the morning. "Your father is itching to get back to the *East Wind,* I think."

"Oh, I know it! Yes, we'll be leaving with you in the morning, but I'll be stopping over at Marcie's in Southport. I'm staying there while you make your next run."

Pat Dorsey was very much like Stormy—he gave way to his feelings. He tried to sound like he was jesting. "Now, I was looking forward to you going with us."

"Well, that's sweet of you, Pat, but Marcie is probably in need of a little company right now."

"I'm sure she is," he said, remembering that Paddy had told him that Marcie had been the closest thing to a mother that Stormy had ever known.

It was more than Dorsey had bargained for to be sitting here on the steps of the Monihan's cottage alone with Stormy.

Dappled moonlight came through the tall, thick branches of the trees and seemed to shine down directly on her golden hair. He reached out to take her hand and asked if she had rested enough to take a little stroll before they went back into the house.

"Oh, I'm rested, Pat," she said as they moved off the step.

Night birds sang their songs and the late summer flowers were in the last flush of bloom, sending a sweet fragrance around the little cottage. They strolled around

the house, where Pat gave way to the impulse to steal
one kiss. He never gave any thought to what he might
be risking, especially after all the things Paddy had told
him about Stormy.

He took one swift kiss and it didn't matter at that
moment what it might cost him. He couldn't resist since
he was walking so close to her and their bodies were
swaying and brushing against one another.

"Stormy, I could say I'm sorry but I'd be lying and
wouldn't do that to you. I've wanted to kiss you since
the first moment I laid eyes on you. You're the most
beautiful lady I've ever seen."

Stormy welcomed the darkness surrounding them for
she knew her face was flushed. She was stunned and
completely unprepared for Dorsey's boldness.

"I hope I didn't offend you, Stormy, but as I said
I'm not sorry I kissed you," he told her, wondering what
she was feeling as she sat quietly.

The truth was she didn't find what he'd done offen-
sive at all. Actually, she had rather liked the feel of
Pat's lips pressed against hers. But she wasn't about to
let Pat know how his kiss had affected her.

She tried to sound more casual than she was feeling.
"I'm not offended but I think we'd better start back
before Paddy and Pa come hunting for us."

Pat didn't argue—he remembered what Paddy had
told him about Stormy's firebrand temper. He'd have
liked to kiss her again, but he dared not press his luck.

He took her arm and they walked back toward the
house. Shortly after they arrived, he and Paddy went
back to the *East Wind* to turn in for the night. Kip and
Stormy retired, too, for they would be getting up early.

Dorsey had sweet dreams that night—he had actually
tasted the honeyed lips of Stormy Monihan. It was
damned well worth the chance he'd taken, even though
he could have riled her and gotten himself in big trouble

with Kip Monihan. Dorsey realized he'd have to be different around Stormy than he usually was with the ladies.

He would have wagered every penny he'd received from Kip this evening that Stormy was still a virgin. He'd like to be the man who first possessed her!

Seven

Stormy bade farewell to Paddy and Pat as she left the *East Wind* with her father. As soon as he had a brief conversation with Marcie Warren, he turned down the narrow pathway to join Paddy and Pat.

Stormy called out to him, "Take care, Pa."

"I will, Stormy, and you do the same. See you in about ten days, honey."

In a few short minutes the *East Wind* was headed south toward Savannah for the next load of lumber to be taken to Norfolk.

Stormy was beginning to look upon Marcie's as her second home. She went directly to the back room to get her valise unpacked.

She proudly rushed out to show Marcie the two skirts she'd made. Marcie inspected them carefully and told her what a fine job she'd done. "You're a good seamstress, Stormy."

"And I'm a darn good cook now, Pa thinks, and I have you to thank for all of it, Marcie."

"I don't deserve so much praise," Marcie declared, following Stormy back to the bedroom.

"Oh, yes, you do—and more," Stormy said as she continued unpacking her valise. As she busily laid her clothes on the bed, she told Marcie she was the closest thing to a mother she'd ever had. When she turned around she saw that Marcie was crying softly.

Stormy rushed to embrace her. "I didn't mean to make you cry."

"It—it just touched my heart to hear you say that, Stormy. These are happy tears, dear."

As usual when the two of them were together, they had spent an enjoyable day and evening before they retired. Sitting out on the step after the dishes were done, Stormy said, "I'm always coming over here when Pa goes off. And I'm going to insist when he gets back this time that you come to our cottage to spend some time, Marcie. It would be a nice change for you. There's no reason why you couldn't, is there?"

Marcie stammered, "Well, I—I suppose not, Stormy. I'd just never thought about it, I guess." Stormy realized that Marcie didn't have Tom's homecoming to look forward to anymore.

"Well, it's settled then," Stormy declared.

Marcie laughed, "We'd better discuss that with Kip first."

"Oh, he'd love it! My pa thinks you're one grand lady."

The feeling was mutual. Marcie had always thought Kip Monihan was a great fellow; she'd always admired his devotion to his daughter. She'd never known Molly as Tom had hired on the *East Wind* shortly after her death but she knew Molly had to have been a very fine woman. Marcie was certain Kip was as devoted to her as he was to his daughter.

During the time Stormy stayed with Marcie, they went into town and Marcie bought a lovely soft gold material to make Stormy a blouse to go with her new skirts. She also indulged herself by buying fabric for a new frock which Stormy encouraged her to do.

In the evenings they sat and sewed together. Stormy loved her new blouse. When Marcie tried on her dress for the final fitting, Stormy said, "Oh, you look so pretty in that color!"

"It's one of my favorite autumn colors. It reminds me of the russet colors in the woods when all the leaves start to turn."

"I don't think I could wear that color but it sure is flattering on you."

Marcie smiled at her. "Stormy, any color would be flattering on you."

When a week had gone by, Stormy told Marcie, "You'd better get busy putting some things in your valise so you'll be ready to go when Pa gets here. I've already started packing."

Marcie found herself reluctant to go along with Stormy's plans. It wasn't that she wouldn't enjoy a few days at their cottage. It was lovely out there in that wooded setting so near the waters' edge. Tom had told her how Kip could go out on the dock to catch fish for his supper any time he wanted to.

Marcie knew from all the things she'd heard about Molly that she took great pride in the little cottage where she and Kip had lived for such a brief time. She doubted that Kip had changed a thing in all the years she'd been gone.

To appease Stormy she went through the ritual of packing and even filled a couple of baskets with the fruit and fresh-picked vegetables her neighbor had brought.

The Hartmens, Marcie's neighbors, quickly agreed to feed her chickens and tend her mare for a week so she could get away. They knew what good friends the Monihans were to Marcie.

Without realizing it, Marcie found herself getting excited about boarding the *East Wind* to spend some time with Stormy and Kip.

On the tenth day, Stormy sensed that her father would

be arriving late that afternoon just as she had when she'd predicted the arrival of Pat Dorsey.

But at five in the afternoon Kip had not arrived and Marcie suggested that maybe she'd better get her cook-stove fired up. "It might be tomorrow before he gets back, honey," she said, trying to console Stormy.

"Don't start a fire yet, Marcie. I still think they'll be coming in soon."

Marcie knew there was no use arguing with Stormy, so she made no effort to go into her kitchen.

Some thirty minutes later the robust figure of Kip Monihan was standing just outside the door. With a broad grin, he greeted the two of them in Marcie's front room.

Stormy leaped out of the chair to fling herself into her pa's strong arms. He gave her a big hug and kiss, then looked over at Marcie with a warm smile.

"You ready to go home with your pa?" he laughed as he finally released her. "Think it's time we gave Marcie a rest."

Stormy looked up at him. "Marcie's going home with us. She could use a change. I'm always coming over here—it's time she spent some time at our house."

"You're right, Stormy. What a great idea. So are you two ladies ready to travel?"

Marcie had no qualms about going now that she'd seen Kip's reaction and knew that he genuinely welcomed her. In fact, he seemed very pleased.

A short time later she was aboard the *East Wind* with Kip and Stormy. She thought a lot about Tom, knowing he'd spent so many days and nights aboard this boat. She could almost feel his presence as the boat surged through the waters toward Cape Fear.

Stormy had gone down to the cabin, so Kip walked over to Marcie. He knew what she must be thinking as she stood looking out over the water. He took her arm with a warm smile and said, "I'm glad you're coming home with us, Marcie. Tom wouldn't want you to stay in the house all the time."

She gave him a nod. "I'm glad I came with you and Stormy, too. In fact, I have to confess I was rather excited about it. I've never been aboard the *East Wind* before. It's a fine boat, Kip."

"You think so?"

"I truly do," she declared.

"Why Marcie, we might just take you on a run one of these days. You and Stormy could have yourselves a whale of a time."

Marcie laughed. "That might prove to be an offer you'd regret, Kip. Two ladies could prove to be a handful."

"I think I could handle it, Marcie."

It wasn't far from Marcie's house to Kip's place at Cape Fear. Somehow, Pat Dorsey never got a private moment with Stormy during the brief trip and he wasn't too happy about that.

It was sunset when they let Kip, Stormy, and Marcie off at the dock. Kip was still leaving Pat in charge of the *East Wind,* so he headed the boat back to Southport. Paddy had invited Pat to say with him for two weeks while they awaited the next run. The rest of the crew would be going to their homes.

It was twilight when Dorsey got all the men paid and the *East Wind* secured at the docks. It suddenly dawned on Dorsey that he'd never given Stormy the little gold heart necklace he'd bought for her in Norfolk.

Jason Hamilton and his crew aboard the *Sea Princess* had left Southport for their destination--Savannah, Georgia—the same afternoon he'd had his encounter with the beautiful Stormy Monihan. But she had made an impact on him—that tiny hand of hers had given one hell of a blow to his face.

For a tiny little minx she had a lot of force in that swing. She intrigued him so much that he wished he could linger longer in that little port.

It was a small place, so a girl like Stormy Monihan would have been easy to track down, he thought. But somehow he never had the chance to do it. After they unloaded their cargo in Savannah, Jason was ready to cross the Atlantic Ocean to return to England.

After all the various rumors Lord and Lady Hamilton had heard about the possibility of war in the States, they were elated to greet their seaman son when he returned much earlier than they'd expected.

The happy-go-lucky Jason just grinned and said, "You see, I told you there was nothing to worry about." What he didn't tell them that first evening he was home was that he was going to return to Savannah in about two or three weeks with an even bigger cargo for the company in Georgia than the one he'd just delivered. He'd tell them about that in a week or so.

Lady Sheila Hamilton sent a message to her daughters and their husbands that afternoon that their brother was home and there would be a gala feast that evening at their country estate. Jane and Angela were unable to get there the first evening on such short notice but Jason's youngest sister, Joy, and her husband came.

That was all right with Jason. Joy was his favorite little sister—she was more like him than his oldest sister, Jane, who was always so serious and straitlaced. The most beautiful sister was Angela but Jason found her a bit of a snob. Joy was just her natural, adorable self and Jason had always found her a delight to be around.

He was so happy that she had found the right young man when she'd married Eric. He was also pleased to see that she seemed just as happy as she'd been a few months ago. He had to say that Jane and her husband Disney seemed to be an ideal match. Jane had put her whole heart and soul into helping him run their lodging inn on the outskirts of London.

Of all the sisters, Angela was the most discontent even though her husband was the wealthiest of the three. Disney had been very prosperous running his inn, which had a reputation as one of the nicest around London. Young Eric was the one struggling to make his fortune but he was making Joy happy and that was all that mattered to Jason.

As they dined in the grandeur of the Hamiltons' spacious dining room, Joy playfully teased her older brother. "Well Jason, what was the most exciting thing that happened to you on this little voyage?"

Knowing she would get a laugh out of what he was about to tell her, he grinned, "The truth is I got slapped by the prettiest little lady I've laid eyes on in a long, long time."

Excitedly, she urged him, "Oh, tell—tell, Jason! I can't wait to hear about this."

"She reminded me very much of Tawny Blair, with one exception. She had a beautiful head of golden hair and eyes as green as the emeralds Mother is wearing."

"So why did she slap you, Jason? What did you do?" Joy asked.

"I rescued her from a bloke who was getting out of line with her but suddenly I found myself the victim of her fury—and what a fury it was!"

"Oh, she sounds exciting! Tell me more, Jason."

"There's nothing more to tell. I left Southport shortly after that so I never saw her again."

"Oh, Jason!" Joy heaved a deep sigh.

"Sorry to disappoint you but don't give up on me.

Perhaps I'll meet this little enchantress again on my next trip to Savannah," he teased his sister.

"Are you going back there, Jason?"

Without thinking, he told Joy, "In a couple of weeks I will be." He suddenly realized he had absentmindedly revealed his plans prematurely.

"You're going back there again so soon, Jason?" Lady Hamilton asked with a distressed look.

"Yes, Mother, but all this talk of war is exaggerated over here. It didn't seem to be that ominous there."

But he knew he hadn't convinced his mother.

Lady Sheila Hamilton was not a lady easily swayed, even by her smooth-talking, handsome son. But she had been pleased to hear that Jason had met a pretty little lady who had obviously caught his eye.

She was impatient because he was remaining a bachelor for so long. She wanted grandchildren while she was still young enough to enjoy them.

His lifelong friend, Lord Bart Montgomery, was already the proud father of two darling little cherubs. Her dearest wish for Jason was that he could find a girl like the beautiful Tawny Blair.

Eight

Back in Cape Fear, Kip Monihan was thinking about marriage for the first time since his wife had died more than fifteen years ago. But he knew it was far too soon to tell Marcie Warren how he felt. The time she'd spent with him and Stormy had changed his friendship with her into something far deeper.

The three of them had had a lot of fun fishing on the wharf and going on picnics down by the water. He knew coming out here had been good for Marcie—she looked radiant.

He'd waited a long time to feel this way about a woman and never really expected something like this to happen.

She'd also calmed some apprehensions he'd had about Stormy and young Dorsey. She'd said, "Stormy's almost sixteen and your Dorsey is very smitten. It's only natural for two young people to become attracted to one another. Remember when you were Pat Dorsey's age?"

"I guess you're right. A woman's bound to see things in a different light than an overprotective father."

She had laughed softly as she told him to think back to when he was Pat's age. "Don't try to tell me you wouldn't have tried to court a beautiful girl like Stormy?"

Kip blushed and grinned as he confessed that he would have broken his neck trying to impress such a pretty girl. "But when it's your daughter—well, you know what I mean, Marcie."

"Of course I do. But when you think about it, Kip, you and I are around them most of the time. They spend precious little time alone."

Listening to Marcie, he found himself mellowing a little. His feelings were shared by his old friend, Paddy. He'd pointed out to Kip that Pat was a fine, hardworking lad and Stormy was bound to have herself a beau. He grinned devilishly when he added, "You might as well not fight it, bucko. Stormy is going to have herself a fellow, and she could do worse than Pat Dorsey."

For the next few weeks Kip didn't fret so much when he saw his daughter strolling arm in arm with Dorsey, who was patiently wooing Stormy with a few sweet stolen kisses. It wasn't easy to restrain himself—she was enough to make any man's blood boil.

His daughter was attracting more than one man's eyes lately and Kip would certainly not have been happy if he knew about the lusty thoughts she had stirred in another boatman. He had no great admiration for the likes of Jed Callihan; he'd learned in Savannah that Jed was trying to underbid him with the lumber company Kip had worked with for over ten years. Kip Monihan had never practiced that kind of dealing in all of his years sailing the coast.

There were a lot of other lumber mills Jed could approach, but he knew that the Oxford Mills had the most prosperous milling trade.

But then Kip didn't like anything about Jed. He was looking for an easy way to earn his money and was a carouser and a heavy drinker.

Stormy didn't know Jed so she didn't recognize him when he cockily accosted her on the street in Southport one day.

Jed had spotted the beautiful Stormy going into the

store so he sat outside on a sack of feed until she came out. He was conceited and considered himself so good-looking that he couldn't imagine any young girl not responding to his charms.

He greeted Stormy as she came out the door with her packages. "Hi there, pretty thing," he said flippantly.

Stormy's green eyes gave him a cold glare as she walked on by, ignoring him. Jed was not used to being shrugged aside. He leaped up from the feed sack and stalked after her, his dark eyes flashing angrily. "Hey, who the hell do you think you are?" he snapped.

Stormy turned around swiftly, her green eyes challenging him. "I know exactly who I am. I'm Stormy Monihan and don't you forget that name, mister. That way you won't be so rude if I come by you again."

"Well, my name's Jed Callihan and don't you forget my name, either, 'cause you'll remember it one day, I assure you."

Stormy had not seen Pat Dorsey coming from the opposite direction until he was right by her side. He recognized Jed and could see that Stormy was angry as a wet hen.

Jed didn't have his usual entourage with him so he didn't wish to start a fight with the husky boatman, who towered over him.

Callihan was basically a coward unless he had others to do his dirty work for him. He had only to glance at the protective manner of Pat Dorsey when he came toward Stormy to know he'd better walk away.

But he couldn't shrug off the fact that Stormy Monihan had looked down her snobbish little nose at him— he wasn't going to forget that, he promised himself.

When Dorsey asked her if the man was bothering her, she assured him that nothing had happened. There were times lately that she rather resented what a mother hen Dorsey could be. He'd become as overprotective as her father. She often felt smothered. "Don't worry about it, Dorsey. I was handling it all right!"

They stopped by the tobacco shop where she headed when she encountered Callihan and then they went back toward the wharf.

As soon as they boarded the boat, Stormy bade Dorsey goodbye and went directly to her father's cabin. Kip found her unpacking her purchases. She looked around to greet him and handed him the pouch of tobacco. "I spent all your money this afternoon, Pa," she laughed.

"Well, I hope you got good buys."

"Oh, I did. Got me and Marcie some material to make new curtains for our kitchen and bedrooms. They're in shreds, Pa."

"I know, honey. So you and Marcie just do whatever you want to pretty up the place," the goodnatured Kip said.

"Thank you, Pa." Then she told him she was going to stay with Marcie when he left in a few days.

"That's fine with me, honey," he replied.

The day Kip and Dorsey were to leave Southport and Marcie was to come to the wharf to pick up Stormy was not Stormy's kind of day. Dark, heavy clouds hung over the small harbor. The air was oppressive and Stormy found herself disturbed that her father was heading south in such foul weather.

"I don't like this, Pa," she said, but he assured her that everything would be all right. His only concern was that she and Marcie travel back to Marcie's cottage before a downpour hit the area. He knew it might be a rough trip.

This was one of the richest cargoes he'd picked up

in a long time. Afterwards he could afford to enjoy a nice long two weeks at Cape Fear. Kip had to admit that he anticipated the time he spent with Marcie as well as with his daughter.

He was relieved once Stormy was in the buggy with Marcie and they were heading back to Marcie's cottage. It was such a good feeling to know that Stormy was with someone like Marcie. With his Irish suspicions, Kip wondered if destiny had not deemed it to be that way.

Once they'd left, he breathed much easier and turned his attention back to his boat and preparing to depart. A few minutes later, Kip's and Dorsey's attention was diverted to a slick-lined schooner plowing through the waters. It moved by them swiftly and was soon out of sight.

"Was that a sight to behold or not, Dorsey? Can you imagine what it would feel like to own such a proud vessel. God, it's beyond my wildest dreams!" Kip declared breathlessly as he heaved a deep sigh.

"I know what you mean, sir. I happened to catch the name—it was the *Sea Princess,* and that is surely a princess of a ship."

Jason Hamilton would have been delighted to know how his schooner was being admired from afar as he headed for Savannah.

Stormy and Marcie were so engrossed in conversation that they didn't hear or notice the buggy coming up behind them. The skies were so dark that it could have been dusk instead of midday.

Neither Marcie nor Stormy was prepared for the buggy to race ahead of them and block the dirt road. Everything happened so swiftly it was like a living nightmare. Marcie found herself restrained by one of the three men as she tried to grab Stormy who was taken out of the buggy by the other two. She screamed at the man holding her and asked why they were doing this. He just gave her a wicked grin.

Never had Marcie felt so utterly helpless or known such panic as when she saw Stormy drive off with those three ruffians.

Frantically, she turned her buggy around and pushed the mare as fast as she could to get back to the wharf in hopes that Kip had not sailed. But there was no sight of the *East Wind*.

She went directly to the authorities and reported what had happened. A half-hour later, she was told to go home—there was nothing more she could do and they'd be in touch with her.

It was a miserable night—Marcie could neither eat nor sleep. She paced the floor and drank coffee until total exhaustion finally forced her to stretch out across her bed.

Jed's buddies were already regretting going along with him on such a crazy stunt once they were aboard his boat. They'd all been drinking liquor for hours.

The only way they could live with what they'd done was to tell themselves that they'd turned the pretty little fair-haired lady over to Jed. What he did with her would be on his conscience, not theirs.

But they also knew that Jed could be a strange one at times—they didn't want to think about what the young lady might be facing at his mercy. But they didn't know Stormy Monihan—or how she was not intimidated by the likes of Jed Callihan.

When she suddenly found herself in a small cabin similar to her pa's, she wondered who owned this boat.

When she was finally confronted by her captor she gave him a smirk. But she said nothing, forcing him to speak first. "I see you recognize me, Stormy Monihan," he said smugly.

"Yes, I recognize you and I'm just as disgusted as I was at our first encounter."

He stood there gazing at her defiant face and arrogant air. He promised himself he would break her before he was through.

Stormy saw the lusty look on his face and she instinctively knew what he had in mind—she was determined he would never boast of possessing Stormy Monihan.

Egotistical as Jed was, he didn't fool himself about this little wildcat—he'd have to take her by force. She'd bounce on him like a mountain cat scratching his eyes out.

He swaggered up to her, still smirking. "You're a liar, Stormy Monihan. I don't disgust you at all. You're afraid of me."

She threw back her pretty blond head and broke into a laugh. "Afraid? Of what, you conceited fool!" But she had hardly gotten the words out of her mouth when she was stunned by a fierce blow to the face from Jed's huge hand. She staggered back against a chair but she didn't fall. She caught hold of the top of the chair to steady herself.

Never had she experienced such hate for someone! Her eyes longed to give way to tears, but she willed herself not to cry.

She hissed at him like a viper, "So now you're feeling like a big man, eh? That's the way with a bully."

"Damn you, woman—you've got a tongue that'll get you killed if I stay here a minute longer," he snapped furiously, and turning around to leave the room.

To choke her pretty throat was not what he had in mind. He wanted to have his pleasure with her and explore every curve of that luscious body.

Stormy heaved a deep sigh of relief once he was gone—utmost in her mind was how she could make her getaway.

She didn't have to look in a mirror to know that she was going to have an ugly bruise on her face but that was the least of her worries.

Jed Callihan had never known such violent emotions. He had only to look at her to be fired with wild passion—but no woman had ever fired a more raging temper in him!

A few minutes ago he could have put his strong hands around that dainty throat. No woman had ever talked to him like that!

Nine

There was one small window and Stormy had no doubt she could wriggle through it. Dare she hope it was not locked on the outside? She bristled with excitement to find it wasn't, and wasted no time climbing into a chair to swing herself up. She saw nothing but utter darkness outside—the sky was heavy with clouds and there was no moonlight to guide her.

She could not tell whether she was dropping to a deck below or into the churning waters the boat was moving through.

Then her feet hit the solid wood of the narrow deck. She stood for a minute to get her bearings so she could swim to shore. At that moment she heard a commotion inside the cabin and Jed's angry voice; he'd obviously returned to find her gone and the window open.

She squatted so he couldn't see her as he peered out the window. She heard him mutter, "Damned little bitch! I hope she drowns!"

Smiling, she thought to herself that she'd rather drown than have him assaulting her, which she knew he intended to do.

She eased out of her slippers and yanked up her long skirt and tucked it tightly around her waist before she dove into the waters. Stormy was a strong swimmer so she never doubted she'd be able to reach the shore, knowing how her father always kept his boat close to the coastline.

But she did find herself exhausted before her feet could finally reach bottom as she neared shallow water.

For the next few minutes Stormy crawled along like a dog on her hands and knees. She could not remember ever seeing a darker night.

When she finally stood up, she tried to scoot her feet along the ground instead of just slowly walking. But as cautious as she was trying to be, she didn't see a fallen tree and fell over it, hitting her head on a boulder.

Stormy found herself sinking into an even deeper blackness.

A farmer and his wife came upon the dazed young lady the next morning but Stormy couldn't tell them who she was or how she got there. The middle-aged couple exchanged glances, apprehensive about what to do with her. But both agreed that they couldn't leave her.

"Come on, dear. Let's put you in the bed of the wagon and get you to the house. You've got an angry bruise on your cheek," Ella Brown said as she took her arm, noticing she had no shoes.

Joe and Ella Brown took her to their house and Ella tended to Stormy's bruised cheek and the bump on her head. Ella gave her a cotton wrapper so she could take off her soiled, damp clothes.

Joe told his wife he was going back to town and ask if a young lady fitting Stormy's description was missing. "It's all I know to do, Ella," he said as he prepared to leave. But an hour later he returned to tell Ella there were no reports of any missing girl. But that little town was some fifteen miles south of Southport.

"Guess we could inquire at Southport when we take our goods to the wharf. I feel sorry for the poor little thing. She must feel so helpless, not knowing who she is. Can you imagine being that way, Ella?"

"No, I can't and I feel very sorry for her, too."

For the next week Stormy was cared for lovingly by Joe and Ella Brown but she was still walking around in a fog. The bump on her head had gone down and the bruise on her cheek had changed colors many times during the week.

She felt like she was in a strange new world and Joe and Ella were the only people there. Ella decided they should take her with them when they went into South-port. "Maybe something there would jog her memory. We've got to try something—she's no better."

Joe agreed as they were hardly in a position to take this young lady on indefinitely as part of their family. Ella had washed and pressed Stormy's skirt and blouse but had not shoes for her. Stormy was in her bare feet as she accompanied them to Southport, their wagon piled high with the goods they were hoping to sell at the wharf.

Ella had noticed the little necklace Stormy wore. Seeing how beautiful the girl was, she said, "I'll bet some young man gave that to you. You're such a pretty little thing—I bet you had a lot of beaus."

Stormy smiled up at her. "You're sweet, Ella, and if I did I can't remember. But I think my necklace is pretty, too."

Ella swelled with compassion for the little lost soul— her green eyes had such a desolate look. Ella had never seen a more beautiful head of hair as this lovely child had. It was so glossy and golden. She'd helped Stormy wash it yesterday with the rainwater she'd caught in the barrel outside her kitchen door.

It was midday when they arrived at the wharf, where people were milling up and down. Ella helped Joe get their goods unloaded while Stormy sat there in the wagon.

Stormy found herself engulfed with a strange feeling—she was not even aware of her sudden urge to leave the wagon. She moved in a trancelike state through the crowd. She walked up the gangplank to a vessel that attracted her—it was such a magnificent ship.

She could probably have never gone unnoticed boarding the schooner but for the fact that Jason Hamilton had gone ashore, as most of his crew had after they'd returned from Savannah. The short stop in Southport was to be their last before they sailed back to England.

Stormy roamed around, admiring everything she saw. She walked down the long passageways and explored behind the doors of the various cabins.

Then she suddenly felt exhausted and curled up on one of the bunks to rest. Before she realized it, she had fallen asleep.

Her sleep was a deep one and when she finally woke up she felt the swaying motion of the ship. What she couldn't know was that that motion had been going on for almost five hours. Stormy might not be able to remember who she was, but she still possessed a curious nature so she rushed to peer out at the billowing waves. As if she were not already in one new world, it seemed that now she was thrust into another, even stranger one.

Where was this magnificent ship heading, she wondered. Wherever it was, it was obvious she was going along.

At least, she did know the name of the ship—she'd seen it on the hull as she boarded. It didn't tell her much but she knew she was on the *Sea Princess*.

Somewhere back there was where she belonged and she knew there had to be someone wondering where she was and what was happening to her. Surely, there was!

Panic engulfed her and she was tempted to rush out the door, but she didn't know who she would encounter when she opened the door. She walked over and sat down in the bunk, propping her legs up and pressing them close to her chest. What kind of insanity had made her a prisoner? Why couldn't she remember who she was?

She had no inkling of how long she stayed there.

One of Jason's crew was walking down the passageway and thought he heard a noise in the unoccupied cabin across from his captain's quarters. Enos Gregory decided that perhaps he should take a look. There was no reason for anyone to be in there and the captain wouldn't like it if they were. This was the cabin which had been furnished comfortably for occasional guests aboard the *Sea Princess*.

It was just as startling to Enos to see the golden-haired beauty in the bunk as it was for her to see him. It took him a moment or two to inquire, "Who in the world are you, miss?"

She stared up at the sandy-haired, ruddy-faced young man. There was no threatening look on his face—just utter surprise.

She flattened her legs down on the bed and those big green eyes looked directly at him. "And who are you?"

"I'm Enos Gregory, a member of this crew. I'll have to report this to Captain Hamilton unless you're here with his approval."

She shrugged. "Then you just go tell your captain, Enos. I'm not going anywhere, since all I can see out that window is water. Do you suppose I might have a cup of coffee?"

She looked like a fair-haired angel to Enos—he could hardly refuse her. Besides, she was so tiny and seemed so helpless. "I'll get you a cup of coffee, ma'am, but then I got to tell the captain."

Stormy smiled and nodded. Enos awkwardly moved backwards out the door. A few minutes later he returned from the galley with her coffee.

"You want to tell me why you're here? Are you a stowaway?" Enos asked.

"No, I'm not," she replied. At least, she had not intended to be.

Stormy sipped the coffee and found it wonderful. She realized just how hungry she was—she hadn't had any food since the early breakfast with Joe and Ella. She knew she should never have left their wagon. They were probably very worried about her.

It was true that they were concerned about the pretty little girl who'd been with them for well over a week. It had been an ordeal for the two of them to feel any great joy over the money they'd made at the wharf after they found Stormy missing. One of them tended to the goods while the other one searched the area. Joe would return to tell Ella he hadn't seen her, then Ella would leave him in charge and go hunt for her.

They remained around the wharf until after the sun went down, then reluctantly forced themselves to return home. "We're going to be well after dark. We've got to leave. I've got my stock to attend to once we get home."

Dejectedly, Ella shook her head and sighed, "Oh, I know she's not blood kin but I've become very fond of the little girl. I'll just pray God looks over her, Joe."

"And so shall I, Ella." He urged the mare up the dirt road.

Joe and Ella were not the only people concerned about Stormy. Marcie Warren had been so upset that she couldn't eat or sleep—she was as at the point of exhaustion. She'd gone out on a daily search for Stormy and checked with the sheriff's office but it was as if she'd been swallowed up. As horrible as it was, Marcie had to tell herself she might have to face the fact that Stormy was dead. God only knew what could have happened to that poor child at the hands of those scoundrels.

The sheriff had turned up nothing and had no clues to work on.

The only consolation Marcie had was that with each day that passed, it meant Kip would be arriving soon. What a shock she was going to have to slam at him as soon as he arrived!

With him and young Pat Dorsey turning this place upside down, Marcie felt they could find her. She could not help but feel guilty that it had happened when Stormy was in her care. But the practical side of her forced her to admit that there was absolutely nothing she could have done to prevent the three robust fellows from doing what they'd done.

She could only hope that Kip would not blame her. If he should, she would be devastated. She was just going to have to live with that uncertainty until he arrived and she informed him about that horrible afternoon.

Ten

Jason Hamilton had just changed the course of his schooner to make his crossing of the Atlantic Ocean. This was probably going to be the last time he would cross until next spring. Nothing would make his mother happier than being told that when he arrived back in London.

But he had to confess he was just a little disappointed that he'd roamed around the streets of Southport for a couple of days with no sight of the young golden-haired girl.

When Enos came rushing up and announced that they had themselves a stowaway, Jason didn't get too upset—it had to happen every now and then. So he dismissed Enos to go about his duties after he asked where he would find this stowaway and Enos told where he might find the girl.

"A girl you say, Enos?" Jason asked with a frown.

"Yes, captain—and a fair-haired angel she is! With eyes as green as the English countryside in springtime."

Jason smiled as he dismissed Enos and went to see this fairhaired damsel Enos spoke so glowingly about. He moved down the passageway toward the guest cabin.

Like Enos, he entered the cabin abruptly to see the girl sitting there holding a cup of coffee. Her golden hair cascaded all around her shoulders, but her bare feet were the first things Jason noticed. Then he saw her delicate features and recognized her immediately.

For one brief second, Jason was speechless; this was the lovely enchantress he'd looked for in the streets of Southport and now here she was on his schooner!

His black eyes flashed as he recognized her, but she merely stared up at him as though she'd never seen him before.

"Good evening to you, miss. May I ask what this is all about and why you're on my ship? I'm Captain Hamilton."

With a look so honest and sincere he could almost believe her, she said, "I can't tell you why I'm here. I just wandered on board from the wharf. I can't tell you who I am—I don't know."

Jason's black brows rose as he wondered what kind of little game she was up to. He well remembered the day she'd given him that firm slap and announced she was Stormy Monihan and that he'd best remember that. He certainly had.

Jason could be calm and patient if he felt the need to. Perhaps three sisters had influenced him.

"I guess you and I had better do a little talking. You have no luggage?"

"I have none—I had no plans to be on this ship when it sailed out of Southport."

"Then why did you come aboard?" he asked.

"I think I was so curious about this magnificent ship. I just wanted to see what it was like so I roamed around for the longest time before I came in here. I was tired so I lay down on the bunk and fell asleep."

The fact that she admired his ship was enough to mellow Jason a little, so he sat down to question her further. She didn't hesitate to tell him about Joe and Ella and how they'd found her at the water's edge. She explained about how she'd lived with them while they'd tried to find out who she was and where she'd come from.

"So you have no memory as to how you got there?"

"I can't recall anything before Joe and Ella rescuing me. It's driving me crazy!"

Jason suddenly felt compassion for the pretty young girl. She seemed so sincere that he was persuaded to believe her. "We'll have to continue this talk later—I've heard about this happening before. In the meanwhile, young lady, we've got to have a name for you," he said as his dark eyes danced over her face.

Stormy thought he was most handsome and he seemed to be understanding, too. She returned his warm smile. "You name me, captain."

Jason sat thoughtfully for a minute before he spoke. "Princess. How do you like that?"

Her green eyes twinkled. "I like it! I like it very much!"

"All right, Princess, I'm taking you to my cabin across the passageway. You're my responsibility as long as you're on my ship. A pretty girl on a ship like this can be a big problem, so I want you in my quarters."

When he got up, Stormy willingly followed him.

"May I ask where we're going, captain?" she asked in her lazy drawl, which intrigued Jason.

"We're heading for London, England, Princess," he said with an amused grin, realizing she had to accept the fact that there was no turning back to Southport. If what she'd told him was true, then who would he be returning her to?

Once they were inside his cabin, he asked her to sit down as he proceeded to speak to her in a fatherly fashion. She could not wander around the ship, he cautioned, and she was not to allow anyone to enter except for his cabin boy.

"There are too many men aboard for you to dare disobey my orders. Do you understand?"

"I do and I won't open the door to anyone but you and your cabin boy, I promise."

Jason prepared to leave when it suddenly dawned on him that she had probably not eaten anything for hours. "Like a snack to tide you over for a couple of hours when Tobias will be serving dinner?"

"I'm starved—a snack would be wonderful if it's not too much trouble."

"You'll have it, Princess. My boy, Rudy, will have a tray here shortly. Lock the door after I go out—I'll be back in an hour or two," he said.

Stormy locked the cabin door as he'd ordered. While she waited for her snack, she began to explore his cabin. She immediately spied pictures of three very pretty ladies on his desk. Such a handsome man must have many lady friends. Stormy had decided she'd never met a more handsome man. She was sure of that even though she could not remember. Captain Hamilton had such piercing black eyes, Stormy thought as she sat alone after he'd left.

A few minutes later a very young man came into the room announcing that he was Rudy, the captain's cabin boy. It was more a meal than a snack he had brought. While she was devouring the good food, she realized he was also preparing a warm tub for her at the other end of the cabin. "Captain thought you might enjoy a warm bath, ma'am. I've got it all ready for you when you've finished eating," Rudy said as he prepared to leave.

Stormy had to struggle to tell him thank you for she had a mouthful of food. But Rudy understood and smiled warmly as he went out the door.

As he left his thoughts were taken back to a few years ago when another lovely lady was in a similar dilemma, clad only in her nightgown when she found herself aboard the Sea Princess. It was a little uncanny how this same thing could be happening again. That lovely lady had been hid in the hold of the schooner while they were in port and Rudy had served her as he had this fair-haired beauty. It brought back a flood of memories to him and he was wondering if the captain was feeling this way, too.

Before they'd arrived in London that time, Rudy had found himself becoming very fond of the beautiful, dark-haired Tawny. He was to learn later that she married Captain Hamilton's best friend, who had been a passenger on that crossing.

Rudy was thinking that maybe this time the captain might win the heart of this little beauty. Something about this little lady reminded him of Tawny Blair and yet, they were as different as day and night.

Jason walked around the deck thinking very much the same thoughts as Rudy. He, too, was very much reminded of Tawny. He had been in love with her and had asked her to marry him, but Tawny had followed her heart and married Bart Montgomery.

Rudy brought a pair of his pants and one of his faded blue shirts to the cabin when he brought the water for Stormy's bath. He suspected that she had no luggage. He also noticed her bare feet.

When Rudy handed her the clothing she felt a sudden flash of familiarity. Was this a garb she'd worn in the past? She cussed under her breath. What *was* her past? Damn it, she had to find out!

Jason was definitely reminded of the past when he entered his cabin and saw her in the dark pants and faded blue shirt. Like Tawny, she sat there in her bare feet. He offered her a pair of his socks but Stormy refused him politely. "I don't need socks. I like my feet bare."

Just as Jason found her slow drawl interesting, Stormy found his distinctive English brogue intriguing. He noticed how intensely she listened when he spoke. With an amused grin, he asked her, "What is it about the way I speak that brings that look to your face?"

"It's—it's nice, I guess I could say. I don't recall hearing anyone speak as you do, captain."

"But then, you have so little that you do remember. As I understand all you remember is the time you spent with that couple, Joe and Ella."

"That's right, but you sound nothing like the people I heard talking while I was there."

Jason chuckled as he prepared to change into a clean shirt. He gave her a gentle pat on the head, saying, "And I have to tell you I find that lazy drawl of yours just as intriguing."

"And why do you call it lazy?" she asked.

"Because I can't think of a better way to describe it."

He stood before her with his broad chest bared as he slipped into a clean shirt and he suddenly noticed how her green eyes were appraising him. He wondered if he had shocked her by being so casual about changing his shirt in front of her. But having three sisters who were constantly rushing into his room when he was home, he thought nothing about it.

Before they arrived in London, he figured she might as well get used to certain things aboard his ship for he had not exactly planned to have a lady passenger aboard.

"Turn your head in the other direction, Princess, while I get my shirt tucked in," he said as he turned his back to her.

He heard her soft little giggle as she dared to taunt him, "Shall I leave the cabin and go across the passageway?"

"I don't think that will be necessary," he said as he tucked his shirt in. By the time he had run a brush through his black hair a few times, he was ready to get himself a glass of his favorite Irish whiskey as always did at this time in the evening. Glass in hand, he took a seat at the table. He made no effort to offer her a drink, knowing she was too young. Actually, she looked like a mere child sitting there with her legs crossed and in her bare feet.

"Ready for a good dinner, Princess?" He had to wonder just how old she was. If he was to guess, he would say about sixteen.

"Well, I'd be famished if Rudy hadn't brought me that tray, but I think I can still enjoy a meal," she confessed.

As he usually did, Tobias served the evening meal to his captain and like Rudy and Jason, he was reminded of a time a few years ago when he'd served a barefoot goddess in the captain's cabin. But this one was different, he thought as she looked up at him with wide-eyed innocence when he was serving her.

Tobias thought about her as he returned to his galley—she was a different breed from the little dark-haired Tawny. There was a certain boldness and daring about her that he could not exactly place.

She ate with such relish that Tobias was amazed at her hearty appetite. When the meal was finished and he had left the cabin with all the dishes, Stormy asked Jason, "I know you told me I can't roam the ship but could you take me for a walk, captain?"

"Would you like to stroll around the deck?"

"Oh, I'd love it!" she declared excitedly.

"Well, let's go. I feel the need for a walk after Tobias's huge meal," he confessed.

"And so do I."

Walking down the passageway in her bare feet, Stormy hardly came to his shoulders.

Eleven

A gusty breeze was blowing across the deck of the schooner as they came from below so Jason took her arm as they moved out on the deck. He quickly realized that the swaying of the schooner didn't seem to be any problem to this young lady—the strong breeze blowing her long hair all around her face didn't disturb her either.

She just laughed and declared, "The next time I take a walk with you I'll have this mess of hair secured under a cap."

They walked over to the railing and watched the moonbeams flash down on the surging waves. Stormy was fascinated by the water's force. She stood by the railing and took a deep breath of the night air. "Oh, Lord—how refreshing it is just to let that air hit your face."

Jason noticed that she didn't flinch at the spray. "You like the sea breeze, Princess?"

"I love it! Don't you?"

"I love it or I wouldn't be a sea captain. The sea and my ship are my loves."

She turned to look up at him. "And what does your wife think about that?"

"I have no wife."

"Then how about your lady friends?"

He laughed. "I don't have much time for *lady friends* as you call them, Princess."

"Now come on, captain—I saw three lovely ladies' pictures on your desk."

"That's my three sisters, not my lady friends."

Stormy couldn't exactly understand why, but it pleased her to hear him say they were his sisters' pictures on his desk. She might not have wanted to admit that she was very much attracted to the tall, handsome sea captain with his piercing black eyes and black hair that curled around the collar of his white shirt. She was very much affected by him and wondered if she'd ever felt this way about a man before.

Jason found himself wanting to ask her so many questions about herself but he knew there weren't any answers she could give him and he was convinced she wasn't playing games with him. He knew only one thing for sure, and that was her name: Stormy Monihan. He wondered if he should tell her that but decided there was time to think about that before they arrived in London.

When they returned to the passageway and came to Jason's cabin, he guided her into the cabin across from his. "I hope you'll rest well tonight, Princess, and remember to keep this door locked all the time unless it's me or Rudy."

She said goodnight and locked the door as he'd instructed. But Stormy didn't feel as secure as she had when she was with Jason Hamilton. Her sleep was restless, as she kept hearing noises outside the passageway. Once she would have sworn she heard the rattling of the knob of the cabin's door; she'd sat up in the bunk to listen for the longest time.

As daylight broke, she found she could relax and sleep more peacefully. When Jason knocked on her door and got no response, he figured she was still sleeping. He went on about his duties but told Rudy to check on her shortly. "Take her on over to my quarters, Rudy. I'd just feel better about her being there." Jason had a qualm about one of the men on his crew where a pretty girl like Princess was concerned. He tried to know his crew very well before he sailed, but he'd had to hire on a couple of new men lately and he was well satisfied with only one of them.

Stormy was awake when Rudy knocked and she leaped out of the bunk to open the door when she realized who it was.

As Jason had instructed him, Rudy ushered her into the captain's quarters and soon he was serving her breakfast.

For whatever reason, Stormy felt safer once she was there and ate her breakfast, feeling relaxed and secure.

It was nice to have Jason come to check on her at midday and assure her he'd take her for another stroll in the late afternoon or evening.

Stormy couldn't know because she couldn't remember her past that what had made her so nervous when she was left in the cabin across from Jason's was that one of his crew whom she'd seen on their stroll was a young man who looked very much like Jed Callihan.

But that evening after they'd eaten and Jason had taken her up on the deck, Stormy pleaded with him to let her stay in the cabin with him. "I'm little, captain, and I'll sleep very comfortably on a pallet. I--I'd just feel safer with you."

"What happened last night that has you so upset? I should know, Princess!"

"I heard footsteps and I don't think I dreamed I heard the knob being turned back and forth," she replied.

When they reached his cabin, Jason guided her inside and locked the door. "You'll stay in here with me tonight."

"Thank you, captain," she said with a sigh of relief. She watched Jason as he strolled over to the cabinet to pour himself a generous glass of Irish whiskey.

"You don't need to thank me, Princess," he said as he took the first sip. What was troubling Jason was something she could not be aware of. This little lady was far more sensuous than Tawny Blair and he longed to make love to her as he had wanted to do the first time he'd laid eyes on her in Southport. Now, here she was in his cabin and he felt protective of her because she didn't even know who she was. He also wanted to know what had happened to her that had been so traumatic to cause her loss of memory.

Absentmindedly, he asked her if there was anything in the other cabin she needed to get for the night and she laughed, reminding him that she had nothing over there to get.

Jason gave her a warm smile, wishing he had something to give her. She didn't even have a nightgown so he had to assume that she slept nude or in her undergarments. That was enough to stir more torment within him.

She said nothing as she sat there watching him rummage through the drawers of the chest. He turned to her and handed her one of his white linen shirts. "At least this will give you a change from Rudy's blue shirt tomorrow. Here, this is my silk robe and while it's going to swallow you, it will cover you when you get undressed."

Stormy thanked him as she took the two garments. Once again she saw that he was searching for something in a huge storage closet and he began pulling out a massive roll of what looked to Stormy like a giant net. "Mercy, what is that, captain?"

"My bed tonight," he said as he began to spread it across the cabin floor.

Stormy gave him a quizzical look. "You have a huge

bed right here—I'll do just fine on a pallet on the floor.
I won't have you giving up your bed for me."

Jason's black eyes looked over at her. "No, Princess—you'll sleep on no pallet. It's not as if I've never
slept in a hammock before—it's not that bad. Besides,
I give the orders on this ship and the captain orders
you to get in that bed," he teased.

She started to protest but he quickly told her, "I'll
turn my back while you get out of the pants and shirt.
Put my robe on and then I'll get this thing hung up so
I can get to sleep."

"You can turn around now," she told him a few minutes later as she stood there in the rich wine-colored
robe with the sash tied around her tiny waist and inches
of the material clustered around her feet. She had to
hold it up to make it over to the bed so she moved
very cautiously.

She sat on the bed propped up on the pillows. Jason
stared at her for a minute, taking in her beauty with
that golden hair fanned out against his pillows. It took
him a minute to break the spell she had cast over him.

"Captain—captain, I'm truly sorry about all this.
You're far kinder than I deserve."

"Now that's not true, Princess," he said, putting down
the end of the hammock to sit down beside her. "I've—
I've enjoyed your company. In fact, why don't you just
call me Jason, eh?" He gave her a warm smile.

"You wish me to?"

"I do," he declared as he gave her a pat on the top
of the head and returned to getting the other end of his
hammock secured. "See how a fellow can rock himself
to sleep?"

Stormy smiled. "I should sleep there—I'm much
smaller than you."

"I don't want you falling out of there and bumping

that pretty head of yours again as you obviously did to have that lapse of memory."

Jason hadn't intended to bring tears to her eyes with his remark about her loss of memory. He heard her sigh deeply, "I wonder if I shall ever remember." A mist of tears came to her eyes.

Jason felt like an oaf as he went over and embraced her, pulling her close to his bare chest. "Of course, you will! I'll try to help you remember if I can. Oh, Princess, don't cry. It upsets me to see tears in your eyes." His lips tenderly kissed the corners of each eye where the tears had dampened her face.

When Jason was about to get up because sitting that close to her was too tempting and he was only human, Stormy reached up to fling her arms around his neck as she'd often done with her pa when she'd been scared. But Jason wasn't her pa and the feelings she stirred within him were quite different.

Instinctively, his lips went down to meet her half-parted lips in a kiss that sparked a flame in both of them that neither of them had anticipated. Jason felt her response to his kiss so his lips lingered. When he did release her, his black eyes were devouring her as he huskily moaned, "Oh, Princess sweeter lips I've never kissed!"

Stormy felt the pounding of his heart as his bare, broad chest pressed against her. All she knew was she wanted him to keep holding her and kissing her. Jason forgot everything except that they were a man and a woman and this golden-haired goddess in his arms was responding to his lovemaking.

He felt the jutting tips of her firm, rounded breasts pressing against his bare chest and a fever like liquid fire rushed through his body.

He heard her soft little purring that told him not to stop but then he was not about to stop anyway—not now! Once again his lips sought hers. God, no wine ever tasted any sweeter! Jason found himself whispering words of endearment as he finally released his lips from hers.

His lips sought the hollow of her throat and his long, slender fingers gently flipped aside the straps of her undergarment so his lips could explore more of her satiny flesh. When he did he felt her suddenly gasp and surge against him.

He let his lips as well as his hands give her tender, unhurried caresses and Stormy's soft moans told him not to stop. Jason would have found that hard to do now for he had removed all her undergarments so he could feel the entire length of her warm, soft body.

Reluctantly, he moved just far enough away to remove his own pants. Stormy felt the length of his firm-muscled body searing her with his heat.

He whispered words of love in her ear and assured her that he realized he was the first man to make love to her. "The first time it hurts a moment or two, Princess, but I'll see that that moment is brief for you, I promise," he murmured huskily.

Her velvety flesh was warm against his thighs. Stormy felt like flames were creeping through her. Her arms clung tightly to his neck as she felt his mighty thrust and that one brief moment of discomfort he'd told her about. But that was quickly forgotten as he sought to love more fiercely.

Like the surging waves in the ocean, they moved as one with a wild, wonderful fury.

For the longest time he held her in his arms—she seemed very content. His deep voice finally broke the long silence: "Ah, love—it matters not what your name is—to me you shall always be Princess—my little green-eyed princess!

Part Two

A Girl Called Princess

Twelve

As it would turn out, the hammock was not used that night—or any of the nights that followed. The rest of Jason's crew might not have had any inkling that the young lady passenger was sharing their captain's quarters but Rudy and old Tobias were not fooled. As discreet as Jason tried to be, he couldn't play his little game and get by with it with these two who had known him for so long.

Stormy was called Miss Princess by Tobias and Rudy, who had never seen their captain in higher spirits.

There was one very distinct difference between this little lady and Miss Tawny: Miss Tawny had detested the sea but this fair-haired miss seemed to love strolling the decks with Jason, letting the sea breeze blow against her face and long hair.

It didn't seem to bother her to pad around in her bare feet. Rudy wished he had a frock to give her as he had to Miss Tawny when she'd found herself an unwilling stowaway. But this time Rudy wasn't taking a dress back to his sister as he'd been on that trip.

Rudy was also thinking that Miss Tawny was luckier than this lady—she knew who she was!

* * *

It wasn't a happy homecoming for Kip Monihan when he arrived back in Southport and went directly to Marcie's to hear the startling news.

Marcie watched him sit down in the chair and cry. She went over to put her arms around him and comfort him. "Oh, Kip, there was just nothing I could do against three husky fellows. Two of them took Stormy while the other one subdued me."

"Why—why would anyone do that to Stormy?" he asked, tears rolling down his ruddy cheeks.

"I've no idea, Kip. I reported it to the sheriff and not one clue showed up. For almost a week I've gone out to search the streets and ask people if they've seen her. I've found nothing, so I had to give up the last three days because I was exhausted."

Kip patted her hand. "I know how much you love Stormy. God knows I know that! This is like a damn nightmare!"

"I know, Kip. I've been living it for over a week."

After they'd talked for a while, Kip got up from the chair. "Guess I better get back to the boat. Paddy and Dorsey have to be told—and I have to check out my house since I've been gone for ten days, Marcie."

Under normal circumstances, Marcie Warren would have never been so bold but this one time she dared to be. "Kip, check your cottage in Cape Fear and get Dorsey and Paddy into Southport. But come back here and stay with me. I'll have supper waiting if you'll come."

With a weak smile he nodded. "I'll accept your kind offer, Marcie Warren. God knows I need your company."

"And I need yours, Kip."

Kip went out the door and down to his boat. When Paddy and Dorsey saw him walking down the path without Stormy skipping along beside him, they both sensed that something was wrong.

They were in a state of shock when Kip told them Marcie's bizarre tale. A cloud of gloom hung heavily over the *East Wind* as it traveled back to Southport. Paddy and Dorsey were glad to hear that Kip was going back to Marcie's as soon as he went by his own cottage. It was best that he was with her right now.

After Kip had let Dorsey and Paddy off at the wharf and they were walking toward Paddy's little four-room house, Paddy shook his head in disbelief. "That man is crushed! First, he loses Molly and now this. It's more than he can handle. I'm glad he's going over to Marcie's. They both love Stormy."

"Oh, I agree with you, Paddy. I must confess—I love Stormy," Dorsey said.

"I kinda figured that out a few weeks ago," Paddy grinned. "I knew the lovebug had bit you when I saw the two of you together."

"Was I that obvious, Paddy?"

"Fear you were, son. Tell you something else while we're talking like this. I think it would be nice if my old friend Kip and that nice Miss Marcie would hitch up. They'd be good for one another."

"Now that you mention it, Paddy, you're right."

They'd come to Paddy's house and were settling in. They were both thinking about Stormy Monihan and wondering where she was.

When Kip arrived at his cottage and went in, it didn't seem right that Stormy wasn't with him. Damned if he wasn't glad that Marcie had asked him to come over. It would have been sheer agony to stay here without Stormy.

He didn't linger any longer than it took him to gather up a change of clothes and the extra pouch of tobacco before he headed for the *East Wind* and Marcie's cottage. He had taken the time to gather up a basket filled with some things from his pantry to take to her. She was such a dear, generous lady but he knew he was also a hearty eater so the basket might help a little during his stay.

It was twilight when the *East Wind* pulled up to the small dock close to Marcie's. Kip had the basket in one hand and his old valise in the other as he walked up the path. But all he could think about was where his little golden-haired daughter was.

It was certainly the tonic he needed to be greeted by Marcie. It helped ease the pain and helplessness devouring him. The delicious aroma of food cooking on her stove whetted his appetite—he was ready for a good home-cooked meal.

Marcie's cottage was like a haven. He knew she was as devastated by what had happened as he was. She'd told him she'd been going through hell for several days when she'd been unable to get in touch with him.

Marcie was like Molly—she enjoyed having her little home glowing with candlelight in the evening. Stormy had never dried and hung herbs from their garden as her mother and Marcie did. It provided a delectable aroma.

Marcie had told him to take his things back to the far bedroom; she'd almost had a slip of the tongue by referring to it as Stormy's bedroom which she now considered it to be.

During the time he'd made his run out to Cape Fear she'd fried a big platter of chicken and prepared potatoes, gravy, and a pan of fresh-baked biscuits. Kip sat down and ate ravenously. They didn't mention Stormy while they ate or did the dishes.

"Damn, Marcie—that was so good! You got to be the best cook in the world."

"Oh, Kip Monihan—you and your blarney!" she laughed. "But I love it so just keep it up."

They could actually allow themselves a little laughter.

"Kip—it's so comforting to have you here. I must admit I enjoyed my dinner more tonight than I have since all this happened with Stormy. I had no incentive to cook for myself."

"I can understand that, Marcie honey. I walked into my place out there on the cove and without Stormy, it seemed ghostly quiet. God, I would have been miserable. I—I needed to be with you, Marcie."

He confessed that being with her had a calming effect on him—he needed a cool, calm head if he was to find his daughter.

Marcie declared, "She's out there somewhere, Kip. I know she is. I just wish we knew where."

"Well, I'm going to pay a call on that sheriff tomorrow morning first thing, Marcie. No, my little Stormy isn't dead. I'd know it if she was," he said as he pointed to his heart.

Marcie told him her feelings about the men who'd abducted Stormy—she was still convinced they were boatmen. "It was the look of them and the garb they wore. Lord, I've had time to think about this over and over again. Stormy was obviously what they came for, so I have to ask myself how they knew we'd be going down that isolated road? One of those young fellows had apparently been stalking Stormy before this happened, I think."

"Did you tell the sheriff this, Marcie?"

"Yes, I did."

Long after Marcie went to bed, Kip sat in her front room pondering who might have enough of a grudge against him to do this.

He could think of no one.

Kip's thoughts about Stormy were also being shared

back in Southport by the young Dorsey. His sharp, keen mind went over everything he could think of. Why would someone have wanted to waylay Kip's beautiful daughter?

As far as he knew, Kip didn't have any enemies. Stormy lived a rather cloistered life, dividing her time between the *East Wind* and Marcie Warren's.

This was Stormy's whole life. Her only contact with the outside world, as far as Pat knew, was an occasional jaunt to town to do some shopping.

Suddenly, he sat up in his bed as though a bolt of lightning had hit him. He remembered the time he'd happened on the scene when that obnoxious Jed Callihan had been trying to push his attention on Stormy. He'd stepped in and led Stormy away, which Pat was sure had not set well with the conceited Callihan.

Pat had to wonder if it was Jed and some of his brawny boatmen who'd waylaid Miss Marcie and Stormy that afternoon. Pat had not liked Jed once he'd discovered who he was trying to woo away Kip's long-time clients. Perhaps he should have mentioned it to Kip when he'd found it out during the time he was making the runs to Savannah while Kip was recovering from his injuries.

He hadn't because none of Kip's customers had accepted Jed's offer to haul their lumber even though he had cut the rate. They wanted to stick with the dependable Kip Monihan, who'd served them so well for many years.

But now Dorsey felt the need to tell Kip—this might be an all-important clue. The next morning he got up early with every intention of heading for Marcie's house, but that wasn't necessary—Kip arrived at Paddy's on his way to see the sheriff in Southport.

Pat told him about Jed Callihan. Kip listened intently—Pat had only to look at his face to know Kip was carefully weighing everything he was saying.

When Pat had finished, Kip spoke solemnly. "Pat, you may have come up with the one clue the sheriff didn't have. I've got some talking to do with Callihan. I knew about Jed trying to undercut my rate."

From the look on Kip's face as he spoke, Pat didn't envy Callihan if it turned out that he had anything to do with Stormy's disappearance. Monihan would surely kill him without a qualm.

Kip got up from his chair. His old friend Paddy had already left to go out on an errand. "I've got to be going, Pat, but I thank you from the bottom of my heart for all this information."

When Kip left Paddy's house, he went to the sheriff's office and got the usual routine report that Marcie had received on each of her trips there for over a week. He did not mention what Pat Dorsey had told him to Sheriff Hartley. Kip knew a lot of eyes and ears out there on that wharf—he was going to do a little investigating on his own. Should he find out anything that would point him in Jed's direction, he'd handle that himself. He was sure young Dorsey would be more than willing to give him a hand.

For over two hours Kip Monihan roamed around the wharf talking to men he knew. All of them knew about the tragic disappearance of his beloved daughter and were willing to keep their eyes and ears open on his behalf.

Kip was about to leave the wharf and call it a day when he came upon the little old lady selling flowers and woven baskets. Knowing how Marcie loved them, he paused long enough to make a purchase.

"Thank you. Thank you very much, sir. I can leave for the day now, but before I do I've something to tell you about your daughter, Stormy. I liked her—she al-

ways had a sweet smile as she passed my way," the old
lady said.

"What can you tell me, lady? I'm a desperate man!"

"Some of Callihan's men have left him. You see, I
hear a lot of things as these young fellows walk by—
they pay no attention to an old woman like me. They
say Callihan stays drunk most of the time, not attending
to his boat. I heard one of them mention your daughter's
name."

"Thank you very much," Kip told her as he dug
down in his pocket to give her a reward.

Kip took the flowers and basket—he was ready to
return to Marcie's. Tomorrow evening he would hit the
boatmen's favorite haunt in Southport, a smoke-filled
tavern called Tides' Inn.

Tonight, he was ready to get back to Marcie's cozy
cottage. As he moved closer and closer, Kip found himself filled with anticipation.

There was no question in his mind that he wanted to
ask Marcie to marry him but he knew she wouldn't
accept. It was too soon after Tom's death and he had
to honor that.

But there was nothing to stop him from telling her
that he loved her, for he did!

Thirteen

It wasn't easy for Kip to spend time at Marcie's and act like a gentleman; the more he was around her, the more he wanted to take her in his arms and make love to her. Marcie sensed this and she knew that they needed each other. She felt no guilt about the feelings she had for Kip Monihan.

There was no betrayal of Tom Warren. He had been her first romantic love and had swept her heart away so swiftly she hardly knew what was happening. For all the years they'd shared she had never thought of loving another man—it had been a most wonderful time in her life that she would cherish forever.

But Tom was gone now and she was alive. The kind of man she had sought to give her heart to in her teens was not the same man she was seeking now that she was approaching thirty.

She could no longer deny that there was something about Kip Monihan that she found attractive. Just being around him gave her the serenity she was seeking.

She worried about Kip when he told her about his plans to return to the Tides' Inn the next night as he would be going up against much younger men.

* * *

Marcie stayed up the next evening until Kip returned well after midnight. She could tell he had learned something that had him churning with anticipation.

In a highly tense mood he went to the cabinet to get himself a glass of his favorite Irish whiskey. As he poured it, he said, "I'm betting Dorsey was right, Marcie. It was Jed and a couple of his hooligans that waylaid you and Stormy. He was irked that she gave him the cold shoulder—Dorsey happened to be coming down the street that day when it happened and escorted her away. It left a foul taste in Jed's mouth—his ego couldn't accept a girl ignoring his so-called charm."

When he told her he was going back to the Tides' Inn the next night, Marcie could not restrain herself. "Oh, Kip—be careful! I want nothing to happen to you."

Perhaps it was the way he was feeling or the whiskey that gave him the courage to take her hand and pull her over to him. Since the hour was late, Marcie was already in her gown and wrapper. She suddenly found herself sitting on his lap.

"Marcie, this is something I must do, but I like feeling your concern for me—and I know how concerned you are for Stormy," he said, looking into her eyes.

Marcie did not know how it happened nor had Kip planned it, but his lips were seeking hers and she was responding.

Kip had waited many years to make love to a woman and Marcie was hungry for a man's kiss. They had only to touch for a spark to become a flaming fire that neither of them wished to put out.

In a trance-like state, Kip gathered her in his arms and carried her to his bedroom. She was too giddy to protest—she wanted Kip to make love to her.

He did not disappoint her. She had never had a man make such gentle, tender love and she had never soared to such lofty heights of passion. Kip Monihan was a very ardent lover and as they lay in each other's arms they were both deep in their private musings.

Perhaps Marcie should have felt guilt about giving herself to Kip, but it seemed right. She knew there was no other man she would have felt that way about since Tom had been dead such a short time. The fact that Kip was much older had not mattered. The truth was, he was more virile than men years younger.

In a deep, husky voice Kip pleaded, "Oh, Marcie! Marcie, don't let this change anything. Don't hate me."

Marcie rolled over to caress his chest. "But it does change everything, Kip."

"Oh, God, I was afraid of that," he moaned.

She laughed softly, "I don't hate you. I think it's love I feel. I'm not sorry it happened."

He sat up in bed and looked directly at her. "You mean that, don't you, Marcie? Damn, I'm happy to hear you say that."

He could see her smile in the moonlight as it shone brightly through the bedroom windows. "I wouldn't say it if I didn't mean it, Kip Monihan."

He bent down to kiss her again and murmur how happy he was. As they lay there together Kip poured out his feelings. "I want us to get married, I want the right to be your husband and lie by your side. You're too fine a lady for me just to live with you. I don't want to wait a year just because it would appear more proper. Hang them! Knowing now how we both feel, don't punish me by making me wait."

"Kip, I have no one to account to and I feel no guilt about what we did. It was surely meant to be. Yes, I'll marry you and we won't wait," she declared.

Kip roared with laughter. "Damn, I never thought this night would end like this. I can't tell you how happy you've made me. If only I could find my little Stormy I would be the happiest man on earth!"

"We'll find her, Kip. I know we will."

For the next few days Kip divided his time between planning his quiet, simple wedding to Marcie Warren and deciding how to deal with Jed Callihan. Paddy and Dorsey were the only ones attending the wedding—that's the way Kip and Marcie wanted it.

It was Kip's idea that they live at his cottage on Cape Fear, where there was more room than at Marcie's. Marcie thought that was a good idea—she wanted to begin their married life in his home instead of the cottage she'd lived in throughout her marriage to Tom.

They were to be married at Kip's cottage in a week, so they began to move some of Marcie's personal possessions. Paddy and Pat helped Kip get some of her furniture loaded aboard the *East Wind* to take to Kip's cottage.

Marcie was delighted when Kip told her, "I want you to make this your home—change anything that pleases you. My happiness is just having you here with me."

"Oh, Kip—I love you so very much!"

A very serious look came over his face. "You know, Marcie, wherever Stormy is, I feel she would wholeheartedly approve of us getting married."

Marcie smiled and nodded. "I feel that way, too, Kip."

By nightfall, Marcie was left alone at the cottage while Kip and Dorsey went around to the various taverns in the town of Southport. It took only three nights of questioning various boatmen for them to single out one of the three men who'd helped Jed as he sought to steal Stormy away.

Denny was a husky fellow but he was no match for

big men like Kip Monihan and Pat Dorsey. By the time they hit him with certain facts they'd found out through the grapevine, he wasn't about to try to cover up for Jed.

Kip's bass voice threatened him, "Don't lie to me, bastard! Tell me exactly what happened that day and what Jed did to my daughter!"

"I—I can only tell you what I saw," Denny stammered. He admitted to being the one restraining Marcie while Jed and Bif Barkley took Stormy. Then he had hightailed it out of there.

"That's the last time I saw your daughter and I think I'm speaking for Bif, too. Jed took her to his boat and we set out for Savannah immediately," he told Kip. He kept glancing down at Kip's huge clenched fists—he had no doubt they were going to beat him to a bloody pulp before this was over.

"Go on," Kip demanded.

"Jed locked her in his cabin and came back to join me and Bif. He was madder than hell—said she was a damned little hellcat but he'd tame her before the night was over. The next thing I know is about an hour later Bif came running up to tell me Jed was like a raging bull. Your daughter had crawled out a small window and escaped. Now that's all I can tell you and that's the honest-to-God truth."

Kip's piercing eyes glared at him. "I think you've told me the truth and you better be damned glad you did. Now get out of my sight before I change my mind."

Kip was glad to hear that Jed had been unable to use his daughter sorely as he'd planned; she had escaped, but what had happened to Stormy after she'd leaped from Callihan's boat?

The thing consuming him was doling out justice to Jed Callihan. Short of killing him, Kip intended to make him pay—and pay very dearly.

The hour was growing late—Dorsey urged Kip to go on home and they'd seek Jed out tomorrow night. Kip reluctantly agreed.

The next evening Kip did not go by Paddy's house to get Pat Dorsey. This was a mission he wanted to go on alone.

Marcie was very nervous when he left the house after dinner.

They had worked around the cottage all day. She had been pleased how her special pieces of furniture had blended in with Kip's. All her clothes and personal possessions were at Kip's so it already felt like home.

She planned to wear the pretty russet-colored dress the night they got married—the one Stormy had thought was so attractive on her.

Marcie had a nice dinner planned after the brief ceremony. She and Kip didn't need anything fancy to make the evening special. They were so very happy.

When Kip gave her a long, lingering kiss before he left, she pleaded, "Oh, be careful, Kip! I'd just die if something happened to you."

"Nothing is going to happen to me, darling. I want to come back home to you," he assured her.

To Marcie's great delight the man she loved returned to her by midnight, safe and sound.

He poured himself a generous glass of Irish whiskey and told her about what had taken place when he went to the Tides' Inn.

Kip settled into one of the comfortable chairs in the front room. With a smug look, he glanced at Marcie. "I think Jed Callihan will remember the name of Monihan for a long, long time. He squealed like a pig as most bullies do when they have to fight their own battles. I found him alone in the tavern and made him show his true colors. I degraded him as he did my daughter and you."

Marcie found herself getting so excited about what Kip was saying that she went to the kitchen for a small helping of his whiskey.

"What happened next, Kip?"

"I taunted him to pick on me as he did two helpless ladies. I was cruel, I will admit, for I announced to the entire tavern how he couldn't take the rejection of a lady who didn't consider him God's gift to women. I asked him, 'What's the matter, Jed? Your overwhelming ego can't believe that a lady finds you crude?' "

"Oh, Kip! You must have had him seething."

"Oh, I had him in a rage—I could see the pulse beating at his temples. He was in a frenzy. I let the whole tavern know what he did to Stormy and announced that I considered anyone who had to lock up a lady to hold her a pretty poor excuse for a man."

Kip told her he had Jed riled enough to accept his invitation to join him outside if he was man enough. Jed could not dare refuse that offer—he would never be able to hold his head up again in the town of Southport.

Jed Callihan found that his youth was no asset when he had to do battle with Kip Monihan. Kip's arms were like steel and his fists were deadly as they pounded Jed's face. Monihan was swift on his feet for such a huge man—he could bob and weave away from Jed's awkward punches.

The patrons gathered outside the swinging doors to witness the fight between Jed and Kip. It took Kip only a short time to have his opponent lying on the ground, a beaten, battered man.

Cheers went up for Kip as he prepared to leave the stilled figure lying there. Kip knew that Jed would never be able to hold his head high again in Southport. Sweet revenge!

Fourteen

Kip's revenge had been sweet but he still had no inkling of where Stormy was or what had happened to her after she'd escaped from Jed. While she was very much on his mind, he willed himself to put his worries behind him for the day he and Marcie were to be married.

His Marcie deserved a wonderful wedding to remember and he wanted that for her. Paddy and Dorsey helped make it a festive evening by bringing baskets of flowers and several bottles of wine. Marcie was overcome with emotion—the two of them were obviously so happy for her and Kip.

Marcie's only regret was that Stormy was not there to share this special occasion. That would have made everything perfect!

She had to be alive out there somewhere, Marcie kept telling herself. She had to believe that!

If there was such a thing as one person's thoughts traveling across the miles to another person who was intensely thinking about them, then this had to be true tonight. Stormy was being bombarded tonight by thoughts she couldn't understand.

It had all begun that afternoon when she tried out the hammock which Jason had hung up but had never slept in since the night they first made love. As he had cautioned her, she had tried to crawl into it but she'd taken a tumble and her pretty head had suffered a sharp blow! For a brief moment she had sat on the floor, stunned.

She'd said nothing about it to Jason when he'd come to the cabin, but all afternoon after the tumble she had experienced flashes of images and faces and she knew they had to be from her past. She tried desperately to put the pieces of this crazy puzzle together.

As she lay in Jason's arms that night a storm hit as they were approaching the English coastline. Jason figured they were less than forty-eight hours away from England. It wasn't a bad storm, but the rain was pelting the small windows and there were sharp flashes of lightning.

Stormy sat up in the bed and announced to Jason, "That's me, Jason! I'm Stormy."

Heavy with sleep, Jason sat up in bed. "What is it, love?"

"I said that's me, Jason. I'm Stormy Monihan. Oh God, Jason, I've finally remembered my name after all this time." There was such excitement in her voice as she sat up in bed that Jason slowly rose to sit up with her.

Rubbing his eyes and trying to rouse himself, he asked, "You sure of that, love?" He'd known all along that Stormy was her name for that's what she'd said when she'd slapped him. He asked her if she remembered anything else.

Like a naughty little girl confessing to her parent, Stormy said, "Well, I wasn't going to tell you, Jason, but I've had strange feelings all afternoon. I've seen bits and pieces of images of people—they must be from my past. You see, I tried to get in your hammock and fell to the floor, bumping my head. Maybe it helped clear my head, Jason."

He listened to what she was saying—he'd heard about

how someone with memory loss could suffer a second blow and it would restore it.

But he had called her Princess for so long that he still wanted to call her that as he urged her to lie back down with him. He felt the need for more sleep before he had to get up to put in a full day of work.

It was apparent that for right now all she recalled was her name or she would have been telling him more.

"We'll talk some more tomorrow, love," he suggested as he pulled her pretty head back on the pillow.

But the next day, Stormy was depressed. No new clues had come to her and it had been a long day since Jason was out on the deck of his schooner. He sensed her mood when he finally turned over the shift to his first mate and suggested that they take a stroll around the deck before Tobias served them dinner in the cabin. "You look like you need a little exercise and some fresh air," he said.

"Perhaps it would help. Oh, Jason—I'm so disappointed. I had hoped I would recall more today but not a darn thing has come."

"Princess, don't try to force anything. It will come— probably when you're not expecting it. Don't get sad on me. We've been too happy lately. I've never been happier than I've been the last few days," he admitted.

She smiled up sweetly, "Oh, Jason, I adore you. You always make me feel so good."

He grinned and bent to plant a kiss on her cheek. "That's the general idea, love, and now I'll tell you something that will brighten your spirits. We've almost reached the coast of England."

His announcement brought no joy to her, for she had nothing to look forward to in England. He realized this when he got no response from her.

"I'm sorry, Jason, but I can't pretend that getting to England thrills me. What have I got to look forward to there. My life is back across that ocean and what family I have is somewhere near Southport."

His dark eyes looked down at her. "Well, you're going home with me until I can get you back to where you belong."

Stormy made no fuss about that for she had no choice. She was grateful that he wished to take her but she had to question what his family would think about him bringing a strange young girl to their home. But he quickly assured her that they would be delighted.

"All my sisters are married now so my parents have a big old rambling house with a lot of unoccupied bedrooms."

He was walking her back down to his cabin for it was getting to be dinner time.

Tobias arrived shortly after they had returned. Instead of having a drink of his favorite whiskey, Jason filled two glasses of wine. "Here, Princess—let's have a little wine while we're waiting for dinner." He hoped that it might relax her—she seemed so quiet and moody.

She took a sip.

"Like it, Princess?"

"I'll tell you in a few minutes, Jason. Right now I'm not too sure," she admitted candidly.

He watched her with an amused smile. He felt certain she'd never drunk a glass of wine before but he figured it was the right time to get her used to the taste.

Then Tobias came to the door and served them a tasty meal. By the time dinner was over, Stormy had decided she did like the wine, so Jason filled her glass again.

Jason had filled his own glass a couple of times. He'd eaten heartily of the roasted hen Tobias had served—it was the last of the chickens in the coop down in the hold. Food supplies purchased when they were in port were always running low by the time they arrived back in England.

Jason could see that the wine had helped her relax by the time Tobias had gathered up the plates and left the cabin. She had gotten up from the chair and crossed the room to the small window.

"It's a lovely starlit night, Jason," she commented as she gazed out the window.

"There's nothing more beautiful than that when you're out on the water," he replied as he lit up one of his cheroots.

"I know, Jason. I think I must have enjoyed the sight many times," she remarked casually as she continued to look out the window.

Jason sat up and frowned. "How would you know that, Princess?"

She turned around to look at him. "I told you I had bits and pieces come to me yesterday. I remember water and starlit nights."

Jason made an impulsive decision. "Princess come here—I need to talk to you." He prayed he was doing the right thing for he would never forgive himself if he was wrong.

"What is it, Jason?"

"Princess, I met you long before I found you here on my ship. It was on the streets of Southport one afternoon. You made quite an impression on me—I thought you were so beautiful."

"We had met before, Jason?" Stormy was frowning.

"Only one brief encounter, love, for a few minutes."

"Tell me more."

"Well, I thought I was playing the gallant gentleman because I tried to rescue you from a fellow who seemed to be bothering you and for one brief moment I found myself holding you in my arms. But the reward I got was a mighty slap on the face. You were in a foul temper and insisted you could fight your own battles without any help from me."

"I slapped you, Jason? Oh, how could I have done that when you were trying to help me?"

Jason grinned, "That's what I kept asking myself, love. But you did slap me and I must say, there's a lot of force in that dainty little hand. When you marched away you told me something, Princess. You said your name was Stormy Monihan and I'd better remember it."

A slow smile came to her face. It was as if the floodgates had opened and something was triggered in her mind. "So that makes me right! My name is Stormy, Jason, as I told you last night." She suddenly broke into a gale of laughter as Jason sat there not knowing what to expect next.

"I'm Stormy Monihan, Jason! I'm also Savannah Monihan but everyone calls me Stormy."

For the next hour she talked to Jason about how she was named Savannah because she had been born just off the Georgia coast on a stormy night and her birth had caused her mother's death. She told him that her father was Kip Monihan and his boat was the *East Wind*.

"We lived on Cape Fear when we weren't making runs on the *East Wind*. My father took me on his boat even when I was a baby. He was my father as well as my mother, Jason."

"Now I understand why you seem so at home on my schooner. Ladies don't take too easily to the sea," he said, recalling how Tawny Blair had detested being on his ship.

"I knew no other life except the *East Wind* and the little cottage on Cape Fear."

She told Jason about all the people dear to her. Jason listened with fascination; whatever block had been in her mind had obviously been swept away. It didn't matter to him that she was Stormy or Savannah—he was content to call her Princess.

He felt the need of another glass of wine and he asked if she would like one. She accepted. As he strolled back over to the table, he asked her, "Tell me, love, if you can remember—how did you happen to be on my ship?"

"I remember as though it were yesterday. I was going with Marcie to stay with her while Pa made his run to Savannah when we were waylaid by Jed Callihan and his hooligans. They abducted me."

"And why would he do this, love?"

"Because I didn't gush all over him like most of the girls around Southport did. I riled him good and he's a bully, so he must have been seeking revenge." She told Jason how she was taken to Callihan's boat and locked in his cabin.

Jason listened intently as she told him she was quick to realize that Jed Callihan was planning to force himself on her before the night was over. After she had angered him so much that he left the cabin to cool off, she had managed to escape through a narrow little window. "I had him so mad that he could easily have killed me right then and there but he didn't want to. He just wanted to pleasure himself and satisfy his wounded ego."

She told him how she had leaped into the water to swim to the coastline and had no doubt she could make it. "I can swim like a fish. I remember the shallow waters and how I stood up. But I have to confess this is where things get foggy again. I do know it was the blackest night I ever remember."

She told Jason that she must have tripped over something and hit her head—then the blackness was really consuming her.

"A nice farmer and his wife found me in the early

morning and loaded me into the bed of their wagon. I couldn't tell them who I was or why I was there—I remembered nothing. I stayed with them for over a week."

"Oh, Princess—you have had quite an ordeal," Jason sighed.

"That brings me to the day I wandered on the wharf and boarded your ship, Jason. Poor Joe and Ella didn't know what to do to help me. Joe had made inquiries but learned nothing so they decided to take me with them to Southport where they sell their produce down on the wharf. While they were involved in unloading the wagon, a sudden urge came over me to wander away."

She realized there had to be something about the sight of the wharf that was taxing her memory. She told Jason she had no inkling of how long she'd roamed around aimlessly before she spied his ship. "It had to be the most magnificent ship I'd ever seen. I remember how intrigued I was and how I was compelled to explore it. No one stopped me, so I roamed all around until I finally came to the cabin. I was exhausted and must have fallen asleep for five or six hours until you were well out to sea."

Jason got up from his chair and in one easy motion he picked her up and carried her back to where he'd been sitting.

He placed her on his lap as though she was a small child. His slender fingers gently brushed the stray curls away from her face. "I know who you are and so do you, Princess. Maybe destiny led you to me, Stormy Monihan. I've got to confess I shall still call you Princess. Can that always be my special name for you?"

She smiled. "Always, if you wish, Jason."

"Thank you, love. It fits you perfectly. Now I've got one question. How did a beautiful girl like you ever get the nickname Stormy when she was named Savannah?"

"Well, as I told you, my pa had me on his boat from the time I was a baby because he had no one to take care of me. One of his men started calling me Stormy because I was a high-tempered little brat and kicked his shins one day. Somehow it caught on and soon everyone, even Pa, started calling me Stormy."

Watching her face as she talked and used her hands, he was thinking that she and his mother would get along just fine. They had a lot in common—he never forgot how lovingly his mother, the daughter of an Irishman, spoke about her own humble background.

If Jason knew his vivacious mother as well as he thought he did, she would be as intrigued by Stormy Monihan as she'd been when he arrived with Tawny Blair in tow.

He wouldn't have to wait too long since the English coastline was not far away! Very soon, Lady Sheila Hamilton would meet Stormy Monihan.

He had to confess to himself that he was curious about what her reaction would be!

Fifteen

The morning they arrived in London the city was shrouded with thick fog and a chilly mist. Jason couldn't see Princess getting off the ship in bare feet and without a cloak.

He asked Rudy and Tobias to remain with her while he made a hurried trip to purchase stockings, slippers, and a light woolen cape.

An hour later, Jason was rushing back across the deck with his purchases. Stormy had no inkling that this was what he was doing when he told her he had an errand to run before they could leave the *Sea Princess*.

When Rudy and Tobias were dismissed, they exchanged smiles. It was certainly obvious that their captain was smitten by the little lady. In truth, she was the captain's lady!

Old Tobias was very sincere as he declared, "I think she'd be perfect for Jason. She could come to love the *Sea Princess* as much as he does. She could be a captain's lady, Rudy."

"Yes, I think she could, Tobias," Rudy agreed.

Tobias and Rudy left the ship to go their separate ways until they were called to serve on the *Sea Princess* again. Rudy planned to spend some time with his married sister and Tobias was going to his own little place on the outskirts of London. Age was catching up with Tobias and he wasn't sure how many more trips he would make with Jason as his galley cook. But Captain Hamilton was a fine man to work for and Tobias hoped to put in a few more years before he retired to his little four-room house.

It had been a very pleasant afternoon for Lady Sheila Hamilton to greet a guest who'd arrived quite unexpectedly about three that afternoon. Lord Addison had gone into the city about two, so Sheila didn't expect him to return before five.

To have Tawny Montgomery ushered into her sitting room was a wonderful surprise for Lady Sheila.

"Tawny, dear, how sweet of you to come by to see me!" Sheila said as she rose from the floral settee. This young lady would never cease to amaze her, Lady Hamilton thought to herself as she led Tawny over to sit down. She was as trim and slim as she'd been the first time she set her eyes on her, which was several months before she'd married Bart Montgomery.

Having her two babies in the last few years had only enhanced the lovely curves of her body. She still wore her beautiful hair loose most of the time unless she and Bart were entertaining or going into London for a social affair.

She looked chic this afternoon in her tailored riding ensemble—Tawny rarely wore any kind of hat.

"You're looking quite fine, Lady Sheila. I trust all your family are, too," Tawny remarked as she sat down.

"As far as I know they are, Tawny. Lord Addison is in the city this afternoon. I've had no news from Angela or Jane but my little Joy was out here the other day. That vagabond son of mine is somewhere out on the sea as usual. Oh, I wish he'd settle down, Tawny."

Tawny laughed softly. "He will one day. Bart swears

hat Jason will fall head over heels for someone one of
hese days."

"Well, if anyone knows Jason it has to be Bart," his
mother declared. "Your little family all well and hearty,
I assume?"

"Almost too healthy, I think at times. Bart sheared
our son's golden curls off yesterday—I almost had to
cry. He said it was time he was looking like a boy
instead of a girl. Our little Joy is getting into more
things than we can keep her out of."

Lady Hamilton laughed. "Oh, isn't it an adventure
raising children?"

"I never realized how much. I'm rather glad I started
my family so young, knowing how much energy it takes
to put in a day with them. Yesterday Bart said he is
ready for us to take a holiday for a week or ten days
in London and leave them here with their nanny. I think
I agree," Tawny confessed.

Instead of afternoon tea, Lady Sheila and Tawny
shared a love of coffee. They sat there for an hour enjoying the coffee and some little cakes Sheila had her
servant serve.

Tawny told her about Bart's fine new stallion, Baron.
"He's magnificent, Lady Sheila. In fact, I rode him over
here this afternoon. Bart wanted me to see what I
thought of him so I just decided to come see you."

"I'm delighted you did, Tawny." She smiled at this
lovely girl she'd yearned so desperately for Jason to
make his bride but she knew things had worked out for
the best. Tawny and Bart Montgomery made the perfect
couple, sharing their great love of horses as well as life
in the picturesque English countryside.

It was almost four-thirty when Tawny announced she
had to be getting back home. "I've been making Baron
wait out there too long. But it's always good to sit and
talk to you, Lady Sheila."

Lady Hamilton walked with her to the door. As Tawny mounted Baron and veered to go down the long winding drive, she spied a buggy. But it wasn't the fancy little buggy Lord Addison took when he went into the city, so Tawny called out to Lady Sheila, "It seems to be your afternoon to have guests."

"I suppose so," she replied as she watched Tawny spur the fiery stallion into a swift gallop. Tawny passed by the buggy so hastily that she got only a fleeting glance of Jason and threw her hand up to wave to him.

But she was curious about the gorgeous blonde in the seat next to him. Surely she had to be the new lady in Jason's life, Tawny figured as she rode on toward her own home.

In a few short seconds a lot of memories paraded through Tawny's mind as she rode the short distance that separated the estates of the Hamilton and Montgomery families.

How close she had been to marrying Jason when she had felt that Bart had played unfair with her; she was expecting their first child and knowing all this, Jason had offered to marry her. She had finally accepted him and left Virginia, sailing back to England with him aboard the *Sea Princess*.

But she had only to arrive back in England with him to know that the ghost of the handsome Lord Montgomery would stand between them. She couldn't love Jason as she did Bart. She felt something more like brotherly love for Jason.

Tawny could not bring herself to play games with him for he and his family were too nice to her so she confessed everything to Jason. She suddenly realized that Jason was just as apprehensive as she was about getting married.

In the end Bart didn't disappoint her and convinced her beyond any shadow of a doubt that he adored her and wanted very much to marry her. The years they had been married had been glorious. Bart had been everything her young romantic heart had dreamed about. She could not imagine a man being a more devoted husband than her handsome English lord.

Lady Hamilton stood at the top of the steps to see who was approaching her home. To her delight, she recognized her black-haired son in the buggy seat—but she also saw the lovely, fair-haired creature sitting beside him. Her Irish curiosity was keenly whetted by the time he leaped down and helped the young lady to the ground.

Jason took Stormy's arm as he led her up to his mother. Stormy instinctively knew who this lady was—he looked exactly like her!

He released his hold on Stormy's arm to embrace his mother. With a teasing grin, he said, "See, mother? I said I'd be back safe and sound." He quickly turned to take Stormy's hand and urge her forward so he could introduce her. "Come here, Princess—I want you to meet my mother. Mother, this is Stormy Monihan."

"Nice to meet you, Stormy. Welcome to our home," Lady Hamilton said.

"Thank you, Lady Hamilton." Stormy was slightly overwhelmed by her surroundings. It was a palace! Jason pointed out the spacious mansion as they'd approached the estate and she'd gasped, "Dear God, this is your home, Jason?"

He laughed and nodded. For a young girl like Stormy who'd lived all her life in a small cottage on Cape Fear or aboard her father's boat, this was enough to leave her a little awestruck. Why, this was like a place that kings and queens lived in, Stormy thought as she found herself led inside the house and down the long hallway. The elegant furnishings were enough to make her feel giddy. She clutched Jason's hand tighter as they walked down the hallway. He and his mother talked and laughed just like she would have done with her own father.

Stormy was already sensing that Lady Hamilton was a warm, loving lady just from the way she acted with her son. Jason and his mother seemed to have the kind of special relationship she did with her father. Now she was curious to meet Lord Addison.

"Stormy, dear—please forgive us for being such chatterboxes but this is just the way it is when this son of mine returns from one of his long voyages," Sheila Hamilton said, realizing how quiet Stormy had been walking by Jason's side.

"I can understand that you're very happy to see your son, Lady Hamilton," Stormy said, managing to smile even though she was still feeling a little ill at ease.

If Stormy thought she was ill at ease, Sheila was aware that she was feeling the same way. She wondered just what Jason meant by suddenly appearing with this young lady.

Once they were comfortable in Lady Hamilton's sitting room, she asked her servant to bring a tray of refreshments. Jason had helped Stormy out of her new brown wool cape—Sheila had only to look at the girl's simple attire to know that she was going to hear a very interesting story from Jason about this lovely young lady once they were alone.

Immediately, Sheila Hamilton remembered how he'd brought another young lady to their home, dressed in similar attire. Now she was Lady Tawny Montgomery.

When they had finished the refreshments, Jason's mother said to her son, "Occupy yourself while I see our guest to her room. Your father could arrive any time so I'll leave you here to greet him while I get Stormy settled in." She gestured to Stormy to come with her.

As they were mounting the stairs, Lady Hamilton confessed, "Your name fascinates me, dear, and I'll be eager to know how you came by it. Now the last name is a good Irish name."

Stormy smiled, "Yes, ma'am. It's Irish."

"And so am I, Stormy."

"Are you now, ma'am?"

"Certainly am. I was born in Ireland and lived there all my life until a handsome Englishman came and stole my heart," she said gaily.

Stormy found it easy to warm to this vivacious lady, as most people did. There was no snobbish way about her as Stormy had imagined there might be, especially after Jason had pointed out this grand house.

Sheila found herself guiding Stormy to the guest bedroom adjacent to Joy's former room. It was decorated in a similar decor in shades of lavender and white.

"I'll send Rebecca up to prepare a nice warm bath which I'm sure you'll welcome after your long voyage. If you'll excuse me for a minute, dear, I've something to get for you."

Lady Hamilton rushed out of the room, leaving Stormy to survey her surroundings. She'd never seen such luxurious furnishings. Her green eyes took in the dainty white dressing table trimmed with gold gilt and the matching little stool with the lavender velvet cushion. Frilly curtains hung at the windows and a lacy lavender coverlet covered the bed, topped with a mountain of little pillows piled at the headboard.

A huge armoire stood against one wall. There was so much for Stormy's curious eyes to see that she had just begun her survey when Lady Hamilton came dashing back into the room, her arms piled high with various articles of clothing. Her experienced eyes had noted that Jason had carried only his valise into the house.

She had gone into Joy's room to fetch a few things

she was sure Stormy could use. She'd brought her a nightgown and robe of pink silk along with an array of lacy undergarments and a pair of cream-colored slippers. There was also one of Joy's simple little sprigged muslin gowns—Sheila had thought that the cream-colored frock with the tiny green print would be something Stormy would feel comfortable in.

Joy had never cared for the gown and had left it behind when she married Eric. It's squared neckline and little puff sleeves made the simple frock similar to the one Stormy was wearing.

Lady Hamilton smiled as she piled the things on the bed. "I thought you might like this to change into, Stormy."

How very kind she was, Stormy thought as she realized Jason's mother had to know she'd brought no luggage with her.

Sheila had no need to mention that there was a gown and robe or the fresh, clean undergarments but Stormy was feeling very humbled by her generous act. Jason had a wonderful mother!

"Thank you, ma'am. Thank you very much," Stormy said.

Sheila Hamilton was an affectionate lady. She walked over to give Stormy a motherly embrace, saying, "Now, I'm leaving you here to enjoy your bath and rest, dear. Jason will come to get you later when we shall all meet again for dinner." She started toward the door but as she went out of the room she turned around. "It's nice to have you here, Stormy."

Lady Sheila left the room and moved slowly back down the stairs to join her son, feeling most curious about the tale Jason was sure to tell her.

No question about it—her son did live a most interesting life as a sea captain. But she knew he would not be a completely happy, fulfilled young man until he had a wife.

Stormy reveled in the luxurious bath. She lathered herself generously with the sweet-smelling soap—the aroma was heavenly. In fact, she was reluctant to leave the soothing warmth of the soapy water in the huge bronze tub. But she knew she must for she wanted to be dressed and ready when Jason came to take her down to dinner.

After she had dried herself with the soft towel, she slipped into the pretty undergarments. Jason's sister must be about her size—her sprigged muslin gown was a perfect fit. Amazingly, so were the soft leather slippers. Stormy was already realizing that this place had cooler weather than Georgia and her home out on Cape Fear, so she was grateful for the warm, silky stockings.

She had got her long hair slightly damp when she'd bathed so she sat down at the dressing table to give it a vigorous brushing.

When she looked at herself a few minutes later, she was pleased. Now she had nothing to do but wait for Jason so she propped herself up on the bed, thinking about how much she'd be telling her pa and Marcie when she saw them.

She felt at ease around Lady Sheila, but now she was pondering how Jason's father, Lord Addison, would react to a strange young lady in his home.

She had become so relaxed propped up against the mountain of silk pillows that she was drowsing when she heard a rap on her door. She rushed to see Jason standing there, looking very handsome in his white linen shirt and finely-tailored blue tweed coat and darker blue wool pants.

His first words were enough to please her. "Well,

how beautiful you look! Shall we join my family, Princess?"

Her green eyes twinkled as she gave him a nod and took his arm. Jason had no doubts that his father would be as intrigued as his mother already was.

Sixteen

At first Stormy felt a little uncomfortable in the company of Lord Addison—he was not the gregarious person that his wife was. Yet, she didn't find him unfriendly. He, too, welcomed her to their home, but in a more sober way. Stormy found nothing about Jason that reminded her of his father. It was his mother he looked like, with his black hair and dark eyes.

She remembered the pictures of Jason's sisters which he kept on his desk aboard his ship. One of them certainly looked like her father, Stormy thought.

Jason had inherited his father's tall, towering figure and long legs, for Lady Sheila was a short lady no taller than Stormy.

They all sat enjoying the wine Lord Addison had requested before they prepared to go into the dining room. He directed his conversation to Stormy. "Young lady, I find myself as fascinated by your name as my wife is. Suppose you might tell us how you came to be called Stormy? You don't appear to me to be a stormy lady."

Stormy laughed. "Well, I fear there are some people who think differently. Actually, Lord Addison, my father named me Savannah since I was born off the coast of Georgia aboard his boat, the *East Wind*. My mother died that night—it was very stormy, I've been told. Pa was in such deep sorrow that my name was not too important. Actually, I think it was his cook, Paddy, who suggested he name me Savannah for that was the port they were trying to make."

She told Jason's parents that her father had raised her on his boat. "My first bed was one of the drawers of the oak chest in his cabin. My nurses were various crew members."

Stormy knew that Lady Hamilton was completely engrossed by her revelation and obviously Lord Addison was, too. He exclaimed, "You have a fascinating tale there, Miss Monihan."

"Oh, please—just call me Stormy."

Lord Addison smiled and urged her, "I shall if you will tell me about that name."

Stormy now saw that he wasn't such a stern, serious man—there was a light side to this dignified gentleman. So she told him about one of the men dubbing her Stormy after she had had one of her tantrums. "I guess I had a temper when I didn't get my way. I must have been a little brat and a problem for my father and the crew when I began to roam around the deck when they were trying to work."

"You must have a very nice father, Stormy," Lord Addison declared.

"The best, sir. Mother and father to me is what he is," she replied.

"And we must let the dear man know as soon as possible that you are safe and in good hands, Stormy dear," Lady Hamilton added.

"Oh, I've already written letters to him and my dear friend, Marcie, and given them to Jason," Stormy said.

"I'm going into London tomorrow, Mother," Jason assured her. "I'll have them on a ship heading back that way, rest assured."

The four of them moved into the spacious dining room. In that quiet, reserved way of his, Lord Hamilton was observing the young lady as well as his son. Like

Sheila, he was reminded of Tawny, but this little lady was different in her own distinctive way.

Lord Addison was not so old that he couldn't admire a feisty little filly when he saw one. There was a certain way those green eyes flashed when she talked which led him to believe she could explode with fury if she was riled. His own beloved Sheila could have a fierce temper when she was vexed. Once when he'd told his wife that he had come to the conclusion that the Irish didn't control their tempers as well as the English, she had just laughed and declared that they didn't even try. "We just let it all out, Addison dear. We don't bottle it up like you Englishmen," she'd added saucily.

It was a most delicious meal. Stormy had never dined in such luxurious surroundings. Her busy eyes took in the many fine silver serving dishes, bowls, and candelabra.

It amazed her that Jason wanted to rough it out on the sea where his living conditions were certainly not like this. All this must not be that important to him. As he'd told her, his stays in London were usually only a few weeks before he took off again.

"This will be the longest period I'll be home," he'd said, explaining that the Atlantic was treacherous to cross during the winter months. So he usually made brief trips nearer the English coastline during that time.

When the meal was over and they returned to the parlor, Jason was thinking how much quieter it was without his sisters. He had to admit he almost missed that little chatterbox Joy, sitting at the table teasing him. He wondered what she would think about Stormy. Would she like her as instantly as she had Tawny Blair? There was no question that she'd been trying to play the little matchmaker—she was devastated when she found out there was to be no wedding between him and Tawny.

Jason invited Stormy to take a stroll in the gardens before she went upstairs to retire. She eagerly accepted his invitation—she was ready to move around after the huge feast.

Lord Addison and his wife watched the young couple go out the double doors leading to the terrace—both were thinking what an attractive couple they made.

"She's beautiful, isn't she, Addison?" Sheila said, looking over at her husband as he was watching them go out the door.

"She's that and more, dear. I think Jason might just be very taken with this little Stormy."

Sheila leaned forward excitedly. "Do you really think so, Addison?"

"I do, my dear. Remember how taken we both were with little Tawny when he brought her here?"

"How could I ever forget, Addison?"

"Well, Jason acted different around Tawny than he does around this little miss. You'll see what I mean, Sheila. As you're always saying, time will tell."

"It always does, doesn't it, Addison?" she said, smiling at him.

Addison suggested that they go on up to their suite. "I don't think the young people will miss us, do you?"

Sheila rose and went over to join him. She reached up to plant a kiss on his aristocratic cheek. "I doubt we'll be missed at all. But you know something, Addison Hamilton? You may fool a lot of people but I have always known that you're a sentimental gent."

He took her arm and smiled. "Keep that our little secret, love."

After Stormy had been with Jason and his parents for three days, Lady Hamilton had to agree with her husband. Jason *was* different around Stormy than he had been with Tawny. When he went in to London, he took her with him as though he didn't want to be apart from her. With Tawny, he had left her at the house to be entertained by his sisters and mother.

But the most startling revelation to Lady Hamilton was the morning the two of them left the house early. Stormy was wearing a pair of faded pants and an over-sized faded blue shirt. She was to find out later that the two of them had worked around the *Sea Princess* all day.

Jason was in the highest spirits when they returned to the house. Sheila had watched them get out of the buggy, lightheartedly and holding hands. If that wasn't love in Jason's eyes, then Sheila Hamilton decided she wasn't as smart as she considered herself to be.

When they came into the sitting room to join her, Sheila learned from Jason that Stormy had pitched in to help him on the *Sea Princess*. "I'm going to hire her on my crew, Mother. She's a hard little worker," Jason had remarked playfully.

"I'll give you a day's work for a day's pay, Jason Hamilton," she replied cheerily.

Lady Hamilton found herself becoming fonder and fonder of Stormy Monihan but she did not want to create any false hopes. She remembered how crestfallen she was when Jason had not married Tawny.

It could happen again, she reminded herself.

But after Jason had been home for two weeks his mother still did not see that look of wanderlust in his eyes nor did he seem bored as he often was after he'd been home this long. He seemed to find utter content-ment in Stormy's company—she was able to keep him happy and smiling as no other girl ever had.

He took her everywhere and Stormy enjoyed all the little jaunts around the city. There was so much to see that she wondered if she'd ever be able to see all of it

before they had to leave. She loved the quaint little
shops and tea rooms Jason took her to in the afternoon.

There were all the beautiful parks and grand palaces.
She remembered the stories Marcie had read to her as
a child about kings and queens. Here in London there
was actually a king and queen living in the palace,
which Jason pointed out.

She couldn't stop Jason's urge to buy her extravagant
gifts. She couldn't believe all the packages they carried
out of a little dress shop on one of their trips into the
city.

She protested violently, "Damn it, Jason—I—I don't
feel right about this. What will your mother think?"

He laughed, "Stormy, you can hardly go around in
that same little frock or the one you arrived in. Our
winter days are too chilly."

Jason seem to know just what a young lady's attire
should be. Stormy figured it was because he had three
sisters, for he gave the clerk very specific requests as
to what she should help Stormy select. When they returned to the country estate, she was outfitted with a
complete wardrobe, including a green velvet cape and
fur muff.

When Stormy saw the beautiful muff, she smiled
sweetly. "I've never worn a muff, Jason."

"You will over here. It will keep those pretty hands
warm," he told her.

She giggled, "Oh, Jason Hamilton—I give up!"

"You might as well, love!"

It was almost twilight by the time the buggy was
rolling toward Jason's home. With a devious grin, he
said, "Princess, in a few weeks that new cape and muff
will really feel good."

She smiled but said nothing. She didn't look forward
to the harsh winter Jason was describing. And there'd
been something else churning inside her for the last few

days. She knew how long it had taken Jason's schooner to cross the ocean and now her letters to Marcie and her father had been on a ship for over a week. She hoped her father would soon receive her letter.

Then he would know she was alive—she was already anticipating getting a letter from him. As nice as the Hamiltons were and as much as she adored Jason, she still yearned to return to Cape Fear.

There was no question in Stormy's mind that she loved Jason Hamilton but now that she had seen the surroundings he had been raised in as the son of a wealthy English lord and lady, she was sure Jason would never ask her to marry him. His bride would probably be the daughter of one of his parents' wealthy friends.

She didn't dare to fool herself about that. No one could have been kinder to her than Lord Addison and Lady Sheila had been. But she was the daughter of a humble Irish boatman and her kind didn't marry into wealthy families like Jason's.

Since the day they'd arrived in London, they'd only had one chance to give way to the passion they'd discovered on Jason's schooner. That had been the day she'd gone with Jason to the schooner and they'd worked around the ship all day. Before they'd departed for the house they'd gone to his cabin.

Once again, Stormy reveled in the ecstasy of Jason's loving arms. She wanted to believe the sweet words of love he whispered in her ear as they lay entwined. But all the time he was telling her how much he adored her, he had never once said he wanted her to be his wife.

Stormy had to ask herself if a man loved a woman as much as Jason said he loved her, then would he not want her to be his wife?

Being Kip Monihan's daughter had instilled a tremen-

dous pride in Stormy. She could never settle for being
a man's mistress, not even Jason Hamilton's, even
though she loved him with all her heart and soul.

Jason had to know she could not stay in London indefinitely—Kip Monihan would make arrangements to
get her back home. If Jason didn't want to part with
her then he would have to ask her to be his wife.

Jason had no inkling of the thoughts in Stormy's
pretty head as they had returned from his schooner that
winter afternoon.

Stormy vowed that she wouldn't submit to his lovemaking again unless he asked her to marry him.

Jason would have to face the fact that she wouldn't
be his mistress.

Seventeen

The next week Stormy met one of Jason's sisters when Joy and Eric paid a visit to her parents' home. Stormy found Joy just as friendly and outgoing as Sheila but she looked nothing like Jason and his mother. Joy had inherited her fair complexion and hair from her father.

Joy was eager to hear Stormy's fascinating tale about how she chanced to be on Jason's schooner. Lady Hamilton knew exactly what thoughts were running through her little Joy's pretty head. She was surely thinking how similar the situation was with how Tawny Blair arrived here with Jason and yet, it obviously wasn't the same at all. Joy could see the vast differences in the two of them. Stormy was as breathtakingly beautiful with her fair loveliness as Tawny was with her dark hair and eyes. But Joy sensed a very different temperament between the two even after she'd been there only a short time.

Her handsome young husband shook his head with a good-natured grin. The chances were that the Montgomerys probably knew about Stormy's arrival and he told Joy that.

"No, they don't, Eric. I asked Mother," Joy quickly replied.

"Remember Joy—a half hour, then we have to be on our way."

Eric was a very patient man who indulged his wife about most things. He knew he would be lucky if he got her away from the Montgomerys within an hour. As usual, he had it figured right. By the time they got to the other side of London on the outskirts of the city, it was getting dark.

But it was hard for Eric to get angry at Joy. Having two married sisters, Eric suspected that his little wife just might be expecting their first child and he could not be happier. It seemed that her waistline had expanded the last two months and her breasts seemed much fuller. So he figured she might just be keeping it her little secret until she was sure. He couldn't wait to hear the grand news!

That evening as Tawny and Bart sat in their dining room she told him about Joy's visit. Bart threw his head back and laughed. "That Jason surely does have the luck of the Irish. First, it was you and now this Stormy Monihan."

Tawny's dark eyes twinkled brightly. "Oh, Bart— wouldn't it be wonderful if she turned out to be the woman for Jason? Nothing would make Lady Sheila happier. She's so anxious for grandchildren of her own. She tells me this all the time."

"I'll ride over there tomorrow and invite Jason and his young lady to dine with us—if that's all right, love?"

"Of course it is. I'd like to meet her. Joy said she was from Southport. That's on down the coastline from where I lived," Tawny remarked as she took a sip of her wine.

"You two southern belles should have a lot to talk about," he said as he smiled across the table.

"It will be nice to see someone from my part of the

world. I'll look forward to them coming over here. Besides, it's been a while since Jason has seen our children."

"Did Joy get to see them this afternoon when she stopped by?" Bart asked.

"No, they were upstairs napping when Joy and Eric came by"

After their meal was finished, Bart suggested a stroll in their gardens. They had walked only briefly when Tawny remarked, "Winter must be coming. I feel a chill in the air tonight, Bart."

"All the more reason to enjoy this stroll while we can. Shall we plan on going into London next month to spend a few weeks? Would you like that, love?"

"Oh, yes. I want to do some shopping, Bart."

He laughed as he pressed her closer to his side. "I was afraid of that!"

"Now, Bart—for the children, not myself. The holidays come so quickly once autumn arrives," she mused.

Bart pulled her around to face him so he could kiss her. It was an ardent kiss—Bart was a man still very much in love with his wife.

Stormy was nervous about meeting Jason's friends even though Lady Sheila had assured her she would like Tawny and Bart. She told Stormy that Tawny came from Virginia. "You two will get along just fine, dear."

She told her how Bart and Jason had been lifetime friends but omitted telling her that that friendship was almost severed forever because of Tawny.

Later when Stormy had gone upstairs to dress, she wondered which of her new frocks she should wear. Finally she decided on the rich green dress with the matching jacket, knowing the night air would be cool as they went the short distance to the Montgomerys' estate.

She knew nothing to do with her hair but wear it as she normally did. She could never manage to put it in the neat coil Lady Hamilton wore, which was very chic and sophisticated. Joy wore her hair loose so Stormy figured she could do the same thing.

As she bathed she was thinking about this strange custom here in England that made certain people lords and ladies. Jason wasn't a lord like his father but this Bart Montgomery was and his wife was a lady. It was all a little confusing.

When she finally emerged from the tub and sat at her dresser in the robe Sheila Hamilton had given to her that first night, she brushed out her damp and tangled hair. Then she dabbed gardenia toilet water to her throat and behind her ears.

Stormy had no jewelry but she didn't need it—her eyes were her gems once she had slipped into the green dress. She was so pleased with the way she looked that she began to relax.

A few minutes later, she was ready to slip into the little jacket as she prepared to go to the parlor to meet Jason. With the green velvet reticule hanging from her wrist, she left the room to go down the steps.

Lady Sheila was sitting in the parlor when Stormy made her entrance—she was quite a vision.

Lady Sheila had only to observe Jason eagerly jumping up to greet Stormy to know that her son was as impressed as she.

Jason didn't hesitate to tell her how beautiful she looked. "Shall we go?" he asked. They bade Lady Hamilton good night and were on their way.

It was only a brief buggy ride. A servant greeted them at the door and ushered them into the parlor which was as grand as the Hamiltons'.

Stormy felt more at ease about her appearance when she got her first glance at Tawny Montgomery, who was wearing her long dark hair in a casual fashion like her own.

Other things also made Stormy feel comfortable as Jason led her to meet the Montgomerys. There was a warm smile on Tawny's face as she rose from her chair. Stormy could tell they were about the same age.

Instantly, she sensed the warmth between Bart and Jason as they greeted one another. As soon as Jason had greeted Tawny, he turned to Stormy to introduce her to his two dearest friends.

"Bart—Tawny—I'd like you to meet Stormy Monihan," Jason said proudly. That was enough to let his old friend know that Jason was very taken with this pretty lady. Bart could understand why.

"Stormy, we've been most anxious to meet you since we heard you'd arrived with Jason," Tawny said as she guided her to a settee.

"And I've been most anxious to meet you. Lady Hamilton tells me you're from Virginia," Stormy said, settling back against the mauve brocade.

That opened the door for an endless conversation between the two women. Bart and Jason exchanged amused grins as they saw them talking so busily. Bart laughed, saying, "I think they have no need of our company, Jason."

By the time they went into the dining room to sit down at the long table with sparkling candlelight and gleaming silver everywhere, Stormy was relaxed and comfortable.

"You have a beautiful home, Tawny," she said as she took the chair Jason held for her.

"Thank you. Bart and I love it here. We lived in his townhouse in London first but I like it better out here in the country. We find it much nicer for raising our children."

After dinner, the two couples talked for hours. The evening had been far more pleasant than Stormy had anticipated by the time she and Jason were ready to go back to his home.

"You see, Princess—they both adored you," Jason said as they pulled up to the front entrance.

"I like your friends very much," she declared.

Lady Hamilton had only to hear their laughter to know that they had enjoyed their evening with Bart and Tawny as she had suspected they would. They were so engrossed in their own conversation that they didn't even notice her sitting in the dimly lit parlor.

She smiled as she prepared to join her husband, who had already retired. Maybe Jason has finally met the young girl to tame his restless heart, she thought as she prepared to mount the stairs.

The long hallway was nearly dark but Sheila Hamilton saw something most encouraging—Jason was embracing Stormy outside her bedroom door. Quickly, she dashed into her own bedroom so they would not see her.

She lingered near the door until she heard Jason's footsteps going back down the hallway to his own room. Once again a smile came to her face.

Jason was smitten by the bewitching little Stormy Monihan!

Eighteen

Kip Monihan rarely took three or four weeks off from his boat but this time he had needed to. Many changes had taken place since he'd arrived back in Southport to hear that his beloved daughter had been missing for almost ten days. He was still unable to turn up any clues as to where she was once she had escaped from Jed Callihan.

But he had satisfied the revenge he sought against Callihan, even though he could not give him any ideas as to where Stormy was.

The one happy moment Kip had enjoyed was his sudden marriage to Marcie Warren, which had eased some of his pain and sorrow.

One day Kip realized he had to get back to a normal life for Marcie's sake. There didn't seem to be anything he could do to find his daughter.

That evening he told Marcie he was going to the wharf in the morning and gather up his men so he could make a run to Savannah the next day. "I've got a load there which has probably been waiting over a week. I can't afford to lose their business, Marcie."

"Of course you can't, Kip."

"You be all right here, honey?"

She gave him a reassuring smile. "Just do what you have to do and I'll handle things here."

So he planned to leave the next morning at dawn's

first light. He went immediately to Paddy's house to inform them that he was ready to make a run down the coastline. Paddy went directly to the *East Wind* to prepare his galley and check on supplies while Kip went in one direction and Pat Dorsey in another to line up all the men for an early departure.

Marcie stayed busy all day around the cottage. She prepared a special meal for the two of them since it would be the last they would share for almost ten days.

She had puttered in the kitchen during the morning, fixing two of Kip's favorite pies. She figured that what they didn't eat this evening he could take with him.

He was constantly telling her that Paddy wasn't much of a baker, so they would all welcome her homemade pies.

By mid-afternoon, she had a huge pot of beans simmering on the back of her stove and a ham baking slowly in the oven. She was dressed in one of her little muslin frocks and her hair was neatly combed.

It was one of those days that everything had seemed to go just perfectly so Marcie was to think later that it had surely been a good omen that it was the day that both she and Kip received a letter from Stormy.

She had torn into hers eagerly—it was enough just to know that the beautiful child was alive and well enough to write. But it was even more intriguing to know about her adventure and how well she'd fared. Staying at a lord and lady's country estate. She could hardly wait for Kip to get home!

Stormy had written every little detail about what had taken place from the moment she was abducted from Marcie's buggy. It was obvious to Marcie why there had been no trace of her in Southport.

Marcie was so excited that she poured herself a glass of sherry as she waited for Kip to return. When she finally saw him coming up the path, she hurried to him.

Kip had hardly expected this enthusiastic welcome but he enjoyed it.

Her face was radiant as she greeted him. "Oh, Kip— she's alive and well! Stormy—she's fine! We got letters today."

"Stormy—letters from her?"

"Both of us! She's in England! Oh, Kip, I don't think I've ever been so happy."

It took Kip a few moments to absorb such glorious news. Then he sat in the front room for a long time, reading the letter his daughter had written to him.

When he had finished, he folded it and gave way to tears of relief.

Unashamed of his unbridled emotion, he muttered, "Oh, God Marcie—I've been so damned scared. I didn't know whether I'd ever see my little Stormy again."

"I know, Kip. I've been feeling exactly the same way," she confessed.

Suddenly, they were both laughing and crying at the same time. They fell into each other's arms and remained there, clinging.

When the embrace was finally broken, Kip announced it was a night to celebrate so he went to the cabinet to pour himself a glass of whiskey. Marcie had another sherry as she put the finishing touches to her dinner.

A bright autumn morning greeted Kip Monihan when he left his cottage at dawn to board the *East Wind* He could already imagine the delighted response he'd get from Paddy and Pat Dorsey when he told them his good news.

An hour later, it was a happy crew aboard Kip's boat as they pulled away from the wharf.

As they traveled along the coast toward Savannah, Paddy posed a question. "Kip, what do we do next to get our little Stormy back home to us?"

"Been thinking about that, Paddy. I'm hoping to be

ucky and run into Captain Murdock when we get to Savannah. He's one of the few sea captains I know who makes the run across the Atlantic. Maybe I can make a deal with him to bring Stormy back here."

Paddy knew that Murdock wasn't making a crossing for another month. He was hoping that Kip would be lucky and catch him when they landed in Savannah. It was likely that Murdock could have already left.

Kip Monihan had carefully thought about what it would cost him to buy Stormy passage back on Murdock's ship should he be preparing to leave for one last trip for England before the winter set in.

He had put a pouch filled with the funds in his valise and had not mentioned this to Marcie when he'd left.

It was smooth sailing as the *East Wind* traveled southward; they made good time, arriving in the early afternoon. The first sight to greet Kip's eyes as his small boat approached the harbor was the *Southern Star.* Murdock was in Savannah and Kip was sure he was getting ready to pull out any time.

The minute they docked, he left Pat in charge so he could seek out Murdock. If he was ever to believe in his Irish luck he had to believe in it this afternoon, for had he been an hour later he would have missed him.

Murdock liked Kip and agreed to his request to bring his daughter back to Southport. Kip told him if he delivered her safe and sound there was another pouch to equal the one he'd just handed him.

Murdock smiled. "Look, Monihan—you hold this for me and have the other one ready when I return. That way I won't spend all this while I'm in England. This will be my last crossing until spring so I'll probably be needing that when I return."

He took the letter Kip had written to Stormy the previous night, hoping he would work a deal with Murdock. Kip stretched out his hand to shake Murdoc[k's] weathered one. "We have a deal, captain!"

"I know the feelings a father has for a daughter, Monihan. I've five of the little darlings."

"Dear God Almighty—I don't know whether I could have managed that!" Kip declared.

"I have to credit a good wife—I was away at sea most of the time."

Kip smiled and gave him a nod. "A good wife you surely have, Murdock."

The two went their separate ways and Kip was in the highest of spirits. Fate had been very kind to him. By the time he arrived back at his own boat, Dorsey was overseeing the loading of the lumber.

It was an evening Kip wished to share with Pat and Paddy. They shared the evening meal together in Kip's cabin after Paddy had worked all afternoon on a hearty meal for the entire crew.

Pat and Paddy were also in high spirits during the evening about his lucky encounter with Murdock. "Lady Luck was riding on your shoulder today, sir," Dorsey declared.

"She was surely there in all her glory!" Kip had to hope she stayed right there on his shoulder for if she did he could see his little golden-haired Stormy in another six or seven weeks.

During the next three weeks, Stormy and Tawny shared many conversations and spent three or four afternoons together. They were never at a loss for things to talk about—Tawny was convinced that she would be the perfect mate for Jason.

She listened as Stormy told her how she loved working around the ship with Jason. "The sea doesn't depress you, Stormy?"

"Oh, no! I find the sea most fascinating. Don't you like it, Tawny?"

"I hate it! I pray I'll never cross that ocean again," Tawny confessed.

"Oh, my goodness—it's good I don't feel that way for I must cross it again to get home."

"And when will that be, Stormy?"

"When I hear from my pa. I wrote him and so now I'll wait here with Jason and his parents. But I will be leaving to return to Southport, Tawny. I must," Stormy said. Tawny saw that determined look on her face. It reminded her of a young girl who was just as determined to get back to Virginia a few years ago.

"I understand your feelings, Stormy. Truly I do. There was a time when the most important thing in my life was to get back to Virginia," Tawny confessed.

"It's good to have you to talk to, Tawny. I—I can't imagine why I was so nervous about meeting you," Stormy laughed.

"I can't either, Stormy. The truth is that it's only been a few years since I was a backwoods girl who liked to roam around the countryside in her bare feet. Believe it or not, I still like to do that."

They both broke into gales of laughter.

Jason was delighted that Stormy and Tawny had formed such a bond in so short a time. Bart wasted no time telling him his sentiments. "If you let this one get away, Jason, then you're a fool!"

"She is something, isn't she Bart?"

"She's like you. She's beautiful and she likes your sea and your ship. I can't think of anything else you'd want. You only meet a woman like that once, if you're lucky. I knew it when I met Tawny. Need I remind you of that?"

"No, Bart—I remember it very well."

What Jason didn't tell him was that he had been offered a deal he was finding hard to refuse and it wasn't crossing the Atlantic. It would be a very brief voyage from England up to Dublin, Ireland. It was a rich cargo, so his fee would be high. Jason figured it would take him only a week at the most.

He was sorely tempted, but he had hesitated even to mention it to Stormy—he knew she would insist on going. On such a short jaunt he preferred that she stay in London with the comforts of his parents' home.

And Stormy did have that reaction when he told her of his plans. Her green eyes looked up at him as he held her in a warm embrace in his mother's gardens. She voiced her most honest feelings. "Jason, I'm not a woman who will be left behind, if you know what I mean. I won't sit home and wait for a man to return when it suits his fancy."

"I'll only be gone about a week—maybe not that long, Stormy."

"You do what you wish, Jason. I have no right to say what I just said, really. But as you must know by now, I'm an impulsive person. My father has always told me that."

He pulled her closer and kissed her, so the conversation about his proposed trip to Ireland went no further. Stormy found it impossible to resist him so she forgot about everything else.

Jason Hamilton made her feel quite different from the way Pat Dorsey had made her feel when she had thought she was falling in love with him. Pat and Jason both had that same happy-go-lucky way, but Pat's hand touching her didn't affect her the way Jason's did. Nor did Pat's kisses stir her desires in the same passionate way.

There was no question about it—Stormy knew she was in love with Jason Hamilton!

Nineteen

The evening before Jason was to board the *Sea Princess* and depart for Ireland, Lady Sheila overheard the two young people having an argument about this trip. She was glad to hear Stormy venting her disapproval—Sheila had the greatest urge to shake her grown son firmly as she'd done when he was a naughty little boy.

Needless to say, she didn't join them in the parlor but she was near the doorway long enough to hear Stormy's voice: "Sorry, Jason, but you're not convincing me it's your fear of running into a storm that's keeping you from taking me along. I've weathered many storms in my life."

Trying to appease her, he promised, "Look, love—I'll take you along the next time."

"There—there just might not be another time, Jason Hamilton!" she warned.

Jason thought how excitingly pretty she looked with that lovely pout. Stormy was surely the perfect name for this divine little creature! She didn't try to restrain that hot little temper, but Jason figured she'd mellow by the time he returned in a week.

Lady Sheila privately applauded Stormy's spunk and spice. She wasn't as sure as Jason was that she'd mellow—she just hoped he would not regret this sudden decision.

Jason figured when he returned with so much money,

there would be nothing to postpone an immediate wedding. He had to believe that would bring a gleam from those pretty green eyes.

There was no doubt in his mind that he loved Stormy Monihan. As his old friend Bart had remarked, he'd be a fool to let her get away. Well, he didn't plan to.

It would be a perfect time for a wedding, just before the festive holiday season, and he'd have the rest of the winter months to spend with his bride. Since Stormy loved the sea, nothing would please him more than to have her go along with him instead of enduring long weeks of separation.

He was convinced that she would be a perfect wife.

Later that evening as the family dined together, Stormy was lighthearted and gay. She gave no signs of being out of sorts with Jason nor did she sit there quiet and preoccupied.

On occasion Lady Sheila had seen all of her daughters at odds with their husbands; they made no effort to hide their feelings as she was certain Stormy was doing.

Sheila could only hope that Jason would not come to regret taking this assignment for the high fee, but she knew of nothing she could do to stop him.

But it almost pleased Sheila when Jason invited Stormy to take a stroll with him in the garden and she politely turned him down. "It's a little chilly out there tonight. I think I'll just stay here in the parlor with your parents. You go ahead," she urged, then turned to Sheila. "Your autumns are cooler than ours back in Southport."

"Oh, I'm sure it's much warmer there. I've heard Tawny say that many times," Sheila declared.

So Jason was left to go on his stroll alone. He didn't walk too far into the gardens but took a seat to light up one of his cheroots. As he puffed on it, he knew why that little minx had refused to walk with him. She was very definitely irked about his leaving in the morning. She could be a spiteful little imp when she wanted to be!

The longer he sat on the bench smoking the cheroot the more he found himself losing patience with her. He was leaving much earlier than she would be getting up in the morning. If he didn't get one last private moment with her tonight then it would be several days and nights before he would see her again. And she had to know that!

Angrily, he stomped out the cheroot and marched back into the house. Much to his chagrin, his father had engaged her in the corner where they were playing checkers. They seemed to be enjoying themselves thoroughly as they laughed and chatted. Sheila was working on her needlepoint when Jason entered the parlor.

She saw the impatient look on his face when Stormy turned quickly around to give him a flippant greeting. "I'm winning again, Jason." She laughed softly and turned her attention back to the checker board.

Addison gasped in despair. "Oh, you are a wicked little player, Stormy Monihan!"

They cleared the board to start a new game. Sheila was amused and a little disturbed that Jason was having such a disappointing time on his last evening home.

When she heard the clock chiming on the mantel, she decided to announce that she was going upstairs to retire, hoping Addison would join her and leave the young people alone in the parlor.

But it didn't work. Jason quickly rose out of his chair to announce that he too was going upstairs.

"Good night, Father. You, too, Stormy. I have to get up in less than six hours," he declared, his black eyes glaring in Stormy's direction.

With a rather startled look, Stormy said, "So early, Jason?"

"I'm afraid so, Princess."

Stormy rose from her chair and walked over to Jason to plant a kiss on his cheek. "Have a safe voyage, Jason, and hurry home."

It took all his willpower to deny himself the long, lingering kiss he yearned for. What a little temptress she was! He had to wonder if she knew how she was tormenting him.

As casually as she'd walked over to him, she went back to the table. Sheila was making her own observations. She had to admire the independent miss from Southport. If any lady was capable of bringing Jason to his knees it had to be Stormy Monihan!

As they walked up the stairway together, Sheila noticed that her son was rather quiet and thoughtful without his usual gift of gab.

She said good night when they got to her door. "Like Stormy, I wish you a safe trip. And hurry back home, son," she whispered as he reached down to kiss her cheek.

"I will, Mother, and take care of her for me until I get back."

"You don't have to worry about that, Jason. We're quite fond of her," his mother assured him as she went through the door.

A dense fog hung over the harbor the next morning as Jason went aboard the *Sea Princess*. It was often this way at this time of year. He was pleased to see that his crew was ready to get the ship moving out of the harbor and on its way to Ireland.

None of them was more anxious to be on the way than Jason. He and his schooner had been out in the water for over three hours before Stormy first stirred in her bed.

When she lazily rose in the bed to see the eerie looking sight outside the windows, she lay back down. The gray fog was the thickest she'd ever seen.

She slept for another two hours before she finally made herself to get out of the bed and get dressed. There was a damp chill to the day so Stormy put on one of her long-sleeved gowns.

Her usual breakfast was a couple cups of coffee and the delicious muffins the Hamiltons' cook prepared every morning. Sheila had observed her coming down the stairs and followed her into the cozy little breakfast room where she also enjoyed her morning coffee.

Addison's routine was quite different from his wife's. He preferred his breakfast to be brought to their suite so he could enjoy it in bed.

Sheila tried to spend more time with Stormy in hopes of making up for Jason's absence. It gave her the opportunity to get to know the young girl much better.

The more time she spent with Stormy, the better she liked and admired her. Stormy had that open, honest way about her. She didn't hesitate a moment to answer Lady Hamilton's questions. Sheila always remembered what her Irish father had said: he didn't trust anyone who wouldn't look him straight in the eye. Sheila had always felt the same way, and Stormy's green eyes certainly looked directly at the person she was talking to.

One day Stormy remarked to Sheila how much she prayed that her letters had gotten to her father and Marcie.

"They may have just arrived in Southport by now," Sheila said. "Jason took them to London the morning after you arrived. Perhaps you'll have a letter from him before too long."

"Oh, I hope so. But my main concern is that mine got to him. I know how much he must have worried about me."

"I can certainly understand that, dear. It would be

horrible not to know what had happened to your child.
I can put myself in his shoes."

During that first seven days Tawny often took Stormy
into London to shop. On one of these trips they stopped
for lunch at the quaint little inn that Jason's oldest sister
and her husband owned. Stormy was intrigued by the
rustic setting at Blair's Inn and listened intently to the
story Tawny told about how Bart had helped his friend,
Disney, purchase the inn. As it would happen, Disney
and the Hamiltons' daughter then met and married.

"Bart asked that he name it Blair's Inn to honor me,
and Disney gladly obliged. So you can see why this is
my favorite place to dine when I come into London. I
have to admit I don't come into the city that often. I'm
a country girl."

As they sat at a small table for two, Stormy told her
she was so glad they had come. Everything about the
place was so cozy. The table was covered with a floral
tablecloth and matching napkins. Little baskets of dried
flowers provided the centerpiece. The wooden chairs
were cushioned with ruffled seats of the same floral
pattern.

Aromatic sprays of herbs were hung from the rafters.
They enjoyed a light cup of soup, then a fish entree.
Stormy had never tasted anything like it. She loved it.

Like Stormy and Lady Hamilton, Tawny preferred
coffee to tea. So they agreed to have one more cup
before they departed.

As they sat leisurely enjoying their coffee, Stormy
dared to ask Tawny something she'd been curious about
for weeks.

"Tell me about you and Jason, Tawny. How did you
end up on his ship the same way I did?"

Tawny smiled, knowing why Stormy was asking her
this. She wanted to be certain that there were no romantic ties between her and Jason. She understood

Stormy's feelings for she would probably have felt the same way.

"Our situations were similar and yet they weren't, Stormy. We both landed on Jason's schooner but you were there because you had no memory of your past. I remembered every horrible detail of mine. I was slipped aboard Jason's ship in the dead of the night—the crew lifted me tied in jut sacks into the hold of the schooner not knowing I was unconscious inside. You see, I had seen two men kill my mother so they wanted to be rid of me. They figured that to put me on a ship sailing for England would be good riddance."

She told Stormy how Jason had discovered her in the hold and taken her to his cabin. "I don't have to tell you how kind and generous Jason can be. I was clad in the nightgown I had on when I'd run from our house after hearing my mother's screams. Jason became my protector until we arrived in London—he took me to his home as he did you."

Then she told Stormy about the handsome Bart Montgomery, who was also aboard the ship. Because of their friendship, Jason had brought Bart to Virginia to purchase a prized stallion, Diablo.

Like Stormy, Stormy was a very honest lady—she didn't try to color the truth. "If you're wondering if Jason and I were romantically involved, I would have to tell you we were. Jason thought he was in love with me and I tried to convince myself that I loved him. But it was Bart Montgomery I truly loved. Jason and I never shared a bed."

She told Stormy how she'd stayed with the Hamiltons until Jason had found passage for her to return to Virginia. "I had to ask myself—if he'd truly been in love with me, would he have let me leave England so quickly?"

She told Stormy how Bart had sailed immediately for

Virginia after he'd found out that Jason had put her on a ship sailing back. "It made me realize just how much Bart loved me. It was a brotherly-sisterly love Jason and I felt for one another and, thank goodness, we both realized that, Stormy. It would have been a disaster if we had married."

"I appreciate you telling me all this, Tawny. I know I probably had no right to ask," Stormy said.

"You have every right if you feel strongly about Jason. I hope you do—I think you're the woman who could make him happy. You see, Stormy—you love the sea and his ship. It would take someone special like you to share Jason's life," Tawny said.

"You're very kind, Tawny, and I appreciate your saying that. I love Jason very much but he will have to learn that everything can't revolve around him and what he wants."

Tawny could only give her an understanding smile. She felt exactly as Bart did, and only hoped that Jason didn't let her get away.

A Stormy Monihan didn't come along too often in a man's life!

Twenty

Stormy was glad she and Tawny had shared such a pleasant afternoon—she truly believed that Tawny had told her the truth. Feeling about Jason as she did, she was glad to have had this talk.

Lady Sheila could see that Stormy was in fine spirits the next morning and was pleased to hear that the two young ladies had such a lovely time in the city. But then, the two of them were so much alike in so many ways.

Yet, they were as different as day and night. Stormy was a fine little sailor from what her son had told her, but she was not the skilled horsewoman Tawny was. Stormy told her that Tawny had promised to teach her to ride a horse. "She found it hard to believe that I have never ridden. The truth is, they frighten me. They're so big."

Sheila laughed. "I'm sure that did amaze Tawny—she's so fond of horses." Sheila recalled how Tawny had once confessed that the ocean scared her, but Stormy had no fear of it.

After lunch Sheila was preparing to visit one of her ailing friends who lived a short distance away. She was just going out the door to her buggy when another buggy pulled up to the entrance. She noticed that the occupant's attire reminded her very much of the clothing Jason wore on his schooner. Her first thoughts were

for Jason when the tall, robust man came sauntering up
the steps to introduce himself and tell her he was seeking Miss Monihan. "I've been sent here by her father,
ma'am. I've a letter from him to give to Miss Stormy,"
Murdock told her.

"I'm Lady Hamilton, Captain Murdock, and if you'll
just come with me I'll get Stormy," she said as she
invited him into the house.

Stormy was in the sitting room, enjoying the bright
sunshine flowing through the windows as she read one
of the books from Lord Addison's study.

"Stormy, dear—Captain Murdock is here to see you
with word from your father. Isn't that wonderful?"

Stormy leaped up and rushed to greet the captain.
He gave the pretty girl a warm smile and wasted no
time in handing her the letter. Then he took a seat as
Lady Hamilton urged him to do.

Lady Hamilton felt that this was a rather private moment and that Stormy and Captain Murdock should have
some time alone. She told the captain she would send
in a tray of refreshments. "I've an errand to go on,"
she said as she prepared to leave the room, hesitating
only long enough to ask him if he preferred tea or coffee.

"Coffee, ma'am," he replied.

"Nice to see you, captain, and I hope you and Stormy
have a nice visit. I'll see you later, Stormy," she said
as she left the room.

Stormy called a hasty goodbye and turned her attention back to her letter.

She was so happy to read that he and Marcie were
relieved to know she was all right. She read it once,
then read it again. The house servant arrived with a
carafe of coffee and some little raisin cakes.

"Pa says I'm to sail with you, Captain Murdock,"
Stormy said as she folded up the letter.

"Yes, miss—he caught me just as I was about to pull out of Savannah. He arranged for you to come back on my ship—I'm to get you back safe and sound, which I promised to do."

A bittersweet feeling consumed Stormy as she was almost hesitant to ask him when he was going to be leaving.

"I'll be here at sunrise Wednesday morn to get you, miss."

This was Monday and Stormy knew if she had to leave without seeing Jason she would be devastated, but she could not refuse to go with Captain Murdock. She knew how hard her father had worked for the passage he had paid to the captain. She did want to return to him but she also wanted to be able to say goodbye to Jason before she left England.

She could only hope Jason would arrive back by Tuesday, she told herself, telling the captain that she would be ready to leave Wednesday morning.

Murdock finished his coffee and prepared to leave. Finding Monihan's daughter had not proved to be the time-consuming ordeal he'd expected.

Stormy walked out to the steps with him and waved goodbye as he pulled away. The next hour she roamed around in sort of a daze. She would be leaving so much sooner than she had expected—her head was whirling from all of it.

Upon her return, Lady Sheila found a young lady torn by emotion. It was just as upsetting to Sheila, but then she also understood why Stormy had to leave and return to her home and her father.

Stormy allowed her to read the letter—it was obvious that Kip Monihan was a devoted, loving father. Sheila knew Stormy had to go with the captain, but she suddenly felt angry and impatient with her son. If he had

not gone away, he would have been here to bid Stormy
farewell.

Lady Hamilton knew that he had no one to blame
but himself if he did not arrive until after she was gone.
She feared that this was exactly what would happen.

The next day she helped Stormy pack her valises.
Stormy gave her a weak smile as she remarked she was
taking so much with her. "I came here with nothing
and now look at all this. I don't feel right about it, Lady
Sheila."

"And why not, dear? It's yours. Don't fret one minute
about that."

"But I do and I'm sad, Lady Sheila. I shouldn't be—
I'm so anxious to see my pa. But I'm also sad to be
leaving you and Jason." Everything had happened so
fast it had an impact on Stormy. She sat down on the
bed and gave way to tears.

Lady Sheila sat down beside her and embraced her.
"Oh, my little Stormy—you say you came here with
nothing. You came here with more than you realized.
Addison and I have not enjoyed ourselves so much in
a long, long time. You gave us much happiness and we
shall never forget this time with you."

"Oh, Lady Sheila—I'll be miserable leaving here and
yet I want desperately to see my pa and Marcie. I've
never been so torn," Stormy sobbed.

Sheila Hamilton held her, letting her cry all her tears.
When they began to cease, Stormy looked at her in that
very direct, open way of hers. "I think I've fallen in
love with Jason."

"Oh, Stormy—Stormy—I pray that fool son of mine
gets back before tomorrow morning because I think he's
in love with you, too. He just may not have the good
sense to know it," Lady Sheila added.

It was not an easy evening for any of them. Lord

Addison was feeling just as gloomy about Stormy's departure as his wife was. He'd become very fond of her.

She had been like a breath of fresh air in this big, spacious house and it was going to seem ghostly quiet without her lilting laughter. She'd given him quite a challenge when they'd played checkers and he'd liked that.

He'd even hoped that Jason would ask Stormy to marry him. He could have sworn that his son was in love with this little golden-haired girl.

But now it would seem that this was not to be. All evening Lord Addison had hoped that Jason would bound through the door with that happy-go-lucky grin of his, but it didn't happen by the time he finally left the parlor to retire.

Knowing his custom of having breakfast in his room, Stormy said goodbye to him as he prepared to go upstairs. He held her in a warm embrace for a few moments. "Young lady, we don't want you forgetting us. You're to come back here to see us again. You must promise me that, Stormy."

"I promise," Stormy said, planting a last kiss on his cheek. Sheila stood observing them, knowing that Addison rarely showed that emotional side she knew so well.

Sheila remained with Stormy in the parlor, suggesting they share a glass of wine before retiring. Like Addison, she had hoped their son would arrive in time.

As they sat sipping the last of their wine, Sheila said, "Stormy, Addison's sentiments are mine. Don't forget us—write as soon as you arrive. We'll be anxious to know you're safe and sound."

"I will write, I promise, and I'll come back, too. I could never forget how wonderful you've been to me and how you welcomed me into your home, Lady Sheila."

The hour was late and Sheila knew she was being selfish to keep Stormy up any later but she hated to call it a night. She also knew that sunrise was only a few hours away.

Stormy felt she had hardly gotten comfortable in bed before she had to get up and get dressed. She caught one of the house servants going down the hallway and asked her to take her valises to the front entrance. She took a final survey of the room she had occupied for all these weeks.

She wore a pretty bonnet Jason had bought her and draped the green fur-trimmed cape around her shoulders. It would be chilly riding in the open buggy to the harbor.

The last thing she did before she left was leave a note addressed to Jason on the dressing table. She had to hope the servant would deliver it to him when she found it.

As he had promised, Captain Murdock arrived— Stormy was glad that all she had to do was walk out the door—goodbyes were too sad.

Stormy was to learn that Murdock was a man of action. As soon as they were aboard his huge ship and she was taken to her cabin, they began to move out of the harbor.

It was a much larger vessel than Jason's slick-lined schooner but it was not as grandly furnished—nor was her cabin adjacent to the captain's. Captain Murdock instructed her to stay in her cabin and keep her door locked.

As she was getting settled in, she noticed that the door from her cabin led to the captain's quarters and realized why he had put her in this cabin. To satisfy her curiosity, she took the liberty of roaming around his quarters for a few minutes. It wasn't as nice as Jason's.

Once she returned to her own cabin, she locked the door. Knowing she was facing many days and nights before arriving in Southport, she occupied herself by carefully repacking the valises which she and Lady Sheila had so haphazardly packed yesterday.

When Captain Murdock came to his cabin late in the afternoon, he found that she had bolted the door between his cabin and hers—he could not have been more pleased. He felt more relaxed about her being on his ship. One beautiful lady with so many men could be a dangerous situation. Apparently, Stormy Monihan knew that, too!

She opened the door when he appeared a few hours later to invite her to join him in his cabin for dinner.

Murdock found Stormy to be very mature for a young lady of seventeen. She was not silly or frivolous as he feared she might be. Truth was, he found her a very interesting dinner partner.

Stormy never ventured outside the cabin except when Murdock came to take her for a stroll, always conducting herself in a most lady-like fashion. He knew she had to realize how the men were eying her.

The only other member of the crew that Stormy had any contact with was Murdock's cabin boy, Danny. He was her slave, for he adored the pretty, golden-haired Stormy.

Twenty-one

There was a terrible void at the Hamiltons' country home the day Stormy left. It seemed so ghostly quiet to Sheila Hamilton—the gray overcast skies did not lift her spirits either. Lord Addison must have been feeling the same way, judging from his somber mood.

Before he left Sheila in her sitting room to go to his study to look over some papers, he suggested she accompany him to London the following day. "Be good for you, dear. Do a little shopping for a couple of hours and later we'll pay a visit to our daughter and son in law. Just might have ourselves a late lunch at the inn. What do you think about that?"

"That's a splendid idea, Addison," she said, her face lighting up.

"It would be a good tonic for both of us—we'll have ourselves a fine day," he said as he bent down to kiss her cheek before heading for his study.

Addison's invitation was enough to brighten Sheila's afternoon—it would serve Jason right, she thought, if he returned with no one to greet him.

Several times during the afternoon she found herself thinking about Stormy, knowing she was several miles out to sea. She could only hope they were smoothly sailing. She was also wondering just how far away from London her wandering son was.

Jason had had to delay his departure from Ireland for

an extra day. A strong storm had moved in over the coast but only for a few hours. Still, it was long enough to delay his departure until the following morning.

The delay tried his patience—he was eager to leave Ireland now that his mission was over and his coffers were enriched. He had had a grand time the afternoon before the storm had rolled in. He had visited some of the shops where they sold some of the nicest woolens and lace. For his father, he had purchased a bright plaid hat with a matching woolen scarf; for his mother he had bought a dozen lovely lace-edged linen handkerchiefs and a wide lace collar.

He purchased the most spectacular gift for Stormy. The moment he saw it he knew that the emerald ring encircled with diamonds was meant to be hers. When he proposed to her it was his intention to slip the ring on her finger.

This was why he was so anxious to start back to London. As soon as the *Sea Princess* docked, he would pay his crew their wages, along with a nice bonus, before he left the schooner to head for home.

The jaunt from Ireland to London went smoothly but the skies were still heavy with clouds.

By three in the afternoon Jason was in the harbor of London and one hour later he was traveling toward home.

There was a gloomy look to the countryside as Jason's buggy traveled hastily down the dirt lane toward the sprawling estate but his mood was far from gloomy. As he went by the Montgomery property, he thought he saw Bart's tall figure going toward the stables. Jason wore a devious grin as he reveled in his private musings. He was about to win the beautiful girl he adored with all his heart.

He was also thinking that he and Bart had certainly had their fair share of beautiful young damsels around

London. There was a time when the two of them were the most sought-after bachelors in the city. Then Bart had married Tawny a few years ago.

Now he had finally found a woman who made him feel the same way. With Stormy Monihan, Jason felt he could be contented and happy forever. He'd never felt like that about any other woman.

With her, he could share his love of the sea and his schooner. That was one of the things that endeared her to him—he wanted the woman he loved to feel this way.

When he arrived at the front entrance, he almost lunged from the buggy and rushed through the front door. The house seemed unusually quiet—there were not even any servants milling around the hall or in the dining room. He made a dash back to his mother's sitting room but she was not there nor was his father in his study.

So he mounted the stairs, taking two at a time, hesitant only long enough at the door of his bedroom to fling his valise inside. Then he made long strides down the carpeted hallway to Stormy's room. He knocked on the door and called out to her but he was met with silence.

When two more raps did not rouse her, Jason unceremoniously opened the door to find no one in there either. The bed was neatly made up but the one thing that caught his eye was how neat the dressing table looked. There were no little personal items lying about as there usually were.

Slowly, he went on into the room, muttering to himself. He looked in the armoire and drawers to find all signs of Stormy and her belongings gone.

A sharp wave of panic rose up in Jason as he quickly slammed the door behind him to march back down the hall to his parents' suite.

But he got the same response. He had only to open

the door to see that there were no signs of them either. He was more than a little perplexed. He went back down the steps directly to the kitchen. If anyone knew what was going on it would surely be old Elsie.

He rushed in through the kitchen door so swiftly that Elsie almost let the pan of tarts slip out of her hands as she was taking them from the oven.

"Lord have mercy, Mister Jason—you startled me!" she declared as she sat the pan down and mopped her brow with the bottom of her apron.

"I'm sorry, Elsie," he apologized.

"You just arrive?" she asked as she walked over to close the oven door.

"Yes, I did but the house seems deserted. Perhaps you could tell me where everyone is?" Jason sauntered over to take a seat on one of the oak chairs by the square table where Elsie had placed the tarts. He helped himself to one. No one made fruit tarts better than old Elsie.

"Your mother and father went into London. They'll probably get back just about any time now, Mister Jason."

Hearing this, Jason somewhat relaxed—he just assumed Stormy accompanied them into the city.

Elsie saw Jason ogling her tarts. Knowing how much he liked them, she urged him to take one, having no idea he'd already done so.

He took another one as he prepared to go up to his room. He was only halfway up the stairs when he swiftly turned on his heel to go back to the kitchen.

It suddenly dawned on him that Stormy wasn't with his parents—that didn't explain her missing belongings.

So once again he took Elsie by surprise. "Mercy, Mister Jason—you in one of your mischief moods?"

"Sorry, Elsie but I needed to ask you something."

"What did you want to know, Mister Jason?"

"Miss Stormy—where is she?" he asked, almost reluctant to hear her answer.

"Guess you wouldn't know about her since you just got home. Miss Stormy left day before yesterday."

"She left?"

"Yes, sir. She's on her way back home. An American sea captain came to get her. Guess she's well out into that old ocean by now. That's all I can tell you, Mister Jason."

Jason just stood there silently, saying nothing. Elsie realized he wasn't happy about the news. "Your parents will be able to tell you more when they get home, Mister Jason."

Distraught and dazed, Jason walked slowly out of the kitchen to the parlor. He went directly to the teakwood liquor chest to pour himself a generous portion of his father's favorite brandy.

He sank down in the brocade chair and toyed with the glass for a moment before taking a sip. He was still finding it hard to accept what Elsie had told him. But he had to—that was why all her belongings were gone.

Jason couldn't recall a time in his entire life when he had been as dispirited as he was at this minute. All his wonderful plans had gone awry and the magnificent ring was not going to be placed on Stormy's finger as he'd planned. What a cruel trick fate had played.

It was enough to make Jason wonder if he was hexed and would never have the woman he loved. She was so far away—they'd already been at sea for two days and nights.

He could only hope that whatever ship she was on would not run into treacherous weather. No question about it, the time was growing short to make a safe voyage across the Atlantic.

He took another sip of the brandy and tried to calm his frayed nerves as he impatiently awaited the arrival of his parents. They could give him answers to all his questions.

He kept looking up at the clock on the mantel and wondered why they were staying in London so late. This was certainly not the homecoming he'd anticipated!

Twilight was descending over the countryside when Jason finally heard the approach of his father's carriage.

His parents seemed to be in a happy mood as they came into the house carrying several packages.

Sheila spied Jason and ran to greet him. The look on Jason's face told them that he had already learned of Stormy's departure.

Sheila walked into the parlor. As she was untying the ribbons of her bonnet, she asked him, "You know she's gone. I can see it in your face, Jason. There was nothing we could do to prevent her leaving and there was nothing Stormy could do but leave. Her father had sent Captain Murdock to bring her back to Southport."

Jason gave her an understanding nod. "I understand, Mother. You couldn't help what happened. My luck just ran out and I didn't get back soon enough."

Lord Addison strolled over to his liquor chest and helped himself to some brandy. He said to his son, "Jason, you've got a lot to learn about life yet, I'm thinking. It takes far more than a run of luck to get what we want out of life."

Jason's dark eyes locked with his father's and he realized that Lord Addison was trying to tell him something.

"I think I've just realized that, Father," Jason confessed dejectedly.

Twenty-two

Jason was restless and discontent. Lady Hamilton was aware of it but she knew nothing she or Addison could do to help him. Nothing around the sprawling country house engaged his interest; he couldn't content himself on cold, rainy days by reading a book as Addison did.

He did accept his father's invitation to go for afternoon walks when the weather permitted. Addison had taken a liking to the plaid hat and scarf that Jason had brought from Ireland and wore it on his daily strolls.

Sheila had tried to let her son know how thrilled she was with her snowy lace collar by wearing it the second night he was home.

Neither of them was told about the exquisite emerald ring Jason had purchased for Stormy. He had put that in a drawer of the chest in his room. Until he could see Stormy's lovely emerald eyes he didn't wish to look upon that ring.

He'd already decided that as soon as he could move his ship out to sea he was heading straight to Southport. But for now, he felt like an animal fenced in by the foul weather assaulting the English coast. Even if he dared to try to leave, it would have been impossible; he had dismissed his crew and they'd spread out in various directions. Jason had always prided himself on the quality of the crew he hired. Ordinary seamen were not eligible.

It had been a long two weeks for Jason since he'd arrived back in London. Sometimes he just went out to the *Sea Princess* to spend the afternoon around his ship or in his cabin. A couple of times he'd gone over to see Bart. They were stunned to learn about Stormy's sudden departure.

Tawny had said, "It must have come as a complete surprise to Stormy too, Jason. Just a few days before she left, we spent a lovely afternoon together—we went into London to have lunch at Blair Inn."

"This Captain Murdock suddenly appeared at the house with a letter from her father, it seems."

As Bart was walking with Jason back to his buggy, he said, "Go after her like I did when Tawny sailed back to Virginia. If you love her, Jason, don't let anything stop you."

"I would have done just that, Bart, if all my men had not left the *Sea Princess.* God, I'd have no idea where to even look for them now. Oh, I could get in touch with Tobias and Rudy easy enough but a cook and a cabin boy hardly make the ship seaworthy, Bart."

"That does pose a problem. What about hiring on different men?"

"Bart, you know my thinking about that. I don't hire just any available seaman to work on the *Sea Princess.*"

Bart shrugged and declared, "Then, my friend, you have a long wait ahead of you. In the meanwhile, want to join me here at dawn for a little hunting?"

"Sounds good, Bart. I'll see you in the morning," Jason replied as he boarded his buggy.

Bart watched the buggy head down his long, winding driveway—he couldn't recall ever seeing Jason so depressed. It was enough to make him recall his panic when he was in a similar situation. He had just returned from an ocean crossing to find Tawny gone and he immediately booked passage to track her down in Virginia.

He'd never regretted it for a minute. He also recalled how his mother, Lady Montgomery, had thought he had taken leave of his senses. Later, they had both laughed about it for she had been as charmed by Tawny as he after she got to know her.

Captain Murdock was glad to see every day that went by, for it meant they were closer to the Georgia coast. He could already tell how much the weather was changing since they'd left London several days ago. When he took Stormy for walks around the deck of his ship, they needed plenty of warm clothing because of the chill winds.

Now that the voyage was coming to an end, Murdock had to admit that Stormy had endeared herself to him. He had teased her by telling her he was going to adopt her. Stormy had laughed, "Sounds like you have all the daughters you need, captain."

They'd had many talks so Stormy had gotten to know him as he had her—she felt she knew his family even though she'd never met them.

But it wasn't only Captain Murdock who'd grown very fond of their young passenger. Most of the crew considered her the most beautiful thing they'd ever seen. They also knew how protective their captain was and none dared to trifle with her. No such incident had happened during the long voyage.

When Murdock took Stormy on one of their nightly walks, he told her they were getting close to home. "We're going to make it before real bad weather sets in. I was sure hoping so."

"Is it pretty rough out here a little later, Captain Murdock?"

"It's very rough—I've done it a few times in my

younger days but I try to avoid it now. This will be my last trip for the next three months," he said.

Three months seemed like an awfully long time to Stormy. Her thoughts strayed across the ocean and she wondered how Jason was occupying himself.

About a week later Stormy chanced to stare out the window of her cabin and saw swooping images descending toward the ship; they had to be gulls. She became very excited—this was a sure sign that land was not far away. For the first time since she'd been aboard, she was tempted to rush outside to ask if they were nearing the Georgia coast.

A short time later, Captain Murdock came into the cabin. She could see the gleam in his eyes as he announced, "We're home, Stormy—almost!"

"Oh, how wonderful! I thought so when I saw the gulls flying around."

"Well, I just wanted to come and tell you myself. Get yourself packed up, missy, and when we get to Savannah you'll come to my house until I can get you safely up to Southport."

She immediately began to gather her belongings together. She also changed her clothes, putting on a warm woolen gown. As soon as she had brushed her hair, she packed away all the smaller articles. She was ready to leave whenever the captain summoned her.

She had been so busy puttering around the cabin that she had not realized that the huge ship was moving much slower. Suddenly she felt no motion at all and leaped over to the window. What she saw caused a bolt of excitement to surge through her: wharves, land, and trees!

Oh, it was a wonderful sight! She'd docked at these wharves many times with her father aboard the *East Wind*. The sadness of leaving England and Jason was swept aside—all she could think about now was seeing her father and Marcie. Dear Lord, she could not even remember how much time had gone by since she'd last seen them! She was thinking about all the stories she would tell when they sat around in the evening.

Never in her wildest dreams had Stormy envisioned seeing a palace where the King and Queen of England lived or even going to such a faraway place as London. There was so much more that she'd experienced in the last few months that now she almost wondered if it was all a dream. Why, she had lived in the grand country home of a lord and lady! They had not been snobbish and haughty—they were just as sweet and nice as her own pa and Marcie.

Once she felt the ship become so still, she became impatient to have Captain Murdock come for her so she could leave.

He didn't make her wait too long, coming through her door with one of his broad grins. "Well, are you ready, little lady?"

"Yes, sir—I am! It's going to be good to put my feet back on Georgia soil," she smiled.

"Ain't no place like it and that's for sure! Got all your belongings? I'll be taking you the rest of the way to your pa's on a friend's boat in the morning. You'll stay with me and my family tonight—like them to meet you, Stormy."

"Oh, I'd love to meet your family, captain. I feel I already know them."

As anxious as Stormy was to get on toward Cape Fear, she had to admit she thoroughly enjoyed meeting Captain Murdock's family. She was warmly welcomed from the minute she arrived until the farewell the next morning.

As they boarded a small boat belonging to Murdock's friend, she told him how much she had enjoyed the evening with his family.

"Aren't they the greatest? I bet my Betsy kept you up all night talking."

"Let's put it like this: if Betsy and I lived nearby we could be great friends. She's a chatterbox like me," Stormy laughed.

"Glad you enjoyed yourself. I can tell my family liked you, Stormy. In fact, my dear wife told me she hoped you could come back and stay longer. So you think about that, missy."

"I promise you I will, Captain Murdock."

Marcie felt a deep compassion for her husband, knowing Stormy was constantly on his mind. But he never shut her out to sink into a black mood like a lot of men would have if they were consumed by concern over a missing daughter. She could not have asked for a more devoted husband.

Three days earlier, he had allowed Dorsey to make the run to Savannah so he could remain in Southport. Marcie knew why—she had seen him looking at the calendar. He'd turned to her as she was finishing up the dishes after dinner to remark, "Murdock should be on his way back from England by now, Marcie."

"Just pray the weather will keep holding, Kip. That's what I've been doing."

With a sheepish smile he confessed, "That's why I decided not to make this run. If Murdock returned with her, I wanted to be here."

Marcie put her arm around him. "Kip dear—I'm glad that you did stay. I love you for loving your daughter so much."

He clasped her small waist and bent down to kiss her. "How did an ugly old bloke like me ever win the heart of a pretty thing like you, Marcie? It never ceases to amaze me, I swear to God!"

"Because you're the man you are, Kip Monihan. If anyone had told me I'd marry so soon after Tom's death I would have called them crazy."

Slowly, they walked into their front room, holding hands. Kip said, "You know, Marcie, there are a lot of different kinds of love that a man and a woman can experience in a lifetime. I'm sure it was the same for you and Tom as it was with me and Molly—it was that first love."

"I'd known no other love."

"And Molly had been my only love, too."

"But Kip, what the two of us have already shared in a few short months means so very much to me. I've never felt so fulfilled. You've made me feel special in a way that Tom never did. I mean no disrespect—I loved Tom dearly as you did Molly. But you have a capacity to love that Tom couldn't or was unable to give to me."

Kip's eyes warmed ardently at her words. "I know you'll understand what I'm about to say, Marcie. I feel the same way. Maybe if me and Molly had been married longer, that wall of reserve would have been swept away. She only gave a part of herself to me, but I've always been a patient man—even back then when I was young."

A teasing smile crossed Marcie's face as she quizzed him, "Who did Stormy inherit her impatient, impulsive nature from? If it wasn't you or Molly, I'm at a loss."

"The truth is, she never looked like me or Molly. It's her Grandma Monihan. My mother Colleen was a wee little lady with a will of iron—her hair was as golden as Stormy's and her Irish eyes as green. My Stormy is exactly like her grandma."

"It's too bad she couldn't have lived to see Stormy."

"Wherever she is, Marcie, I'm sure she knows about Stormy. Knowing my ma, I have no doubt she's up there in heaven feeling very smug that my daughter turned out to be just like her."

"Oh, Kip!" she laughed, flinging her arms around his neck. Her kiss was enough to flame his desire to make love to her.

Once again, Marcie was to know the love this man could make her feel and she eagerly abandoned herself to it. This man who was many years older had made her feel like she was sixteen again, experiencing the thrill of her first romance.

Twenty-three

The small boat plowed through the coastal waters at a fast clip—the weather was perfect, but it took awhile to travel from Savannah to Southport. The sun was setting much earlier already, a sure sign that winter was approaching.

Monihan's cottage was just south of Southport, but Murdock figured that after he collected his fee he could well afford to treat his old buddy, Stan Tolliver, to a night's lodging and a good meal before they went back to Savannah.

Tolliver's boat, *Tidewater*, pulled into Monihan's dock about five in the afternoon. Murdock sensed Stormy's excitement as he took her luggage and guided her up the path.

A swift breeze wafted through the tall cypress trees as they walked. Murdock said, "Ah, Stormy, we're here just in time, I think. Winter is surely on its way."

"I'm so glad you're safely back here with your family, captain—and I'm glad I'm home."

"Luck was with us, missy." There was no time to say more for he saw Kip Monihan rushing toward them. He'd spied them coming up the path and his long legs strode hastily toward them. Then he took his daughter in his arms and swung her around in sheer exuberance.

His voice was cracking with emotion. "Oh, Stormy! My little Stormy, I've waited so long for this moment!"

Murdock stood back to observe the happy reunion. He could certainly understand Kip's agony, having daughters of his own.

By the time the three of them had gone to the cottage and Stormy had had a reunion with Marcie, Murdock was ready to rejoin Tolliver, who was waiting for him in the boat.

While Stormy and Marcie were absorbed in conversation, Murdock took the opportunity to tell Monihan what a wonderful daughter he had. "She was a grand little sailor—no problem at all, Monihan. I'm very fond of Stormy and she endeared herself to my family last night, too. She spent the night with us so I could bring her here this morning."

"I'm beholden to you, Murdock, and your fee doesn't begin to repay you." He walked over to the desk in his front room to pull out the leather pouch with Murdock's money.

Monihan saw the warm embrace Stormy gave Murdock and knew that they had developed a strong friendship.

He accompanied Murdock down to the dock and thanked him once again. "I feel I still owe you, Murdock," he said as the captain boarded Tolliver's boat.

"You owe me nothing, Kip. Stormy was good company and I'm just glad we got here when we did. It's getting rough out there."

The three of them enjoyed a grand and glorious evening. Marcie could not have been happier because Stormy was thrilled that the two of them had married. It was very important to Marcie that Stormy approved.

Once they had eaten dinner and the kitchen was put in order, the three of them retired to the front room. The rest of the evening Marcie and Kip were spellbound by the tales Stormy had to tell.

For a young lady who had not yet celebrated her

eighteenth birthday, Stormy had already lived a very exciting life. She did not hesitate to tell them she was in love with Jason Hamilton.

"He sounds like a very nice young man, Stormy, and he certainly took good care of you. That's enough to make me feel kindly toward him," Kip said.

"His family was just as nice, pa. You wouldn't believe the mansion they live in."

"Well, you may find it hard to adjust to this humble cottage of ours after all that luxury," Kip teased.

"Ah, Pa—you know better than that! This is home—the only home I've ever known. Nothing is dearer to me than this little cottage."

She had noticed all the special touches Marcie had added—it had made the little cottage look nicer. It was only right, for now it was Marcie's home, too. But she had also seen that nothing had been changed in Stormy's room. When she finally retired, she unpacked her beautiful new clothing along with all the other luxurious articles Jason had given her.

She had noticed how Marcie's eyes admired her cape with the fur-trimmed collar. Now that Stormy was back in Southport, she wondered how often she would wear these elegant ensembles. They all seemed too fancy.

When she undressed and slipped into her nightgown and robe, she realized what a completely different life she'd had in England.

The nightgowns in the chest were simple little batiste gowns—no lavish edgings of French lace—and her robe was a simple cotton wrapper. It was certainly not like the fancy robe she was wearing.

It suddenly dawned on her that life was not going to be the same for her as it had been before.

By the time she dimmed her lamp in this room that had been hers for as long as she could remember, she realized it would take time to adjust to these surroundings. This was her home—why did it all seem so different?

As she lay looking out the window into the darkness, her thoughts strayed back across that ocean. She thought about the Hamiltons and especially Jason, wondering if he'd been very upset to find her gone.

She also thought about Tawny and Bart and regretted she hadn't been able to tell them goodbye. At least she and Tawny had shared one wonderful afternoon together.

For the first few days after she'd arrived she spent time with her father, the two of them taking long walks and talking endlessly. She also spent time with Marcie and helped her around the house.

In quiet moments alone she wrote to Jason and Lady Hamilton, telling of the voyage and her safe arrival as well as the happy reunion.

She also wrote to Tawny and the Murdock family in Savannah. When they were all completed she turned them over to her father. Kip took the letters, remarking, "Seems you made yourself a lot of good friends in a few months, Stormy."

"I sure did, Pa, and I love each and every one. They were wonderful to me."

Kip had been observing her, as any doting father would, to see if there had been any changes in his daughter. There was no question that she had changed in ways Kip could not quite pinpoint yet. He hadn't said anything to Marcie but knowing her, he would have wagered she'd also observed the changes. But if she had, she hadn't mentioned anything.

Stormy was the same lively, talkative girl she'd always been, but Kip saw a more mature, sophisticated young lady than the young girl who'd been abducted last summer. He figured that being around the refined English family for several weeks had made a strong impression on Stormy.

One afternoon after she'd been home about a week, Stormy took a stroll out on the wharf by herself. Kip had gone into town and Marcie was puttering in her kitchen. She found time hanging heavily on her hands and felt restless.

It was quiet out on the water—she didn't even see any boats. She had to admit that she wasn't looking forward to the endless days of winter.

She was wearing one of the simpler gowns she'd brought with her. Dear Lady Sheila had such a wonderful sense of humor. She'd laughed about her morning gowns being actually her dressing gowns for she didn't get up as early as Lord Addison did.

Their way of living was so different from her pa's and Marcie's, Stormy thought as she began to stroll back toward the house.

In her kitchen, Marcie went about rolling out a couple of pie crusts. She'd seen Stormy go out in her pretty woolen gown. There was a time when Stormy would have saved that for a special occasion, but now she had so many dresses to choose from.

Not once had Stormy put on her old faded pants and loose-fitting blue shirt. She had the feeling that Kip might have liked to see her in her old garb, but she could hardly fault Stormy for wearing the soft woolens or lovely sprigged gowns she'd brought back which were so much nicer than the ones in her old wardrobe.

Stormy had only gone a few steps up the path when she heard sounds out in the cove and quickly turned to see a familiar sight: the *East Wind* moving toward the wharf. She dashed down, knowing it had to be Dorsey.

She threw up her hand and began to wave excitedly. What a wonderful sight it was to see the *East Wind!* The glorious sight to Dorsey was to see her standing on the wharf. His heart began to pound harder and harder as the boat came closer to the wharf and he could see her. Other hands began to wave to her. An air of excitement ignited on the deck. Kip's daughter was home!

As soon as the *East Wind* docked, Pat leapt out to give her an amorous embrace and a kiss—with all the crew watching. Stormy was not prepared for such a display. She'd forgotten about Dorsey and their brief little romantic interlude once Jason Hamilton had come into her life. Now Dorsey was expecting to take up where they'd left off when she was abducted.

Stormy was embarrassed when she heard the crew laughing and quickly stiffened in his arms, wiggling free of his embrace. But Dorsey was so engrossed by the sight of her that he didn't notice. "God, Stormy— you're the best thing these eyes of mine could behold!" he declared.

"It's very good to be home, Pat," she said. Some of the crew called out to her and welcomed her home. She turned from Dorsey to thank them, calling out, "It's so good to be back."

About this time a sleepy Paddy had roused to amble out on the deck. A big smile broke on her face as she rushed to him and flung herself into his arms.

"Prayers are answered, little one," he said, his voice cracking with emotion.

She locked her arm in his as he, Stormy, and Dorsey walked up to the cottage together. When Kip returned from town, he was to find a very gala celebration in his little cottage.

Twenty-four

Stormy had to face a dilemma she had not thought about once she returned home and saw Pat Dorsey once again. It was obvious he'd assumed their relationship would resume as it was when she had disappeared. In fairness to him, Stormy had to admit that she had been attracted to him and willing for him to court her for those brief weeks before Jed Callihan had played his evil tricks on her.

Most young ladies would find Pat Dorsey very attractive—there was a certain charm about his cocky, assured manner. Obviously, there was a time when she had been drawn to him, but that was before she'd met Jason Hamilton and fallen in love with him.

She didn't want to hurt Pat's feelings—he had always been nice to her and she also knew how much her pa depended upon him.

Things had changed a great deal since the time they were courting and she was a naive little innocent. She knew that she might have appeared to be a feisty little vixen then but she wasn't. She knew nothing about men or what it was like to love a man. Jason taught her that and now she knew about passion sparking in a man's eyes and the fires of desire in his lips when he kissed her.

What she didn't know was how to handle Pat Dorsey—

she could not love him when she felt such strong feelings for Jason.

Pat made frequent trips to see her. If she told him the truth, he would become so angry he would probably leave her father. She didn't want that to happen.

So she played for time in hopes that the answer would come. Stormy's dilemma was obvious to Marcie. Knowing Stormy's devotion to her father, she also suspected the reason why she refused to offend Pat.

Marcie had only to listen to Stormy talk about Jason Hamilton to know that he was the one who'd tamed Stormy's romantic heart.

But he was in England and Stormy was here. Marcie saw how disturbed Stormy was each time Dorsey arrived at their front door.

Marcie kept hoping Stormy would approach her about the situation, but she didn't so Marcie remained silent.

Now that Stormy was home safe and sound, it didn't come as any surprise to Marcie when Kip told her he was making the next run to Savannah on the *East Wind*.

But she was slightly stunned when Stormy announced she wanted to go with her father. Kip was so thrilled that he didn't question her motives.

Stormy noticed the quizzical look on Marcie's face and later confessed why she wanted to make the run. "I'll have the opportunity to see the Murdock family and it will probably convince Dorsey that I'm not ready to settle down. He's becoming far too serious. I can't marry him, Marcie."

"I understand, Stormy," Marcie replied. She knew Stormy's real reason: her heart yearned to marry another man.

A few days later, Marcie bade Kip and Stormy goodbye and watched the two of them walk down the wharf. Seeing Stormy in the faded pants and loose tunic carried her back to the time when Kip had first started leaving his young daughter with her when he and Tom walked to the wharf.

Life was so unpredictable, she thought to herself. Now she was Kip Monihan's wife and Tom was dead. The young girl she'd taken care of was now a young lady and her stepdaughter.

The sight of Stormy accompanying Kip was an unexpected delight for Dorsey. His heart swelled with anticipation—now they could share many stolen moments together.

The look on Kip's face was enough to tell him how happy he was to have his pretty daughter once again by his side. He rushed up to greet them, his eyes directly on Stormy. "Didn't expect to see you here this morning, Stormy," he smiled down at her.

"I surprised you, eh, Pat?"

"It's a nice surprise though. Must be that you've missed the old *East Wind*," he said.

"Can't deny that. Well, I'll leave you two to get on with your business while I get settled in the cabin," she said as she took her little brown valise and made her way to her father's cabin.

She wore an amused smile as she walked away. That conceited Pat Dorsey was probably thinking she was making this trip so she could be around him but he would be in for a few surprises, she suspected, before this run was over.

Stormy kept herself very busy in the cabin most of the afternoon—some housecleaning chores were very much in order.

Since Dorsey had made the last run, the cabin had a month's accumulation of dust. She cracked the small window to allow some fresh air in.

When Kip finally arrived late in the afternoon he found her padding around the cabin in her bare feet.

She'd pulled her thick blond hair away from her face in one long braid down her back.

"Well, you're a busy little beaver, Stormy."

"It had been shut up so long, Pa, it had a musty smell and dust was everywhere. I was just trying to air it out a little."

"Don't know what I'd do without you and Marcie. A man is a lost soul without a lady, I truly believe," he declared. "Been down to say hello to Paddy yet?"

"Haven't had time, Pa, but I will in a minute."

"Might be that we'd have a much better supper tonight if he knows you're aboard," Kip laughed.

"Oh, Pa!" she giggled.

A short time later she was breezing toward the galley to see Paddy. It was a happy surprise for Paddy to see her dashing through the door.

"Well, look who's here! Kip didn't tell me you were going to be with us," he declared, wiping his hands on the tail of his apron.

"He didn't know," she confessed. "I decided to come at the last minute."

"Well, then, I guess I got to fix a special meal. Now, it ain't going to be that fancy fare you were used to eating over there in London town but it'll be good eating," Paddy grinned.

"Oh, Paddy!" She walked over to hug his neck. "You're the best cook in the world. You fed me all my life and I turned out to be pretty healthy."

"By lord, you have, haven't you? Never thought about that until just now. Guess I'm a good cook after all," he chuckled.

"You know you are. Guess I better not take up any more of your time or I won't get that good meal, will I?"

"You and a whole bunch of other people!"

Stormy left and Paddy turned his attention back to his stove.

It was a disappointment to Pat Dorsey that Stormy didn't roam around the deck as she had in the past. In two days at sea, he'd only seen her once.

Since she was walking around the deck with her father, he could hardly intrude so he didn't try to join them. Pat was beginning to ask himself if Stormy was deliberately trying to avoid him, which was enough to wound his ego.

One of the boatmen who'd sailed with Kip for several years had casually mentioned, "That little Stormy ain't exactly the same little gal she was before that awful thing happened. Guess that's why she's staying close to the cabin. Lord, I remember that little rascal running all around this deck all the time."

Dorsey had to agree with Gus—the changes in Stormy were obvious to him, too. He found her much more reserved.

She'd seemed very stiff that first afternoon when he'd eagerly leaped off the boat to welcome her home. He'd just assumed she was a little shy about the two of them being observed by the rest of the crew. But during the following week when he'd gone over and they'd taken strolls, he'd been very aware that he could hold her hand but one kiss was all she'd allowed him.

He'd assumed that could be due to the trauma she'd been through so he had vowed to be patient and understanding.

On the few strolls they'd taken, Stormy apparently had had no desire to tell him anything about her ordeal, so he hadn't prodded her. Nor had she spoken about her voyage aboard the English sea captain's schooner and her stay in England with his family.

The last few days he'd been pondering about this Captain Jason Hamilton he'd heard Kip speak about with great admiration.

The third night out, Dorsey spied Stormy roaming around the deck after the evening meal. She was not looking for Dorsey. In truth, she hoped she would not run into him. She was taking a stroll because Kip and Paddy were playing cards and sipping a little whiskey.

Her thoughts spanned the ocean as she stood in the moonlight. She was remembering Lady Sheila's description of their holiday season. Instead of a turkey, Elsie baked a goose and made Yorkshire pudding. She told Stormy about the thin-sliced salmon they ate with brown bread. Stormy had eaten a variety of fish all her life but it wasn't until Jason had taken her to one of the little London tea rooms that she had tasted a scrumptious Dover sole.

She smiled as she recalled dear Lord Addison. He was such a tall, trim gent—it amazed her that he consumed that mammoth breakfast in bed every morning. Lady Sheila had confided that he always had his bowl of hot porridge with fresh fruit, eggs, sausage, bacon, and kippers. It seemed like a tremendous feast to Stormy and Lady Sheila agreed. She had no desire to eat so much in the morning.

She was so engrossed in her thoughts, she didn't hear Dorsey walking up behind her. When he addressed her, she rather resented the intrusion.

"Well, we finally meet, Stormy. I'd been wondering when I was going to see you," he said as his arms reached out for her. She saw the look in his eyes and knew instinctively he was going to kiss her.

She attempted to whirl around as she made a light-hearted remark about being busy in her pa's cabin, but she wasn't swift enough. Dorsey's arms enclosed her and his lips covered hers.

But Stormy's lips were cool and didn't respond.

Dorsey was experienced enough to realize it so he quickly released her.

"Sorry, Stormy—guess I assumed too much," he said with a frown on his face.

Stormy realized she had wounded his pride and sought to soothe him. "Pat, I could never play games with you—I think too much of you for that. But too much has happened to me over the last months. I'm—I'm not the girl I was back in the spring. I may never be that girl again. I want us to be friends, Pat, but that's all. I—I can't be serious about any man right now."

Dorsey admired her honesty and accepted what she said. He took her arm to lead her back toward her cabin. "I'll always be your friend, Stormy. I'm glad you were honest—I can respect that. Like you, I don't have time for silly games."

She managed a weak smile. By the time they parted company, Stormy felt a little guilty—she was hardly being honest with Dorsey. She was just trying to calm him so he wouldn't be angry with her. If she had been completely open and frank, she would have told him she didn't want him to kiss her for there was only one man's lips she longed for—Jason's.

But that would have been too cruel, so she told him that little white lie.

When they'd said goodnight, she declared, "Thanks, Pat, for being so understanding. I—I truly want very much for us to be friends."

He gave her arm a pat and assured her, "And so we shall be, Stormy. I do understand. Hey, I'm a very patient man."

"Good night, Pat, and thanks," she said, eager to get back inside.

Their brief conversation made things easier for Stormy during the run. She felt more relaxed around the boat and felt free to roam around the deck.

As the days went by, she found herself having a greater respect for Dorsey—he seemed to accept the fact that they were only to be friends.

But in truth, Dorsey was hardly ready to accept that. He just didn't want to rile Stormy. He was determined to win her and was willing to give her a little time if that was what she needed after the trauma she'd been through.

Stormy Monihan whetted Pat's interest as no other woman ever had.

Part Three

Love's Fury

Twenty-five

It didn't seem to matter where he was or who he was with, Jason could not find any escape from his memories of Stormy Monihan. The essence of her was overwhelming whether he was home with his mother and father or out on the *Sea Princess*.

Every fiber in his being cried out to him to throw caution to the wind and get some kind of crew together and sail for the States and claim the woman he loved.

When Joy and Eric came to have dinner at his parents' house in late October, Joy was absolutely shattered to hear that Stormy had sailed for the States.

"Dear God, Jason—you let her leave?" Joy asked her older brother, disbelief in her eyes.

"I couldn't stop it, Joy. Her father sent for her while I was on a mission to Ireland."

Joy had always adored her brother, but she was out of patience with him. Once again, he had allowed a beautiful lady to flee. She wondered if Jason would ever feel strongly enough about any woman to fight for her as Bart Montgomery had to win Tawny Blair. She would always see Bart as a hero—he had been the first man she'd had a crush on when she was a teenager.

Folding her napkin neatly by the side of her plate, Joy declared in a tone of voice that made her mother and father exchange glances, "Then why don't you do what Bart did? He couldn't stand it when Tawny sailed back to Virginia. Go to her, Jason!"

"I might just do that, Joy," Jason said. Everyone's eyes were on him. Lady Hamilton quickly changed the subject to the approaching holidays. "You and Eric will be here with us, won't you, Joy?"

"Oh, of course we will, Mother. I can't imagine being anywhere else," she smiled over at her mother.

"Jane and Disney will be here for Christmas Eve but not for Christmas Day. They plan to have the inn open and have to serve the lodgers over the holidays," Lady Hamilton reminded Joy.

"And how will they manage to tear themselves away for Christmas Eve? Lord, that inn consumes all their time, it seems to me. I never get to spend much time with Jane anymore," Joy complained.

"That's true, Joy, but Jane loves what she's doing so I guess that's all that matters. She and Disney have made a good life for themselves."

"And what about Angela?"

"Poor dears—they're going to try to divide Christmas Eve as well as Christmas Day between both of their parents' homes," her mother said. Lady Hamilton knew that it would please Joy to hear that Tawny and Bart were dropping by for a while on Christmas Eve. "So you'll get to see them and your little namesake."

"Oh, that's good news!"

Jason excused himself from the family circle to go outside and enjoy a cheroot. He didn't enjoy all this talk about the holidays. Being surrounded by his sisters and their husbands made him the odd man—his sister Angela was always trying to match him up with one of her little social butterflies.

The minute Angela had found out about Stormy going back home, she'd brought one of her friends to their country home. He'd already told his mother to put a bug in Angela's ear. As he'd requested, Sheila had urged her to forget about trying to line Jason up with her friends. "Jason just isn't interested, Angela."

"Jason obviously intends to end up an old bachelor," Angela sighed. "Or could it be that he's moping over Stormy Monihan? Lord, he may never see her again."

Sheila smiled. "Oh, I wouldn't say that, dear. I wouldn't say that at all."

Stormy had been back in Cape Fear for a few weeks when her three letters arrived in England. Lady Hamilton read hers a couple of times before she finally folded it up. It was wonderful to know that she had arrived safely back with her father.

Jason would have a nice surprise awaiting him when he returned from the city this afternoon.

A few miles away, Tawny had also read her long, newsy letter from Stormy. She spoke about the signs of autumn everywhere, and for one fleeting moment, Tawny found herself feeling a bit homesick for Virginia. But her little daughter had only to toddle toward her to remind her that this was her home now. The day she married Bart Montgomery, England became her home— and she truly loved the English countryside now.

Stormy wrote about her regret that she'd had not time to come over to say goodbye, but that she was so glad they'd had that nice afternoon together. At the end of the letter she wrote that she missed them all very much.

The last thing she wrote was that she hoped Jason would understand why she had to leave when she did. She'd had no choice.

Like Sheila, Tawny had folded the letter and put it on her desk. She had to satisfy her curious nature, so she decided to ride Baron over to see the Hamiltons. She felt sure they had gotten a letter, too, but just in case she wanted to let them know that Stormy had arrived home safe and sound.

Sheila saw her galloping up the long drive and suspected that she, too, had heard from Stormy. She went to the front door to greet her. Sheila was reminded of the young seventeen-year-old Tawny she'd first met when she dismounted and came rushing up the steps.

"I heard from Stormy, Lady Sheila. I just had to come over to see if you did, too," she exclaimed.

"Yes, I did and Jason has a letter waiting for him when he gets home," Sheila said, urging her to come inside.

"Oh, I'm so glad," Tawny declared as she followed Sheila back to her sitting room.

For the next hour, the two of them sat enjoying coffee and little cakes as they talked of nothing but Stormy Monihan. They compared the news in each of the letters.

Tawny had always been able to talk frankly with Jason's mother since the moment they'd met. She even confessed her brief moment of yearning for Virginia again when she'd read Stormy's letter.

"It's beautiful back there in the autumn, Lady Hamilton. But then I have only to look out on this countryside to know how lucky I am."

"Ah, Tawny—I've lived a lifetime in England but there are times when I yearn to see that gorgeous green of Ireland. It was where I was born and raised for the first eighteen years of my life."

"Lady Hamilton, I truly don't know what I'd have done without you through the years. You've been like a mother to me—Jason is awfully lucky to have a mother like you."

"Tawny, that's so sweet of you—you could almost make me cry." Sheila might not have been blessed by having her as the daughter-in-law she'd hoped for but they had remained very close and that was enough.

Hardly a half hour after Tawny left, Jason and his father arrived back home. It was a happy Sheila Hamilton who greeted them.

The first thing she announced was that they had news of Stormy. She immediately saw the fire spark in Jason's black eyes so she wasted no time in handing him the letter. And he wasted no time, either, as he rushed up the stairs to his room. Addison and Sheila exchanged smiles as they went on into the parlor where he took a seat to read their letter.

As soon as Jason was in the privacy of his own room, he anxiously read her letter. As he read her words, he could easily envision her lovely face. The letter ended all too soon for Jason. He found himself wanting to read more, so he read it over again.

When he finally laid the letter aside, Jason was filled with many conflicting emotions. Nothing could have made him happier than getting that letter. To read how sad she'd been to have to leave while he was away lead Jason to believe she did feel as strongly about him as he did about her.

But the letter had also made him ache with renewed loneliness and yearning. He had no inkling how long he paced around the room and stared out the window into the early-evening darkness. A lot of reckless thoughts were parading through his mind—he had just about convinced himself to give way to his gnawing impulses.

Jason was able to disguise his true feelings as he dined with his parents that evening. For once, Lady Sheila was fooled by his happy-go-lucky manner. That was exactly the way Jason wanted it for the time being.

But he didn't linger long with them after the evening meal. Sheila told her husband, as the two of them sat in the parlor later, "I'll bet Jason is up in his room writing Stormy a letter, Addison."

"You think so, dear?"

But a couple of hours later when the two of them went up to their suite, Addison noticed that the lamp was still burning in Jason's room. He commented to his wife as he opened the door for her, "Then it must be a very long letter he's writing, dear."

"Well, Jason was never one to write a letter, as you know, Addison."

It was no letter Jason was writing but a long list of things he intended to do the next day. Everything he was about to do went against rules he'd set for himself when he'd acquired the *Sea Princess*. He knew he couldn't meet his own standards in terms of a crew if he wanted to sail from England at this time of the year.

Tobias and Rudy would go with him—he had no doubt about that. It was the rest of a crew Jason would have to gamble on if he wanted to take on that tempestuous sea.

The men around the harbor or in the taverns on Fleet Street were a reckless breed that he had always tried to steer clear of.

But he had decided to chance it. It told him how driven he was to get to Stormy Monihan—he was finally fully convinced that he was truly in love.

The next morning Jason went into London and by the time he returned at dusk, he had recruited Tobias and Rudy to join him on this wild venture.

Lady Luck surely had to be riding on his shoulder, he figured, when he chanced to run into his first mate, Dewey, down by the wharf. Jason didn't know whether he agreed to ship out with him because he was bored or if it was the higher wages Jason was paying. Whatever it was, Jason didn't care—he knew he had three very dependable men.

We've got your authors!

If you seek out the latest historical romances by today's bestselling authors, our new reader's service, KENSINGTON CHOICE, is the club for you.

KENSINGTON CHOICE is the only club where you can find authors like Janelle Taylor, Shannon Drake, Rosanne Bittner, Sylvie Sommerfield, Penelope Neri and Phoebe Conn all in one place…

…and the only service that will deliver their romances direct to your home as soon as they are published—even before they reach the bookstores.

KENSINGTON CHOICE is also the only service that will give you a substantial guaranteed discount off the publisher's prices on every one of those romances.

That's right: Every month, the Editors at Zebra and Pinnacle select four of the newest novels by our bestselling authors and rush them straight to you, usually *before they reach the bookstores*. The publisher's prices for these romances range from $4.99 to $5.99—but they are always yours for the guaranteed low price of just *$4.20!*

That means you'll always save over 20% off the publisher's prices on every shipment you get from KENSINGTON CHOICE!

All books are sent on a 10-day free examination basis, and there is no minimum number of books to buy. (A postage and handling charge of $1.50 is added to each shipment.)

As your introduction to the convenience and value of this new service, we invite you to accept

4 BOOKS FREE

The 4 books, worth up to $23.96, are our welcoming gift. You pay only $1 to help cover postage and handling.

To start your subscription to KENSINGTON CHOICE and receive your introductory package of 4 FREE romances, detach and mail the card at right *today*.

We have 4 FREE BOOKS for you
as your introduction to
KENSINGTON CHOICE
To get your FREE BOOKS, worth
up to $23.96, mail the card below.

FREE BOOK CERTIFICATE

As my introduction to your new KENSINGTON CHOICE reader's service, please send me 4 FREE historical romances (worth up to $23.96), billing me just $1 to help cover postage and handling. As a KENSINGTON CHOICE subscriber, I will then receive 4 brand-new romances to preview each month for 10 days FREE. I can return any books I decide not to keep and owe nothing. The publisher's prices for the KENSINGTON CHOICE romances range from $4.99 to $5.99, but as a subscriber I will be entitled to get them for just $4.20 per book or $16.80 for all four titles. There is no minimum number of books to buy, and I can cancel my subscription at any time. A $1.50 postage and handling charge is added to each shipment.

Name _____

Address _____ Apt. _____

City _____ State _____ Zip _____

Telephone ( ) _____

Signature _____

(If under 18, parent or guardian must sign)

Subscription subject to acceptance. Terms and prices subject to change.

KC0895

We have
4
FREE
Historical
Romances
for you!

(worth up
to $23.96!)

Details inside!

AFFIX
STAMP
HERE

KENSINGTON CHOICE
Reader's Service
120 Brighton Road
P.O. Box 5214
Clifton, NJ 07015-5214

He figured that this would help compensate for the ones who might be shiftless. Before he left the city he ambled into the Dover Tavern and approached two robust seamen enjoying their ale.

When Jason approached and offered to buy them another ale, he told them of his plans. They exchanged glances and one of them remarked, "Captain, you got to be one brave seaman or crazy in the head to start across the Atlantic at this time of the year."

"I lay claim to neither but I'm one of the best sea captains you'd ever sail with," Jason boasted arrogantly.

A slow grin came to both faces. "Hell, I'll go with you. Rather be out there than sitting the winter away here. How about you, Bruno?"

"I'll go if you will," the other man chimed in.

When Jason left London that late afternoon he had five of the crew he needed. His spirits were soaring by the time he arrived back home.

But he still had no plans to say anything to his parents just yet.

Twenty-six

Sheila Hamilton knew something was brewing when Jason kept going into the city daily, though he gave no hint of what he was up to. She had to say she was glad that he seemed so happy in the evenings.

Because they were so much alike, Jason sensed that she was carefully scrutinizing him across the table as they dined. He also knew she was extremely curious about everything that went on in her family.

Knowing what he was going to do just before the Christmas holiday, he had taken one afternoon to buy everyone in his family a gift. She had also observed him that afternoon when he'd entered the house, his arms filled with packages.

She wondered if Jason was just enthused about the coming holiday. Then her practical Irish side took over and she made herself face reality: Jason was buying his Christmas gifts early because he wasn't going to be here at holiday time. He was leaving—and quite soon, if she knew her son as well as she felt she did.

She remembered the challenge her darling Joy had tossed at him last week, reminding Jason what Bart Montgomery had done to claim the woman he loved.

Lord Addison was not surprised when his son decided to make his announcement. He had expected it since the day the three of them had received Stormy's letters. He couldn't fault his son, even though he knew the treacherous weather he'd be facing. If he was a young man like Jason and he was in love as he'd been with the lovely Sheila O'Reilly, he would have done exactly the same thing. So he had no intention of trying to dissuade him.

Addison Hamilton knew that passion was the strongest force in a man—he was not so old that he'd forgotten that!

Never had any woman caught his eye and held it as Sheila had throughout all the years they'd been married. It was truly an amazing union for they were complete opposites. But her vivacious ways had been able to penetrate his quiet, reserved manner. In their private times together, she could bring out a side of Addison Hamilton that no one else ever saw.

To this day, it was true. But Addison also knew that Sheila needed what he could give her. She liked that safe, secure comfort he had always provided. She found him a forceful, masterful man in that quiet way of his.

He was glad for Sheila's sake that the day Jason left to board the *Sea Princess,* the sun was shining and there was not a hint of bad weather.

He watched his one and only son leave the house, secure in his belief that Jason would return. He also hoped that he returned with the woman he loved.

He did all he could to assure Sheila that he would be fine. He made a point of telling her, "Burt Montgomery did it a few years ago, Sheila. Why shouldn't our Jason be as bold?"

Addison had made his point. She smiled, declaring, "So he did, Addison, and so shall Jason."

She no longer had a sad look on her face—Addison was grateful for that.

The next few days, she became completely absorbed in her plans for the holidays—she was no longer moping around, consumed with worry about Jason.

She had asked him what they should tell the family.

"Tell them the truth, Mother. Tell them I've gone to Cape Fear after the woman I love," he laughed. "That should provide fuel for endless conversation during the holiday."

"Oh, Jason," she laughed. "You're impossible! Do you really think we're such busybodies?"

"Just an ordinary family, Mother, especially when there's one son and three daughters," he teased with an impish twinkle in his eyes.

When the two of them parted company and Sheila was left in her sitting room, she was thinking it would be worth being without him during this holiday if he returned with Stormy Monihan as his bride. She could already imagine what beautiful children the two of them would have.

Out on Cape Fear it was the greatest holiday Kip could remember. His daughter was back home and he had a new wife, who was making it a special holiday— her first Christmas in her new home. The little cottage was aglow—the mantel was decorated and wreaths were hung at all the windows. Kip was going to the woods to cut one of the tall fir trees.

The cupboard counter was already lined with applesauce cakes, tins of cookies, and a mountain of fruit pies.

Paddy and Dorsey had been invited to share the holiday with them. In the evenings, Marcie knitted various gifts. When Kip was out on his run, and had worked on his gift—woolen gloves and a cap to pull over his ears.

Trying to get Stormy's green sleeveless vest finished was proving to be an ordeal—she was around the house so much of the time. She suggested to Kip that he urge

Stormy to accompany him to town on Saturday so she might finish it and sew on the gold buttons.

Marcie thought Stormy seemed more relaxed and content since she'd returned from the run. She had had a nice visit with the Murdock family and talked about them often.

Stormy didn't mention her frank discussion with Dorsey to Marcie or Kip, but that was one reason Stormy was more relaxed.

Marcie began to notice that Dorsey wasn't coming over as he had been. She called Kip's attention to this. "The two of them have a fuss out on your last run, Kip?"

"Don't think so, Marcie. They seemed friendly enough to me." But he realized that Marcie was right.

Could it possibly be that young Dorsey had found himself a new girl? Since he was staying over at Paddy's when they were in from their runs, Paddy would know.

It certainly didn't seem to be bothering Stormy, so he decided it shouldn't concern him either. What did concern him was that Stormy had not once traveled the short distance into Southport as she used to do so often. He had to conclude she was fearful of an encounter with Jed Callihan. He didn't want to see her become a prisoner in the cottage.

The next day Marcie had to go to town to do some shopping but Stormy sweetly declined again. Actually, Kip's suspicion that Stormy had a fear of Jed Callihan was wrong. She had no fear of him at all. She figured Jed to be the worst kind of coward—a bully only when he had a bevy of buddies to back him up.

Her reason for remaining at the cottage when Marcie went into town was to give herself time to do the delicate work on the gown she was stitching for her gift. She had about an hour of embroidery left and it would be finished. She was delighted with her handiwork.

By the time Marcie returned, she had done the final stitches and put it away. Working on her pa's shirt proved to be no problem—she didn't have to concern herself with whether Marcie was in the house.

But now, she was ready to go into town for she needed gifts for Paddy and Dorsey. She had an idea for Paddy but Dorsey's was difficult.

She knew what she was going to make for Paddy—she'd seen his old, ragged apron when she'd gone on that last run. She was going to make him a new apron with big, roomy pockets.

The next day Marcie was taken completely by surprise when Stormy announced, "I'm going to make a run into town, Marcie. Need me to pick up anything?"

Marcie was in the middle of rolling out a pie crust. "I can't think of anything, honey," she stammered.

Marcie watched Stormy guide the buggy down the drive a short time later, thinking how different she looked now than she had a year ago. There was no doubt about it—Stormy had been very influenced by her stay in England and certainly by this Lady Sheila Hamilton she talked so much about. Marcie even saw it in the way Stormy dressed now.

Marcie turned her attention back to her pies, thinking that she'd have good news for Kip when he returned with the fir tree.

His Stormy was not afraid to go into Southport after all!

Stormy would have been amused if she'd known her dear pa had been concerned about her. She did not fear Jed Callihan or any other man!

Twenty-seven

When Stormy returned to the cottage in the afternoon, her arms were filled with packages. Marcie looked up from her knitting to ask her if she'd bought out all of Southport.

"Hardly, but it's getting close to the holiday season so I've gotten caught up in the spirit, I guess," Stormy said as she laid the packages in the chair and removed her shawl.

"I built a fire—there was a chill in the cottage. I got us a pot of stew on the stove and came in here to knit after you left. Your pa went off without a jacket. He's going to be chilled when he gets in," Marcie said.

Stormy ambled closer to the hearth for a few moments.

When she was comfortable, Stormy picked up her packages and her shawl to take them to her room. "Your stew smells wonderful, Marcie. It's a good night for it."

Later when the three of them sat down at the kitchen table to eat Marcie's hearty stew with generous chunks of beef, potatoes, carrots, and onions, Stormy told them about her plans to make old Paddy an apron.

Kip roared with laughter. "That old Irishman will be thrilled—he'll wear that apron for the rest of his life."

"Maybe I should make him two, Pa," she offered.

"Might be a good idea."

"Then I'll do it," she declared. That evening after

she'd helped Marcie in the kitchen she left them alone in the front room and cut out the aprons.

As Kip and his wife sat in the cozy warmth, he felt mellow as he thought about how wonderful the holidays were going to be with Stormy back home. And, this Christmas he had a loving wife. He couldn't have been happier!

Jason couldn't have asked for a more perfect late-autumn day when he left the harbor with his new crew aboard the *Sea Princess,* but he knew that this day would be the exception before he reached his destination. He had some grave misgivings about a few of the men he'd been forced to hire. But Dewey was a good first mate so between the two of them, Jason figured they could keep the schooner running.

At the end of the first day out, Jason went to his cabin to have his evening meal, beginning to feel a little more relaxed. He didn't stay up as late as he normally would have. A few hours of sleep and he would relieve Dewey at two so he could get some sleep. Dewey would then take the ten-to-six shift the following day.

They had decided on this routine before they'd shipped out, but Jason found it rough to get to sleep at ten in the morning.

Often when Jason's head hit the pillow he thought of Stormy and how he was taking leave of his senses to attempt such a foolhardy journey.

The new sailors on the *Sea Princess* had to wonder what this journey was all about, for they carried no cargo. All Jason had told his old seafaring buddies was that he was going to the States on business. But the three of them were doing a lot of speculating. Tobias and Rudy had many conversations in the galley about this mysterious trip. It just wasn't Jason Hamilton's way to set out on a voyage without a skilled crew.

Tobias had known Jason longer than Rudy or Dewey. "The captain is driven by a very powerful force," he said.

"A powerful force, Tobias?" Dewey queried.

"The powerful force of love, laddie. Nothing as strong as when a man finds himself in love with a fair young lady like Miss Stormy."

"So he's going to Miss Stormy?" Rudy asked.

"I'm declaring it to you, Rudy. Remember he said we were going to Southport? Miss Stormy talked about living near there. You want to make me a wager?"

Rudy grinned and shook his head, "I'm no fool, Tobias. Likely it is you'd win."

On their tenth day out of London they were hit by a squall that quickly turned to sleet. Jason hoped that this wasn't going to keep up for the next several days and nights. The icy pellets pounded against his face and the chilling winds cut through his thick jacket. But after about three hours, it suddenly ceased just as he was turning the helm over to Dewey.

Dewey saw he was chilled to the bone. "Have a good, stiff shot of brandy, captain. We rode this one out, all right."

Jason did help himself to some brandy the minute he entered, then got out of his wet clothing. But the chill was still with him as he sat in a woolen robe waiting for Tobias to serve his dinner.

Tobias's crock of steaming beef stew and fresh-baked bread was exactly what he needed. He ate heartily, feeling the warmth permeate his body.

As soon as Tobias picked up the dishes and bid Jason good night, Jason went immediately to bed. It took only a few minutes for him to fall asleep. His last thought was about how nice it would be to snuggle up to Stormy's soft, warm body as he had some months ago.

God, how wonderful those last nights aboard the *Sea Princess* had been, once Stormy had finally surrendered to his lovemaking.

But once they'd arrived in England, those precious moments had stopped—except when she had accompanied him to the harbor. Then they'd finally given way to their passion. He missed that terribly, he had to admit.

His first mate was luckier than Jason had been—they didn't run into any more freezing rain for the rest of the night. But as the sun rose the next morning at a few minutes before seven, there was a thick gray sky overhead.

The good night's sleep had done wonders for Jason— he was ready to take over from Dewey. Tobias's hearty breakfast of eggs and ham, along with biscuits and two steaming cups of coffee, had fortified him to meet the day.

During the morning hours, Jason sauntered around the deck noticing how some of the seamen cast him a wary eye.

When he first took over the *Sea Princess* after his uncle had left the fine schooner to him, Jason had learned that his crew had to be a little in awe of him.

But he had always tried to temper that by proving that he was a fair-minded man. His old crew knew this, and by the time this journey was over these men would know it, too.

Twenty-eight

The weather turned so foul along the Carolina coast that Stormy rarely saw boats or ships plowing through the waters. Kip was staying close to the cottage these days. He and Paddy spent afternoons playing cards and he and Pat often went out for a day of hunting. They were usually lucky enough to provide a nice meal for all of them.

Stormy had had plenty of time to finish all her gifts, for the weather forced her to stay indoors. But time was hanging heavily on her and she was thinking of things she hadn't dwelled on earlier. Why hadn't she heard from Jason, Tawny, or Lady Hamilton? They had surely received her letters weeks ago.

She often checked off the number of days since she'd left there.

Ever since she had returned from the run with her father, Stormy found that her bond of friendship with Pat Dorsey deepened. When she was around him, as she often was, she had to respect Pat and the fact that he hadn't tried to force his kisses on her. They often took walks when he'd come over for dinner. He took her hand as they strolled around the countryside in the early evening.

They talked about everything in an easy, relaxed way. Yet, there was those times that Stormy saw passion flare in Pat's expressive eyes when they were in the seclusion of the nearby woods.

Once she had stumbled and would have fallen had Pat's strong arms not caught her. She knew that he held her longer than was necessary but she had not protested. Later, she had justified it by telling herself that Pat Dorsey was a very attractive and sensuous man. Most young ladies would find him very appealing with that witty charm of his.

It had been a long time since a man's arms had held her and she had to admit she missed it. With the exception of her father, Marcie, and Paddy, Pat Dorsey was the only person who was ever around.

Stormy was beginning to feel a certain kind of discontent lately—she wasn't sure what had brought it on.

She was also beginning to wonder if she had been a fool not to give herself a chance with Pat after she had first returned instead on insisting they just be friends. She might never see Jason Hamilton again.

If the truth were told, she and Pat Dorsey had more in common than she did with Jason. After all, his background was similar to hers and her father respected and admired Pat very much. He had shown a devoted loyalty to Kip, which was very important to Stormy.

Had she been terribly unfair to Pat—and even to herself? Perhaps when she had returned from England she should have picked up her life where she had left off. But she had been so affected by the fairytale existence she'd lived in England. The fine mansion where the Hamiltons lived had seemed like a palace.

The tall, dark, and handsome Jason Hamilton was the man of her dreams—she'd envisioned him so often when she was sailing on her father's boat when she was fourteen and fifteen.

That was about the age she had been when she became aware of nice-looking young men around the wharf and on various boats around the harbor.

Until Jason had unexpectedly come into her life, she had to admit that Pat Dorsey had attracted her as no other young man ever had. But she and Pat had just begun to get to know one another when it was interrupted by that devious, scheming Jed Callihan.

Every now and then Stormy thought of that stormy afternoon when Jed and his buddies had overtaken her and Marcie in the buggy. It had changed everything in her life. Had it not happened, she would probably never have fallen in love with Jason.

She had no regrets about that—even if she was never again to know the feel of his strong arms or his kiss. She shuddered to think what would have happened to her and the nightmare she would have lived for the rest of her life had she not escaped from Jed's boat that night.

She also had to ask herself if there had been no interruption of their courtship whether Pat would have been the first man she would have surrendered herself to instead of Jason Hamilton.

She had to admit quite honestly that it might have happened that way. So maybe now she should give Pat another chance and try to forget her hope that Jason would sail into Southport and claim her for his bride.

A little voice inside her kept reminding her that he had plenty of time while she was at his parents' home to proclaim his love and ask her to marry him. But he hadn't. Not once had Jason mentioned marriage.

She was too young to mope around like a lovesick calf waiting for a young man who might never come after her, she decided.

The next time Pat Dorsey came over to the cottage, she suggested that the two of them take a walk—Pat was more than willing to oblige her. To his delight, she seemed more like the Stormy he'd fallen hopelessly in love with. She was in a lighthearted mood and never looked more beautiful than she did that afternoon. The cool air brought a flush to her cheeks and her green eyes sparkled.

Her gloved hand was nestled in his as they walked—Pat was deeply affected by her closeness. It was difficult for Pat to suppress the urge to pull her around to face him so he could kiss her.

But he dared not risk ruining this wonderful time they were sharing on this brisk winter's day. Stormy would have to let him know she wanted him to kiss her after what she'd said on the *East Wind*. Pat was a proud man—he'd plead with no woman for her affections. He'd never done that and never would—not even for Stormy Monihan.

As he continued to guide her along the narrow path through the woods, he figured that her happy mood was possibly because of the approaching holidays. Perhaps Marcie's enthusiasm was rubbing off on Stormy.

He was wondering what he might get her and Marcie for Christmas Eve night since he and Paddy had been invited over there for the evening.

When they finally stopped to rest for a minute on a fallen tree trunk, he asked, "Help me, Stormy—suggest something I might get for Marcie. Me and Paddy wanted to bring her a gift on Christmas Eve. She's been so darn nice to both of us."

"Marcie would appreciate anything you brought her, Pat. She is nice, isn't she? I'm so glad she and Pa got married 'cause I loved her for so long. Marcie's been the mother I never had."

"And she loves you. Probably why Kip didn't hesitate to marry her, knowing you would approve. That would have been very important to him."

It was at this moment that they spied a playful little

raccoon chasing another one down from the tree. Excitedly, Stormy turned to call Pat's attention to them.

In the motion of turning her head a strand of her hair had suddenly tangled with one of the big buttons on Pat's jacket.

"Hold still, Stormy, and turn slowly back toward me so I can get you untangled," he declared as he moved slightly toward her. "Now just be still and I'll have it undone in half a minute."

His long fingers gently began to pull her hair away from the button. But as he bent toward her face, which was only inches away, he saw her half-parted lips. A certain look in her eyes invited him to meet her in a kiss.

There was nothing about his kiss that repulsed Stormy. Sensing this, the kiss lingered longer than Pat had expected.

When he finally released her lips, he looked into her eyes to see if she was angry—but anger did not seem to be there. "I'm not going to apologize, Stormy. I couldn't help myself."

"I don't expect an apology, Pat. Maybe I wanted you to kiss me so let's just leave it at that for right now, shall we?"

"Shall we get started back to the house?" He was feeling too elated to push his luck any farther.

"I guess so," she said and smiled sweetly up at him.

"Well, I don't want to get my face slapped if I tried to kiss you again," he said playfully.

"Oh, Pat!" she gaily laughed as she rose and took his hand.

Stormy did not realize that Pat Dorsey's cockiness was a coverup for his seriousness. Not even Kip Monihan had detected what old Paddy had slowly begun to see. With Dorsey living at his place with him, Paddy had slowly become aware that there were two very distinct sides to this young boatman.

It was next to impossible for Paddy to get him to talk very much about his family or his past. When Pat did make a few comments, they were brief. What little he had said had led Paddy to believe that both of Pat's parents were dead and he had been on his own for years.

The truth was, Pat had left home at the tender age of thirteen to escape brutal beatings from an overbearing father. He had loved his mother and felt she loved him but there was little she could do to stop her husband. Pat never returned home after he left but he did keep in touch with an older sister. It was through her that he learned of his mother's death three years after he'd left home, so there was never any reason to return.

As far as Pat was concerned he had no father—he was dead! It was probably the reason he admired and respected Kip Monihan so much. It would have been nice to have had such a doting, loving father. The good-hearted, generous Paddy was also his idea of what he'd liked to have had in a father.

Pat knew that one of these days he was going to have to find his own place—he had his own ideas about what he wanted in a home. It was very important to him to own his own little cottage someday.

For the time being, Pat decided to stay on with Paddy a few more months. But when spring came he would start searching for a little house.

When he'd come in early that evening, Paddy was preparing their supper. Pat insisted he go stretch out in his chair after the meal and he'd clean up. Reluctantly, Paddy went—but he wasn't used to anyone else doing the chores around his place.

Later Pat joined him and confessed, "Damned if I

can figure Stormy out, Paddy. She's a complicated woman!"

Paddy roared with laughter. "I quit trying to figure women out a long time ago, son. Guess that's why I decided to be a bachelor. Hell, I can't figure myself out a lot of the time."

But Pat didn't feel that way. He wanted a wife and a family, a home to call his own. He wanted to share his life and his home with Stormy Monihan.

Twenty-nine

The next afternoon Pat sauntered slowly along the main street of Southport looking in the shop windows for Christmas presents for Stormy and Marcie.

He finally decided to go into Worthington's Emporium and wander up and down to see if something caught his eye. He went by various racks of ladies' apparel but he would not have dared to choose anything like that. Kip might not have approved.

Paddy had told him that Kip was buying Marcie and Stormy gold lockets so he passed by the jewelry counter. So what did that leave, he asked himself as he slowly ambled back toward the front door.

For several minutes, the pretty little clerk behind one of the counters had been eyeing the trim, firm-muscled Pat Dorsey as he'd roamed around the store. He was one handsome gent, Rebecca Branson thought as her blue eyes followed him. Anticipating that he would come her way, she dabbed some of the newest essence on her wrist and behind her ears. It was called "Carolina Jasmine"—a very intoxicating scent.

The aroma reached Dorsey as he approached the counter where she was smiling at him. He was thinking how the fragrance reminded him of Stormy—she was always picking wild jasmine during their strolls and tucking the cluster behind her ear.

He walked up to the counter. "May I ask what that is—that smell?"

" 'Carolina Jasmine,' sir? You like it?" Rebecca asked.

"Sure do. Think I'd like a bottle of that."

"Yes, sir." The new essence was one of the most expensive toilet waters at the emporium.

As she was getting the toilet water, Dorsey decided to get Marcie a bottle, too.

"Ma'am, now I'm going to need your help. You have something that smells like lilacs?"

Rebecca gave him her most charming smile. "Worthington's has any floral fragrance you wish. I have a lilac toilet water I'm sure your lady would love."

"Then I'll take a bottle of the lilac, too, miss."

Rebecca was not only thrilled about the two nice sales but she was intrigued by the man making the purchases. She envied the lucky lady receiving these gifts.

When she had packaged them and Dorsey had placed the money in her hand, she smiled up at him. "Pleasure to have served you, sir, and come back to Worthington's. I'm sure your lady will be very pleased."

Dorsey smiled, "I hope both of them will be pleased, miss." He turned toward the front entrance of the emporium.

The pretty little clerk thought to herself that it wasn't too surprising that a handsome fellow like that could squire two ladies.

He was feeling very pleased about the gifts. Now he could begin to relax, for buying gifts for Paddy and Kip would not be as difficult.

Old Paddy was certainly in need of another pair of pants and Pat had noticed how worn Kip's wool jacket was. So the next afternoon he made another trip to the emporium to shop for them.

Once again, the young lady at the fragrance counter

had seen him enter and she immediately anticipated that he might be coming her way again. But Dorsey went in the opposite direction.

She was disappointed, but after an hour had passed by, she figured he had left.

Pat had left within a half hour—it didn't take him long to buy Paddy a pair of pants and Kip a wool jacket.

Now he was ready to enjoy the holidays with the Monihan family—and Stormy had given him every indication that it might be the best holiday he'd ever known.

Kip and Marcie were very aware of the change in Stormy's attitude toward Pat. In a way Kip was glad she and Pat seemed to have rekindled the romance that was just budding when she'd disappeared.

When she'd first returned home and talked endlessly about the dashing young Jason Hamilton, Kip had to figure she'd left her heart back there. He could not even confess to Marcie that such a union would have made him unhappy for Jason would surely have taken Stormy back to England with him.

Another thing had also bothered him: the Monihans and the Hamiltons were not the same kind of people. How under God's green earth could he have found anything in common with an English lord and lady?

Besides, Pat was a fine young man and hard-working, too. If Kip was any judge, it was pretty obvious he was more than fond of Stormy and had been for a long time.

From all that Paddy told him, Dorsey was not one to carouse in the taverns around Southport. The more he thought about it, Dorsey might just be the right husband for Stormy.

It wasn't exactly marrying Dorsey that Stormy had on her mind but he was making it possible for her to get her mind off of Jason. At least, she wasn't as disappointed every day when there was no letter from him.

Now that she'd had time to really think things out, she could well imagine that Jason was very upset to find her gone. She'd tried hard to accompany him on that trip to Ireland but he'd refused. He could even think she'd left England while he was away out of spite.

She had been cool and aloof that last night. Jason was a very proud man so he could have thought she was saying a final farewell by leaving while he was away.

But if he received her letter he had to know that was not her intention. Could her letters have gone astray? She hadn't heard from Lady Hamilton or Tawny either.

She knew her life had to go on, with or without Jason, and she was determined that it would. Right now that meant enjoying Dorsey's company—she had to admit he was a very engaging man. She had felt more like her old self the last week because of their lighthearted good times together.

For now, that was all she wanted. If Dorsey wanted to hold her in his arms briefly and kiss her, she didn't object. Should his arms and lips become as demanding and forceful as Jason's had, she wasn't so sure of how she'd react.

As Stormy and Marcie sat working on a garland, they talked about how both of their lives had changed over the last year.

"Stormy, I feared at first that it would take you a while to adjust to your former life, but now I'm not concerned at all," Marcie declared with a warm smile.

"I'm just fine, Marcie, really I am." Since the time she'd arrived back in Cape Fear she hadn't brought up the name of Jed Callihan except when she had told them how everything had happened. But now she didn't find it too painful. "Marcie, what happened to Jed? Is he still around here? Dorsey hasn't mentioned anything about him, nor has Pa."

"We've heard various rumors, Stormy. Someone told Kip they'd seen him down in Savannah. The one thing we do know is he lost a lot of his crew after your pa and Dorsey beat a couple of them up pretty good."

She told Stormy how the confessions of those two were enough to set Kip on Jed's trail. "Kip wanted to kill him but he stopped just short of that."

She explained how they were still in the dark after Jed had told Kip she'd jumped off his boat. "We were more perplexed than ever—it seemed you'd literally been swallowed up. Poor Kip didn't know where to turn," Marcie said.

Stormy shook her head. "I can imagine what a state Pa must have been in."

"Your pa's a remarkable man, Stormy. He went through a private hell worrying about you, but he didn't allow that to stand in the way of our wedding. No one could have had a nicer wedding than we had. That's the wonderful thing about Kip—he has so much love to give," Marcie declared.

"I know, Marcie. I always knew how strong he was, even when I was very young. I must have absorbed some of that from him or I wouldn't have been able to face Jed locking me in his cabin. Otherwise, as protected as I'd always been, I would have just stayed there trembling with fear and not dared to do what surely saved my hide."

"Well, thank God you did what you did, honey. I shudder to think what would have happened. You spooked him, Stormy!"

Stormy laughed, "You know, Marcie—you're right! That's exactly what I did with old Jed—I spooked him but good!"

* * *

Just before Christmas, everything changed for Stormy. She just happened to look at her calendar to check off the weeks she'd been home and it suddenly struck her like a bolt of lightning: she could be carrying Jason's child! She should have been aware of it four or five weeks earlier, but she'd been caught up in the holidays and was trying not to think about Jason.

Now she realized she had to whether she liked it or not. She recalled the last time she'd lain in Jason's arms—they'd made passionate love in his cabin on the *Sea Princess* just a few days before he'd left for Ireland. Nine days later she'd left with Captain Murdock and three weeks after that she'd arrived back here. She should have been aware of the possibility of being pregnant much sooner.

Now she had to face that, but she was determined not to let it mar the Christmas holiday.

Whatever it took, she was determined to be happy and excited through the holiday. She'd worry about her dilemma later.

She soothed her frayed nerves by telling herself she could always marry Dorsey and save shaming her pa and Marcie. But that repulsed Stormy for it went against her nature.

As much as Pat Dorsey seemed to adore her, Stormy knew he was a proud man. She doubted that he'd marry her if he knew she was carrying another man's child.

Thirty

That brisk, cool morning that Jason left, Lady Hamilton was delighted when she woke up and saw a bright sun shining. The next few days had been chilly but it was still sunny so she was happy for Jason's sake.

But these nice days were not to linger, and when the foul weather moved in over London, Lady Sheila paced around the house with grave apprehensions about her son.

Dense, thick fog moved in and then came the rains. As the temperatures dropped, the rain turned to sleet.

Lord Addison did not attempt to make his weekly jaunt into the city. Besides, he figured Sheila might need his company for he sensed her mood and knew Jason was occupying her thoughts.

Watching her fret and fume, he decided to have a talk with her. That evening after dinner, he handed her a glass of sherry. "Sheila, love—you're upsetting me by the way you're acting the last few days," he said.

"I've upset you, Addison? What did I do?" she asked, unprepared for what he'd just said.

"You have. Our son is no babe anymore. He's almost twenty-eight years old. You've other family to consider. There are your daughters and there is a husband—me!"

For a moment she said nothing and then a mellow warmth came to her face. "Oh, Addison—I'm sorry! But when does one quit being a mother?"

"Never, nor is there a time you quit being a father, Sheila. But there is a time that you are no longer in control of your children. Ours are all grown now, Sheila. Jason is the only one not married but he set out on this voyage knowing full well what it would be like. Whatever happens, you and I can't fret about it. So get your thoughts on our holidays and forget Jason for awhile."

Rarely did Addison make such a demand. She never took it lightly when he did for he was usually right.

"You're right, Addison," she said as she reached over and put her arms around his neck and gave him an affectionate kiss. As she did, she was aware that it was this force of his that had kept her so completely fascinated all these years.

A weak man would never have held her love for so long.

Jason was to find himself sorely tested over the next ten days. The weather became more treacherous every day. He could see why all the old sea captains were convinced that the Atlantic Ocean should never be crossed once winter set in.

So far, his slicked-lined schooner was doing a fine job—they'd gone through a couple of harsh squalls and everything had turned out all right.

Dewey hadn't said anything to Jason and he wouldn't, but he was more than anxious to see that Carolina coastline. He didn't give a damn if they quartered there until the winter months were behind them—he had no one to rush back to England to be with like a wife or lady friend.

As he recalled when they were in the Carolinas a few months ago, he'd spied many a pretty little miss around the port cities so he figured he could easily enjoy himself there for the rest of the winter.

Dewey wasn't fooled about this madcap voyage any more than Tobias or Rudy were. It had to be that golden-haired siren, Stormy Monihan, calling out to him. He knew how that could make a man take leave of his senses. It had happened to him more than once and he'd thrown caution to the winds just as Jason had done.

He was not as handsome as the captain but he'd had his fair share of the ladies. Something about seamen seemed to intrigue them. Perhaps it was the adventuresome life they led, Dewey had concluded.

But he'd never asked a lady to marry him—he knew that absence did not make the heart grow fonder. Being a seaman, he knew he would be away from a wife for weeks at a time. He was not yet ready to settle down with just one woman and he certainly wasn't ready to give up the sea.

So he had decided to remain a bachelor for a few more years. He wasn't yet thirty, so he figured he still had plenty of time to meet the right young lady and have himself a family.

As he prepared to take over the shift from Jason, he was thinking that according to his calculations they had to be about halfway to their destination.

When he joined Jason, he asked him. Jason said, "Got to that point this afternoon, I think, Dewey. Keep your fingers and toes crossed that it will keep going as well as it has so far. I knew you're feeling just like me, Dewey. I miss our old buddies—this will be the one and only trip I'll ever make like this. In fact, I'm hoping to pick up two replacements once we reach Southport."

"You mean just have two extra hands?" Dewey asked.

"That's right. The weather will naturally be a bigger challenge going back—we might want to stay in the Carolinas until spring," Jason remarked. He had a reason for saying this to Dewey; if he was lucky enough to be taking Stormy back with him, he would think twice about such a dangerous crossing with her aboard.

"I wouldn't object to spending a few months in the Carolinas," Dewey admitted.

"Good! I'm glad to hear you say that, Dewey."

"I guess you know that we'll lose some of the crew if we do?"

"I'd thought about that but I figured it wouldn't be that hard to replace the ones we'd lose. Few are worth fretting about."

"Well, you got a point there," Dewey grinned. Jason put on his cap and prepared to turn the helm over to Dewey.

Hamilton suddenly turned sharply around with a devious grin as he told his first mate, "Guess there's no reason not to shoot honest with you, Dewey. This trip to the Carolinas is to claim myself a bride. If she refuses my proposal I'll end up the biggest fool in the world."

An amused smile broke on Dewey's face. "Guess you could say I sorta had that figured out, captain. I can't say I blame you and I'll wager she'll say yes, sir."

Jason gave him a shrug as he ambled on down the deck. For a few days he'd been debating whether to tell Dewey—after all, he was his first mate and he'd been with him almost as long as Tobias and Rudy.

Each mile the *Sea Princess* plowed through the choppy waters was getting closer and closer to his golden-haired Princess, Jason thought as he made his way to his cabin.

It wasn't exactly as he'd planned it—he would rather have his wedding back in England with his family gathered around. But if Stormy agreed to be his wife then he'd be more than happy to marry her in her part of the world with her family. It mattered not to Jason where they were married—the only thing that did matter was that Stormy became his wife.

He sat at his desk and studied his charts while he waited for Tobias to bring his dinner. If he had no delays he would certainly make the Carolina coast a few days before Christmas. He felt a certain boyish excitement about the holidays that he hadn't felt since he was an adolescent.

He thought about the magnificent emerald and diamond ring he had for Stormy; he was sure those lovely eyes of hers would light up when she saw it.

Jason slept sound and deep that night, his thoughts on Stormy and his arrival in Southport. It was a calm night and Dewey had no problems to deal with as far as the crew was concerned.

When Jason got up the next morning it was a pleasant sight to be greeted by a clear blue sky. He dressed, hastily drank a couple cups of coffee, and ate the rolls Tobias brought—then left to relieve Dewey.

For whatever reason, he was in the highest of spirits as he left his cabin to go up to the deck. Dewey welcomed the sight of him—he was more than ready to get some sleep. Jason sensed that and didn't engage him in any lengthy conversation as he took over the helm.

The skies stayed a beautiful blue for the entire morning as the *Sea Princess* moved along at a fast clip. Jason kept thinking that if his schooner kept moving at this pace it wouldn't be too many more days before they reached the Carolina shore.

But weather is as unpredictable as the sea, so by the afternoon those blue skies began to change. Jason scrutinized the skies carefully for the next two or three hours as he sauntered around the deck and stood at the railing.

He was also very aware of the angry waters slapping at the hull. The crew's mood had seemed to change— and so had Jason's.

There had been no golden sunset before Dewey appeared to take charge. The sky was an awesome red, and Jason didn't like that. Dewey had chanced to look out the small window of his cabin, and he didn't like the signs either.

This would probably not be a pleasant night like the night before had been!

Thirty-one

The same bright blue sky that had greeted Jason was also around Southport and Cape Fear when Kip roused from his bed. He was almost tempted to think about making a run down to Savannah when he saw a sky like that. But Kip also knew how quickly it could change at this time of the year, so he shrugged that idea aside.

He slipped slowly out of the bed, for Marcie was still sleeping soundly. Once he was dressed he went into the kitchen to build a fire in the old cookstove and filled the coffee pot.

The fire was going furiously, so Kip went to the pantry to take down the shank of ham and the slab of bacon.

He found himself ravenously hungry so he got busy preparing a hearty breakfast. He hadn't spent much time in the kitchen since he'd married Marcie, but this was one of those rare mornings that she seemed content to remain snuggled under the coverlet.

Kip felt perfectly at home in a kitchen, but then he'd had to do more cooking than most men. As he puttered around that morning, he thought that he'd possibly fed his baby daughter foods that she shouldn't have had, but at that time, he didn't know. Somehow and someway, everything had worked out. Kip was sure he'd had a guardian angel riding on his shoulder or he'd never have made it through that first year.

Maybe it was his tremendous love for his young daughter that had seen him through.

His private musings ceased as a sleepy-eyed Marcie came into the kitchen and saw the platter of ham and eggs and pan of hot biscuits.

"Well, Kip Monihan—you're a handy man to have around," she smiled as she reached up to kiss his cheek.

"Now you just keep thinking that, Marcie honey," he grinned. He thought she looked awfully pretty this morning with her long hair hanging down her back.

The two of them sat down—Marcie also found herself with a hearty appetite. They ate Kip's feast with such relish that Marcie began to laugh when she looked at the empty platter. "We were two hungry wolves this morning, Kip."

Stormy heard their laughter as she entered the kitchen, thinking how happy the two of them were. She could not have been more delighted just to stand there and watch them before they realized she was there.

Kip glanced up to see Stormy. "Come on, honey, sit down and I'll fry you some eggs."

"No, Pa—sit back down. I'm not that hungry. All I want is some coffee."

"Oh, Stormy, you put me to shame. You should have seen what I just ate," Marcie said. "That pa of yours is a darn good cook. He spoiled me this morning. Think I'm going to sleep late every morning."

Stormy laughed, "Marcie, that's exactly what you should do."

"Well, I'll leave the two of you here and go get dressed. If Kip can do all the cooking then the least I can do is clean it up," Marcie declared as she rose from her chair.

Kip finished his coffee before leaving Stormy in the kitchen, telling her he had some wood to gather for their fireplace as well as the kindling box. He carried in several armfuls of split wood and stacked it under the roof of the back porch. At least they'd have dry wood—Kip didn't trust those skies by late morning. Maybe it was his boatman's instinct.

Kip had not said anything to his daughter, but he thought she looked pale and wondered if she wasn't feeling well. She had never been much of a breakfast-eater but she usually had one of his biscuits.

The truth was Stormy didn't feel well. She'd felt queasy as soon as she had gotten up. For a while she'd just sat on the side of her bed before putting on her wrapper. She hoped a cup of strong coffee might help but it hadn't.

She left the kitchen before Kip returned, knowing how perceptive he was where she was concerned. By the time she got back to her bedroom, she was thinking it was a terrible time to feel ill. She just couldn't ruin everyone's Christmas!

Stormy had always been so healthy that she was not prepared for this. It had all happened so suddenly. When she returned to her bedroom, she just wanted to curl up and pull the covers over her. But she didn't. She went through the routine of dressing and brushing out her hair.

As she was brushing her hair, she remembered the many talks that she and Marcie had had as she was growing up. Marcie did try to assume the role of her mother, enlightening her about what it meant to become a young lady. Marcie had had a lengthy talk with her the time she'd had her first period, which had happened when they were together. She and Marcie had never discussed what a lady experienced in early pregnancy, and Stormy could not bring herself to bring that up.

Stormy was convinced that what she was experiencing was what they called "morning sickness." When she coupled this with the fact that she hadn't had a period for over six weeks, she had to face the stark reality that she was pregnant!

The father of her baby was far away across the Atlantic Ocean, so Stormy knew she would have to assume the responsibility.

When she could no longer conceal her condition from Marcie and her pa, then she'd have to tell them the truth and have her baby, who would have no father. She would be an unmarried mother.

Another possibility was to marry Dorsey, who she knew would eagerly marry her if she enticed him. Her baby would have a name and she would not disgrace her family—but the time would come when Dorsey would know the baby wasn't his.

She looked at herself in the full-length mirror and was pleased to see that she showed no signs of pregnancy as yet.

So Stormy felt she had some time to mull it all over. She decided that for the next few days, she would forget about her plight and try to enjoy the holidays.

She went to the kitchen to get the big wicker basket, telling Marcie she was going to the woods to gather pine cones. Before Marcie could reply, Stormy was out the door. Marcie was pleased to see that she was so lively. Like Kip, she had thought Stormy was pale and might not feel well when she first appeared in the kitchen.

Kip finished getting in a big supply of wood and told Marcie he was making a run into town. "Need some tobacco in case bad weather moves in. Can I get anything for you, honey?"

"Sugar and flour, Kip. Otherwise, I think I'm fine."

The quiet of the woods was exactly what Stormy needed. She wished that the sudden awareness of her condition had not come until after the Christmas holiday. Her spirits had been so high and now they were so low.

She roamed about, picking up pine cones until she had the basket filled but she still wasn't ready to return to the cottage. She sat and propped her back up against a tall sycamore tree, then gave way to the urge to cry. She cried out to Jason about how desperately she needed him now. There was no one to hear her but the creatures of the woods. "Oh, Jason—it is you I love and want to marry but I may have to settle for Pat as my husband and the father of your child. What a sad thing that would be," she sobbed.

She let all the anguish flow out of her, and when she finally dried her eyes, she knew that coming to the woods had been a good tonic. By the time she was on her way back to the cottage, she held her head high and walked briskly. She had plenty of love surrounding her even if she didn't have Jason Hamilton. She knew that her pa, Marcie, and Paddy would stand by her as they always had. That was all she needed, she told herself.

One small baby wouldn't be too much for her to handle. Women have babies every day. It wouldn't be the end of the world. Married or not, Stormy would still be proud for she knew she was no wanton woman.

The people who really mattered knew she wasn't either. As for Dorsey, time would tell about just how much he loved her.

From the time Stormy left and she returned to the cottage, the skies were no longer blue. Masses of moist air flowed in over the cove and brisk winds were whipping Stormy's hair around her face. She had to grip her shawl firmly to keep it from blowing off her shoulders.

She'd had no inkling that Dorsey had been trekking through the woods from Paddy's place to their cottage. He'd seen her get up from the ground and pick up her basket but he was too far away for her to hear him if he had called out. But his long stride was quickly closing the distance between them.

When he was within calling distance, he beckoned and she turned with a surprised look. "Dorsey—what are you doing out here?" she asked him.

"Taking the shortcut to your house," he grinned. "Beats walking down the dirt lane, I've found out."

She laughed softly, "Pat, I guess I didn't realize you'd done that much walking from Paddy's when you'd come over."

With his usual cocky air, he said, "Hey, Stormy—remember, I'm a boatman. I don't have a buggy or a horse so my two feet have to get me where I want to go."

She laughed, "Guess boatmen don't find the need of buggies, do they? Pa never owned a buggy either, nor has Paddy."

"A buggy is not my first goal though. I want a place to call home. I want a cottage like Kip has. Can't tell you how beholden I am to ol' Paddy but I won't be satisfied until I own my own little place. Owning my little piece of ground and a small house is very important to me."

Stormy listened to him and realized Pat had not really revealed too much about himself. There were many sides of him she did not know.

About the time they arrived at the house, Pat said, "Got to tell you if these skies had been looking when I started out as they are looking now, I'd probably have stayed at Paddy's. We're going to have some foul weather coming in before the night's over."

"You think so?"

"Know so. I got a sense about storms," he said.

When they entered the house, Kip was sitting in the front room and greeted the two of them. He'd just gotten back from town. Like Dorsey, he felt the bad weather moving in. He smiled, "Well, let it come. Got myself a supply of tobacco and a lot of dry wood."

"I'm glad I got Paddy plenty of wood before I left this afternoon. Like I told Stormy, I might not have walked over here if the skies had looked like this when I'd started out," Pat said.

"Well, since you have, you might as well stay and have dinner with us, Pat."

Pat grinned. "I'll chance walking back to Paddy's in bad weather any time after one of Marcie's dinners."

So the four of them sat in Kip's kitchen that winter night and enjoyed Marcie's delicious dinner. Pat had eaten her chicken and dumplings before and swore they were the best he'd ever had.

It always pleased Marcie to see everyone enjoying her cooking. She was the first to leave the table. As she passed by the window, she noticed ice pellets hitting the panes. "It's sleeting cats and dogs, Kip," she said.

"Doesn't surprise me, honey."

Pat got up from the table to look out the window, saying, "I hate to leave so soon but I think I should head back."

Pat made a fast exit into the darkness. His long legs set a fast pace—he wished he had his wool cap, but when he'd left Paddy's the sky had been so clear and blue he'd put it in his jacket pocket.

Stormy's thoughts were about Pat for the next hour, knowing he was out in that foul weather. She knew he would take the shortcut so he'd get back to Paddy's sooner.

Thirty-two

Kip was glad he'd listened to his instincts earlier and stored a good supply of wood for the cookstove and fireplace. There was enough to keep the cottage warm and cook their meals for a couple of days.

When the clock struck nine, Kip figured Dorsey had most likely arrived at Paddy's and was having himself a good, stiff drink.

He put another log on and he and Marcie sat cozily by their fireplace. If it had to sleet and snow, at least she had everything ready for the holiday and Kip's trip into town had taken care of his needs for the next week. He knew it would take a lot of bad weather to keep Dorsey and Paddy away from Marcie's feasts on Christmas Eve and Christmas Day.

Hearing how the winds were howling, Kip could well imagine what it would be like out on the open water off the coast. He damned well wouldn't want to be out there tonight.

The *Sea Princess* plowed through the water in a south, southwestern direction—the bad weather had not reached them as yet, but the sky hung heavy with clouds.

Jason changed his course to due southwest and could have sworn he felt a sudden change in the temperature.

He yanked his wool cap down over his ears and buttoned up the front of his jacket.

For the next hour a bone-chilling rain swept across the deck of the schooner—but soon those drops became ice pellets. An hour later, the deck was too treacherous to walk across. Jason's crew moved with caution, but some of them hit the deck with a mighty thud.

By the time Dewey came up on deck, he wasn't prepared for the sudden ice storm, which had been going on unrelenting now for several hours.

It was no happy-go-lucky Jason Hamilton he encountered—there was a very serious look on his captain's face when Jason said, "It's a bitch out here, Dewey."

"I can see that, captain. How long has this been going on?"

"From the moment I changed our course to the southwest. It hasn't let up for a minute," Jason replied.

"Well, go get yourself some supper and some rest. Before this night's over, it may take both of us to see the *Sea Princess* through this one."

"Get me if you need me, Dewey. Now I mean that," Jason said.

It might have sounded crazy to some but a sea captain loved his ship with the same intensity that he loved a woman. Dewey knew it had been a taxing time for Jason—he looked weary and haggard. He understood why after he had been at the helm for an hour. If only the bloody winds would calm down, it would not be such an angry sea.

By the time he'd been in charge for two hours, Dewey was cursing the simpleton seamen serving as their crew. Two of them had managed to slip on the icy deck and injure themselves, so Dewey was working the schooner two hands short.

Jason wasted no time crawling into his bed—total exhaustion made him fall asleep almost immediately.

When he woke up the next morning, Jason was relieved that once again they had survived a nasty storm. Another night had passed and he was miles closer to the Carolinas.

He hoped Lady Luck would just keep riding on his shoulders. He wasn't that far from his destination now. Once he got there, he'd already made up his mind that he'd stay on through the winter months before he attempted to cross the ocean again. Tobias and Dewey had been his loyal, devoted friends—he would not endanger their lives again regardless of what might happen between him and Stormy. But he had to hope that when he left in the spring he'd be taking her back to England with him.

Jason was to greet a beautiful day when he went on deck to take over for Dewey. Dewey told him they had two hands injured.

Jason took time to study his charts—he was very close to the coast now. He was feeling very smug that he had managed to cross the treacherous Atlantic Ocean and felt very confident that he was going to make it to the Carolinas and Stormy.

Dewey shared Jason's feelings. His shift had gone very smoothly, so he was taken by utter surprise when he was strolling around the deck and chanced to see a fierce display of lightning in the south skies. Alarmed, Dewey wondered what would happen before the night was over. He didn't have to wonder for long.

The fury of this storm had stretched along the Carolina coast all the way up to Savannah. Winds lashed unmercifully, tossing the *Sea Princess* wildly. The schooner was pitched so violently that Jason roused from his sleep and rushed to the window.

He yanked on his pants and shirt, then put on his boots and jacket. Grabbing his wool cap and gloves, he rushed out of his cabin.

Torrents of ran whipped at Jason as he got up on deck. He struggled to find Dewey to see what damage they'd already suffered. He already knew what Dewy had had to cope with because of this unseasoned crew.

The howling winds were so loud that Dewy didn't hear Jason calling out to him, but Jason finally made his way to him.

"We've lost one man, Captain. Washed overboard. Couldn't save the poor sonofabitch. This damn storm came in so fast, it seemed to explode right over us. There was no warning."

Jason ordered his crew to move away from the railings. He knew what a bunch of greenhorns he'd hired, but he still had to protect them, idiots though they were.

In his galley below, Tobias knew that something fierce was going on. He sent Rudy up to the deck to find out.

What Rudy saw was enough to scare the hell out of him. He ran back down to the galley. "Tobias, it's hell on that deck tonight. Don't know whether we can ride this one out. Never seen anything like it."

He had hardly gotten those words out when the schooner gave a mighty heave, which caused Tobias and Rudy to sprawl on the galley floor.

Old Tobias had been luckier than the younger Rudy. He had been flung to the floor but he'd only received a harsh blow to his shoulder. One of Tobias's cast iron pots had hit Rudy's ankle with a mighty blow and crushed it. Rudy found that he could not move without suffering excruciating pain.

The blow stunned Tobias for a brief moment—he saw the expression on Rudy's face and knew he was in great pain. Tobias started to crawl toward him—the ship was pitching too fiercely for him to get up.

He was amazed that the lanterns were still hanging on the walls and providing light.

He had only to look at Rudy's bloody foot to know that the young man's injury was serious. Rudy urged him, "Don't try to get up yet, Tobias. You might fall again. A little bleeding ain't going to kill me."

"You're right, Rudy. Surely this old girl will quit swaying so much before long. Thank God we didn't lose our lanterns."

It seemed like ages before Tobias could finally manage to lift himself up and get a cloth drenched with water to press around Rudy's foot. He raised Rudy's foot and laid some towels underneath it.

"Thanks, Tobias," Rudy said. Propping up the foot seemed to ease the pain.

Once he had a thick compress on Rudy's foot and it was resting on the towels, he wondered what kind of havoc had gone on up on deck. He imagined there were injuries, so he figured they would need hot water and plenty of coffee.

Thirty-three

By the time the storm blew over, Dewey was too exhausted even to go to the galley for a cup of coffee. All he wanted was to lie in his bunk at the end of his shift.

Jason began his next six hours at the helm by gulping down three steaming cups—it revived and warmed him after the freezing downpour. Like Dewey, he fell on his bed at the end of the shift.

Both men welcomed the calm sea, hoping it would last for the next few days until they hit the Carolina coast. Had he not been so weary, Jason would have known that the storm had thrown them well off course. He knew it would take some time for the crew to check for damage. He had doubts that the ship had escaped unscarred.

Tomorrow, he would know what he was up against but tonight he was just grateful that his *Sea Princess* had ridden out such a fierce storm!

A coat of ice covered his jacket and cap by the time Pat Dorsey walked into Paddy's house. He was glad he'd had his gloves in his pocket or his hands would have been stiff. The little bucket of chicken and dumplings from Marcie was frozen by the time he got to the front door.

Paddy was sitting in his rocking chair. "Good god-damn, son—you look like an iceberg! Get over here by the fire and thaw out!"

Pat grinned as he did exactly that. "It's a bitch out there tonight, Paddy."

"Told you, son, that a man can pay a hell of a price when he goes courting."

"Ah, but sometimes it's worth it, Paddy. I've got something for you—wait until you taste Marcie's chicken and dumplings."

He picked up the little bucket and marched into the kitchen. "Had supper yet, Paddy?"

"Just a little snack—I figured you'd be gone for the evening or maybe the whole night after that sleet started."

Pat added some kindling to the cookstove. "Going to have some coffee. Want me to heat up your chicken and dumplings, Paddy?"

"Guess you might as well."

While the coffee and chicken warmed, Pat got out of his damp shoes and socks. He also went out on the porch to get more logs for the fireplace.

A little later Pat was sitting in the other chair by the hearth drinking the hot coffee, and Paddy was thoroughly enjoying the chicken and dumplings.

They could still hear pellets of sleet hitting the window panes.

Pat didn't have to be told how much Paddy was relishing his meal. There was a twinkle in his eyes as he finished the last bite. "Kip's going to replace me on the *East Wind* with Marcie spoiling him so. That woman is one hell of a cook!"

Pat had to agree. But he also knew that Kip would keep Paddy on his boat as long as the old man wanted to be there. But Pat also knew Paddy's time was running out. He'd been with Kip Monihan for over eighteen years—a lot of runs and a lot of cooking. Pat had seen a frailty come over Paddy during the time he'd shared this house. He was not the same man he'd known only a few months ago. Something was ailing the old Irishman and Pat knew it. He still had that quick wit and glib tongue, though.

Pat was absolutely convinced Paddy was not feeling too well when Paddy handed him a small leather pouch filled with money. "Want you to do me a favor, Pat. Want you to go to the emporium and get Marcie and my little Stormy some gifts. Got a bottle of good Irish whiskey I'm taking to old Kip."

"I'll do it, Paddy," Pat assured him.

The next day, Pat left the house to go to the emporium. He chose a pair of gloves and matching woolen scarf for Stormy and a woolen shawl for Marcie in a pretty plaid he thought she would like.

Pat made another purchase. He had already bought a gift for Paddy but he had noticed how worn his old blue sweater was—he'd probably had it for years. So he bought Paddy a new one in a rich shade of burgundy.

When he was ready to leave, he heard a soft feminine voice calling behind him, "Hello, there." He turned to see the pretty little clerk who'd waited on him when he had bought the toilet water.

"Hello, miss," Dorsey greeted her as she hastened her step toward him. It was obvious she was leaving, too, for she was wearing a bonnet.

There was no denying she was a most attractive young lady. Had Pat Dorsey not been so enamored of Stormy Monihan, he would have been attracted to her.

"Looks like you've had another shopping spree, mister—by the way, what is your name?" she inquired.

"Pat Dorsey, miss," he said.

"Well, it's nice to see you again, Pat. I'm Rebecca Branson. Ask for me if I can help you purchase toilet water for your lady." Her blue eyes surveyed his handsome face carefully to see how he was going to respond to her remark.

"Now, I'll certainly do that, Miss Branson."

They went out the front entrance together. The winds were strong, so Rebecca gathered her cape tighter around her for the long walk home.

She paused for a moment. "Seems winter is coming early this year."

Pat responded, "And it looks like a rough one!" He headed down the street and wondered if she was expecting a ride. She stood there hesitating for a moment but he had no buggy so he couldn't offer her a ride home.

Rebecca bade Dorsey goodbye as she began the long walk to the house where she and her mother lived—a little two-bedroom cottage similar to Paddy's. Her father had been able to buy the small house and lot just a short time before he died. Rebecca was grateful for that since she had to support herself and her ailing mother.

Pretty as she was, Rebecca didn't have time for gentleman friends. Putting in a full day at the emporium and tending to her mother in the evening took up all her time. That only gave her Sunday to attend to all the chores.

Few young men had whetted her interest as Pat Dorsey had when she first saw him. She found him so handsome that her heart seemed to flutter wildly. She found herself envying the young lady he was buying the toilet water for that day.

She had not even celebrated her twentieth birthday when she'd had to assume such a large burden, but Rebecca was clever and a shrewd planner. With the help of a discount at the store, she'd managed to acquire a nice wardrobe. She shopped frugally for food and supplies—there was nothing left over for luxuries or frivolous times.

She looked like a delicate blonde beauty, but Rebecca was no fragile, pampered female. But she did daydream about a handsome young man coming into her life. She'd often had thoughts about Dorsey.

As she walked home against the brisk winds, she found herself daydreaming about him. Seeing him again rekindled her interest. Perhaps it was her romantic heart that felt it was meant to be that they keep meeting. That thought warmed her as she walked along toward her house.

Paddy was pleased with the gifts Dorsey had purchased. Now that he had gifts to take to Stormy and Marcie, he was ready to enjoy the Christmas holiday.

He didn't have to buy a Christmas gift for Pat. He had decided a few weeks ago to give him his father's gold pocket watch. He'd become very fond of the young man, and since he had no son to pass the watch down to, he figured he'd give it to Dorsey.

In a way Paddy had began to look upon him as his son the way he looked upon Stormy as his little daughter. Pat probably didn't realize that his company and companionship had filled a lot of lonely hours for old Paddy.

It had been a special comfort to him the last few months for Paddy had not been feeling well. However, he never suspected that Pat's perceptive eyes had seen that.

Paddy appreciated how Pat always carried in all the wood. He'd also saved Paddy having to trek to the store, insisting that he would buy the groceries if Paddy furnished his lodging.

Since it had been several weeks since the *East Wind* had made a run, Paddy knew that Kip wasn't aware of how his health had been failing. Truth be told, Paddy was already aware that he might not be up to making the runs when spring came. The last run had taken its toll.

It wasn't a fact that Paddy enjoyed facing, but he had no complaints. He'd been with Kip over eighteen years—the Monihans had been the only family Paddy had had until Dorsey came into his life. To have shared his life with a man like Kip Monihan had been a blessing, Paddy thought.

Pat could have gone over to see Stormy that evening—the weather wasn't that bad—but he stayed home with Paddy. They had their dinner and Pat cleaned up the kitchen. Paddy seemed a little livelier during the evening and Pat was glad of that.

Paddy retired a few hours earlier than Pat. Sitting in the quiet solitude of Paddy's front room, he did a lot of thinking about the idle months ahead until spring finally came. He didn't like all this time on his hands, so he decided he would scout around Southport the next day to see if he could find a job to make some extra money.

For Paddy, it was great to have the time to rest up and take it easy. He was sure Kip was also enjoying the time off with his wife and daughter. But the chores around Paddy's small cottage didn't fill enough of the long days and nights for Pat.

By the time he went to bed that night, he decided he was going to do a little exploring around the town. But it was more than a job he planned to check into.

He was going to ask some questions about places for sale—he had no idea what a little cottage like Paddy's would cost.

Should he persuade Stormy to marry him, he'd certainly want them to have their own place. Regardless of what she'd said, he was convinced he couldn't change her mind in time. There was no more sentimental time of the year than the Christmas season, he reminded himself.

Maybe during the time he'd see her Christmas Eve and Christmas Day, he'd find that perfect moment to convince her he was the man for her.

His Irish arrogance and conceit refused to believe she didn't have some feelings for him. In fact, Dorsey believed she was fighting those feelings. At first, he reasoned that she was feeling strange around him because they'd been apart so long, but she'd been home long enough now for any feelings like that to have ceased.

So now Pat was convinced that Stormy was affected more deeply by her experience with Jed Callihan. Perhaps, that was why he'd learned very little about that period of time when she'd been his captive. Dorsey could start boiling with rage when he dwelled too long on the subject of Callihan. His wild imagining could drive him crazy as to how far the bastard pushed himself on Stormy. Whatever had happened, he knew Stormy would keep that her secret.

Somehow, it never dawned on Dorsey that she never talked with him about the English sea captain and her long voyage to England—or the many weeks she'd spent with his parents.

It was only with Kip and Marcie she'd talked endlessly about Jason, Lord Allison, and Lady Sheila Hamilton. When she'd been in Pat's company she never remarked about the magnificent sights Jason had shown her or the quaint little inn where they'd dined. If she had, Pat would have seen that excited sparkle in her eyes and known immediately why Stormy had no desire to become romantically involved with him.

Had he known all this, Pat Dorsey would not have felt so self-assured and cocky!

Thirty-four

By the time Jason realized that his schooner was off course by probably a hundred miles, he was facing another dilemma. He had four ailing seamen running high fevers from exposure to the freezing rains during the storm.

He'd told Dewey he was making straight for Savannah—then they'd follow the coastline up to Southport. At least they'd be close to land should they run into another siege of foul weather.

This was enough to lift Dewey's spirits—the last few days had made him wish he hadn't agreed to make this journey.

Dewey and Jason had a crew of unhappy men. All of them were ready to see land—with four men laid low, the rest were having to work much harder.

Tempers were short and snapping. Dewey and Jason had both been seafaring long enough to know they had a highly volatile situation.

When he had taken over the shift from Dewey the next morning he felt they might see land before Dewey took over again early that morning.

By midday he stood by the railing for several minutes surveying the unpredictable skies. What he saw was enough to make him leery—they could be heading into another storm.

He kept his eyes on the skies constantly during the

next two hours. Old Tobias was curious when a young seaman brought a message from Jason as he'd served him some lunch. "Captain wants you to boil up some extra coffee, Tobias."

The galley cook quizzed him at once. Was there something brewing up there? Tobias had not had a chance to take a glance out the window.

"Just thick as pea soup as it has been most days we've been out here," the young man said.

"Well, the captain must have a good reason to make such a request this early in the day. Must see something. Realized a long time ago he sees things in that sky I'd never know were there," Tobias remarked as he got busy filling his pots.

An hour later, the coffee was brewed and ready and Tobias did take the time to go to the window. His eyes were not as keen and trained as Jason Hamilton's but he didn't like what he saw. The sea was unusually calm.

Well, it was out of his hands, he told himself as he strolled over to sit down. As he often did, he shut his eyes for a while. Tobias sat there for over an hour, his hands resting on his lap, and slept as soundly as most people do in bed.

But suddenly he jerked up in the chair when a sound like a wailing banshee roused him from his sleep. Sprays from the angry ocean pelted up again the window of his galley and Tobias rushed over to look out.

"Oh, God almighty! Lady Luck better be with us again or we'll never ride this one out," he muttered to himself when he saw the high pitching waves battering the hull.

Tobias felt himself tossed to one side of the galley— and then to the other side. The old seaman sank to the floor and braced himself in the threshold of the doorway. This was where Billy, the young seaman, found him. His first concern was that Tobias had been injured but he quickly realized he was all right.

"Figured this was the safest way to keep from getting hurt," Tobias said. "Better grab on to something yourself, lad. This is going to be a rough ride, I'm thinking."

Everyone aboard the *Sea Princess* was having a rough ride. Dewey had actually been flung out of his bunk onto the floor. He immediately scrambled for his clothes and began to get dressed as quickly as he could.

Jason would be sorely in need of his services. He slammed his hands into his jacket and pulled the wool cap down over his head as he rushed out and made his way down the passageway and across the deck.

Dewey barely made it up to the deck when he swore the demons from hell were released right there on the *Sea Princess*. In one fleeting second, his eyes beheld the right side of the ship lashed so severely that the tumultuous wave washed over the entire deck. In horror, he saw God knows how many men washed out to sea.

That was the last thing he saw before something slammed into the side of his face and he fell into a bottomless pit of blackness. Only a few seconds before, Jason had also been rendered helpless by some flying object smashing into the deck. He, too, lay unconscious.

Of all the men aboard the *Sea Princess*, old Tobias and Rudy were in about the safest place they could have been.

Like all seafaring men, Captain Murdock found it hard to wait out the winters. Going to sea as many years as he had, it was like a fever in the blood—he felt like a fish out of water when he wasn't out there. He pondered how he could ever give up the life he loved.

His old buddy Captain Al Brunson understood Murdock's feelings and shared them. He, too, was growing older like Murdock, but now he was alone—his dear wife had died last year and he didn't have the brood that Murdock had sired.

The two of them got together a couple of afternoons every week to play cards and drink a little whiskey. Brunson lived in a little house on the shore, walking distance from the harbor in Savannah. The windows in the front room offered a perfect view of the ocean—that was why he and his wife had settled in the house years ago.

His wife had told him she loved that view because she could always spot his ship coming back into port.

Murdock's wife never knew when he might reappear when he went over to his friend's house to play cards. But being the independent lady she'd always been, she had her own dinner at the scheduled time and left his food on the back of the stove.

She had her own job as a tutor to many local children—she and Mick had always had an understanding about that. She'd met and married him but she'd also assured him she wouldn't be one of those wives who waits and twiddles her thumbs while he was out to sea. That was probably the reason their marriage had lasted. It had been blessed by five lovely daughters. Only one remained at home—their youngest, Janet.

Sue Murdock didn't like the looks of the sky as she bade her last little student good afternoon. She was also glad Janet was home and wondered if Mick was paying any attention to the storm brewing in the bay.

Anytime a hard blow came through, she felt—and always had felt—safe in this old two-story house. It had weathered many a fierce wind.

But the one about to assault the coast of Georgia was one of those freakish storms that hit with such suddenness that there was no time to take cover.

Little Jeff had not been gone more than fifteen min-

utes when Sue heard her shutters rattling. Branches
from the trees were bending and breaking from the
force of the winds.

"I just hope Father hasn't started walking in this,"
Janet remarked as she stood at the stove stirring the
stew.

Looking at the clock, she said, "I'd wager he's still
sitting in Al's front room. It's too early for him to have
started home."

Where her husband was concerned, Sue was exactly
right. But he and Al had put their cards down—their
attention was turned in the direction of a fancy, slick-
lined schooner foundering off the coast. The ship's only
ace in the hole was that the winds were sweeping them
closer and closer to the coast.

Brunson gulped down the last of his whiskey as he
reared up from the table. "They're going to be needing
our help, Mick!"

In the blink of an eye, both men were up and into
their jackets and yanking on their woolen caps.

They rushed over to the wharves to see how many
men they could muster. In the driving rain and wind, a
handful of seamen had clustered in the warehouses.
They offered to help Murdock and Brunson rescue what
was left of the *Sea Princess*.

The fine schooner had many scars by the time they
managed to get it moored. The few survivors were taken
into the warehouse and covered with jute sacks as there
were no blankets.

It would be another half hour before wagons would
arrive to get the poor devils. Brunson took two of the
fellows and Murdock loaded the other three to take to
his place.

One young man with copper-colored hair was able
to talk and identified Jason as the ship's captain and
Dewey as the first mate. The hefty older fellow was

Tobias, the cook, Rudy told them. He then informed Murdock that he was the cabin boy.

Rudy and one young seaman were loaded in Brunson's wagon and taken to his home. Murdock traveled in the other wagon with his three passengers.

He carried the older fellow into the house first and gave Sue a brief explanation about what had happened before he dashed back out to get his second passenger. Once all three of them were upstairs in the vacant bedrooms, Sue took charge of old Tobias and Murdock attended to the captain. Janet was left in charge of Dewey to see that he was covered with warm blankets before she left to get a basin of warm water.

Dewey roused to feel the gentle touch of Janet's hands washing the dried blood from his face and the side of his head. He closed his eyes, deciding he had died and gone to heaven. This was surely a lovely angel hovering over him. There was no rain beating at his face and it seemed so quiet and peaceful.

It took several minutes for the older fellow Sue was attending to quit shaking from either chill or fright. When his eyes fluttered open, she assured him, "You're safe now, sir. Just relax and rest."

Tobias looked up to see the kindly and caring face of the lady looking down at him, so he did exactly as she'd told him to do. He closed his eyes and relaxed.

Mick Murdock saw that the captain might need the services of a doctor. Sue came to have a look at him. It didn't take her too long to tell Mick, "You better go fetch Doc Miller. His arm is broken and he may have other injuries we can't handle."

"Think you and Janet will be all right if I leave?"

"Of course. Be on your way."

Mick went to fetch the doctor and Sue went back to the room Jason was occupying. On her way she stuck her head in to see Janet, who was taking care of that young man. He appeared to be lying restfully on the pillow—Janet had washed his face of all the dried blood and mud. Then Sue walked across the hall to the young man who seemed to be the most seriously injured.

It was good to hear him moan—he'd seemed so life-less earlier. Mick had done a good job of cleaning off his face, but she wanted to get his shirt off before Mick got back with the doctor. She took her scissors to it and then slipped it slowly out from under his back. Then she quickly pulled the coverlet and blanket up as he still seemed chilled.

As if he was grateful to her for covering his bare shoulders, Jason's eyes slowly fluttered open. Sue thought he had the blackest eyes she'd ever seen.

"Where—where am I?" he mumbled weakly.

"You're in Savannah, young man, and in good hands. Just rest until my husband gets back with Doc Miller and keep that left arm of yours still. Got an idea it's broken."

Jason was willing to take her word for that—he was too damned weak to move. So he closed his eyes and did as the woman had told him to do. It was just a bloody good feeling to feel warm under the blanket and be dry!

At least, they had made it into Savannah!

Thirty-five

Old Tobias was feeling like moving around the room after three days of complete rest and Mrs. Murdock's excellent care. Dewey's only impairment was a slightly sprained ankle so he too was moving around the room but with a little limp.

Janet had brought him a walking cane that morning when she brought up his breakfast tray. He had found it a great help so he got out of bed to get a little exercise.

These were certainly the most kindhearted and nicest people Dewey had met in a long, long time. He'd always remember how they'd opened their home and their hearts to him, Jason, and Tobias.

And he couldn't have had a prettier nurse. Those first two days she bathed him and shaved him with such a gentle touch that he swore she had to be an angel! By yesterday he knew he was getting better—as she was bending over him to examine his swollen ankle, he was suddenly fired with the wild desire to kiss her rosy lips.

Her warm chestnut brown hair was tumbling around her shoulders while he lay there thinking how he'd like to run his fingers through it.

When she'd suddenly rose to find him staring so intensely, there was a twinkle in her hazel eyes as though she was reading his thoughts.

She smiled impishly, "I think you're going to live,

Dewey." But she had a gentle way of being bossy and admonished him not to put too much weight on that foot yet if he wanted the swelling to go down quickly.

"Yes, ma'am," he grinned as she turned to go toward the door.

Later as she was helping Sue in the kitchen she remarked how attractive she thought Dewey was. "Don't you think he's handsome, Mother?"

"Both of the young men are very good-looking, dear, and both of them seem very nice," Sue replied, trying to suppress her amusement. She'd already sensed that Janet was enjoying caring for the young seaman.

Mick had taken over the care of the older fellow—he was too hefty for Sue or Janet to try to support him when he got out of bed.

Jason's firm, muscled body had obviously taken the worse punishment. Doc Miller had been unable to find out what was causing the stiffness in his left leg which was hampering him when he tried to get up from the bed.

It seemed the entire left side of his body had taken the brunt of whatever had rendered him unconscious.

At least, Jason was glad his brain had not been affected. All he could think of, now that he was rested and gaining strength from all the meals Mrs. Murdock was feeding him, was what he would find when he could go to see his schooner.

It was sheer frustration to Jason that he couldn't make his damned left leg work right so he could get down the stairway and make his way to the harbor. A broken arm would not have stopped him but that leg did!

But Dewey had kept him company that afternoon and he assured Jason, "Give me another day or two and I'll be able to get down to see what it looks like, captain. Tobias can't and you sure aren't up to it."

He had also paid a visit to Tobias's room and he'd learned what neither he nor Jason had known: they had both been knocked senseless.

Mick Murdock had told Tobias that there had only been five survivors on the *Sea Princess*. Tobias then told Jason, "Seems Rudy was the only one able to talk. He and one other fellow are over at Murdock's friend's house."

Jason was shaking his head dejectedly as he listened to Dewey's terrible news about the loss of life. Also, he knew now that his schooner surely had to take a terrible beating that night. It had been a devil's tempest they'd sailed into.

After Dewey had left the room he lay there staring at the ceiling and found his thoughts drifting back to England. His mother had told him she often had forebodings. "You'll have them too, Jason. There's Irish in you, too," she said.

Her words were certainly ringing in his ears as he lay there—he had certainly had very definite forebodings just before the fierce storm hit.

He was absolutely convinced that his mother was right—he would never take it lightly if he felt that way again.

Two days later, Rudy found his way to the Murdocks' rambling two-story house as Captain Brunson had directed him. The worst of Rudy's injuries were numerous cuts on his face and arms and some ugly bruises. His injury during the earlier storm wasn't as serious as Tobias had thought. Young Billy hadn't been so lucky—he was in Brunson's back bedroom with a broken leg. Rudy had been helping Brunson tend to him and going over to Murdock's to check on Jason, Tobias, and Dewey.

Old Brunson could tell that young Rudy was anxious about his friends so he'd urged him to go to Murdock's this afternoon. "Me and Billy will be fine. I'll be around all afternoon and Billy sure as hell ain't going nowhere," he'd chuckled.

So Rudy had walked from Brunson's shoreline cottage over to the Murdocks' house; it wasn't all that far away, he discovered.

Janet greeted him at the door and Rudy introduced himself. She invited him inside. "I'm Janet Murdock."

"Nice to meet you, Miss Murdock," Rudy said, quickly removing the old cap Brunson had given him.

As she guided him up the steps she remarked about how he had come out of the wreck better than the others.

"Yes, ma'am. Me and Tobias were down in the galley and not on that deck like the captain and Dewey," he said. All the time he was climbing the stairs, he was thinking how pretty she was.

"Well, which of the gentlemen would you like to visit first?" Janet asked. "And by the way, you didn't tell me your name."

Rudy blushed and apologized, "I'm sorry, Miss Murdock. Rudy McCormick, ma'am."

"Well, Rudy, it's nice to meet you, too," she said warmly and smiled. "So whose room shall I take you to first?"

"I'd like to see the captain, ma'am."

"All right, but please just call me Janet, Rudy. We're very informal around here."

"Well—well, all right, Janet," Rudy stammered, feeling awkward and unsure of himself around this pretty young girl.

"See, that sounds better. Captain Hamilton will be glad you've come, Rudy. He's been concerned about his ship and what happened to everyone," she remarked.

"Captain Hamilton is the best. Been his cabin boy for quite a while now. I don't just consider him my captain but my friend," Rudy said earnestly.

"That's very nice, Rudy. My father is a sea captain, too."

"Well, I'll be darned! Didn't know that," he replied as she suddenly stopped by one of the doors.

"Just go on in, Rudy. This is Captain Hamilton's room. Would you like some coffee or tea?"

"Oh, no, ma'am!"

With a twinkle in her warm hazel eyes, she said, "Well, if you or the captain decide you'd like some, then just come down to the kitchen and tell me."

"Thank you, Janet," he grinned, this time remembering to call her Janet.

She turned to go and he went on into the room. Seeing Rudy lifted Jason's spirits. He visited with Jason for almost an hour before he finally got up to go see Dewey and Tobias. And he didn't want to be away from Brunson's place too long with Billy the way he was.

"Glad you came out so well, Rudy," Jason declared. "Come back when you get the chance. Looks like I'll be here a while longer."

"Knowing you, captain—you'll be back before you know it," Rudy assured him.

"Well, I'm anxious to know how that lady moored out in the harbor is doing, too," Jason confessed to his cabin boy.

"I'll try to find out for you, captain," Rudy told him as he prepared to leave and go to Tobias's room which Jason had told him was just next door.

Rudy had a nice visit with old Tobias and was pleased to see that he was in fair condition. He told Tobias the news about Billy and that there were only five of the crew left alive.

From Tobias's room, he went to Dewey's. He seemed

in the best shape of any of them—Rudy found him moving around the room with the aid of a cane. Dewey was delighted to see Rudy.

"Damn if you aren't a sight for sore eyes!" Dewey laughed as he hobbled over to give Rudy a warm embrace. Like Jason, Dewey was grateful that Rudy had been spared that fateful night.

"Dewey, you look pretty good! Glad to see it! Billy got a broken leg. Seems we all found ourselves some real friendly people here in Savannah."

"Sure did, Rudy. Couldn't ask for nicer people than the Murdocks—you've obviously found it the same with whoever you're with," Dewey said as he sat back down on the bed and motioned Rudy to sit.

"I'm staying with an old friend of Murdock's. They were the ones who came to our aid that afternoon, Dewey. But for those two old seamen, we might have all ended up in that raging sea."

"Well, I'll be damned. I didn't know that!"

Rudy laughed, "You and the captain didn't know anything when you were loaded onto that wagon and brought here."

"Guess you're right. I really haven't seen Murdock that much since I've been here. With three of us blokes to attend to, each member of the family gives a lot of their time. The daughter has been tending to me and Mrs. Murdock has taken charge of the captain. Murdock took charge of Tobias."

"Then I'd say you were the lucky one, Dewey. I met Janet—I'd have bet you had the prettiest nurse," Rudy laughed.

"You're right about that," Dewey readily agreed with him.

When Rudy prepared to leave, Dewey asked the distance between the house and the harbor. He was delighted to hear that it wasn't that far away.

"Good—I want to try to get there and see what happened to the *Sea Princess*. The captain is most anxious to know and he has to rest so I hope I can give him a report."

"I'll go with you, Dewey, when you go," Rudy said.

"Come for me day after tomorrow, Rudy. I'll have myself in shape by then," Dewey promised.

Rudy left the house without getting to see the pretty Janet again as he'd hoped. He was a little disappointed.

Rudy's visit to the Murdock home had been like a tonic to his seafaring buddies. Old Tobias had been delighted to see his little red-haired friend—he would have been devastated if the sea had swallowed Rudy.

With Rudy by his side, Dewey had no doubt he could make the jaunt to the harbor to survey the *Sea Princess*. He was in the highest of spirits when Janet came to check on him a couple of hours later.

Rudy had spurred Jason to get out of bed and make that stubborn leg function.

After he'd worked for almost an hour, the leg had a dragging motion to it but by God, it was an improvement. It was enough to urge Jason to keep pushing himself to the limit and beyond!

Tomorrow he would do better, he vowed as he finally sank down on the bed exhausted.

Thirty-six

Southport was lucky—it didn't receive the full brunt of the storm that Savannah got. Only the outer winds hit to their coastline. Three or four days later, the word drifted up to Southport about the beating the Savannah area had taken.

When Kip returned to the cottage from town and told Stormy and Marcie about the news, Stormy prayed that Captain Murdock and his family had escaped any harm.

The last week had not been pleasant for Stormy—she didn't like this game she was playing with her father, Marcie, and Dorsey. It wasn't her way but she didn't know what else to do.

By now, she was convinced she was never going to hear from Jason Hamilton but what had really surprised her was that she hadn't heard from Lady Sheila or Tawny. She was wondering if she'd been naive to believe that they'd truly liked her. She didn't like the thought that she'd been fooled, for she considered herself perceptive about people. But right now she wasn't sure about anything. She didn't want to think it was only for Jason that Lady Sheila and Tawny had been so sweet. That would have wounded her deeply.

There was one thing she *was* very certain about—she was pregnant with Jason's child. Perhaps that way why, the night before, she'd made Pat a promise to consider marrying him after the holiday was over. She had not given him a definite yes but neither had she told him no.

To get away from the cottage, she offered to go into town to get some extra flour and sugar for Marcie. Pat and her dad had gone hunting for wild turkeys.

But she didn't guide her buggy directly to Holcombe's Grocery Store. She gave way to the sudden impulse to go to Paddy's knowing Pat wasn't there.

Paddy couldn't have been more delighted by her unexpected visit. He invited her to come and sit with him by the fireplace after she'd flung off her cape.

The two of them had not been sitting there long before Stormy was pouring out her heart to him as she'd often done when she was a child.

As he'd done when she was a little tadpole, he reached out his weathered hand to pat the crown of her golden head. "There, honey, it will be all right. Dorsey's asked you to marry him. I know he loves you, Stormy."

"But I don't love Dorsey like I love Jason, Paddy," she sobbed.

"But sugar, Jason isn't here and Dorsey is and there's a wee babe to be considered in all this. That babe deserves a name, Stormy. A sacrifice has to be made, as I see it. You said you didn't want to hurt your pa and Marcie and bring shame on them. There's also yourself to think about, too. To have a babe without being married makes you a tainted woman and that sweet babe you'd have a bastard, Stormy. That's the way it is."

Stormy knew old Paddy was not trying to be cruel or unfeeling—he was just telling her the truth.

"Marry Dorsey and who knows? Everything might work out just fine. Maybe his love would be strong enough to make up for your lack of it. He's a good, honest man, Stormy. You know I wouldn't say that if I wasn't convinced."

He reached up to wipe away a tear from her lovely

cheek. His voice cracked with emotion as he said, "Ah, little Stormy, you've just given me a reason to want to live a lot longer. I want to see what this babe of yours will be like. I recall the night you made your entrance into this world on a stormy night and I helped Kip get you all settled in that drawer."

Her eyes warmed with love for the old man as she confessed, "Guess that's why I came to you, Paddy. I didn't know where to turn and I just couldn't bring myself to talk to Marcie or pa about this yet."

"Guess that's another reason for me to stick around—so we can still have our little talks, eh?"

"Oh, Paddy—you better! I don't know what I'd do without you," she declared with such sincerity that Paddy had to believe her.

"Well, I'm going to be around for a while, Stormy, just for you," he promised.

Stormy stayed at Paddy's for over an hour before she left to attend to the errands for Marcie. She was feeling much better—baring her soul to Paddy lightened her burden.

Back at Paddy's there was an old man sitting in his rocking chair feeling exactly as Stormy was feeling. A burden had also been lifted from him—Stormy had not realized that in coming to talk to him she'd made him realize there was a reason to keep living. Lately, Paddy had felt dejected and depressed. Age was catching up with him and he was pondering what he would do if he couldn't go out on the *East Wind* with Kip. If he was confined to this house all the time, he'd have no reason to live. But Stormy had given him a reason.

It had meant everything to Paddy that Stormy had come to him to bare her soul—he'd never forget this special moment as long as he lived.

In the late afternoon when Pat returned he found Paddy in a happy mood, but Paddy mentioned nothing about Stormy's visit. The next morning Paddy didn't tell Pat where he was going when he left the house. Dorsey was pleased to see that old Irishman was so lively.

But Pat was beginning to wonder just what Paddy was up to when he had not returned by midday. He was about to go to Southport to see if he could spot him when a gentleman in a buggy came rolling up to the gate with Paddy sitting beside him.

Pat watched from the window as Paddy bade the fellow a fond farewell and ambled slowly up the pathway. Something on his face told Dorsey that the old man was in good spirits. There was no question about it—old Paddy had come to mean a lot to Pat.

When Paddy came in and saw Dorsey in the front room, he figured that the young man had seen him arriving with his old friend, Dennis Walker. But Paddy didn't tell him what he'd been up to.

As the two of them were putting some supper together, he teased Pat, "Going over to see your pretty lady friend this evening?"

A gleam came into Dorsey's eyes. "Thought I might just do that, Paddy. Think you could keep yourself out of trouble if I left you alone?"

"Don't worry about me, Pat."

Paddy was acting so chipper that Dorsey didn't hesitate to leave as soon as they'd eaten their supper and he'd helped Paddy get the kitchen in order.

By eight, Dorsey was on the front porch of Kip's cottage preparing to knock on the door as Stormy came rushing out the front door. They both gave way to laughter as she almost slammed into him.

"Well, I must say I don't usually get that kind of welcome," Dorsey said, smiling down at her.

"I'm sorry, Pat—I—I didn't mean to bump into you like that," she declared as she stepped back. She was going out the front door to get a breath of fresh air after she and Marcie had finished putting the kitchen in order.

Dorsey couldn't keep from taking her into his arms. His lips sought hers as she stood looking up at him so temptingly.

When he slowly released her, he murmured in her ear, "Oh, Stormy, don't leave me hanging like this any longer. Say you'll marry me—and soon! If you're not sure right now, I'll convince you I'm the man for you. We're alike, Stormy—you and I."

Had she not had the talk with Paddy she might not have answered Dorsey the way she did but she surprised him by telling him she would marry him.

Pat Dorsey was soaring to the heavens when he heard her say that and felt her soft body clinging to his.

"Oh, Stormy, we'll be happy. I'll swear it!"

Stormy could not dampen his happiness that moment by confessing to him that she was carrying another man's child. But she would before they were married— she could never lie to him.

For the longest time he just held her in his arms. This was the best holiday he'd ever had. Stormy had promised to marry him.

With a boyish enthusiasm, he suggested, "Let's go tell Marcie and your pa! God, I want to shout it to the world—Stormy Monihan has promised to be my wife! But right now, I'll settle for your pa and Marcie."

Stormy laughed softly. His gaiety was infectious and she was also beginning to feel excited. Paddy had been right—Pat would make her a good husband.

He was witty and charming, as well as affectionate. And she had always considered him handsome. What else could she possibly want in a husband?

She had thought for months that he was very much in love with her and now there was no doubt in her mind.

They entered the room where Kip sat puffing his pipe and reading the local paper. Marcie was stringing cranberries into a garland that she would drape around the Christmas tree.

There was such a radiant gleam on both of their faces that Marcie just sat there for a second, thinking to herself that if she ever saw a couple in love it surely had to be Stormy and Pat.

She had to believe that their courtship had taken a more serious turn in the last day or two, she thought to herself.

When Pat proudly made his announcement, Kip let the paper he was reading drop from his hands and took the pipe out of his mouth.

"I asked her a few minutes ago, Kip, and she said yes. I hope we have your approval," Dorsey said.

Marcie was already jumping up to give the two of them a warm embrace but Kip was still trying to find his tongue. He was taken completely by surprise by Dorsey's announcement. His eyes went to Stormy's face—she seemed to be happy.

"All I want is my daughter's happiness, Dorsey," Kip said. He'd known for a long time how smitten this young man had been with his daughter but it was Stormy he was not sure about. Somehow, he had the feeling that Pat had not completely captured his daughter's impetuous heart. Kip felt that the man who'd actually managed to do that was across the ocean. He couldn't forget the look in Stormy's eyes when she'd told him and Marcie about Hamilton.

He could only hope that Stormy wasn't giving way to her impatient nature because the young Englishman had not appeared in his schooner. She had to know that the ocean was too treacherous for any sane sea captain to try to make a crossing right now.

Dubious feelings gnawed at him and he rose to give

them his blessings as Marcie had. His all-knowing eyes continued to survey his daughter's face.

Marcie was asking the two of them, "So when will we be having a wedding?"

Stormy quickly spoke up. "Oh, Marcie—we won't even get into talking about that until after the holidays. Maybe even after the first of the year."

"Hey, Stormy, not too long after the holidays now that I've got you to say yes," he declared.

Everyone broke into laughter—even Stormy. But she was serious about what she'd told her family. She had no intention of rushing into a wedding just a week or two after the holidays. Marcie needed a rest after all the cooking and baking she'd been doing.

The end of January suited Stormy just fine!

Thirty-seven

It seemed to Sue Murdock that any time she spied Janet sitting in a chair in the evening lately, she was engrossed in her knitting. The needles were working at such a pace that it amazed Sue for she could never learn the skill. Mick proudly wore the dark blue vest she'd knitted and Sue was already putting to good use the gray neckscarf and matching gloves Janet had made for her.

Sue's curiosity was whetted now about what she was working on so feverishly, so she inquired, "What are you making now, honey? You're the hardest working young lady I know."

"Well, Mother, I figure we'll have three guests gathered around our Christmas tree and I couldn't stand not to have gifts for them. So I decided to make poor old Tobias a pair of warm socks—his feet always seem to be cold. Right now I'm finishing up a pair of wool gloves for Dewey and I thought I would knit a scarf for the captain."

Sue had always known her Janet was a kindhearted person but once again she was reminded that she was also very thoughtful. Sue had not given any thought to the fact that there would be three more here for their Christmas holiday until now when Janet had mentioned it.

"What a sweet gesture on your part, Janet! I'll have to see what kind of little gifts I can get for the three of them, too," Sue declared. She left her daughter in the parlor to go check on supper.

She told Mick about what Janet was doing when he came strolling into the kitchen a few minutes later.

Mick helped himself to a cup of coffee and sat down at the table. "That Janet is a true angel, I'll swear she is. Some lucky bloke is going to have himself a hell of a good wife someday."

"Well, I told her I'd get some little gifts for them, too," Sue said.

"I'll do that for you, Susie dear," Mick said. He knew exactly what would please the captain and Dewey. They were both running short on the cheroots he'd borrowed from his friend Brunson. Jason had mentioned that he'd give his right arm for a smoke so Mick had taken a few from old Brunson's jar.

So he'd go to the tobacco shop and purchase cheroots for Jason and Dewey and a pipe and some tobacco for old Tobias. Tobias had been using one of Mick's old pipes.

When he told Sue what he had in mind she thought it was a grand idea.

"Truth is, Sue, they're not going to be leaving Savannah in that schooner for many, many weeks. 'Course, I'm sure the minute Captain Hamilton is back on his feet he'll probably find lodging for himself and his men at the inn."

Jason had had a lengthy discussion with Dewey just the day before about finding lodging somewhere else. They couldn't expect to impose on these good people much longer.

Dewy had been able to go down to the harbor and spot the *Sea Princess*. He was happy to come back to tell Jason that she was moored in the water as though she were waiting for them to come to her. "At least she's topside, sir."

Jason gave Dewey and Rudy another assignment

when they could manage to do it. "Check on an inn where we might get three rooms and meals, Dewey. I'll be able to get down those steps very soon now, I think."

"Sure will, captain. Me and Rudy will start looking tomorrow. I'll try to find someplace near the harbor."

Jason had always found Dewey to be a dependable guy. Now he was having to allow him to be his legs until he could get himself mobile again. He was slowly making progress but not as quickly as his impatient nature desired.

During those long days he'd been confined to the upstairs bedroom of the Murdock house, he'd written a long letter to his parents but Mick had told him that no trans-Atlantic ships were coming or going out of the Savannah harbor. Only ships making short coastal runs were pulling into the port. So Jason's letter would have to wait.

Jason was pleased to see that Tobias could move around—he seemed more like his old self—and each time he saw Dewey he seemed to be limping less and less.

Jason's biggest incentive to get that leg working was to travel up the coastline and find Stormy. To be this close was absolute torment.

As he would have expected, Dewey came into his room excited and pleased after Rudy had come back to the house with him.

"Got us a perfect place, Captain Hamilton. Right close to the harbor so it'll be handy to the *Sea Princess*. We'll start repairs when you're up to it. A real reasonable rate, too."

Jason knew that before he could do anything about their lodging he had to get out to that schooner and pray that the money pouches in his cabin were still there. The other thing that was troubling him was making sure that Stormy's ring was in the same place with his pouches.

The next day Mick loaned young Rudy his buggy so he could take Jason and Dewey to the harbor. Getting down the steps at the Murdock house had not been as taxing as Jason had expected and the ride was no problem at all.

Boarding the *Sea Princess* was a challenge but with Dewey and Rudy there to help, he managed. The deserted decks and the mud-caked hull gave the *Sea Princess* the look of a forlorn lady, Jason thought. Never had he allowed her to be so unkempt. He had never loved anything so passionately as he had that schooner until he met Stormy Monihan. To see it this way was devastating!

Getting below deck was another challenge, but he made it. Once inside, he suggested that the two of them look around. "Rudy, check the galley so we can report back to Tobias—he'll be anxious to know what we found."

"Shall I come back to your cabin then and help you back to the deck to meet Dewey?"

"Yes, Rudy," Jason replied as he went to sit down. He suddenly found himself feeling weary.

There was a fetid, moldy odor to the room that was sickening to Jason. His cabin, which contained some of his prized possessions, looked nothing like he remembered. His massive desk was no longer where it belonged and all his books lay in a pile on the floor. He shook his head dejectedly as he slowly surveyed the place. What a vicious bitch that storm had been!

He wondered if it could ever be put back in order. Suddenly, he noticed something that seemed to be a true miracle. That old chest still stood exactly where it should have been. How that could have happened when his heavy desk had been moved he would never understand!

He walked over to it and frantically began to search

the drawers—he found Stormy's ring and the pouches of money. Absolutely nothing in the chest had been stolen or damaged.

When Rudy came back he scurried around and found the brown leather valise and packed all the belongings Jason had piled on his bed. "Seems you lucked out, captain. Old Tobias wasn't so lucky. Pots and pans are all right but the floor is a solid sheet of broken glass. All his dishes must be broken."

Jason put Stormy's ring in the pocket of his jacket. Rudy put the three leather pouches in an old leather bag.

"Anything else you'd like me to do for you, sir?"

"Don't think there's much more we can do here today, Rudy," Jason said. Rudy had never seen such a sad look on his captain's face and he understood why. It was depressing to see this cabin. Rudy didn't know whether he was just imagining it, but he would have sworn he saw tears in Jason Hamilton's eyes as they left the cabin.

Rudy suddenly realized that the captain should remain in the cabin until he could get the luggage up on deck and then he would be able to help him back up. Jason sat back down. Damn, it was a miserable feeling to be so helpless! Jason had never been helpless before and he didn't like it one bit!

But he had to admit to himself that he'd changed his thinking about a lot of things. He had never realized that a man could be humbled so!

When Rudy was dropped off at Brunson's cottage, Jason pulled a generous amount of money from one of the pouches to cover anything Rudy and Billy might need as well as their wages. He then gave Rudy more money and told him to give it to Captain Brunson. "This is for everything he's done for you and Billy."

He also told Rudy that he planned to get them lodging at the Sea Gull Inn within the next three or four days. "Dewey will let you know, Rudy."

"Yes, sir—thank you, captain!" Rudy said as he jumped out of the buggy. He couldn't recall ever having this much money in his hand. No one better tell him that Captain Hamilton wasn't the most goodhearted man in the world! He knew he was holding more than double the wages he and Billy had earned and Captain Brunson was getting a most generous reward for the care he'd provided.

Dewey and Jason traveled the short distance to the Murdock house. By the time Dewey had helped him back up the stairs, Jason had to admit, "Dewey, I'm one bloody tired son of a gun! I'll settle up with you tomorrow."

Jason stretched out on the bed for the rest of the evening. When Mrs. Murdock brought his supper tray he found it a tremendous effort to prop himself against the pillows.

Like a mother hen, she gently admonished him—she reminded him of his own mother. "You tried to do too much today, captain, and don't try to tell me you're not paying for it now."

Jason gave her a sheepish grin. "I can't argue with you, Mrs. Murdock. I am paying for it."

"Then behave yourself tomorrow!"

"Yes, ma'am, I promise!"

At least his appetite had not been affected—he ate every morsel. An hour later when Janet came in to pick up the tray, she found Jason sleeping soundly. He slept for twelve solid hours before he finally woke up the next morning at eight.

Part Four

Calming the Tempest

Thirty-eight

Hoping he might save some steps for Janet and Mrs. Murdock, Dewey went to the kitchen to offer to take Jason's breakfast tray up to him. But Jason was still sleeping so he took the tray into Tobias's room.

He waited almost an hour to take the second tray up for Jason. This time he did find him awake and dressed.

But before Jason eagerly dug into food, he reached down by the side of the bed to pick up the leather pouch. He wanted to settle with Dewey. Jason figured he'd earned not just wages, but a handsome bonus.

Dewey protested that Jason was being far too generous, but Jason grinned, "Hey, remember, Dewey—I'm the captain."

Jason put another pile of money on the bed. "Think you might get over to the Sea Gull Inn and get us some rooms, Dewey?"

"Sure can. In fact, I'll go as soon as I get your tray back down to the kitchen."

A short time later Dewey was preparing to walk to the inn, but Mick Murdock wouldn't hear of it and insisted he drive him there. "Now you young fellows don't have to rush so. Besides, Susie is going to be mad as hell if you leave before Christmas."

Dewey laughed, "I think she's already made that clear

to the captain. No, I think it's the day after Christmas that the captain is planning to move over to the inn."

"Well, guess we'll have to settle for that. You'll find the Sea Gull a nice place. It's like a landmark around here. Been there for a long time and run by the same family. Sons have taken it over from their fathers for at least two or three generations," Mick said.

A few minutes later they came to the two-story white frame inn. A long, narrow porch extended across the front of the building and there was also a similar porch on the second landing.

The proprietor gave Mick Murdock a big smile when they came through the door. "Good to see you, Mick!" George Duncan told him as he came striding up to shake his hand.

Mick shook his hand and introduced Dewey. "This young man and his two friends need lodging and meals, George. They're with me and Susie right now."

"Think we can take care of your friends, Mick," George said. There were vacancies on the lower level as well as the second floor, but Dewey picked three rooms on the lower level for Tobias's and Jason's sake.

Dewey paid for a week's lodging and meals before he and Mick left the inn. He had some money left over to give back to Jason.

"Got any other little errands to run, Dewey? I've got nothing going this morning," Mick told him.

Since Jason had paid him his wages, Dewey could buy himself a change of clothes. He hadn't been as lucky as Jason—he'd found nothing left of his personal belongings.

"I could use some clothes, sir. Would—would it be all right if we stopped by the store?"

"Sure, Dewey," Mick said as he turned the buggy toward the main part of town.

Mick pulled up to the mercantile store where he and

Sue did most of their shopping. As they walked in, Mick told Dewey to take all the time he needed.

A half-hour later Dewey had indulged himself far more than he'd planned to. But after all, he figured he deserved it. Chances were that he and the *Sea Princess* were going to be in this port city of Savannah for a long time.

Now he had a nice warm wool jacket and he could return the one he'd borrowed from Mick, which was much too large. He'd also bought two pairs of dark blue pants, three shirts, and several other articles he needed.

Mick saw that Dewey had been quite successful by the packages he was carrying.

"Ready to head for home, now, son?" Murdock asked

"Think I'd better before I spend all my money," Dewey laughed.

Mick held up a little package. "Spent a little money myself. Got my Susie some of that sweet-smelling stuff she likes for Christmas," he told Dewey.

A person didn't have to be there under the Murdock roof too long to know that Mick was very devoted to his family. Dewey found him a very interesting fellow with all his tales about the sea—he'd been a sea captain for many a year. But he was also a very devoted family man.

While Dewey and Mick had been gone, Jason had hardly been idle. He wasn't quite sure whether he could make it down that stairway on his own but he decided to try it.

Before he attempted that venture, he stopped by Tobias's room to visit with his old cook. As he had done with the rest of his men, he paid Tobias the money he owned him plus the additional bonus.

Jason gave the old man a warm, comradely embrace. "Tobias, you're looking more like yourself."

"I am and I have to thank Mick Murdock. One fine gent he is, captain."

"The whole family is fine, Tobias," Jason said as he sat down on the end of the bed. He told Tobias of his trip out to the *Sea Princess* and what he had found.

Tobias shook his head, glad he had not had to see the fine schooner in such a state. Jason assured him that his galley would be put back in proper order.

"Tobias, we'll be leaving the Murdocks the day after Christmas. I've sent Dewey to get us rooms at the Sea Gull Inn."

"Guess we can consider ourselves lucky, can't we, captain? Our *Sea Princess* was a lucky lady."

"I feel we were very lucky, Tobias," Jason said as he rose to leave.

An hour later Jason had made his way downstairs to find Sue Murdock. He paid her generously for the services she and her family had provided for him and his men.

Sue Murdock had been very reluctant to take so much money, but Jason Hamilton had insisted and she'd found he could be a very determined young gentleman.

She thanked him graciously and said firmly, "Now I insist that you all spend the Christmas holiday with us, Captain Hamilton."

"I promise you, Mrs. Murdock. We'll be delighted to share the holiday with you and your family," Jason said, giving her one of his charming smiles.

When he returned to his room Jason sat staring out the window, thinking of the lovely girl who had been his reason for making this ill-fated trip. Nothing had worked out as he had planned. Here he was, still many miles away from her—but now he could turn his thoughts and energy to making his dream come true. That meant he had to concentrate all his energy on the *Sea Princess*.

As soon as she was put back in shape he could get on to Southport and the woman he loved so much that he'd risk everything to claim her as his bride.

Pat Dorsey didn't know that a man could be as happy as he was the night he left Kip's cottage with Stormy's promise to marry him.

It was an elated young fellow who came busting through Paddy's door that night. Exuberantly, he told Paddy the happy news and, needless to say, Paddy was overjoyed to hear it. But he was a little surprised to hear that it had happened this quickly.

But then that shouldn't have surprised him—Stormy had always been an impetuous, capricious little imp!

"And when is the big day, Pat?"

"Don't know just yet, Paddy. Stormy wants to get the holidays over first. Marcie has all she can handle right now. Can't be too soon for me, I can assure you!" Pat grinned as he removed his jacket and strolled over to hang it on the peg.

When he took a seat he told Paddy of his plans to find some kind of job to earn during the months before they'd start making runs again.

"More than ever, I have to find something. Me and Stormy have to have our own place."

"That's understandable, son. I'd feel the same way," Paddy said. "Sounds like you've got a lot cut out for yourself, young fellow."

Pat stood and smiled down at Paddy, "That's why I'm getting to bed early. I'm starting out early in the morning to see what I can find."

Paddy found himself sitting alone in his front room all evening. He usually was the one hitting the bed before Pat.

He felt a little sad about Pat moving out into his own

place but Paddy knew that sooner or later it was bound to happen.

True to his word, Pat was up and had the coffee pot brewing by the time Paddy crawled out of bed. Still in his nightshirt, Paddy ambled slowly into the kitchen.

He shared breakfast with Pat, insisting he'd do the cleaning up since Pat had done the cooking. Pat gave him no argument as he went to get his jacket—he was eager to get on his way.

By midday he'd made a stop at the livery and talked to the manager of the lumber mill. Many boatmen in Southport were trying to earn extra money—Pat was wishing he'd gotten the idea sooner.

He stopped at one of the grain stores but once again he was turned away. He figured it was pointless to go by the warehouse—it wasn't all that busy around there. But then again, he thought there might be the possibility they could use a handyman to build some new stalls or do repairs before the spring busy season.

Dick Carpenter told him he didn't have anything right then but he added, "I'll get word to you, Dorsey, if I do need an extra hand."

Dorsey thanked him and was turning to leave when Carpenter called to him, "Hey, Dorsey—just happened to think of somewhere you might try."

"Yeah, where's that, Dick?"

"Holcombe's Feed Store. One of Frank's men messed his back up about a week ago and he might just need a man if this guy's going to be laid up for a while."

"Thanks a lot, Dick. I'll head over that way right now."

A half hour later he had not only talked with Frank Holcombe but he had himself a job. Frank had only to look at the firm muscled Dorsey and figure he could handle the sacks of grain. He was definitely in need of another man and had no inkling of when Whitt would be back.

"Be here at seven in the morning and we'll give you a try, Dorsey," Holcombe told him.

"I'll be here, Mister Holcombe," Pat promised. As he walked back toward Paddy's house he swore he was running a streak of luck. It had started out being a discouraging morning but now he was going home with more good news to pass on to Paddy.

Paddy was happy to hear his news. He also realized that Dorsey was going to be around only in the evenings once he started to work for Holcombe, so he'd have to start handling all the many chores Dorsey had been doing during the day. Pat had spoiled him, Paddy realized.

But then since Dorsey's announcement last night about his engagement to Stormy, Paddy realized he would have to accept the void it would make in his life. Things would be like they'd been before Dorsey had come to stay.

But Paddy reminded himself that he'd lived alone since he'd been eighteen.

He'd lived long enough to know that nothing in life remained the same. He'd become quite accustomed to living the solitary life when he wasn't sailing with Kip and rather enjoyed it. However, he wasn't that able-bodied anymore, so he didn't look forward to getting through the long winter after Pat left.

He didn't like the frail, old man he was becoming!

Thirty-nine

Frank Holcombe was pleased with his new hired man—it didn't matter to him if Whitt came back or not. Dorsey could work circles around Whitt any day of the week.

In the course of their conversations, Dorsey mentioned that he was getting married. When he told Holcombe the name of the young lady, that got Holcombe's attention. He'd known Kip for years and he'd heard about his beautiful daughter, Stormy.

"Well, I'll be damned! So you're marrying Stormy?" Frank exclaimed.

"Yes, sir. That's another thing—I need to find a house for us. But I have to get some money saved up before I can do that," Pat grinned.

"I'll keep my eyes and ears open, young man," Frank told him as he turned to walk away. Frank didn't have to keep his eyes and ears open—he knew of a little cottage that was vacant and would soon be offered for sale but he wasn't ready to say anything to Dorsey right then. He wanted to get to know this young man a little better.

The little cottage was next to his own property where he had a fine two-story frame house. But the plot of ground was very small. It was where his widowed mother had lived until she died a few months ago—

Frank had been in no hurry to put the property up for sale.

Dorsey had worked a full week before the feed store closed to observe the Christmas holiday. Holcombe wished Dorsey a happy holiday and told him to give his regards to Kip and his family.

"You and your family have a wonderful holiday too, sir," Pat said as they parted.

Dorsey's back was sore from the busy day he'd put in—he was glad Holcombe had closed the store an hour early. A good warm bath and a change of clothes would make him feel much better. He knew he'd have to hasten his pace so he could get to Paddy's house quickly if he hoped to get that bath in and be dressed by the time Kip arrived in his buggy to pick them up.

Paddy was all decked out when Dorsey came rushing through the door. He did manage to have his bath and be dressed when Kip arrived.

Dorsey would have found it hard to describe this Christmas Eve night but he knew he'd never experienced one like it.

From the minute the three of them arrived at Kip's front door, it was like entering a special wonderland. The enchanting smells of pine and cedar mingled with scents of bayberry and holly. The fireplace crackled and flamed brightly. The huge evergreen was standing in the corner colorfully decorated with gifts piled under it.

Stormy was sheer perfection as she greeted them, looking so festive in her green woolen gown. It was a gown Jason had purchased for her and Stormy had remembered that when she was dressing. For a moment she felt a wave of sadness wash over her, but then she put thoughts of Jason aside so she could enjoy the evening.

Marcie was lovely in her berry-colored gown she

met Paddy and Pat at the door, giving each of them a warm embrace.

Dorsey figured that this was surely what Christmas Eves were supposed to be like, even though he'd never known one like this.

They sat around Kip's table, lit by candlelight, and enjoyed a magnificent meal. Later they gathered in the front room to exchange their gifts. There had been laughter and singing. As the hour grew late, Kip poured Paddy, Pat, and himself a glass of his favorite Irish whiskey. Marcie decided it was a night when she and Stormy should have themselves a glass or two of sherry.

Once again, Stormy found her thoughts drifting back to England and the Hamiltons. She remembered how Lady Sheila loved her sherry wine and how the two of them shared special moments in her sitting room.

It was obvious that Kip, Paddy, and Pat were enjoying themselves as they sipped their whiskey. When the clock struck midnight, Marcie knew she had to get to bed if she was to get up to cook the turkey for their feast tomorrow.

She winked at Stormy and softly suggested, "If they want to stay up all night, that's fine—but I've got to get some sleep."

Stormy's glass of sherry had made her more than ready to lay her head on a pillow. She was weary after the long night's festivities.

"We'll see you gentlemen in the morning," Marcie said as she bent down to kiss Kip on the cheek.

Stormy made no such gesture toward Pat. She couldn't explain it even to herself later but she felt no desire to do anything but smile as she said good night. It was not to her bedroom she went but to Marcie's sewing room. Paddy and Pat were to share her room tonight.

As she was undressing, she asked herself what had

happened during the evening that had so suddenly depressed her. She didn't know, but something had.

Long after she had gotten into the narrow little daybed and pulled the coverlet over her she lay there wide-eyed. As weary as she'd thought she was, she suddenly found she couldn't sleep. So she allowed herself to relive the evening.

It was true that she had a moment of melancholy when she'd put on the green gown and thought about Jason. But that had passed by the time she'd gone into the front room and joined the festivities.

She greeted Paddy and Pat with an affectionate kiss when they arrived. At that moment, she'd felt the desire to do so but she was questioning why she'd had no desire to kiss Pat good night.

Her mood had not changed during dinner. What was it, she kept asking herself, that suddenly changed the evening for her? She had been so thrilled with the lovely green vest from Marcie and she was delighted with Paddy's music box. It became even more precious to her when Paddy told her it had belonged to his mother. "I wanted you to have it, honey," he'd said. She'd rushed over to kiss him and thank him. She also thanked him for the gift he'd had Pat buy for him.

Kip's gift had been a delicate gold necklace which she immediately put on.

Marcie took a turn at opening some of her gifts. Kip had bought her a lovely necklace similar to Stormy's—she was as thrilled as Stormy had been. Dorsey's gift was next and Marcie was delighted with the lilac toilet water.

Stormy opened Pat's gift last. It was also a bottle of toilet water. The fragrance he'd picked was jasmine—not her favorite. She liked gardenia—she used the small bottle she'd brought back from England very sparingly. Now she knew the moment she had become depressed:

it was when she had opened Dorsey's gift and she'd received a bottle of toilet water just like Marcie's. It made her realize just how much Jason had spoiled her.

For the rest of the evening, Stormy was pondering whether she had made a disastrous mistake when she'd promised Pat she'd marry him.

It was true that she had never lain in Pat's arms and allowed him to make love to her as Jason had but instinctively she knew that the rapture would not be there if she did. As handsome as he was and as charming and witty, Pat Dorsey was not Jason Hamilton!

Stormy wondered if she would ever know that glorious ecstasy again!

For all of Christmas day, Stormy could not shake her mood. Nothing she did seemed to lift her spirits. She'd put on one of her prettiest frocks and worn her father's necklace. She dabbed some of the jasmine toilet water Dorsey had given her behind her ears and at her wrist, but she just didn't like it. Pat had obviously found it pleasing or he wouldn't have given it to her.

It was not until they'd had dinner and all the dishes were washed and put away that Pat finally found a moment to be alone with Stormy. He was beginning to wonder if they'd be surrounded by her family and old Paddy for the entire day.

It wouldn't be long before Kip would be taking him and Paddy back to Southport, so Pat grabbed the opportunity to take a stroll with her so they could have at least a few brief moments alone. "I need to walk a little after that huge meal," he said.

Stormy went to the room to get her cape. The days were shorter now—the sun was going down earlier so by late afternoon there was a chill in the air.

"Shall we go, Pat?" she asked as she draped the cape around her shoulders.

He was already anticipating her kisses as soon as

they reached the secluded wooded area. He was aching to hold her in his arms and feel her soft body pressing against him.

Pat kept glancing down at her—she looked so breathtakingly beautiful with her golden hair blowing away from her face.

"It was a wonderful holiday, Stormy, but damned if I thought I'd ever have a moment alone with you," Pat said lightheartedly.

Stormy laughed, "That's the way it is when a family gathers for the holidays."

"Well, I wouldn't know, Stormy. All I know is this was the best Christmas I've ever had."

"You mean your family didn't get together for holidays, Pat?"

"Nope."

Stormy realized she really knew nothing about Pat's background as she did about Jason and his family.

She wondered why Pat was always so reluctant to speak about his family. If he was to be her husband, she felt she had the right to know something about it. "If we're to be married, don't you think we should be able to talk about anything?"

"We will, Stormy, but not today." He shrugged her request aside because he didn't want to spoil this special moment.

He wasted no more time, pulling her around to kiss her. Stormy felt the hunger in Pat's lips as they captured hers. It was not her nature to play games—she tried to give him the response she knew he expected.

"Oh, God, Stormy, you smell so sweet," he murmured huskily as his lips trailed to the side of her cheek and his nose nuzzled her hair.

Waiting so long to be with her and finally getting to kiss her had filled Pat Dorsey with flaming passion. His hand moved from her waist to cup one of her breasts. Never had he been so bold and Stormy reacted quickly by pulling his hand away. "No, Pat—we're not married yet!" There was a sharp tone of indignation and when he looked into those green eyes he saw contempt.

"God, Stormy! I know that but we're going to be soon if I have my way," he muttered. His eyes searched her face—he was feeling confused and hurt by the way she'd reacted. Most ladies liked his caresses and he would have expected Stormy to feel the same way.

So he reluctantly suggested they start back, and Stormy readily agreed.

"Yes, it's getting a little chilly out here. The wind seems to be coming up."

They were both very quiet and thoughtful as they walked the short distance back to the house. But Pat couldn't let her go into the house without telling her, "Stormy, I didn't mean to offend you. I'm just a man very much in love with you."

A wave of guilt washed over Stormy. She understood this, and why shouldn't she? She knew how a woman responded to a man she loved. She well remembered the ecstasy she'd felt when Jason had caressed her.

Poor Dorsey—she was not being fair and she knew it! Had it been Jason's hand caressing her she would have melted in his arms as she always had when he touched or kissed her.

She had even pretended it was Jason holding her instead of Dorsey—her eyes were closed but that didn't change a thing. Nothing about Dorsey was the same as it was with the man she truly loved!

There was only one Jason Hamilton and he was back in England!

Forty

Marcie and Stormy stood on the porch to wave good-bye to Paddy and Pat as Kip put the buggy into motion to get them back to Paddy's before dark.

When they had disappeared, Marcie and Stormy went back into the house to warm themselves by the fireplace. "Oh, it was a beautiful Christmas, wasn't it, dear?" Marcie exclaimed, still glowing from all the excitement.

"It was perfect," Stormy lied. She couldn't bring herself to feel like Marcie was feeling. God knows, she had certainly tried. She had tried desperately!

But she did manage to fool Marcie and Pat managed to do the same thing after he and Paddy arrived home. Like Marcie, old Paddy was still churning with excitement from the holiday.

Dorsey had a perfect excuse to retire to his room—he had to get to the feed store bright and early in the morning.

"Well, the holiday's over, Paddy, and I have to get up early so I'll be saying good night to you," he told the old man. It was not a matter of being sleepy—he wasn't. But he did want to be by himself so he could think.

Dorsey finally came to the conclusion that Stormy was just having one of those strange times that he'd heard other fellows discussing. He'd heard the men on the *East Wind* talking about their ladies getting cranky at certain times of the month. Pat could think of nothing else that could have made her react as she had.

Since he had been seventeen, Dorsey had had a high opinion of himself where the ladies were concerned. He knew he was pretty good-looking—he also knew he had a winning way about him.

But Stormy was a complex lady. She had challenged him as no other woman ever had. Never had the cocky Dorsey waited so long for a woman to surrender to his Irish charm. But his patience had been sorely tested the last two days. It would never have entered his mind to ask himself if his kisses and caresses just didn't excite Stormy.

By the time he was ready to go to sleep, he had come to the conclusion that he was going to have to be a little more assertive with his bride-to-be. She might as well get accustomed to the fact that he was to rule their roost, not her.

Thoughts about Stormy were put aside as he got up the next morning and walked to the feed store. After the long hours he put in, he was too weary to walk over to the Monihans in the evenings after he and Paddy had supper. He just wanted to take a warm bath to soothe his aching muscles.

At the end of the second week of working for Holcombe, Pat was made an offer he couldn't refuse. Frank gave him a most reasonable deal on the cottage and land, with Pat making payments out of his weekly salary. Frank figured that Pat would feel under obligation to work for him through all the winter months. He knew that Kip Monihan wouldn't be making runs for another twelve weeks.

On the weekend, Pat went over to the Monihans to tell Stormy his exciting news. Fred had already turned the key over to him so he could show it to Stormy over there. He thought the little house was the perfect honeymoon cottage.

He felt Fred had been most generous when he'd included the cookstove and the kitchen table and chairs in the price.

So Dorsey was in the highest of spirits when he jauntily walked over to tell Stormy about the cottage he'd purchased. Now that he had a place for them to live he didn't figure they'd have to have the entire place furnished to make it livable, so he saw no reason that they should wait to be married. He didn't figure that Stormy would want a fancy wedding any more than he did. Marcie wouldn't have to do that much for the two of them to have a simple wedding in Kip's front room. Then they could leave for their own little place for their honeymoon.

With a boyish eagerness, he boasted to the Monihans and Stormy about what he'd accomplished in the last two weeks. Kip gave him permission to take the buggy to show Stormy the little cottage.

Everything was happening too fast for Stormy—she was the one least enthused about Dorsey's news. She sat stiffly in Marcie's buggy as Pat guided the bay toward this cottage he'd purchased.

When they arrived, she saw that Pat had described the outside of the cottage exactly, with its picket fence and gate. It was a small plot of land but a very pretty front yard and lovely flowerbeds.

He led her through the front door into a small front room with a fireplace. There were two bedrooms and a kitchen. The kitchen was the only room with furnishings—Pat told her they were included in the sale price.

It didn't take long to make a tour of the small cottage and Stormy carefully surveyed every corner. By the time they were moving back toward the front room, Pat's exuberance was still with him. "Can't see why we should delay getting married any longer now, Stormy. We've got ourselves a home."

"Oh, Pat—there's a multitude of things to do before we could live here," she said as she smiled up at him.

"What do you mean, honey?"

"Furniture for the other rooms, for one thing. Pots, pan, and dishes for the kitchen as well as linens for the bedroom. We can hardly sleep and sit on the floor, now can we?"

He grinned sheepishly, "I guess I hadn't thought about all those things. So when do you think we should set our wedding date, Stormy?"

"Let me think about that, Pat, once this place is gone over and cleaned up. There's a bed to buy and some things for the front room. When the kitchen is equipped and the bedroom furnished completely, then we can talk about a wedding date. The front room doesn't have to be furnished completely but there are some things we'd have to have to make it livable."

Pat listened—and what he heard was enough to tell him there was to be no wedding for several weeks yet. It told him how naive he was about providing a home for a bride.

As he was taking her back to her house, Pat was a little crestfallen. He was also feeling stupid that he had not been more aware of all the things she mentioned. Hell, he hadn't thought about the bed or the linen nor had he thought about the pots and pans. So there was no possibility of setting a date today as he'd hoped when he'd gone over to Kip's that morning.

Stormy was going back home feeling as disillusioned about Pat Dorsey as she had been a week ago. All her life she had admired the strength and masterful way her father had taken charge. He had been her first "knight in shining armor" and then she'd met Captain Jason

Hamilton. She saw the forceful, energetic way he moved around the *Sea Princess* and she'd admired that.

Pat Dorsey might be able to take over running the *East Wind* for her pa, but Stormy was convinced that Pat was not the man to fulfill her need as a woman. He didn't have the power and force of Kip Monihan or Jason Hamilton.

Today, Stormy had decided that she could not possibly settle for anything less.

It was not Kip but Marcie who first noticed Stormy's disenchantment with Dorsey. Knowing her as well as she did, Marcie could see that Stormy was not yet ready to talk to her so she didn't try to press her.

But Marcie was already wagering that a wedding would never take place between Stormy and Pat Dorsey!

Jason Hamilton could not say it was one of his happier holidays —Christmas back in England at the country house was a grand affair, and he missed it terribly. How different the traditions were between the two countries! The Murdocks served roast turkey but his family always served roast goose. Mrs. Murdock had an array of pies but at his home his mother always served Yorkshire pudding. Then there was that delicious little dish of heavy cream and berries, which he loved.

Nevertheless, it was still a gala scene at the Murdocks' that evening as he, Tobias, Dewey, and Rudy joined the family for the festivities. Billy was still not up to making the trip over from Brunson's place.

For the first time in his life Jason suddenly realized just how much his family and his home back in England meant to him. He vowed that when the Christmas holiday came around next year he would be out in the country to share this time of the year with them.

But then Jason had changed his thinking about many

things lately. Lying in that bed had given him a lot of time to think. His lifelong friend, Lord Bart Montgomery, had been far smarter than he. When he'd found the lady he loved he had left his randy bachelor days behind and married the beautiful Tawny Blair. Bart Montgomery was the happiest fellow he knew.

A man couldn't sail the sea forever. Jason had stared death in the face that night on the deck of the *Sea Princess* and the last thought rushing through his mind before he fell into that bottomless pit was that he had not really begun to live. He wanted more out of life than just the sea and his ship. He wanted a wife and children like Bart had. That would be the legacy that would live long after he was gone—his children.

He noticed that Rudy couldn't take his eyes off pretty little Janet—obviously he was lovestruck over the Murdock's daughter. But Jason had also gotten the idea that his first mate was rather taken with her as well, so that provided a little entertainment for the rest of the evening.

Janet seemed to like the attentions of both of them, showing no preference. Tobias was obviously aware of it, too, as he looked over at Jason and gave him a knowing wink.

Later when he and Jason were sitting near each other Tobias bent over to whisper in his ear, "Think Dewey's got himself a little competition over there, captain." Jason nodded in agreement.

Tobias was delighted with his new pipe and leather pouch filled generously with tobacco. Mick urged him, "Try it out, Tobias. My Susie isn't fussy about a man smoking in her house."

So Tobias filled his pipe and sat there enjoying Mick's gift. He knew he was also going to enjoy the warm woolen socks little Janet had knitted for him.

Jason admired the neck scarf she'd knitted for him,

but it also reminded him of his own sister, Jane, and how she was always knitting articles of clothing for him. It seemed that everything tonight was reminding him of home and England.

If his thoughts weren't roaming in that direction, they were traveling up the coast to Southport where Stormy and her family were most likely sharing an evening similar to theirs.

Come next Christmas, he vowed that the two of them would be together for the holiday. Nothing was going to separate them ever again. But for right now it was sheer torment to have to delay the journey up the coast.

There was one thing that the Hamiltons and the Murdocks had in common at the holiday time—the wassail bowl. The Murdocks' wassail was always enjoyed by Sue's family and their guests. There was a difference in that she had used wine instead of ale in her wassail. But Lord Addison preferred ale so that was how Lady Hamilton had her cook prepare theirs.

As it had been with Kip's family, the Murdocks feasted on Christmas Day since the exchanging of gifts was done on Christmas Eve.

Early in the evening a sudden quiet fell over the parlor that had been so alive with laughter and gay conversation the previous night. Sue had to admit to Mick that she was ready to sit and relax.

Tobias was so stuffed from all the food he'd eaten the last two days that he could have fasted for the next two. Jason was ready to retire to his own room so he could sit alone and make plans for the next few days.

Only Dewey lingered downstairs and it wasn't hard for Jason to figure out why. He had a disgruntled look when Janet graciously accompanied Rudy to the front door as he was leaving for Brunson's place. Rudy had wished that Billy could have been with them tonight. Since Dewey's room was next to his, Jason was aware that he hadn't come upstairs so he figured Dewey was hoping to catch Janet alone to have a few minutes with her.

Much to his chagrin, Dewey never found that moment. Once Rudy and Janet walked out on that front porch Rudy was not in that big a rush to get to Brunson's after all. Dewey gave up after he had paced around the parlor for almost a half hour. For the first time he was irked at the likeable Rudy.

When Sue Murdock came back into the parlor, Dewey quickly excused himself and said good night. Sue's all-knowing eyes had observed the two young men and she knew that Janet had two admirers.

Somehow, it seemed the young red-haired Rudy's boyish charm had won out over the older and more handsome Dewey!

By the time Dewey had climbed the stairs to his room, he was no longer angry with Rudy. After all, he'd had a lot of lady friends through the years and this was probably the first time young Rudy had ever been in love. So how could he be angry with him?

Dewey could recall that first time he was lovestruck. God, it was glorious! There was nothing to compare to that very first time.

The truth was that Janet deserved a nicer fellow than he was, and he knew of no nicer young man than Rudy!

Forty-one

As they'd planned, Jason and his entourage moved out of the Murdocks' home the day after Christmas. Jason graciously thanked them for their kind hospitality. Sue had said as they were saying their farewells, "I still feel guilty about all that money you gave me, captain."

Hamilton patted her hand as he assured her, "And I'd feel guilty had it been any less, Mrs. Murdock."

Mick took them to the Sea Gull Inn in his buggy— Jason was more than pleased with the ground-level rooms Dewey had picked out.

They were hardly settled in before Jason dispatched Dewey to the livery for a flatbed wagon to enable Billy and Rudy to move into their rooms.

Jason wanted his men with him as they would have been if they were on his ship. Of the five of them, he had two able-bodied men in Rudy and Dewey. He was also getting stronger every day. Old Tobias was at least able to look after some of his needs.

There were a lot of idle men around Savannah eager to earn some money, so Jason hired as many as he could. The ship was in need of a good airing—it was most important to get the hold completely clean and dry so he could survey it for cracks or leaks and be sure it was seaworthy again.

Carpenters were hired to repair all the splintered timbers. Pails and mops were busy in all of the cabins. Jason was determined that the *Sea Princess* would be as meticulously ordered as it had once been. With all the windows open and the winter breeze wafting through the cabins and passageways, that sickening musty aroma decreased.

By the end of the first week, Jason and Dewey made a careful inspection of the hold. Miraculously, the lower hull had suffered no damage. It was as dry as a bone!

It pleased Jason to report to old Tobias that his galley was in proper order. He asked Tobias to give him a list of all the things he would need so they could restock it.

Jason became a familiar figure to many Savannah merchants as he purchased supplies. One merchant received a tremendous sum when Jason purchased the many items on Tobias's list.

Jason was pleased when the lower level of his schooner was restored to its original shape. When he was ready to get working on the deck, he was forced to take a two-day rest. A rainy period had set in but it worked to Jason's advantage—the rains washed some of the dried mud away from the deck.

On one of those rainy days, Jason spent some time in his cabin sipping his favorite whiskey. Some things he could never replace and he'd come to terms with that. All the books that had lined his bookcase were gone forever. What had amazed him was how some of the champagne and wine had ridden out the storm.

Jason had been so occupied that it had not dawned on him that a new year had started and he had had another birthday. Hell, his twenty-eighth had come and gone and he hadn't even thought about it!

Like Billy, who was beginning to exercise that broken leg of his, Jason was doing the same thing with his injured arm. The arm had been idle so long it was not that easy to make it move.

When the rains ceased, the crew Jason hired were

ready to go back to work on the *Sea Princess*. Repairing the topside would be a major undertaking because of Jason's high standards. Old Tobias was dazzled by the cleaned, restored, and restocked galley.

It was mid-January—a long time after Jason had figured he'd reach Southport and Stormy—but he was very pleased that his ship was finally being restored. His next move was to hire a crew for the trip up to Southport.

Jason was to find out that his name had been tossed around the wharves by the men who'd been working for him repairing his ship. They praised his fair and generous wages.

The next day the four seamen sought out Jason Hamilton. Jason could tell right away they weren't greenhorns. So he hired them on.

When he was about ready to leave Savannah he was sitting up late sipping his whiskey when something came to him like a bolt of lightning: Could it be possible that the man who came to their rescue that terrible night and took him, Tobias, and Dewey to his home was the same Murdock who'd come to England to take Stormy home to her father?

Why had he not have thought about that before? He must have been very dazed when he'd been brought to the house by Captain Murdock.

Jason sat there, seemingly in a trance. He knew instinctively that he was right. But he vividly recalled that his mother had told him that a Captain Murdock had come to the house to deliver a message to Stormy from her father and he was to take her back home.

Now that Jason wasn't concentrating on his ship, he had time to do some thinking. He wondered why Captain Murdock had not associated him with the Lady Sheila Hamilton he'd met in England. He was convinced there could only be one old sea captain in Savannah named Murdock, so he had to be the one.

Jason was also asking himself another troubling question: Had Stormy not spoken of him at all during that long crossing with Murdock? If she had, would not Mick have recalled the name of Jason Hamilton?

He had no doubts that Stormy was out of sorts with him when he left to make the jaunt to Ireland so now he began to wonder if she'd no longer loved him when she left England.

What if he arrived in Southport to find his beautiful Stormy married to someone else? This ill-fated voyage would have been for naught!

Jason tried to fight back such thoughts. He was restless—he knew he had to satisfy his curiosity about Murdock, so he headed for his place.

Jason found Mick and Janet in the kitchen. Janet was tending to their supper for Sue was tutoring a young lad in her parlor. Jason accepted Murdock's invitation to join him for a cup of coffee.

Jason came straight to the point, asking him if he was the Captain Murdock who'd come to his parents' estate to deliver the message to Stormy.

"Holy Moses, I thought you were never going to make the connection," Mick roared with laughter. "Didn't think I should say anything at first because you were in a state of shock. But I just knew that when Rudy told me you were Captain Jason Hamilton you had to be Lady Sheila's son."

"So you were waiting for me to say something?" Jason grinned.

"I was, but then you had only two things on your mind once you got back to yourself: your men and your ship. I admire you for that, young man."

"Can't deny that, sir," Jason grinned.

"Well, I guess you could say I felt like I knew you and your family long before I was to meet you. Me and little Stormy had a lot of talks on our way back here."

"When you and Captain Brunson rescued us, you had to be thinking what a foolhardy sea captain I was to have ventured across the ocean this time of year," Jason remarked.

"When Rudy told me your name, I knew why you'd done it. A man can do a lot of crazy things when he loses his heart to a beautiful girl like Stormy Monihan," Mick grinned.

Jason's black eyes sparked with amusement. "You're a sly fox, Captain Murdock. But you're right, I admit. I'm usually more sane. But I was a man in torment when I returned from Ireland and my mother said Stormy had sailed back with you. I couldn't wait out the winter, even though I knew I was sailing with a miserable crew. I had only my galley cook, Tobias, Dewey, my first mate and my cabin boy, Rudy. I hired the rest in desperation."

"A good crew means everything to a captain," Mick told him.

"Oh, did Dewey and I find that out! Believe me, I won't leave the Carolina coast until I have a good crew and until the winter is over," Jason declared.

"So tell me how you came to Savannah instead of Southport?" Mick asked.

"A storm had thrown us off course so the *Sea Princess* had veered to the south. I was heading for Savannah instead of Southport," Jason told him.

"Well, son—you've just had a slight delay. Got a feeling you'll be heading for Southport soon," Mick grinned.

"Yes, sir. Sometime this next week."

Mick told him he hoped he'd come back this way before he sailed back to England.

"Oh, I promise to do that, Captain Murdock. When I sail for England I'm hoping I'll be returning with Stormy as my bride. Wish me luck, captain," Jason grinned.

Forty-two

The week after the Christmas holiday when Pat had taken Stormy over to see the little house he was going to purchase, it was obvious to Marcie that Stormy was not as enthused as she expected her to be.

She was aware that Pat didn't stay long before he started back to Southport. Knowing Stormy as well as she did, Marcie concluded she was glad that he'd hurried off. For whatever reason, she figured that the two young lovers had had a spat. She said nothing until Kip went out to chop some wood.

Seeing Stormy sitting quietly in a chair, she asked, "Stormy, you didn't like the house?"

"It's very nice, Marcie but I'm irritated with Pat. He seems to think we could be married and moved in there in a couple of weeks—that would be utterly impossible!"

Marcie smiled, "I guess most men have no idea of what it takes to make a house ready to live in. Kip knew, for he'd been running this house for years before I came along. I had little to do."

"There are no furnishings. I told Pat there are no linens for a bedroom or pots and pans for the kitchen. Dear God, there are a million things to get and that's not the half of it! The place needs a thorough cleaning—it's been vacant for months. Obviously, Pat never gave that any thought."

"So he wants the wedding to take place much sooner than you do?" Marcie asked.

"There will be no wedding this month and I told him so," Stormy said. She paused for a moment to look back at Marcie before leaving the room. "Right now, Marcie—right now, I'm not even sure I want to marry Pat Dorsey!" Marcie's heart went out to Stormy. She was troubled and Marcie knew it!

"Oh, honey, don't marry Dorsey or any man unless you're sure," Marcie pleaded as her eyes searched Stormy's face.

Long after Stormy had left, Marcie sat thinking that she wouldn't say anything to Kip about this conversation. She knew how much he thought of Dorsey but that didn't matter if he wasn't the right man.

Marcie knew that a bride-to-be should be happy. She didn't know what Dorsey lacked that Stormy was seeking in a husband. As awkward as it might become, Marcie knew she was going to stand by Stormy—she just hoped that Kip's loyalty to Dorsey would not blind him.

Marcie knew how Pat Dorsey had ingratiated himself not only to Kip but to Paddy. Stormy loved both of them dearly—it would be terribly hard for her to change her mind, knowing how the two of them felt about Pat.

After all it was Stormy, not Kip or Paddy, who would be living with Pat.

Dorsey didn't come by the cottage for the next six evenings, and Marcie sensed that Stormy was just as glad that he didn't. In fact, as the week wore on, Stormy's mood got more and more cheerful.

Marcie was delighted to see her acting more like her old self. She couldn't remember seeing Stormy looking more beautiful. She had taken the buggy and gone into town twice that last week and on both trips she paid a visit to Paddy.

What Marcie could not have known about nor did Stormy choose to tell her, was her confidential talk with Paddy. Stormy had not planned it that way but somehow it had just happened.

Now that she was grown up, she found that she could still cry her heart out to that old man as she had as a child. He always seemed to understand her.

Paddy would never know how much their talk had helped. It was good just to have someone to confide in. While that had not been the reason for her visit, she was glad that everything had happened as it had.

It meant a lot to know that Paddy seemed to understand her feelings about Dorsey—now she could only hope that her pa would feel the same way.

It had alleviated the guilt she'd felt since Pat had bought the little cottage. Paddy had pointed out that Pat could always use that small a house even if he was a bachelor.

As Paddy had also pointed out, she could always play a waiting game. At least, she could gamble for another two or three weeks. Past that, she wasn't so sure!

It was a pleasant evening at Kip's as the three of them sat around the kitchen table having the evening meal. Kip quizzed Stormy about how old Paddy was. "Marcie told me you paid him a visit this afternoon. That was mighty thoughtful of you, honey. I got to get over there."

"Well, he was just fine, Pa. Like you, he's probably getting the itch to get out of that house and back on the *East Wind.*"

"Well, about eight more weeks and maybe me and old Paddy will be doing just that."

"That doesn't sound too long, Pa, the way you say it," she smiled.

"It isn't, honey, when you consider that we've already had about twelve weeks of winter."

Marcie sat quietly observing the two of them. Stormy seemed so relaxed and contented, talking with her dad. She wondered if her mood would stay the same when Pat came over to see her, which he was bound to do in a day or two.

The next evening, Pat was at their door. Marcie thought to herself that Dorsey was a sly one—he'd timed his visit just right to be there around the dinner hour. But she could hardly fault him for that. Most men liked a good home cooked meal.

She greeted him at the door instead of Stormy, who was still in her bedroom. "Come on in, Pat, and make yourself at home. Kip's outside and I'll call Stormy."

She went to Stormy's bedroom to announce that Pat was there, then called to Pat, "Got to get to my kitchen or my supper will burn."

As she stood over her stove, she had a clear view of the front room—Stormy didn't seem in any rush to greet him. Marcie was thinking that Dorsey might consider himself experienced where the ladies were concerned but she wasn't so sure. She found it odd that he never brought Stormy a little gift as most young men did when they were courting a young lady, especially one so beautiful.

She hadn't said anything to Kip but she'd found Pat's Christmas gift to Stormy inadequate. To have given Stormy a bottle of toilet water, the same gift he'd bought for her, surely hadn't impressed Marcie. She had expected Pat to buy Stormy a ring since she'd accepted his proposal. She was sure Stormy had expected more than a bottle of toilet water.

She didn't know what Kip was doing, but she wished he'd come on into the house. She'd seen Pat get up and begin to pace, finally coming into the kitchen.

In his cocky way he remarked to Marcie, "Well—
wonder what's happened to my girl."

"Perhaps she's finishing dressing or brushing her
hair. You'll have to learn a little patience," she smiled.
There was an air about Pat that could be annoying to
Stormy now that she'd agreed to marry him. Pat had
been acting a little overconfident. That could be the
worst mistake he could make with a girl like Stormy.

When Stormy did appear, the first thing Pat did made
her bristle. He clasped her waist and boldly helped himself to a kiss with Marcie standing there watching them.
Marcie saw how Stormy's eyes had green fire in them
as she quickly jerked away. She laughed uneasily and
declared, "My goodness, Pat!"

"Hey, I haven't seen my girl in days. A man has a
right to kiss his bride-to-be," he replied. Then he informed her that he'd bought a bed the previous day.

If Pat could have read Stormy's thoughts, his ego
would have been badly wounded. The idea of sharing a
bed with him left her cold. Truth was, everything he
said or did seemed to rub her the wrong way so she
began to fidget around the kitchen, pretending to help
Marcie so she wouldn't have to go to the front room
with him.

Luckily, Kip came in and greeted Pat, "Didn't know
you were over here, Pat." Stormy was delighted when
Kip invited him to come to the front room with him.
"We'll let these little ladies get our dinner on the table.
I'm starved."

Marcie felt sorry for Stormy—she saw how she
seemed to sigh with relief when she was finally rid of
Dorsey.

Stormy didn't have to say a word to Marcie about
how she felt. Marcie already knew. And she was certain
there would be no wedding—Stormy would never go
through with such a farce.

Marcie announced that dinner was ready and both men wasted no time coming to the table. Kip ate heartily and Pat ate like a starved wolf. When the meal was over, Stormy got up from the table to help Marcie clear away the dishes. Marcie said, "Honey—if you want to spend some time with Pat, I can do these dishes."

"No, Marcie—Pa can entertain Pat. I'll—I'll help you," Stormy responded hastily.

It didn't take long for the two of them to put everything in order, so Marcie and Stormy were soon ready to join the two men in the front room. Kip sat in his favorite chair on one side of the fireplace and Marcie sat down in the one on the other side.

So Stormy went over to join Pat on the settee. She'd hardly sat down before he suggested the two of them take a stroll. "I got to be leaving soon, Stormy. Got to get to the feed store at seven," he said. It was one of those times when Stormy really perplexed him. Hell, he hadn't had ten minutes alone with her and she didn't seem to care.

He left a few minutes later, feeling completely confused when she smiled sweetly and said quite casually, "Oh, I don't think I want to brave the chilly air tonight, Pat. In the winter, afternoons are best for a stroll."

Pat could hardly protest with Kip there. Had they been alone, he could have assured her that his arms would keep her warm.

Kip glanced over at Marcie as Pat sat there for a few seconds, slightly stunned by her dismissal. For once, he lost his glib tongue.

Pat awkwardly said his goodbyes to Marcie and Kip, expecting Stormy to accompany him outside. He suggested she put a shawl around her shoulders.

"I won't need a shawl. I'll just say goodbye at the door, Pat," she said. She had no desire to have him kiss her again. If he didn't get the message, she thought, he was pretty thick-headed.

Kip wondered if Stormy was not feeling well. His daughter wouldn't think twice about braving the cold to be with the man she loved.

But this was not the man Stormy loved!

Forty-three

Dorsey walked out into the night but he felt no chill—he was angry and indignant about the way Stormy had treated him. It was even more embarrassing because Kip and Marcie had been there. It was the ultimate insult when she wouldn't even step out on the front porch with him.

As he walked back to Paddy's, Dorsey was wondering if he'd asked an ice maiden to be his wife. For all those sensuous looks and that tempting body, did Stormy have ice in her veins?

Dorsey was a hot-blooded man with a healthy sexual appetite—he knew he would never be content with such a woman. But Stormy had never given him that impression until just lately.

His arrogance would never have allowed him to question whether Stormy Monihan would have submitted to this bossy individual he'd become since she'd accepted his proposal.

Knowing Stormy as he did, he should have known better. Her independent nature, had been evident from the start.

So Dorsey returned to Paddy's with a badly-dented ego. Paddy had only to look at him to know he was in a foul mood. It was apparent that things had not gone well between him and his lady, so Paddy didn't ask any questions.

The way Dorsey was slamming things around as he put his jacket on the peg and yanked off his boots, Paddy knew he was blowing off steam. So he just sat there puffing on his pipe and reading the *Southport Journal*.

When he did venture out of the chair to pour himself another cup of hot chocolate, he asked Pat if he'd like one. But Pat politely refused. "I'm full of Marcie's stew," he muttered.

"Had stew, did she? Marcie makes good stew."

"Yeah, it was good. That was about the only thing that made the damned long walk over there worth it. Thought Stormy might have been a little excited about the bed and chair I bought but she sure didn't seem to be."

Paddy chuckled, "Take it from an old bachelor, Pat. An old secondhand bed and chair is not what gets a young miss all excited. Now you mention a pretty dress, a fancy ring or a string of pearls and I guarantee those green eyes would sparkle."

"Hell, Paddy, I don't have the kind of money to buy Stormy those things."

"Know you don't, but you're missing the point. I'm sure Stormy doesn't expect that from you, but then you shouldn't expect her to feel elated about a bed and a chair. That ain't the way it works with women, son." He took his cup and moved back into the front room. Knowing what he knew since he and Stormy had had their talk, he realized that Pat couldn't know that she had far more important things on her mind.

Pat said good night and went to bed, his mind still in a state of confusion.

Back at Kip's cottage, Stormy told her pa and Marcie good night shortly after Pat left. She knew that the two of them were curious, and she wasn't up to any questioning.

Once Kip heard her bedroom door close, he turned to Marcie. "What was going on here tonight? They don't act like young lovers to me."

"I don't think there will ever be a wedding between those two, Kip. For whatever reason Stormy accepted Pat's proposal, I think she regrets it. She doesn't love him."

"Then she should tell him if that's the way she's feeling."

"Perhaps she doesn't wish to hurt him, Kip. Maybe she's trying to find a way to do it. We can't judge her too harshly, dear." Marcie also wondered if Stormy was concerned because she didn't want to cause friction between her father and Dorsey, which she pointed out to Kip.

"Hell, Marcie—Stormy's happiness is the only thing that's important to me. I guess I better let her know that—and quick."

Marcie smiled, pleased to hear him say that. "Tell her, Kip. Tell her tomorrow."

"I will. I'll go ask her to go out on the *East Wind* since I've got a few little jobs to do out there. It'll give us a chance to talk."

"That's a wonderful idea, Kip. She'd like the two of you being alone."

The next morning Kip asked Stormy, "You want to help your pa do a few things out on the *East Wind,* honey?"

"Sure, Pa, but isn't it a little early?"

"Not really. Go get those old pants so you won't ruin any of your pretty dresses and we'll be on our way."

He teased her about missing seeing her in her old clothes.

She grinned, "Well, I've missed it too, Pa. I won't

be long." She rushed out of the room with the girlish enthusiasm that Marcie remembered so vividly. It had been a marvelous idea to take her out on the boat.

But Stormy had a shock when she tried to fasten the old faded pants. She couldn't make them meet at the waistline, but luckily the tunic covered that up.

She sat down at her little dressing table and put her thick hair in two long braids. When that was done, she got her old blue wool jacket from the peg, realizing that she had not worn it lately. She realized she hadn't worn any of these clothes since she'd returned home.

Meeting Jason Hamilton and living with his family had had a tremendous influence on her. More and more she was beginning to notice the changes in herself.

But for today she was returning to her old self with her faded pants and shirts, accompanying her pa down to the wharf.

She rushed down to join her father who was waiting for her. He greeted her with a warm smile. "Ready, honey?"

"I'm ready, Pa," she replied with a perky look on her face that reminded him of her when she was a little girl. For one brief moment he found himself wishing she was still a youngster. But whatever her age, Stormy had been the great joy of his life and always would be.

Marcie said goodbye and stood at the front door watching the two of them walk down the path hand in hand. She was thinking it was sort of like time standing still for she had often watched the two of them depart together like that.

Marcie had no idea how long they would be. After she'd eaten lunch, she left Kip a note and drove the buggy into town.

She made a stop at the grocery store and went by the post office. Stormy had received two letters from

England—Marcie smiled for she knew Stormy would be delighted. She had seen the disappointment on Stormy's face when she'd received no word from them week after week. It seemed to Marcie that she'd finally given up for she never mentioned it anymore.

During the morning hours Kip worked up on the deck making some simple little repairs. Stormy swept Kip's cabin of the dust that had accumulated over the last five or six weeks—then she mopped the floor. While that dried, she went down the narrow little passageway to old Paddy's galley to warm up the coffee they'd brought. Then she spread out slices of bread and ham.

When she had everything ready she went to the deck to summon her pa. Kip was more than ready for a cup of coffee. "You timed that just right, Stormy. I'm just about through. How about you?"

"Got the cabin all spic and span for you, Pa?"

"Ah, you're a good daughter, Stormy. I'll say it again—I'm about the luckiest man in the world to have a daughter like you and a wife like Marcie."

They sit down at the table after Stormy had poured the coffee. They put the slice of ham on Marcie's homemade bread and began to eat ravenously.

Kip laughed. "Reminds me of the past, honey, when you were sitting there eating like a little pig with your hair in braids. You never liked it flying around over your face, you'd tell me when you were a little tadpole. Oh, Stormy—we had ourselves good times even though it was probably not the way a little girl should have been brought up."

"Pa, I'm glad it was the way it was. I have memories that other little girls could never have. I'd take nothing for the way I was brought up by you and old Paddy. I never doubted that I was loved and loved dearly," she declared fervently.

"Thank you, Stormy. That means everything to me. You were surely loved and still are."

Kip didn't know how to approach the subject he wanted to discuss with Stormy, so he decided to just come right out and ask her. "Stormy, I get the impression that you aren't as taken with Dorsey as you must have been when you promised to marry him. For God's sake, honey, don't marry him if you don't love him!"

Kip's words were like an answer to a prayer for Stormy. They were all she needed to hear to make the decision that had been gnawing at her since before the Christmas holiday. In a moment of weakness and desperation, she'd promised to marry Pat but now she knew it was only because she faced having Jason's baby alone.

The past few weeks had proven to Stormy that it would be torment to doom herself and her unborn baby to a loveless marriage. So would she face disgrace? At least she would be free—and her baby would surely be loved.

As time had gone by, she had become more and more repulsed by Pat's arrogance—how quickly he would sink into a sulky mood if everything didn't go his way. No man was going to be her lord and master, Stormy vowed.

Her talk with Paddy had bolstered her courage and now her pa had completely convinced her to listen to her feelings.

Stormy's green eyes locked with her pa's. "Now I'm the one thanking you, Pa. I'm glad we had this time together and time to talk. I can tell you right now that my promise to Pat will have to be broken. I—I don't love him as a woman should love a man, and I can't settle for less."

Kip rose from the table and bent down to kiss the top of her head. "You just do what you have to do, honey. I'm behind you all the way. I only want what will make you happy, Stormy."

When they went back to the cottage that afternoon, Stormy was feeling happier than she had in a long, long time!

Forty-four

Marcie had only to see the two of them walking gaily up the path to know that they had had a wonderful time together. Kip and Stormy were quite a pair! They were like no other father and daughter she had ever known.

Theirs was a very special relationship—it would always be that way and Marcie understood this, so she never felt excluded. She was just grateful for the wonderful life she'd had since she married Kip.

When they entered the front door, Kip's thick mane had been blown down over his forehead by the stiff breeze. Stormy looked radiant.

"Getting chilly out there," Stormy declared as she dashed over to the fireplace and rubbed her hands together.

Kip walked over to kiss his wife. The look on his face told her all she needed to know. Kip had enjoyed his time with his daughter.

Marcie reached over on the table next to her chair and picked up the two letters. "Honey, you finally got letters from England."

Stormy's heart began to flutter erratically as she reached out to take them. She knew that Marcie must have seen how her hand was trembling. For a fleeting moment she just held them and looked down at them before she announced that she was going to her room. She wanted to be by herself when she read them.

When Stormy rushed out, Kip looked over at his wife with a big smile. "She's a happy girl, Marcie. It was so good to spend time with her today. I—I thank you from the bottom of my heart for not resenting our time together. Some women would be jealous."

Marcie smiled. "Jealous? Oh, Kip, wouldn't I be silly when you give me so much love! I couldn't be happier that you and Stormy had such a nice day together."

"You're quite a woman!" he said as he reached over to kiss her.

As they sat by the fireplace, he told Marcie how their day had gone and about his lengthy discussion with Stormy. "There will be no wedding. She doesn't love Pat, Marcie, so I wouldn't want her to marry him. I support her—I think she needed to know that."

Marcie smiled and nodded. "Pat won't take her news too graciously, Kip. You may lose him."

"So be it. The *East Wind* was running for years before Dorsey joined me," he assured her.

As soon as Stormy got to her room and flung her jacket off, she tore open the two letters. She read Lady Sheila's letter first, hoping the other letter was from Jason.

She'd written to Stormy about how lonely she and Lord Addison had been after she'd left, but it was the last two pages that Stormy read two or three times. She wrote about how devastated Jason had been when he'd returned to find that she'd left. Lady Sheila confessed that she was very concerned about Jason, who had set out for the Carolinas to find her. She also wrote that she knew how much Jason loved her for him to risk such a crossing.

At the end of the letter she stated that she prayed that Jason had arrived in Southport before her letter.

Reading Lady Sheila's letter and knowing that Jason was coming to her made her swell with happiness. *He did love her!* She lay back on her bed with a huge sigh, thanking God she hadn't allowed Dorsey to talk her into a hasty marriage.

She was trembling with excitement. More than anything, she had yearned for Jason to come to her and declare his love. But her excitement changed to anxious concern when she chanced to notice the date of Lady Sheila's letter.

She could remember how long it had taken when she returned with Captain Murdock. She also recalled how long it had taken the *Sea Princess* to sail to England. She quickly realized that Jason should have been here by now.

With this thought hanging so heavily, she couldn't enjoy Tawny's letter as she would have otherwise. But it was nice to read that she wished that they'd had more time together and that she hoped one day they'd see each other again.

It was a sweet, long letter and as Stormy folded it and put it with Lady Sheila's, she realized that a part of her had remained in England. The brief time she'd spent with Tawny had made her feel like they were old friends. Growing up, she'd never had a friend her own age to talk with. Her young life had been dominated by men like her pa, Paddy, and the boatman. Perhaps that's why she and Marcie had become such good friends.

When she finally left her bed, she had one desire: to get out of those uncomfortable, tight pants. She found it far more pleasant to slip into one of her gowns, but she noticed that the sprigged muslin was a little snugger than it used to be. As she sat at her dressing table to brush out her braids, she prayed that Jason wasn't lost at sea. Life couldn't be that cruel, she kept telling herself.

She also knew that all she could do now was wait.

Once she had changed her clothes and read her letters, she knew she should be getting into the kitchen to help Marcie. Before she left her room she picked up Lady Sheila's letter so her pa and Marcie could read it. She was filled with mixed emotions: part of her could not have been happier and part of her was deeply concerned for the man she loved.

Kip understood her feelings—he could not bring himself to lie to her so he didn't try to. "Time will tell, honey. We'll all do a lot of praying for this young man," he said as he gave her a comforting hug.

She looked up at him. "Jason's not dead or at the bottom of the sea. I'd know it, Pa. I'd feel it right here." She placed her hand over her heart.

"You just keep thinking that, Stormy," he said.

Of all nights, she had no desire to see Pat arrive now. Since the time she'd arrived back home from England, she had considered him presumptuous to hit their front door at the dinner hour. She didn't know her pa's or Marcie's feelings about that, but it had vexed her.

Marcie was always gracious and warm to Dorsey as was her pa but Stormy had to wonder what both of them were thinking privately.

Stormy didn't have to concern herself about Pat tonight—he was occupied elsewhere. Frank Holcombe had offered him the delivery wagon to get some furniture to his new house.

Pat was feeling very smug about the deal he'd made on a settee, two walnut side tables, and an overstuffed chair. That was enough to furnish the front room of his new house. Dorsey was convinced that Stormy could not complain about these furnishings—they were finer than the ones in Kip's cottage.

When he got the four pieces moved into the house, he surveyed the room. It looked fine to him. He muttered to himself, "Don't think Stormy could say that this isn't a fine looking room."

His pride was still badly bruised by her attitude. He might work for her dad but when they married, he was going to be the master of his house. Neither Stormy nor Kip would rule his home, he vowed.

He went out the front door and locked it. He was preparing to climb back up in the wagon and pull out to the dirt road when he spied a very attractive sight walking down the road carrying a heavy sack of groceries. The little lady was so petite that the sack seemed to overwhelm her. By the time he guided the wagon out to where she was walking, he recognized her as the pretty clerk from the emporium.

He called out to her, "Hello, there!"

With a surprised look, Rebecca glanced up to see the handsome Dorsey sitting in the wagon. She was so weary from lugging the heavy bag she could hardly manage a smile.

He leaped out of the wagon and asked her if she was heading for home. "You have a very long walk, much less carrying a sack like that. Here, give it to me," he insisted.

"I have no choice, Pat. I have to purchase groceries for me and my mother so one does what one has to do."

"Come on, I'll get you on home. Truth is, Rebecca— I don't have a buggy either so I usually walk wherever I go. My boss let me borrow his wagon tonight to get some furniture moved into my new house."

"Well, my goodness—we'll be neighbors. I don't live far from here," she said as he helped her up into the wagon.

Dorsey could see what she meant as he drove the

wagon a short distance, pulling up in front of a little frame house surrounded by a picket fence. Dorsey insisted on carrying the groceries into the house.

As they'd traveled she had explained that she lived with her widowed mother, who was a semi-invalid.

They entered the dimly lit front room. She guided him to the kitchen, then breezed around to light two lamps. "Excuse me just a minute, Pat, while I look in on Momma," she said.

It gave Dorsey a brief moment to look around the kitchen and see that everything was spic and span. From what he'd seen in the front room and kitchen, there was nothing fancy but it had a clean, orderly look.

When she rushed back into the kitchen, she was unbuttoning her coat. "Oh, I thank you, Pat. Please, have a seat and I'll put on a pot of coffee. That's the least I can do. Mother's asleep right now. Poor dear—she sleeps a lot. I always come in at night not knowing what I might find but I have to work so she's alone during the day. I—I can't afford to hire someone to stay with her."

Dorsey found himself sinking down into the kitchen chair just listening to her talk but all the time she was moving around the kitchen. She laid her coat on the sofa with special care and in a few seconds she had fired up the smoldering coals in her stove to start a pot of coffee.

She was intriguing to watch because she moved with such grace. Quicker than he could bat an eyelash, she had emptied the entire sack of groceries and put them away as she continued to talk with him and ask questions about himself. She wasn't a frivolous girl—she had listened to everything he'd told her. He got the impression that Rebecca didn't waste time—she had to make every moment count. When the coffee was ready, she poured two cups and sat down with him.

Her lovely blue eyes looked at him as she smiled. "You're welcome to share our dinner, Pat. Nothing fancy—just a home-cooked meal if that would interest you."

He muttered a weak protest, which she quickly shrugged aside. Pat laughed, "Well, being a bachelor it's hard to turn down a good meal. But you must promise to let me help with the dishes."

"We'll see," she laughed as she rose from the chair and prepared to set the table. She did accept his offer to put another log in the fireplace.

It amazed him how fast she moved. She was quicker than Marcie, who was the only woman he'd ever watched move around her kitchen.

When she had her pot of creamy potato soup simmering, she brought out a loaf of fresh-baked bread and a peach pie she'd baked the night before. She explained that she baked at night because she got in too late to prepare anything elaborate for dinner.

An hour later, Dorsey was enjoying the tastiest potato soup he'd ever eaten. Then Rebecca served him a generous piece of her juicy peach pie as she set up a tray for her mother, who wasn't feeling strong enough to come to the table.

Dorsey sat eating the pie and thinking what a remarkable young lady Rebecca was. Only after she had tended to her mother did she sit down long enough to have her pie and another cup of coffee.

As he'd insisted if he stayed for dinner, he helped her with the dishes before he left. When he told her good night, he thanked her for a lovely evening.

She smiled. "It will be nice to have you for a neighbor, Pat. You must come again."

Rebecca didn't realize how much she had soothed Pat's shattered ego. She'd seemed to welcome and enjoy his company, as tired as he knew she must have been, and that had impressed him.

As he traveled toward home, he knew old Paddy would be wondering why he was so late. But Pat didn't figure he had to explain to Paddy where or how he spent his time.

Pat was asking himself a lot of questions. He'd spent time with a pretty young lady tonight who welcomed his attention, which Stormy certainly hadn't done lately. He could not deny he was attracted to Rebecca Branson, so maybe he wasn't ready to be married after all.

He wasn't dependent on Kip for wages since he had money coming from Frank Holcombe. By the time he pulled the flatbed wagon up in front of Paddy's, he realized he didn't have to wait for a wedding to move into his new house. The house was his and he could move in any time he wanted to.

He was thinking he'd like to be over there instead of at Paddy's. By the time Pat neared the house, he had made a decision: he wasn't waiting to move over there.

He was hoping Paddy would not be sitting in the front room when he came in the door. Chances were he wouldn't be that lucky.

Forty-five

As Pat expected, the old man was sitting by the hearth puffing on his pipe. His first question was to ask Pat if he'd had a nice evening at Kip's.

"As a matter of fact, I was not over at Kip's tonight, Paddy. I bought some furniture today so I was hauling it to my house in Frank's wagon." Pat considered that was enough to tell the old fellow.

"You're going to have that place all furnished before too long, aren't you son?"

"Yes sir—sure am," Pat said as he took off his jacket and hung it on the peg.

Paddy didn't think anything about Pat not lingering too long with him. He figured he was tired after lugging sacks all day at the feed store and all the furniture moving after work.

Pat just thought it was best that he and Paddy not get to talking too much tonight—he knew how that old man could ask questions. He didn't feel like being quizzed.

A lot of things were prodding at Pat. Since the time he had started working for Frank Holcombe he had begun to realize that he could make as much working for him as he could for Monihan. But marrying Kip's daughter meant there was no question about it—once spring arrived, he would have to quit his job at the feed store and start back working on the *East Wind*.

But Pat had also began to realize that Frank liked
him and his future might lay in the feed store instead
of on the *East Wind*. Pat knew he would have to make
a decision soon, for spring would be coming in about
three months.

He figured he would know by that time how it was
going to work out for him and Stormy. There was no
question that Stormy Monihan was still the most exciting woman he'd ever met. She'd affected him as no
other woman ever had. But he was a very possessive
man and he wanted a woman who would give herself
to him completely. He was wondering lately if Stormy
would be able to do that.

Pat didn't want to settle for less!

And he didn't intend to settle for less now that he'd
spent an evening with the pretty little Rebecca Brunson.

Stormy shared the news from England with her father
and Marcie. She immediately saw the look on Kip's
face when he'd asked her when the letter had been written.

"He's been gone quite awhile, Stormy. That fine
schooner should have made it here by now, honey.
They're known to make rather good time."

"I know, Pa, and that's what's got me so worried. I
fear he's met with foul weather, because I remember
what Captain Murdock told me when we were crossing.
He said that would be his last trip until spring."

Kip had to agree with Murdock's decision—he would
have felt the same way. This young Captain Hamilton
had to be a most daring devil to venture out on the
Atlantic at this time of the year or even weeks ago, as
he'd obviously done from what his mother had written
to Stormy. If he loved Stormy enough to do such a
foolhardy thing, then Kip could only pray that he had

not met up with bad weather. He hesitated to express his thoughts to Stormy. Yet, he didn't want her living with false hope.

If the young man left England when his mother said he had, then he should have arrived over two weeks ago. Once the young Englishman started out from England he had to keep going—there was no port in which to take refuge until he reached the east coast of the States. He was at the mercy of the Atlantic in winter.

Kip had only to look at his daughter's face to know how concerned she was. Now he understood so many things. Being allowed to read Lady Sheila's letter, he had to conclude that she approved of her son's love for Stormy. She was just concerned about his safe arrival here in the Carolinas. It was a sweet, warm letter—now he understood why Stormy felt so sad about leaving England. Living that many weeks with these fine people, their ways had started to become Stormy's ways. That's why she seemed so different to him and Marcie when she'd first returned.

Kip was glad his daughter had had the experience of living with this English family. It had been a grand experience that few girls like Stormy ever know. His young daughter had actually seen Buckingham Palace, where the King and Queen of England reside. It was a time in her young life that she'd never forget.

And he could understand now why Stormy enjoyed the lifestyle of this English family so much. How could he fault her for loving the beautiful surroundings of the country estate, as well as the lord and lady residing there. Apparently, his little daughter had quickly adjusted to their way of life and they'd just as quickly come to love her.

But when he and Marcie were in the privacy of their bedroom, he confessed, "I fear the young man will never arrive, Marcie. God, I pray some miracle brings

him safely here. Otherwise, I think my daughter will
have a broken heart."

Kip's sentiments were hers as well.

Stormy knew her pa was trying to spare her the harsh
truth about what he was actually thinking. Once alone
in her room, she'd checked off the number of weeks on
the calendar since Jason had left England.

The thought of him and his sleek schooner lying on
the bottom of the ocean left her devastated. Her lovely
face reflected her sleepless night when she walked into
the kitchen the next morning.

Marcie had only to look at Stormy to ask her,
"Honey, are you ill? You look like you feel terrible."

She didn't try to hide the truth. "I do feel terrible,
Marcie, but it's not that I'm ill. I'm so worried about
Jason that I couldn't sleep last night. I—I just know
he's dead."

Marcie dropped her dish cloth and rushed over to
her. Her arms went around Stormy but her soft voice
was firm. "Don't say that, Stormy—don't even think it.
That's not like you to give up so easily, Stormy Monihan. I'll not listen to such talk."

All Stormy could manage was, "Oh, Marcie." Tears
began to flow so Marcie just held her and let her cry.

When the sobbing ceased, Stormy looked up. "Oh,
Marcie, now that I know he was coming to me, I know
he loves me as I hoped. I—I just don't know what I'll
do if he's dead. It was always Jason, Marcie, and it
always will be. I know that now. I never loved Pat. I
just tried to convince myself I did."

"I know that, honey. Thank God you know that before a wedding took place, Stormy," Marcie declared.

"I must tell Pat the next time he comes over, Marcie.
There's no reason to delay," Stormy declared.

"The sooner the better, Stormy," Marcie agreed.

Stormy nodded. It was not the time she'd planned to tell Marcie her secret, but she impulsively blurted, "I'm carrying Jason's child, Marcie. I've known since Christmas."

Marcie was momentarily stunned by Stormy's confession but she quickly recovered. "Oh, sweetie—one wee babe isn't the end of the world. Your pa and I will be there to support you and your baby. Everything will be just fine. But all the more reason why you must tell Pat that your wedding is off."

"Oh, Marcie—Marcie, what would I do without you? I hadn't planned to tell you just yet but somehow, it just came out. Pa doesn't know yet. I—I'll tell him in a day or two," Stormy promised.

"If that's what you want, Stormy, but this is too much for you to carry alone—I'm glad I know. I won't say anything to Kip if you don't want me to. I'll wait for you to decide that."

"Thank you, Marcie. I know I have to before long. God, I'm already expanding so much I could hardly wear my old pants. My gowns are pinching me, too, so I must tell him soon."

"It will be all right, Stormy. Kip is a most understanding man—I don't have to tell you that. You've never had any reason to doubt that he worships you," Marcie pointed out.

"I'm the luckiest girl in the world to have Kip Monihan for a father—I've always known that, Marcie."

As it had been after she'd had her talk with Paddy, a great release swept over her now that she'd told Marcie.

Marcie laughed softly. "Oh, Stormy, I guess we both feel the same way about that man. I've also felt I was the luckiest lady in the world that he asked me to be his wife. Kip changed my whole life around. Can I make a confession?"

"You know you can, Marcie. Lord, after all I've told you, I think you could tell me just about anything," Stormy declared with a smile.

"Well, Tom was my first beau and I was very young when we married. I truly thought I loved him and I was a most devoted wife all the time we were married. He was a good husband and a kind man. When Kip came to tell me about what happened to him, I was devastated. Loving another man at that point in my life was the last thing on my mind."

Marcie rose to get the coffeepot and then sat back down. "Because we've always been so close I feel free to speak so frankly, dear. Perhaps it's why I can understand how you feel about your Jason Hamilton. Kip brought something into my life that I'd never known, even after all the years I'd been married to Tom. Kip made me feel so completely fulfilled as a woman that I knew I'd never truly loved until he taught me its true meaning. Oh, Stormy, he's made me so very happy!"

"Oh, Marcie, I'm so glad we've had this talk," Stormy declared. Her tears had dried and she sipped her coffee, feeling relaxed and contented.

Neither of them was aware that Kip had been about to join them when he'd been privy to Marcie's words of endearment. He decided that this was the kind of mother-daughter interlude that he shouldn't interrupt. But his broad chest swelled with delight as he listened to his pretty wife speak so glowingly about him.

He moved quickly backwards and went out the front door, then he walked down the little pathway and through the gate. From there he made his way through the woods to the wharf. He looked out over the water, thinking what he would give to see the sight of that slick-lined schooner. He knew that would make his little Stormy so happy—but there was no boats in sight.

At least there was a clear blue sky, but he feared

Stormy's young man had battled some fierce storms in the last weeks that could have overwhelmed him regardless of how skilled a sea captain he was.

It wasn't hard for Kip to understand why Pat Dorsey would have seemed colorless to Stormy after the dashing Jason Hamilton. He had become her hero following her traumatic experience with Jed Callihan.

All those weeks in England with Jason and the Hamilton family had given a new dimension to Stormy's life that Kip's honest nature made him admit that he could not have given her. He was glad she'd had that opportunity.

Kip had changed his opinion about the Hamiltons after Stormy allowed him to read the letter. He felt he could sit and talk with this lady, and feel relaxed. There was no hint of the snobbish lady he might have expected.

He was thinking that he'd like to meet her to express his gratitude for her generosity to his daughter. Knowing instinctively how she must love her only son, Kip could understand her concern. He could well recall the many days and nights when he didn't know if his daughter was alive or dead.

Some might not have considered Kip Monihan a religious man but they didn't know how many prayers he'd said for his Stormy. And they'd been answered!

Now Lady Sheila's son needed his prayers, and he'd get them!

Forty-six

It was a rather strained evening at the Monihan cottage that evening when Pat Dorsey appeared. He had had apprehensions about how Stormy would greet him after their last encounter—he had truly been reluctant to go over there. But it had been almost a week since he had called on the Monihans, so he felt he should make an appearance.

The last week had been a taxing one for Dorsey—he was in a state of confusion. He owed Kip a degree of loyalty, he'd asked his daughter to marry him, and he was still living under the roof of Kip's old friend.

For once in his life, Dorsey wasn't so sure of himself. As it would happen, Stormy greeted him at the door. Ironically she was feeling grateful that she didn't have to delay telling him any longer.

As it was usual after the meal was over, Stormy and Marcie remained in the kitchen to wash the dishes while Kip and Dorsey went into the front room to enjoy a smoke.

As soon as they finished the dishes, Stormy and Marcie went into the front room to join Kip and Dorsey.

It took Dorsey by surprise when Stormy asked him, "Pat, want to take a stroll?" He saw that certain look on her face that had first intrigued him. She was a most complex young lady but that was what had been so refreshing.

"Sure, if you're willing, Stormy," he responded immediately.

"I'll get my cape," she said as she went out of the room. In a few minutes she returned with the green cape draped around her shoulders. "Shall we go?" she asked.

Marcie knew what she was going to do and Kip suspected that was why she'd invited Pat to take a stroll. He and Marcie watched the young couple leave but neither of them expected them to be gone long.

It wasn't a half-hour before Stormy returned alone. She had seen no reason to prolong the agony for either of them. It was a chilly January night and even with her cape around her, Stormy felt the chill.

She told Pat she had a reason for asking him to take the walk. "I can't marry you, Pat. I don't love you. I'm— I'm no good at playing games. I respect you too much to go through with a loveless marriage—it wouldn't be fair to either of us."

Pat was speechless, even though he knew things had not been going smoothly between him and Stormy. But he hardly expected this. His ego was wounded—he felt like he'd been stabbed in the gut. In a sharp, snapping tone he finally uttered, "So you've suddenly decided that you don't love me, eh Stormy?"

"No, Pat—it was not sudden. I've thought about it for the last few weeks. I take a promise most seriously; all I can say is that when I said I wanted to marry you I must have thought I did. But I became convinced I didn't love you—as a woman should love the man she's to marry—the last few times we've been together." She was aware that Dorsey wasn't taking the news too graciously.

"Well, I guess there's nothing more to say, Stormy. Too bad you didn't let me know this before I went and bought that house," he declared indignantly.

A sly smile crossed Stormy's face—she had no guilt about that. "Remember, Pat—I wasn't consulted about your plans as a bride-to-be should have been. One day, you'll find a young lady to share the house with you and until that time, it will be perfect for you."

Pat found himself becoming more riled by the minute. They had not strayed far from Kip's cottage. He turned sharply. "I'll let you see yourself back to the cottage. I'm on my way."

Stormy turned back to the cottage without saying good night to him. More than ever, she knew why she was not in love with Pat. When she reached the front steps she sat in the dark alone for a moment before facing her pa and Marcie.

But she didn't mind facing them and telling them that Pat had been told. She had hoped he would have been more the gentleman. She wondered if he wouldn't work for her pa any longer. She also wondered if he was the man her pa thought him to be.

All she knew was she was glad the evening was over and she was free of him. Maybe now dear Marcie wouldn't have him as her dinner guest so constantly.

Pat kicked at the ground as he walked along in the woods. For the first time, he admitted to himself privately that Stormy had to be enamored of that English sea captain. He had just been someone to pass the long winter months with until her Englishman arrived. The closer he got to Paddy's, the more convinced he was that Stormy Monihan was not the adorable little angel old Paddy considered her to be. She was a conniving little minx!

Knowing how doggedly devoted Paddy was to the Monihan family, Pat also made another decision by the time he reached the front steps. He figured he'd move on over to his little place. But he wasn't going to say anything to Paddy about it yet.

He wasn't in any mood to say anything to Paddy about Stormy calling off their marriage, either. He entered the front door and greeted Paddy, who was sitting in his favorite chair, puffing on his pipe.

He should have known that Paddy would ask about Kip—Dorsey gave him a brief reply that the Monihans were just fine. He didn't linger any longer than it took him to get out of his jacket and hang it on a peg. "Good night, Paddy. Got to get up early to make a delivery for Mister Holcombe," he lied.

He did plan to be up early but not because he had to make a delivery. He planned to stop by the general store before he went to work so he could purchase what he called a "batching outfit." He wouldn't need much to get by for a while. A pot and a skillet, a tea kettle, a few pieces of silverware and dishes and he'd be fine. By the time he left the store he'd made all these purchases, along with a couple of blankets.

Frank saw him come in with his arms filled with purchases and teased him, "Been out spending all your money?"

"Anxious to get settled in at my new place. Thought I'd get moved on in, Mister Holcombe, so I could start getting some things done."

"You've got a lot of things to tote home tonight, young fellow. Take the wagon again, Pat," Holcombe offered. He turned to his office but turned around to ask Dorsey, "You got yourself any wood hauled in over there yet, son?"

"No sir, I haven't," Pat said. He was beginning to realize he had a lot to learn about owning a place.

Holcombe told him to help himself to enough wood to get by until he could get his own supply.

Dorsey worked very hard for Frank Holcombe that day, telling himself once again that he should think seriously about staying there instead of going back on the *East Wind*.

He also took advantage of having the wagon. He stocked up on groceries and loaded enough logs to last for a few days. He hadn't given any thought to the fact that he was going to need wood to warm his house and cook his meals.

By the time he'd unloaded the wood and put his groceries away, Pat was thinking he might just move in tomorrow night. He didn't need a wagon to move his belongings from Paddy's.

However, when he was unpacking the dishes, skillet, and tea kettle, Dorsey realized he'd forgotten some necessary items like a dishpan and a water bucket. He also needed towels, wash cloths, and a bar of soap. Dear God, he had no inkling of what a man had to have when he lived in his own place!

Paddy knew something was gnawing at Dorsey when he came in from Kip's and his curiosity was whetted even more when the young man was two hours later than usual in coming home. He'd kept the pot of beef stew warm, adding kindling to the cookstove, but he had the feeling that Pat wouldn't be with him much longer.

He scrutinized the young man carefully. "Had a busy day today, Pat?"

"I did, Paddy—a lot of deliveries. Holcombe has a very prosperous store," Pat remarked as he took his jacket off

"Well, you'll find the stew still warm, Pat. Had mine quite awhile ago," Paddy said.

"Sounds good to me. I'm starved!" So he didn't hesitate to devour not one but two bowls.

He decided he would tell Paddy about him and

Stormy. He saw no reason not to. After all, sooner or later, he had to know. Pat figured that tomorrow night would be his last night at Paddy's.

After the two of them had talked for a while, Pat made his announcement. He expected a surprised reaction from Paddy but he hardly batted an eyelash. It was as if the old cook already knew. His only comment was, "It's your life, Pat. Better the decision be made before the marriage than afterwards."

"You're sure right about that, Paddy. So seeing that there is to be no wedding, I've no reason to delay moving into my house. I don't have to have it as fancy as Stormy would have wanted it."

"I understand, Pat. I'd probably feel the same way," Paddy said.

Later when Pat was lying in bed, he questioned Paddy's calm reaction to both of his announcements. Knowing how close Stormy and Paddy were, he didn't doubt for a minute that she'd already told him that she intended to call off the marriage.

The look on Stormy's face when she came into the front room and flung off her cape told Marcie and Kip that she had broken her engagement.

"Well, I told him. I—I trust I haven't lost you a good man, Pa, come springtime. He didn't take it too graciously, shall I say," she added.

"Don't worry about me, Stormy. I've got a lot of good men. Pat is a good boatman but if he leaves I'll just hire someone to take his place. You did what you had to do," Kip said as she sat down beside him.

Marcie thought it was the right moment to go make all of them some hot chocolate. She saw Kip put his strong, reassuring arm around his daughter. She knew how much that had to mean to Stormy, who was carrying such a heavy burden right now.

Never did she doubt for a minute that Kip would give her all his love and support when he was told about the baby, even if she was forced to have it without a father or a husband.

Forty-seven

The end of January was the coldest time of the year in the Carolinas, but it didn't seem that way this afternoon to Stormy as she set up the buggy to go to town. Kip was going with her to visit Paddy while she did some shopping for Marcie.

Stormy let him off and proceeded to the mercantile store to pick up some thread and various articles Marcie needed. She and Stormy had been working the last week to let out all those gowns Stormy had brought back from England. It was amazing that Kip hadn't detected any change in his daughter's figure.

Stormy did her shopping in a leisurely way to give Kip enough time for a nice visit with Paddy. She browsed around the store for a while before she finally paid for her purchases and started for her buggy.

She suddenly saw a familiar figure rushing up the street toward an attractive lady about her age with the same shade of golden hair. Pat Dorsey greeted her warmly, planting a kiss on her lips. The girl seemed as enamored with him as he was with her.

Stormy stopped for a minute, wondering if she should go the other way—but why should she? They were no longer betrothed, so she kept walking in the direction of her buggy.

Stormy was amused as she got closer and closer. Pat had wasted no time finding himself another lady. More than ever, she knew she had been wise not to marry Dorsey.

By the time she passed by them, they were completely engrossed in each other. Then Pat caught sight of her and stared directly at Stormy. There was a devious twinkle in her green eyes as she greeted him, "Afternoon, Dorsey."

She didn't stop to hear his stammering reply as she sashayed on to her buggy. But Rebecca Brunson had taken very definite notice of the striking young lady. She asked Pat Dorsey who she was. Rebecca knew that pretty lady was no casual acquaintance!

Pat spent the rest of the evening trying to explain who Stormy Monihan was and how well he'd known her. By the time he said good night he was not so sure he'd convinced Rebecca it was all over between him and Stormy.

Rebecca's kiss was cool—she wasn't sure Pat was being completely honest with her. In fact, she was having second thoughts about a lot of things about Pat. He was a handsome Irish rogue and Rebecca was asking herself if she'd been blinded by his charm.

He had become a distraction—she was not getting her chores done in the evenings. After he'd left, she'd been staying up a couple of hours later to get things done, but it was telling on her the next morning.

The next afternoon, when Pat walked home with her, she told him she couldn't invite him to stay for dinner. "I've got to get caught up on a few things," she said politely.

"Hey, I'll help you, Rebecca," he offered.

"No, Pat," she smiled. "You distract me."

"Then I'll see you tomorrow night."

She laughed. "Pat, I've got two full nights of work to do. I might as well be honest with you. My evenings aren't free to do as I wish. One or two a week is all I can possibly spare."

Pat left, accepting her terms. But he figured she was still slightly miffed about the Stormy incident. It never dawned on him that he had eaten there nightly for the last week and poor Rebecca had been forced to buy extra groceries which she really couldn't afford.

As she was fixing dinner just for her mother and herself, Rebecca was certainly made aware of it. She was doing a lot of thinking. Dorsey hadn't brought her a bottle of toilet water as he had this Stormy Monihan—nor had he given her a bouquet of flowers or a tin of chocolates.

She also noticed that her mother was sitting in the front room after dinner instead of going directly back to her room. Rebecca was delighted to see that she was feeling much better and remarked about it.

"Well, honey, I can hardly sit out here in my nightgown when there's a young man in the house, so I have been going back to my room. Heavens, when it's just you and me I can even come to the kitchen table in my nightgown," she added with a smile.

"Oh, mother—I'm sorry. Pat has been making a pest of himself," Rebecca said.

"No, honey—I've been happy that you've had a little company lately. Believe me, Rebecca, I know you have had very little fun in your young life. But I guess I have been asking myself whether this young man has been asking too much of you by having supper here every night."

"Well, you're absolutely right, Mother. By inviting himself to eat here every night, Dorsey has made my weekly grocery money fall short. I can't allow that to continue," Rebecca assured her.

Mary Lou Branson was glad to hear her daughter talk so wisely but then she'd always had a level head on her young shoulders. When she'd finished the cup of tea Rebecca had served her before she started to wash up the dishes, she was ready to get back to her bedroom. But it had been nice for her and Rebecca to have some time together without that young man under foot.

Pat went home in a disgruntled mood because for the first time in eight nights he had to prepare his own dinner. All the time he puttered around the kitchen, he cussed and blamed Stormy. He could see why Rebecca had been jealous as this feisty little green-eyed girl sashayed by and greeted him with that teasing glint in her eyes. Damn that little vixen!

He was still thinking that when he sat down to his meager meal. If it hadn't been for Stormy, he could have been over at Rebecca's eating one of her delicious dinners.

The cocky Dorsey figured she might pout tonight and tomorrow night but she'd welcome his company after that. He was convinced he was the first beau Rebecca had had for a long time. She'd be eager for him to come over again in a night or two.

But Pat was to have a rude surprise the next afternoon when he met Rebecca—she was still not ready to invite him in for dinner.

She said she wanted some time without Pat around in the evenings. She also wanted to get her pantry supplied with some extras.

She also felt she had to be more considerate of her mother's freedom to roam around the house when she felt like it. So she told Pat a little white lie. "I can't have company for the next few nights, Pat. Mother hasn't been feeling too well the last day or two."

"Well, damn, Rebecca—are you telling me I can't come over for a few nights?" he asked.

"I'm afraid I am, Pat. But right now it doesn't matter what you or I want. I must consider my mother's best interest," she said, watching the expression on his face. What she saw didn't impress her.

She saw a man who was selfish and self-centered. Whatever she'd first found so exciting about him was suddenly swept away.

A young lady like Rebecca who was so completely unselfish had little patience with a man like Dorsey. When she walked away from him that afternoon, she knew there was no future for them.

She could have told Dorsey that afternoon that he had no reason to blame Stormy for her coolness. He had only himself to blame!

With the help of Mick Murdock, Jason had recruited a crew. As Mick pointed out, "You don't have to have the best just to get you from here to Southport. You aren't making a crossing until spring, so you'll have time before then to pick and choose your men."

"That's what I figure, sir."

"Well, me and Sue are going to hold you to that promise to bring your bride to see us before you leave for England," Murdock reminded him.

"Oh, I promise you that, captain. I just wish I could be as sure as you seem to be that Stormy will say yes. Absence doesn't make the heart grow fonder. She wasn't too happy about me leaving her to make that run to Ireland. I wanted to make all that money so I could offer her marriage."

Mick laughed, "If that little imp had known that, I would probably never have got her to come with me, Jason."

"Well, Captain Murdock—my father is a wealthy man but I'm not. I may never be wealthy but if I am

I want to do it on my own. I don't want to live off my family's wealth."

"I admire you for that, young man," Murdock said.

The crew was a few hands short when Jason prepared to leave for Southport but the weather was calm—Jason planned to travel close to the coastline.

Tobias could not have been happier to be back aboard the *Sea Princess* and puttering around his galley. This galley was his home, the crew his family.

Jason knew that his old comrades like Tobias, Dewey, and Rudy were excited about being aboard and beginning to plow through the waters of the Georgia coastline.

They'd left Savannah in the late afternoon and it seemed like old times for Dewey to come to his cabin and make his report. "A full moon and a nice, gentle breeze out there. Smooth sailing tonight, sir," Dewey said with a smile.

Later, Dewey shared the evening meal with his captain. They proposed several toasts as they dined together. In a serious tone, Jason remarked, "It was an experience, wasn't it, Dewey?"

"One I'll never forget," Dewey replied.

"I promise you, Dewey—I'll never be this reckless again. We won't return to England until there are signs of spring."

"That sounds good to me, captain. Who knows, by that time I might just find myself a pretty Carolina girl like you did," Dewey jested.

As Dewey left Jason's cabin, he said, "I'll see you around midnight, sir."

At the midnight hour, Dewey reported that they had a far better crew than they'd had during the crossing.

"We're traveling at a nice, fast pace. I think we're going to be in Southport sooner than you'd expected."

"Can't be too soon for me, Dewey," he responded.

By dark the next afternoon, the schooner had reached Santee Point and was ready to enter Long Bay. Jason sauntered across the deck and gave orders to Dewey that the *Sea Princess* would stay there for the night. His short crew had been on duty over ten hours and they deserved a rest so he curbed his impatience to get to Southport.

Dewey realized that Jason Hamilton was a far wiser sea captain than he'd been before that ill-fated night back in December. Now he knew he wasn't invincible. That storm had conquered him.

Dewey knew he'd stared death straight in the eyes. He didn't like the feeling at all and realized that he had a lot of living to do yet. As he'd seen the changes in Jason Hamilton, Dewey realized he was going to quit frittering away his time in port cities with pretty girls just to pass the time.

He wanted to find himself a pretty girl he could fall in love with as his captain had. He wanted to get married and be a father before he died. Hell, the years had been going by more swiftly than he'd realized. He was almost thirty-five years old.

Jason wasn't the only one that storm had made an impact on, Dewey had to admit.

Tobias and Rudy shared the same feelings—all of their lives would be forever changed.

Forty-eight

For the first two weeks after Dorsey had moved, he'd been so occupied with his job and courting Rebecca Branson that he'd given no thought to Paddy. But since he was no longer free to go to Rebecca's and he was weary of eating his own cooking, he decided to walk over to Paddy's after work. A pot of his beef stew or potato soup would sure taste mighty fine. But Pat didn't find Paddy at home. The house was dark, so he turned and started to walk home.

As he made the long walk, he was thinking that his luck had surely run out. The idea of going home to eat fried eggs and ham again tonight left him in a foul mood.

Ironically, Dorsey had missed Paddy by only a few minutes. By the time he'd walked around the bend in the road and out of sight, Kip was driving Paddy home. Marcie had baked a fat hen with all the trimmings so Kip had brought Paddy over for dinner.

When they were traveling back, Kip asked Paddy when Pat had left, and Paddy told him. There was a hint of disappointment reflecting in Paddy's voice when he said, "Thought he might drop by every now and then to visit me but he hasn't." With a weak smile, Paddy added, "Well, you know what they say—out of sight, out of mind. Guess that's what happened to Pat."

Kip made no comment but he felt Paddy was feeling

a little disillusioned about the young man he'd befriended for so many months.

Kip was beginning to wonder if he had given Pat
Dorsey a higher rating than he deserved. It wouldn't
surprise him if Pat didn't join him on the *East Wind*
when spring came in eight weeks. But that wouldn't
disturb him as much as losing his old galley cook; he
knew that Paddy's health would have to improve in eight
weeks or he wouldn't be able to make the runs.

Paddy could barely cook a little for himself, so he
hardly had the energy to cook for a crew.

When Kip returned home and he and Marcie were
sitting alone in the front room, she mentioned her concern for Paddy. "I can't believe how much he's failed
in the last three months. We must look in on him more
now that Dorsey is gone," she said.

"I've already decided that, honey. Love that old man.
He helped me raise Stormy—I'll help him any way I
can. It isn't that far from his house to ours."

After Kip had taken him home, Paddy felt warmed
by the pleasant evening with Kip, Marcie, and Stormy.
As usual, Marcie had served a magnificent meal. Kip
Monihan was the luckiest man in the world to have such
a lovely wife and daughter. If he had ever envied any
man, it would have been his old friend.

Talking about Dorsey with Kip turned his thoughts
to the young man. He wondered if he'd been a sentimental old fool to have given Pat the heirloom watch
at Christmas. Perhaps he had been too generous with
Pat all along. The more he thought about it, the more
he felt that Pat should have contributed something to
his lodging and meals long before he did. That young
man was a hearty eater and he'd cost Paddy a lot of
extra money.

He asked himself another question: was Pat a taker
from people who befriended him? He'd constantly ac-

ocpted Kip's and Marcie's hospitality, eating over there all the time. The truth be told, Pat had given far less than he'd received from all of them.

Maybe Stormy had seen this side of him, even though she'd promised to marry him just before Christmas. He had no doubt that finding herself pregnant had urged her to accept Pat's proposal for he knew what a prideful young lady she was. The last thing she would want to do was bring shame to her pa.

But he also knew Stormy well enough to know she was desperate when she'd confessed to him that she loved another man and carried his child. That was why he'd advised her not to marry Dorsey even though she was pregnant.

He knew he and Marcie would stand by her and he certainly knew he would. Better the baby have no father and Stormy no husband than for her to endure a loveless marriage.

Jason was greeted by a glorious morning—before this day was over he would be in Southport. Kip Monihan greeted the same morning—after he and Marcie had breakfast, he went for a stroll in the woods. It was just not a day to linger in the house.

For an hour, he roamed around the wooded area near his cottage. When he was returning, he saw his daughter going down the path leading to his wharf. Each day she went out to see if she could see Jason's schooner anywhere in the distance. His heart went out to her when she always returned to the cottage, a desolate look on her pretty face.

It was the one time Kip couldn't comfort his daughter and he knew it, so he said nothing.

It was midday before she finally left the wharf—he thought she might want to go to town with him and

Marcie, but she said, "I think I'll just stay here, Pa. I'm—I'm going to write Lady Sheila. I've waited long enough to answer her letter. Oh, Pa, it's the last week of January. Jason should have arrived almost a month ago." The agony in her eyes was enough to tear at Kip's heart—he could only give her an understanding nod and a warm embrace.

When he and Marcie left for town, Stormy sat in the chair by the fireplace to write to Lady Sheila. It was a painful letter to write and it would certainly be a painful letter for the dear lady to read.

Stormy was writing and stopping to wipe her tears by the time she began the second page. On the first page she'd described the wonderful reunion she'd had with her family and the happy holiday they'd shared. It was when she started to write the second page that the mist came to her eyes.

Had Stormy been standing out on her pa's wharf about an hour later, she would have seen the magnificent schooner plowing through the water toward Southport. Jason knew he would have to go to Southport to get directions to Cape Fear.

Jason left Dewey in charge of the *Sea Princess* when he arrived at the small wharf which he hoped was Kip Monihan's place.

In long, striding steps, he walked up the pathway to a cottage. His chest was pounding with wild anticipation as he mounted the steps to the front porch. Stormy heard footsteps and sighed as she put aside the pad and pen. She figured it had to be Dorsey. He was the last person in the world she wanted to see.

She was in no hurry to answer the rapping and brushed away the dampness on her cheek—it seemed she could only write a sentence or two without starting to cry again.

Then she opened the door and saw her handsome Jason standing there! She gasped and flung herself into his arms. With his one good arm he held her tightly as he whispered over and over, "Oh, Princess—is it really you?"

"Oh, Jason—I thought you'd never get here," she sobbed, but these were tears of joy. He was holding her so close that Stormy was not aware that one arm remained idle.

After he'd kissed her several times she smiled and took his hand to lead him into the house. It was only then that she noticed Jason's arm was in a sling and his wool jacket was just flung over that shoulder. She asked him what had happened.

"I'll tell you all about that later, love. Come here—I only need one arm to hold you anyway," he said as he led her over to the settee and pulled her down on his lap.

Her long lashes fluttered as she asked him, "Oh, Jason—I'm not dreaming, am I? We're really together?"

"You're not dreaming. I'm here and I'm not leaving until I can take you with me as my bride, Stormy. I've waited a long time to propose to you, Stormy Monihan. I intended to just as soon as I got back from Ireland."

Nothing he could have said would have made her happier. She put her hands on either side of his face. "Nothing else matters now."

She was very careful of his arm and kept wiggling around to be sure she wasn't leaning against it. "Jason, you know my curious nature. I must know what happened to your arm."

So he told her about the storm and how they ended up in Savannah. "I would have been here over a month ago but the *Sea Princess* was damaged and I lost all my crew. By the time we were rescued there were only five of us left."

She was glad to hear that old Tobias and Rudy had been spared, as well as Dewey.

She told him she had been writing a letter to his mother. "Jason—I couldn't write for crying. I don't think I would have wanted to live if you had been swept down to the bottom of the sea. Seeing the date of the letter your mother had written, I feared something had surely happened to you. I remembered the crossing I made with you and I also knew how long it took when Captain Murdock brought me home."

"I'm a much smarter captain now, Stormy. We won't make our crossing until spring arrives. I know I acted recklessly but I wanted so desperately to get to you," he said. The look in his eyes was so warm when he told her he wanted them to be married as soon as possible. "I hope your family won't object."

"Nothing could stop me from marrying you, Jason," she firmly declared.

His arm brought her close to him and he murmured in her ear, "Oh, Princess—I've learned that time is too precious to waste. My arms have ached to hold you for so long." His hungry lips took hers once again.

Neither of them was aware that Kip and Marcie had entered. Marcie was the first to spy Stormy and her handsome young man, lost in their own private world.

Marcie smiled and motioned to Kip to look. She whispered, "It's him, Kip. It's Jason Hamilton. Oh, thank God!"

So they quietly slipped back into the kitchen to give the young lovers a few more moments of privacy.

Forty-nine

Stormy got a fleeting glance of Marcie so she gently nudged Jason. "My folks are home, Jason." He lifted her off his lap and stood up to greet Marcie and Kip as they entered the room.

Kip stepped forward to shake his hand. "I don't think Stormy has to introduce us, young man. You can only be Jason Hamilton."

"Yes, sir—I am." Jason was as tall as Kip so they looked each other in the eye. Kip could see why his daughter was so smitten with the fine-looking young man.

"Jason, this is my wife, Marcie. All three of us have been anxiously awaiting your arrival after Stormy got your mother's letter," Kip said.

"I was just as anxious, Mister Monihan. But as I told Stormy, I was delayed for over a month in Savannah," Jason said as Kip urged him to have a seat.

Jason told Kip and Marcie what he had yet to tell Stormy—how Captain Murdock and his buddy Captain Brunson had rescued him and his crew.

"I'll tell you, Mister Monihan, I'm very beholden to those two. Captain Brunson took in two of my men and Captain Murdock, your friend, took me and two of my other men. His family nursed us back to health," he informed all of them.

"Murdock is a fine man. That's why I trusted him to bring my daughter home safely."

Jason grinned and looked over at Stormy. "Captain Murdock and I got a few laughs about the irony of everything that happened this last year."

"Well, I think this calls for a good shot or two of my Irish whiskey. What would you say to that, Jason?" Kip grinned.

"I'd say that sounds like a fine idea."

Marcie figured she and Stormy should join them so she went to the kitchen to pour two glasses of her sherry.

When Jason took the glass of Irish whiskey Kip offered him, he saw no reason to postpone his reason for being here. "I'm not usually a reckless sea captain but I was a desperate man when I got home from Ireland to find that a Captain Murdock had taken Princess."

Stormy started to giggle. "Pa, he named me Princess because when Jason found me on his schooner I didn't know my name or who I was. Remember I told you about that?"

"I remember, honey. I think Jason gave you an awfully pretty name," Kip declared.

"I thought it fit her perfectly," Jason smiled as he reached over to kiss her cheek. He felt no restraint about that for Kip Monihan had to know he loved his daughter. He took Stormy's hand and announced to Kip and Marcie, "I want to marry your daughter as soon as possible. As I told her a while ago, I've come to realize that time is too precious to waste. But I promise I won't cross that ocean with my beloved bride until spring comes."

Kip smiled, "That's all I would ask—you two have our blessing. I know you love one another and Stormy's happiness is all Marcie and I want."

"Mister Monihan, you've made me a happy man!"

Jason felt the warm, inviting atmosphere in the little cottage as Stormy had felt it when Jason had taken her to his parents' home in England.

Because he was feeling so relaxed around Kip and Marcie, especially after two generous glasses of Kip's whiskey, he began to fumble in his pocket for the ring. When he found it, he turned to Stormy with a glint in his eyes. "Give me your hand, Princess. I've waited long enough to do this, too." He slipped the exquisite emerald and diamond ring on her dainty finger. It fit perfectly. Stormy was awestruck by its beauty—all she could manage to say was, "Oh, Jason—Jason. It's gorgeous!"

"Just like you, love. The emeralds reminded me of your eyes when I saw it in a store in Ireland."

"You got this when you were in Ireland?"

"I did but I had no finger to put it on when I got home."

Kip and Marcie sat exchanging glances and smiling. They both felt they were sharing a special moment with Stormy and Jason.

Jason certainly endeared himself to both of them when he gallantly rose up from the settee to bend down on his knees and look up at Stormy as he held her hand to ask her, "Stormy Monihan, I'm asking you to be my wife. Will you marry me?"

Stormy smiled. "Jason Hamilton, I could marry no one but you."

It suddenly dawned on Marcie that she had a dinner to cook. She'd done nothing the last two hours but sit in her front room enjoying the company of Jason Hamilton.

Kip offered his wife a helping hand in the kitchen when Jason suggested he take Stormy aboard the *Sea Princess* to see Tobias, Rudy, and Dewey.

So the two of them left the house to go down to the

wharf and look at the sunset. Jason recognized the green cape she had flung around her shoulders.

Kip and Marcie watched them stroll down the path. Marcie looked up at her husband. "Isn't he handsome, Kip? What beautiful children they'll have," she sighed.

Kip laughed and gave her a hug. "What a romantic lady you are!"

She smiled and rushed into the kitchen—she had no time to waste if she wanted to have a nice dinner on the table in an hour.

Kip set up the table and sliced one of her fresh-baked loaves of bread. He set down plates for the pie she'd baked this morning. "Lucky you baked those two cherry pies. We've got a dessert to offer the young man," he remarked as she was preparing to put the floured pieces of chicken into hot grease in the cast iron skillet.

Out on the *Sea Princess,* Tobias had started preparing the evening meal for the crew. He didn't expect that their captain would be dining aboard.

All was well with Jason's world this evening. He was walking in the sunset with his girl and his ring was on her finger.

He could hardly fault his crew for staring at Stormy as he escorted her across the deck to his cabin. Rudy had already lit the lanterns. He grinned, "Well, does it look the same to you, love?"

She surveyed the cabin. "Almost, Jason—all but the missing books and empty shelves over there."

"Lost all of them, Princess. You can't imagine the condition I found this lady in when I was finally able to check the damage. But that's over with now. Come, shall we go to the galley so you can see Tobias? Think I better tell him I'm not dining here tonight," he said, taking her arm.

Tobias was sitting at the table taking a rest when he looked up to see the two of them entering his galley.

He jumped up and wiped his hands on his apron. "Good Lord—Miss Stormy! What a sight you are!"

She rushed over and he gave her a big bear hug. She smiled, "Oh, it is good to see you. I thought you all would never get to Southport."

He chuckled, "We sorta had grave doubts about that ourselves, Miss Stormy."

"But we did, Tobias, and here we'll stay until spring. By the way, there's going to be a wedding. You're the first to be told. Tomorrow night we'll be dining here to celebrate the occasion. Think you might fix us a fine feast?" Jason asked.

"A grand meal for a grand occasion, I assure you, captain," Tobias said with a broad smile.

"Well, we'll let you get back to your cooking—we'll be leaving shortly," he told the old cook. Stormy told Tobias goodbye and said she'd be looking forward to seeing him tomorrow night.

As they left the galley and walked down the passageway, Rudy spotted them and came dashing up. Once again, Stormy left Jason's side to embrace him. She'd become very close to Rudy during that crossing for he was the one bringing trays of food to the captain's cabin when Jason was occupied and couldn't join her. It was also Rudy's old faded pants Jason had borrowed for her.

All Rudy could say was, "Miss Stormy! Miss Stormy!"

She gave him a warm smile. "Oh, Rudy—I was so happy to hear that you were one of the lucky ones."

Jason stood there, pleased to see how much Tobias and Rudy liked and admired his lady. He knew that Dewey surely had to know by now that they were aboard. He restrained himself from doing what he truly yearned to do. But for the fact that they were due to get back to the Monihans' and Marcie was preparing dinner for them, he would have liked to take her back to his cabin, lock the door, and make love to her as he'd ached to do for so long.

Tomorrow night would be theirs, he promised himself. Tomorrow night they'd dine in the privacy of his cabin. Tomorrow night would be their night to lock themselves away from the rest of the world.

After waiting so long, he tried to soothe his impatience by telling himself that twenty-four hours wasn't too long.

Marcie had no reason to be concerned about her hastily prepared dinner. Her huge platter of crispy, golden-fried chicken, bowls of mashed potatoes, and creamy gravy whetted Jason's appetite—he ate ravenously, which pleased Marcie.

"Princess—you got to get Marcie to teach you how to fry chicken like this," he declared.

She admonished him sweetly, "I'll have you know I can fry chicken, Jason Hamilton. But I'll admit it's not as good as Marcie's."

"You're a very good cook, Stormy," Marcie quickly responded.

It was a wonderful evening. After dinner, they discussed wedding plans.

Jason smiled, "Our honeymoon will be spent aboard the *Sea Princess*. In fact, the schooner will be my home until we sail for England. I prefer it to living in a lodge or inn."

Jason told Kip that he knew he'd be losing some of the crew during those idle weeks but that Murdock had told him he'd be able to find a lot of good seamen in Southport by the time he was ready to sail.

"He's right and I can help you, Jason, when that time comes," Kip said. "I'm glad you're going to be here that long—we'll have a chance to get to know one another as Stormy did with your family."

Jason grinned sheepishly, "And I guess I better start calling her Stormy now that I'm here."

They all laughed. Stormy teased him, "I'll answer to either name, Jason."

The hour was late when Jason rose to return to the *Sea Princess*. But before he left, he invited Kip on a tour of his schooner the next day. Kip realized how proud Jason was of his schooner and eagerly accepted the young Englishman's invitation.

Long after he and Marcie had gone to bed, they lay there talking endlessly about the young man. "The more I'm around him and talk to him, the better I like him, Marcie."

Marcie shared her husband's feelings.

Sleep didn't come easily to Stormy—she was thinking about tomorrow evening when they would finally be alone again. She was delighted to hear him tell her folks that their honeymoon would be spent aboard the *Sea Princess*.

It was the perfect place. It was there that they'd made love for the first time.

Fifty

Kip thoroughly enjoyed the tour with Jason—he was a little overwhelmed by the vastness of the schooner. His daughter was certainly not going to be in cramped quarters. Jason's cabin was as large as his front room and kitchen combined.

He met Tobias, Dewey, and Rudy as he walked around with Jason. Old Tobias was quick to tell Kip what a grand dinner he was cooking for Stormy that evening.

"I'll tell her, Tobias," Kip promised.

The three of them had found Kip Monihan a likeable, friendly fellow with that same outgoing manner as his daughter.

With just as much pride, Kip took Jason on a tour of the *East Wind*. Jason enjoyed seeing where Stormy had spent so much of her time when she was growing up.

Living on the boat and making those runs up and down the coast, Jason understood why she'd been such a "good little sailor," as Captain Murdock had called her. Jason knew he could have looked the world over and not found a more perfect woman for him.

When he returned to Kip's cottage, he didn't linger long. He told Stormy, "I'll be here to get you at five-thirty, love. I have to make a trip into Southport and pay my crew. I figure the minute they get paid, they'll head for town."

She laughed, "I'm sure of it."

She had already chosen the gown she was going to wear. All day long she had kept looking down at her finger, admiring Jason's ring. More than once, Marcie had raved about the beauty of it.

Tobias had sent one of the crew down to the wharf that day so he could fix a fine fish dinner and his special herbed rice, which he knew Stormy loved. He'd baked a plum cake with a delicious sauce.

Jason had picked a favorite white wine to be served with their meal. Since it was the time of year it was, he could not find many flowers—he had to settle for pots of narcissus. But he had not forgotten the fragrance Stormy loved, so he purchased a bottle of gardenia toilet water. Ironically Branson waited on him.

As handsome as he was, Rebecca wasn't interested in any young man. She was just there to work so she could keep her job, for she had a new burden on her small shoulders. Her mother had died four days earlier and she had to meet the expenses of the funeral.

Promptly at the appointed hour, Jason arrived at the Monihan cottage looking very dashing in his gray tweed pants, white linen shirt, and gray wool coat He looked completely different than he had in the captain's garb. Stormy was instantly transported back in time—he was dressed as he was when they'd made their jaunts around London.

Marcie thought Stormy looked just as elegant in her long-sleeved emerald gown.

When the two of them left, Marcie and Kip sat down at the kitchen table to have their dinner. Marcie said, "Can you imagine what a special night this is for them, Kip? Last night they shared the evening with us but tonight is theirs."

Kip smiled, "I'd thought about that, Marcie."

* * *

From the minute she arrived aboard the *Sea Princess,* Stormy truly felt like a princess. His cabin was the perfect romantic setting, with the sweet-smelling flowers and glowing candles. Rudy had set up the table and covered it with a frosty white tablecloth.

Jason took off his coat after he'd helped her remove her cape. He served the two of them some of his favorite white wine, which they were still sipping when Tobias arrived. There was a smug look on his chubby face as he lifted the platter containing the delectable fish, generously sprinkled with his favorite herbs.

"Hope you enjoy it, Miss Stormy. I fixed this especially for you," he said, smiling down at her.

"Tobias, it looks delicious. Need I tell you how much I always enjoyed your meals?"

When Tobias had all the side dishes on the table, he left. Jason smiled across the table at her. "Guess I know how I rate with Tobias. After you, I come first."

"Oh, Jason," she said softly. "It not only looks delicious, it smells divine, doesn't it?"

"Well, let's not deny ourselves any longer, love."

It was the best fish dinner Tobias had ever prepared and they told him that when he came back an hour later to gather up the dishes. It was sweet music to his ears.

Jason followed his cook to the door and closed it after Tobias. He wanted no more interruptions for the rest of the evening.

He went back to the table to finish the rest of his wine. There was a devilish glint in his eyes as he asked, "You decided on a wedding date, love?"

"Just as soon as I can get myself a wedding gown, Jason."

"Are you going to make me suffer that long? It takes weeks for a gown to be made. Remember, I have a mother and sisters so I'm aware of the time that involves," he sighed.

"Oh, Jason— No, I just want a pretty gown. It won't be special-made since it will be a simple wedding. Marcie and I are going into Southport tomorrow to see what we can find in a nice little dress shop there," she soothed.

"Good! I'd marry you tonight if we could. You look stunning in that lovely green gown," he said, getting up from his chair and walking around the table to take her hand. His black eyes were aflame with desire and Stormy sensed his passion. He had only to bend down to kiss her for a liquid fire to flow through her.

As it always had been when they'd made love, Jason's long, slender fingers could remove her clothing so quickly that suddenly there were no barriers between them. His nimble fingers seemed to sear her flesh, causing her desire to blaze just as heatedly as his.

He murmured her name softly as he told her how wonderful it was to feel her velvet-soft flesh once again. Then his lips were caressing her and Stormy was arching up to press against him. She felt the firm muscles of his thighs pressed against hers. Swiftly, both of them found themselves being carried away to their own special rapture. Like the fury of a fierce storm, they were tossed to and fro like an undertow clashing against a giant wave.

It was so sweet to lie in Jason's arms as the calm came over them after their storm of passion. They lingered in Jason's bed for another hour before they reluctantly got up to get dressed. Once more they realized they had to part company—Jason had to get her back to the cottage.

"You see why I'm so anxious for us to be married, love? Then we won't have to part. I can lie with you in my arms all night long," he told her.

"It won't be long, Jason. I promise you it won't be,"

she vowed, still feeling breathless from his fierce love-making.

It was a busy week at the Monihans'. Marcie and Stormy went into Southport twice to get everything they needed for the wedding. On the first trip, Stormy found the perfect gown. It wasn't a bridal gown but Marcie said it made her look like a bride. It fit Stormy to perfection. It was white silk with a fitted bodice and long sleeves. The low-scooped neckline was edged with delicate seed pearls.

Marcie had insisted that she buy some white silk slippers. Stormy didn't realize that Marcie had made a secret purchase: a lovely blue satin gown, matching negligee, and a blue garter. It was just something she wanted to do for her stepdaughter.

While Marcie and Stormy made their trips into Southport, Kip and Jason spent hours together. They roamed the woods and went hunting. Jason told Kip that he and his father often went hunting at the country estate.

Kip was pleased that his Stormy was marrying a down-to-earth man he could enjoy spending time with. They found much to talk about even though they came from very different backgrounds. Jason might be the son of an English lord, Kip thought, but there was nothing pretentious about him.

When Marcie and Stormy had gone on their second jaunt to Southport, Kip took Jason over to meet Paddy. "He's her second father, Jason. He was there with me the night Stormy was born when we were riding out a fierce storm much like the one you did. Don't know what I'd have done without Paddy."

Even before he met Paddy, Jason knew he was going to like the old man. When the two of them met, he found he was right. Paddy saw why Stormy couldn't settle for Dorsey when she'd known this impressive young man. Only an hour in his company convinced Paddy he'd advised Stormy wisely.

Paddy liked the way his dark eyes looked directly at him as he and Kip and him had prepared to leave. He'd told Paddy, "I'll be seeing you at the wedding, Paddy."

"You can bet you will, Jason. Nothing would keep me away. That would be like not seeing my own daughter get married. Guess I don't have to tell you she's like my daughter?" Paddy grinned.

"Paddy, Stormy had told me so much about you I felt I knew you before we met," Jason smiled.

It was only after he and Kip were climbing back into Kip's buggy that Jason broke into a laugh and said, "I called her Stormy for the first time! I knew it would happen sooner or later."

Kip laughed, "Guess you're right, Jason."

After Kip and Jason had left his cottage, Paddy sat doing a lot of thinking. Stormy was getting herself a fine husband and father for her babe—a far better man than Dorsey. He couldn't deny he was going to miss her when she sailed away with her husband. But if he knew Stormy as he felt he did, she would be returning to Carolina fairly often to see her pa and Marcie.

It had been a fine afternoon for Paddy to meet Jason Hamilton. His spirits were high when he went into his kitchen to warm up the pot of soup he'd made at midday. He was thinking to himself as he put a bowl and spoon on his kitchen table how he'd been fooled by Pat Dorsey and how quickly he'd seemingly forgotten that he even existed. Pat had not darkened the door since the evening he'd moved out.

But Paddy knew a lot of people in the small port city and he'd heard that Pat was squiring another young lady—so he hadn't wasted much time after Stormy had called off their marriage. It was enough to tell Paddy that Pat had not truly loved Stormy.

Those first rumors were true for Pat had often been seen in the company of Rebecca Branson but those were old rumors. Rebecca had not allowed Dorsey to come back into her life after her mother had become very ill two weeks before she died. That was enough to discourage Pat from trying to pursue Rebecca any more. He was searching Southport for another pretty girl. Rebecca had too much responsibility to concern herself about Pat's sudden disappearance.

But three weeks after the funeral, Rebecca put some order in her life. She was paying off her indebtedness and was no longer looking drained. She was also finding she finally had some free time in the evenings. She'd even had time to make herself a new challis skirt and a blouse of pale blue silk to wear with it.

The next day she'd worn them to work, pinning her mother's brooch on the blouse. She felt she looked very elegant. All day she had noticed how the gentlemen walking by the counter had ogled her and smiled so she figured she had to look very attractive.

Looking for a gift for Stormy and Jason, Dewey ambled up. It was a good excuse to speak with this blue-eyed beauty. Rebecca asked if she might help him.

Dewey noticed a sweet fragrance. It reminded him of flowers. He gave her a smile and confessed, "Honestly don't know, miss. I was thinking about a gift for a lady but I don't know what she would like."

"Well, I might be able to help you. All ladies like a nice toilet water. Do you know what fragrance she likes?"

"Can't say I do, but I sure like that fragrance."

She smiled at him. "You must be talking about the new fragrance I'm wearing. Its hyacinth. Here, let me get a bottle of it for you." She reached back on the shelf and took one of the bottles, removing the top. "Is this the one that pleases you?"

"Oh, yes, ma'am!" Dewey exclaimed.

"As a matter of fact, I haven't had time to display the bottles I just got in," she said.

"Well, I'll take two of those," he declared without even asking the price. Dewey was deeply engrossed in her loveliness—he hadn't had a pretty lady impress him in a long, long time.

As she was packaging his purchase, she asked, "You aren't from Southport, are you?" She was aware of his accent.

"No, miss—I'm from England," Dewey said as he counted out the money for his purchase.

"Well, I hope your lady enjoys this fragrance," Rebecca said as she took his money.

"Oh, this is a gift for my captain's lady and I hope she does, too. Guess that's why I was a little lost as to what to purchase. I would know the fragrance my lady liked," he assured her with a teasing glint in his eyes.

That was the end of Dewey's first encounter with Rebecca. But having a lot of time on his hands the next two days before his captain's wedding, he went back to the emporium just to gaze at her from a distance to assure himself she was as beautiful as he'd first thought.

After sauntering around the emporium two afternoons later, he was convinced she was even prettier. Dewey told himself there were a lot of weeks left before spring. He might be just as lucky as Jason before he shipped out of Southport. He didn't even know her name but that didn't matter to Dewey. All he knew was she had the loveliest blue eyes he'd ever seen.

It was a simple wedding—just what Jason and Stormy wanted. After Jason left the *Sea Princess*, Tobias and Rudy lingered on the schooner to take a bottle of champagne to his cabin for the two of them when they returned later that night. Tobias was sure there would be a wedding cake over at the Monihans' but he wanted to bake one, too. So he placed it on the table as Rudy brought the champagne and glasses before they left the schooner. Dewey had walked over earlier with Jason and old Paddy was already there.

Jason had only one regret about the wedding and that was that his dear mother and father could not be with him and Stormy since the two of them adored his bride so much.

When they did return to England in the spring, he and Stormy would have to have another wedding ceremony for the benefit of his family. But at least his mother would know the joy of being there when their firstborn arrived.

His keen eyes and sensitive hands had detected the changes in his little princess the afternoon he'd arrived. He was sure she was carrying his child after they'd made love. Her wasplike waist had expanded slightly and her breasts were fuller.

It was one of his torments when he found she'd left England with Captain Murdock. The thought that she was carrying his child and an ocean divided them was pure agony for Jason. He knew that when she would become aware of it, she would be alone back here in Carolina.

The one thought that gnawed at him and drove him to take the risky voyage was that his princess would marry some young local gent to avoid the shame of having a baby without a father or a husband. He knew her fierce Monihan pride!

He thanked God that had not happened—all that was behind them now. Now he was wondering how long the little imp was going to make him wait to make her announcement. He had no intention of saying anything until she did—then he'd let her know he couldn't be happier!

It was after midnight before he and Stormy finally left the cottage. Marcie had prepared a fine dinner for the ten guests. The minister and his wife left shortly after the dinner but for the remaining guests, it was a night to celebrate. Kip didn't have to take Paddy back to Southport—he'd told him to plan to spend the night since Stormy's bed would be unoccupied.

Jason had to admit he was glad to see Tobias nudging Dewey and Rudy toward the door. Dewey and Paddy had become friends quickly and were enjoying Kip's Irish whiskey more than the champagne.

Stormy had noticed that her proud Englishman was not wearing his sling when they'd stood side by side to take their vows. But she also knew that his arm was paying the price by the time they were returning to the schooner.

She let him know she was aware of it. He tried to make light of it, asking, "Now why would you think that, love?"

"I saw you flinch when Paddy gave you an exuberant pat on that arm."

"I'll only have one wedding, my darling Stormy, and I bloody well wasn't going to stand beside you with my coat flung over that damned arm. My arm will be fine," he assured her, giving her a strong embrace with his good one.

"I'll let you get by with that tonight but tomorrow you put that sling back on until that arm is strong enough, Jason Hamilton," she said, smiling up at him.

He bent over to give her a kiss on the cheek as they walked across the deck. "Already becoming the bossy little wife, aren't you?"

"Only because I love you, Jason. I want that arm to

heal properly, so please do as the doctor told you. We have the rest of our lives to be together. We're together now—we're married now so nothing else matters to me, Jason."

"Oh, love—you express my feelings so completely! Nothing else matters," he agreed.

When they arrived at his cabin, they knew Tobias and Rudy were responsible for the romantic scene that greeted them. They saw the cake with its frosty white icing and the bottle of champagne glowing in the candlelight.

She surveyed everything and exclaimed, "Oh, Jason—we couldn't have asked for a lovelier wedding. I have only one regret."

"And what is that, love?"

"I wish Lady Sheila and Lord Addison could have been with us tonight."

"We'll have another ceremony just for them, Princess," he promised.

Jason had been calling her Stormy more and more in Southport, but at special, private moments like tonight, she would always be his Princess!

Fifty-one

After making love, Stormy lay encircled in Jason's good arm. Now he knew what true love was all about—what a gem he had in his wife!

He had decided he was tired of waiting for her to make her announcement. Stormy was so open and honest that he knew she'd tell him the truth.

In a low, husky voice he asked, "What are we going to have, love—a boy or a girl?"

He felt her stiffen and she stammered, "Jason, isn't it a little soon for that?"

"Not if I've got it figured right, love. I'd say in about six months our little angel is going to arrive." He wore an amused smile and was glad the cabin was dark.

She sat up in bed and asked indignantly, "Jason Hamilton—how did you know I was pregnant?"

"Who better than me? Who knows that little body of yours more intimately? After all that lovemaking we'd done during the crossing I had suspected it was a possibility by the time we arrived in England. As I told you, I took the assignment to Ireland so I could ask you to marry me. Oh, Stormy it was hell to find you gone when I returned. I thought if you were carrying my baby we couldn't let an ocean separate us. I couldn't wait for spring—you could have been heavy with my child."

Stormy reveled in the great love Jason felt for her as

she lay back down and snuggled close to him. Both of them felt the need for sleep, but as it was about to come, she softly drawled, "I love you so much, Jason Hamilton."

"And I love you, Stormy Hamilton," he said with a lazy smile.

It was the first time she had been addressed as Stormy Hamilton and she liked the sound of it. So it was a sweet, contented sleep they enjoyed on their first night as husband and wife.

It came as no surprise to Stormy after they'd been married six weeks when Jason started to talk about some plans he'd been making. The days were getting longer—a sign that spring was coming soon.

He smiled, "Guess I'm anxious to head for England so I can get you settled comfortably, love." What he didn't mention was that she seemed to be growing a little bigger with each week that went by. But he didn't have to—Stormy was very aware of it.

She could no longer conceal her condition and hadn't tried to after she and Jason had been married a couple of weeks. Marcie and Kip had only to observe the two of them together not to be upset that a baby would be coming some three months early.

Kip soared to the heavens when he found out he was to be a grandfather. He teased Jason, telling him they'd better be prepared for a visit from him and Marcie within a year.

"I figured that this just might get you and Marcie to England. I'd love to have the two of you. We have beautiful countryside there, too."

Jason had finally found a ship sailing for London so he was able to get a letter sent to his parents. By the middle of March, they would know he was alive and well. He also knew how excited they would be that he and Stormy were marrying and that he'd be bringing her home soon.

By the end of March, Stormy and Marcie had been to the dress shop to have new gowns made to accommodate Stormy's swelling body. By that time, all of her possessions were over at her husband's cabin so Stormy's old room became a guest bedroom. Paddy often stayed with them for the weekend or a couple of nights during the week.

He and Kip had had a very serious talk and Kip had reluctantly accepted the fact that he would have to start searching for a galley cook for the *East Wind*. Kip and Jason often went down to the wharves to seek crew members as Kip had two to replace. He hadn't seen, or heard a word from, Dorsey.

Jason hired three able-bodied men—he knew instinctively they would be good seamen. Kip hired a cook who reminded him very much of a younger Paddy. He took an instant liking to Corky, who was in his forties and like Paddy had no family.

Heading home one day, Jason laughed as he told Kip, "I better leave before too much longer or I might just lose Dewey. Think he's found himself a pretty little girl in Southport. He might just decide to stay."

"Don't think so, Jason. But I wouldn't rule out the possibility of having two brides on the *Sea Princess* instead of one."

"Never thought about that, I've got to admit. Well, if Dewey finds himself a lady I'd be happy for him. It's about time he got married," Jason said.

He gave no thought to Dewey for the next day or two—he had other things on his mind. Never had Tobias's pantry been stocked as well as it was by the next day. Jason tried to think of everything that would make the crossing more pleasant for Stormy. He'd even stopped by a bookstore to line his empty bookshelves—he knew she'd be spending a lot of time in the cabin alone.

Finally Jason announced to his crew and to the Monihans that they would leave on the first day of April. Kip would have been very sad except for the fact that his daughter was so gloriously happy. Jason promised that if they didn't come to England he'd bring Stormy back to see them the next springtime.

Kip had gone over to get Paddy so he could spend the next two days with him and Marcie. "Thought you'd like to be at our place, so you could say goodbye to Stormy. They're leaving the day after tomorrow."

Of course, Paddy was delighted by Kip's thoughtfulness. Like Kip, the only reason he wasn't sad about Stormy going so far away was that she was so happy and had herself such a fine young fellow. He'd observed them over the last month and a half and was satisfied that she had a husband who would take good care of her.

Tobias and Rudy were all fired up about finally getting back to the sea. Dewey was the only one who seemed somewhat disturbed about something. He'd finally cornered Jason out on the deck and asked him, "Could—could I have the next two days off, captain? I got a little unfinished business to take care of."

"A girl, Dewey?"

"Seems I've lost my heart to a Southport girl just like you did. Want to ask her to marry me and take her back to England if I can get her to say yes," Dewey confessed.

"Then you better not waste any more time with me and go try to sweet talk her. Just be back on the *Sea Princess* by departure time—that's all I ask," Jason said.

"I'll be here, captain. You know that. Wish me luck," Dewey exclaimed excitedly. Jason watched him dash across the deck. He did wish him luck and he hoped Dewey would be sharing his cabin with the lady he loved when they sailed.

But he didn't say anything to Stormy that evening when they were dining in their cabin. The young lady might not consent to Dewey's proposal.

He'd insisted that they dine on the *Sea Princess* since Stormy had seemed so tired after packing all day. Tomorrow night they would have their last evening with Kip, Marcie, and Paddy and Jason realized it could be an emotional time for his little bride.

But he had been very aware of something else this last week—Stormy's petite body grew heavier, the walk from the wharf up to Kip's was exhausting for her.

When the next evening was over and they'd returned to Jason's cabin, she told him, "Oh, Jason—I'm glad the goodbyes are over. I don't like farewells. The morning I was to leave with Captain Murdock, Lady Sheila and I stayed up late that night and said our goodbyes. The morning I left, she didn't come downstairs and I didn't want her to because we'd have both been crying."

"Mother's so much like you," he told her. He urged her to come over so he could unfasten her gown. She was ready to get into the comfort of their bed.

Jason didn't linger long after she had snuggled under the coverlet for he had to get up early.

As he climbed the stairs up to the deck the next morning, Dewey was there. "Told you I'd be here. I got my little bride all settled in my cabin. I'm anxious for you and Stormy to meet her. She's a nice girl, captain."

"I'm sure she is, Dewey. You and your bride will have to dine with us tonight," Jason said.

"Thank you, captain—we'd be delighted," Dewey said as he turned to leave. They'd been together so long that Jason didn't have to give him orders—Dewey knew what his captain expected of him.

Stormy was still lying in bed when she felt the motion of the schooner beginning to move. It was exciting, so she got up and looked out the window. She stood there for a moment marveling at how swiftly the schooner moved compared to her pa's *East Wind*.

As Jason had promised, they were traveling southward toward Savannah and Captain Murdock's house. That evening Tobias served dinner to Jason, Stormy, Dewey, and his new bride.

The two young ladies recognized one another immediately but neither of them said anything. The feisty little lady Rebecca had seen that day with Dorsey in front of the emporium had changed. She was now heavy with child but she was still as beautiful.

It was apparent to Rebecca that Captain Jason Hamilton worshipped his wife. It was a most pleasant evening for her—being aboard a ship was a new experience. She already warned Dewey she might get sick. Dewey had assured her if it happened it wouldn't be so unusual. She was glad she made it through dinner and was still feeling just fine.

The *Sea Princess* arrived in Savannah late the next morning and remained until the following day. Jason and Stormy had a jubilant reunion with Mick and Sue Murdock. Sue had prepared a feast and insisted that Tobias, Rudy, Billy, Dewey, and Rebecca join them.

Mick was quite a jester, and said, "I'll tell you, there are no prettier girls in the world than the ones living up and down this coast. Seems you two guys plucked up two of the best."

They all said their farewells to the Murdocks late that night—Jason wanted to make an early departure so they didn't stay overnight.

When they were in the seclusion of Jason's cabin, Jason told Stormy, "Dear God—I think we'd better head for England quickly or I could have been taking *three* brides back. Did you see how Rudy was looking at Janet all night?"

Stormy laughed, "I guess I didn't."

"Well, I knew he thought Janet was special when she was nursing all of us. But tonight he couldn't take his eyes off of her."

"Well, Rudy's young yet. He has some time before he should think about getting married," Stormy remarked as she slipped out of her gown.

"Tell that to a young man when he's bitten by the lovebug," Jason laughed.

Stormy was propped up on her pillows and in her nightgown, smiling up at him as he prepared to dim the lamp. "Well, look what happened to me when that bug bit me."

"How glowing you look, love!" he teased as he darkened the room.

"Come on to bed, Jason. That silken tongue of yours won't reward you tonight. I'm exhausted!"

"This silken tongue has already rewarded me—I have the woman I love and she carries my baby. What more would I want?"

Stormy realized how delighted he was about the baby—she sighed contentedly as she snuggled against her handsome husband.

The crossing was a smooth one. Stormy and Rebecca spent many hours together—the two of them had become very close friends by the time the *Sea Princess* neared London.

They both agreed that their associations with Dorsey had been a waste of their time. Stormy told her how she and Pat had got acquainted when he'd worked for her pa and Rebecca told her how she'd met him. In the end, they agreed that Pat tended to use people who were taken in by his charm.

Stormy liked Rebecca because they had a lot in common. She was a frank, honest person who had worked very hard to support herself and her mother. Dewey and Jason were pleased that their wives had become such good friends.

Dewey said to Jason, "We've been out of Savannah ten days now and we couldn't have asked for more perfect weather."

"Stormy is my good luck charm," Jason said. "In fact, we've been making such good time we could dock a day or two sooner than I'd figured, Dewey."

The sooner they arrived in England, the better Jason was going to like it. Stormy didn't even want to take an evening stroll as they'd done nightly when they'd first left Savannah. But he understood why it took so much effort that she just preferred to stay in the cabin. But she missed their strolls and having the sea breeze whip at her face. Often she opened the window and just stood there to feel the refreshing breeze.

Never had she expected to get this huge—it made her feel depressed when she saw Rebecca looking so trim and slender. On one of her moody days, she remarked to Jason, "What a miserable sight I must be, Jason!"

"Don't you talk like that, Stormy! I wouldn't want to spank a pregnant lady. You're always beautiful to me, love. You'll hurt our baby's feelings when it hears you talking like that," he teased her playfully.

"Oh, Jason—Jason," she began to laugh. He was always able to lift her spirits.

As she'd learned many things from her boatman father when she'd accompanied him up and down the Carolina coast, she was absorbing knowledge from being a sea captain's wife. That's why she got very excited the afternoon she spied something fluttering high in the clear blue skies. Jason had told her when he spotted sea gulls he knew that land wasn't far.

She wanted to rush out of the cabin and up on the deck to tell Jason that she thought she'd seen some gulls but she restrained herself.

Jason had seen them, too, but he wanted to be sure it was the shores of England they were approaching before he came to tell Stormy.

By the time he was convinced, he dashed down the steps churning with boyish enthusiasm. With a broad grin, he rushed in to tell her, "We're home, love! We're home! You get your pretty self dressed and I'll do your packing."

"Oh, Jason—I'm not helpless."

"You don't need to be bending down. Just get one of those pretty gowns on and comb your hair—you know, all the things you ladies do. Now you just obey your captain's orders," he admonished tenderly.

She did begin to dress—she wanted to look nice when she arrived at the country estate. She put on one of her prettiest gowns, a bottle-green silk with velvet cuffs and collar. Then she laid her green bonnet and reticule on the bed as Jason busily began to stuff things into the various valises.

Down the passageway, Dewey made the same announcement to Rebecca. He didn't linger in their cabin, dashing back up on deck. He knew it wouldn't take him that long to pack his one valise—he always traveled light.

He did hesitate one brief moment and stood with a sheepish look. "Rebecca, I might as well prepare you. Didn't leave my cottage in such fine shape when I took off so suddenly with Jason."

Rebecca smiled, "I'll love having a little cottage to

clean and a kitchen to cook in after so long on the ship. So if it's a mess, I'll clean it up. It's just going to be so good to walk on the ground again."

Dewey gave her a quick peck before he left, telling her he'd come to get her when they docked.

Jason had told Stormy the same thing, so she sat down to wait for his return. She was beginning to feel as excited as he was. In a way, she felt like she was coming home—she remembered how sad she'd been when she'd had to leave England.

Now, England was to be her home and it was here her son or daughter would be born. She sat with an amused smile, realizing how all her girlish daydreams had come true. She had never imagined that she'd be living anywhere but Cape Fear or the Carolinas—and certainly not across the ocean!

But she firmly believed that destiny deemed that she and Jason Hamilton should meet. That meeting was to bind them together forever!

Fifty-two

Jason had hired a carriage and sent two of his husky seamen to load the valises into it before he moved Stormy out of the comfortable cabin. Tobias and Rudy came to say their farewells to her. The two of them planned to stay behind on the schooner after the captain and his lady left. Tobias was very meticulous about how he shut his galley down at the end of a voyage. Rudy planned to help him and spend a night aboard before he traveled on to his aunt's home in a small town twenty miles out of London.

Dewey had also engaged a carriage to take him and his new wife to his cottage on the outskirts of the city. But his carriage would be traveling in the opposite direction from Jason's.

Rebecca came to Jason's cabin to tell Stormy goodbye—the two of them promised to keep in touch. Stormy smiled, "We'll both have some adjustments to make, Rebecca, but once we're settled in, the four of us will have to get together from time to time."

"Oh, I hope we can, Stormy. You can't know what it meant to me to have you during the crossing. As much as I love Dewey, it was a little frightening to leave Southport and come to this strange country. Guess that's what convinced me how much I love him. I was willing to do it but I was scared. But then I met you and Jason. Our afternoons together made me feel relaxed."

"Well, your company was just as important to me, Rebecca. You kept me from being lonely and depressed, especially once I was confined to this cabin."

Rebecca gave her a warm embrace as she prepared to go meet Dewey. "I'll hope to see you, Stormy, before your baby arrives. Take good care of yourself."

"Oh, Jason will see to that," Stormy said with a soft laugh. Neither of them had heard Jason enter.

He smiled and asked, "Well, are you two ladies ready to disembark?"

Their carriages went in different directions as they all waved to one another. Rolling toward the outskirts of London, Stormy reached over for Jason's hand. Her eyes were warm with love as she said, "It seems we've traveled down this road before."

"We have, love, and it was a miserable winter's day— remember?"

"I do. You'd gone out to buy me a cape as we left the schooner."

Stormy didn't need a wrap this late spring day—she felt quite comfortable in her long-sleeved gown. Jason thought she looked utterly adorable in her little green bonnet. Pregnant or not, she was a saucy little minx!

On this lovely spring afternoon, neither of them knew that if their departure had been delayed a few more weeks they would not have been allowed to leave Savannah.

Fort Sumter in Charleston, South Carolina, was fired upon April 12 and captured on April 14. All southern ports were blockaded due to a direct order from President Lincoln. The conflict between the North and the South had begun.

Mick Murdock and Kip Monihan had to face the stark reality about the rumors they'd heard for months.

Kip was just happy to know his daughter was out on the seas with her English husband.

Stormy had never seen the English countryside in the spring—it was lovely. Wildflowers were already blooming in the meadows lining the country road and trees were budding profusely. She sat beside Jason knowing she was going to love her new home.

Suddenly she saw the two-story stone house towering above the fenced-in front grounds of the Hamilton estate. She sensed Jason's excitement as the carriage turned in the long, winding drive heading toward the front entrance.

Lady Sheila sat in the parlor having a glass of sherry—she was so absorbed in her private musing that she hadn't heard the carriage approach. Addison was still in his study. She knew that the weeks of uncertainty about Jason had taken a toll on him. He had decided it was time to sell his shipping lines—he was getting too old to handle it. He'd always hoped his only son would be taking over for him but that might not be, he reasoned realistically.

He knew his curious Irish wife wondered what was keeping him so occupied lately but there were a lot of business records to go over. He dared not tell Sheila just yet what he had in mind.

Jason's letter hadn't arrived in England, even though he had delivered it to a ship which sailed a few weeks before he did.

When Addison joined her in the parlor, Sheila sat slowly sipping sherry, deep in thought. She was wondering if she'd be able to enjoy the roast beef tonight, knowing it was Jason's favorite.

She knew that she and Addison had to go on with their lives but it was hard to believe that her handsome son would never come dashing through the front door or sit at the dining table with them again.

Addison had greeted her and was walking over to the liquor chest to get himself a drink when his keen ears heard a carriage rolling up to their entrance. He went ahead and poured a glass of his favorite liquor, grumbling to Sheila, "Now who could be arriving at our dinner hour? I'm sure it's not Jane and her husband. I would expect that the other two would not be so presumptuous. We taught them better manners than that, Sheila."

"Well, I'm not expecting Joy or Angela so I've no idea who it could be. We'll know shortly—Clovis is going to the door." She took a quick sip of her sherry but almost choked on it—the voice she heard talking to Clovis was very familiar! Her knees went weak and she stammered almost in a whisper, "Dear God, Addison—it's our son! It's Jason!"

Nothing could have been more glorious to the Hamiltons than the sight of their beloved son coming into the parlor with a broad grin, his hand holding Stormy's.

He was very much alive, looking quite hale and hearty. The beautiful Stormy was glowing in her pregnancy. Jason embraced his mother and held her close as he felt her trembling, knowing the hell she'd been through. Addison warmly embraced Stormy. He didn't try to be his usual dignified self. There was a mist of tears in his eyes as he murmured, "It's so good to see you two—this time I'd venture to say that you're Jason's wife."

She laughed, "I am Jason's wife."

Lady Sheila was bubbling with happiness—she would finally know the joy of being a grandmother. It was not a matter of getting to know and like her new daughter-in-law—she already adored Stormy Monihan.

It was a festive evening which Lady Sheila and Lord

Addison enjoyed far more than the holiday season. But by nine, Stormy was ready to collapse. Jason saw her to his old room and got her comfortably into bed before he rejoined his parents. The three of them talked unceasingly for the next two hours.

Jason must have been a little tired himself for he slept until noon. But it was almost three in the afternoon before Stormy roused from the sweet comfort of Jason's bed. She had a late brunch in the room before Lady Sheila sent her maid to prepare a warm bath for Stormy.

Jason had had a late lunch with his parents—it was sweet music to their ears to hear him say he had no plans to go to sea for a long time. "I've got a son or daughter arriving before summer is over and I intend to be here. Don't want to be away from my wife and child for weeks at a time, Father," he told Addison.

Addison was encouraged to think that Jason would now be willing to run the Hamilton Lines. It took a lot of willpower for Sheila not to send word to Joy, Angela, and Jane that their brother had returned home. Out of concern for Stormy, she postponed alerting them for another day. She could see that the voyage had taken its toll on Stormy and Sheila felt she needed another day and night of rest before the family gathered together.

Lady Sheila's mind was whirling with ideas. The bedroom adjoining Jason's had to be converted into a nursery and work on that had to begin immediately from the way Stormy looked. She wanted her to have the best care—her own doctor would attend to Stormy and the delivery.

Jason had to laugh when his mother asked him, "When is our baby to arrive, dear?" He had told her he figured it would be about the first of July but they'd probably know more about that once Stormy saw Doctor Winston.

Addison and Sheila had been intrigued with Jason's tales about the Carolinas and Stormy's family. "Kip Monihan is Irish like you, Mother. You'll like him and Marcie very much. He loves to hunt like you, Father," Jason added.

Two days of resting and being pampered by all of the Hamiltons did wonders for Stormy. When the family gathered on the third night, she wasn't sure which created the most excitement—the fact that Jason was home or that he was to become a father.

The warmth of Jason's family made her feel very loved—it meant everything to her.

The next three weeks left Stormy bedazzled by what Lady Sheila could do when she set her mind to something. A door had been cut in one of Jason's bedroom walls. Everything had been stripped from the guest bedroom. New carpet had been laid and the walls had been painted a pale pastel.

The room truly took on the appearance of a nursery when the furnishings were brought in. Stormy had never seen such a lavish cradle. There was a tall chest to hold the baby's clothing—there was even a rocking chair. Stormy felt exhausted just watching Lady Sheila move around, filling the drawers with enough clothes for two babies.

Jason was just as amazed by the excitement their first grandchild was generating in his mother and father. While Sheila and Stormy had been occupied with planning the nursery, he and his father had been spending a lot of time together. Addison had approached his son about taking over the shipping lines because otherwise he would have to sell it.

"I always planned it to be yours, Jason. You're my only son. But if you still wish to be a sea captain, then I'll sell the company before I'll allow it to degenerate. I'm not up to handling it anymore," Addison confided.

"I'll take over, Father, and hope to do as well as you've done. If I hadn't met Stormy, I would probably still want to roam the seas. But right now, I have no desire to wander. Stormy's changed my life, Father."

"Oh, I've seen the change, son, since you've returned home. And I like it. You're a wiser, man, Jason. I've no doubt that Stormy played a very important role but something else made an impact on you, too. For the first time in your life you had to face the fact that you aren't invincible. An angry sea nearly conquered you! You faced death, Jason, and that changes any man's thinking. I've been there a time or two," Addison Hamilton added.

"You're right, Father. It made a bloody impact on me and I'll be the first to admit it," Jason confessed.

Fifty-three

For a while Jason said nothing to Stormy about some things he'd been thinking about privately. He knew they had to remain at his parents' estate until Stormy had the baby and for a few weeks after that. But he did not want to stay there too long—he wanted them to have their own home.

As much as he adored his mother, he was already seeing how she could become a possessive grandmother. It was not "our baby" as she was always calling it. It was his and Stormy's baby!

So he began to search the picturesque countryside for a place that might be for sale and would make the perfect home. He also felt that Stormy would wish to be the mistress of her own home and she could never be that as long as they lived with his parents.

They didn't need a spacious mansion like his parents had or acres of land—they needed a much smaller place.

He couldn't believe his good luck. As he'd told Dewey, Stormy was his good luck charm. He'd been coming home from the shipping office on a late afternoon when he spied a sign on some property just up the road from Bart Montgomery's property. The layout of the grounds and the two-story stone house appealed to Jason the moment he saw it. He quickly guided his gig into the drive toward the house.

The house was surrounded by a garden and flower-beds, which had been planned and planted long ago but had been neglected. A caretaker greeted him when he arrived and asked if he was interested in seeing the house. Jason told him he was.

So Jason took a tour of the house. It had a nice size parlor and dining room. He followed the caretaker up the stairs to the second landing where there were three roomy bedrooms. There was a carriage house at the back with living quarters above where the caretaker told Jason he was living.

Jason was anxious to make a deal right away when the caretaker told him the asking price but he dared not buy their future home without Stormy's approval. He just wondered if she was up to coming there to see it. If she liked the grounds and the first landing, he knew she'd like the second floor so she wouldn't have to make the effort to climb the steps.

When he came home late that afternoon and told her about the home he'd found, she got very excited and quickly said she was up to going over to look at it. While she'd said nothing about her feelings to Jason, she did want them to have their own home. As much as she adored Lady Sheila, she could be very bossy. Stormy knew that might cause problems after the baby was born—*she* intended to be in charge of her child, not Lady Sheila.

So the next afternoon he took her over there. He'd grinned as they were traveling, saying, "Lets this be our little secret for a while, love. As far as Mother knows, I'm taking you for a jaunt around the country-side."

"I understand, Jason."

He had only to lead her around the ground level of the quaint little stone house for her to exclaim, "Oh,

Jason—I love it! It's a little dream house. I don't need to go upstairs from the way you described it."

He gave her a hug. "I hoped you'd feel that way, Stormy. I fell in love with it when I first saw it but I wanted you to see it before I bought it. I'll make the deal tomorrow. Now, let's head for home. But as I said before, let's keep this our little secret for a while."

"I won't say a word, Jason," she promised. "You know your mother is expecting us to live with them, don't you?"

"I know, Stormy, but I want you to be the mistress of our own home. That's why I don't intend to say anything until after our baby's born and you're able to move. In the meantime, I can be getting it ready."

"Oh, Jason, now I have two things to look forward to. I can't wait for our baby to arrive so we can move into our new home."

Stormy's spirits were higher than they'd been for weeks. The last months of her pregnancy had been very draining. She told Jason as they were going back to the estate, "Jason, this has to be a big boy I'm carrying. A little girl wouldn't make me so large."

But Jason had laughed, "Don't be too sure, love. We could be having a chubby little girl." He remembered how huge his own mother was when she was carrying his younger sister, Joy.

The outing that afternoon was the last one Stormy would have before the birth—she was more comfortable resting during the endless month of June. But for Jason, it was a very busy month. Part of his day was spent at the shipping lines, another part overseeing work being done on their house.

The grounds were manicured and the inside of the house was completely cleaned, repainted, and decorated. By the end of June all the furnishings had been delivered. He was very pleased with the warm, inviting look of the parlor and dining room.

Their bedroom was lavish-looking in a soft shade of mauve—he knew Stormy liked that color. The bedroom adjoining theirs was done in white and pink.

Joy was the only one he'd taken into his confidence—the two of them had always been close. She'd helped him choose the furnishings for the nursery.

She laughed, "You must think you're having a daughter, Jason."

"Can't tell you why, Joy, but yes, I think it's going to be a beautiful little girl who looks like Stormy," he admitted.

It truly amazed Joy how one little lady had so completely changed her restless brother. He'd been home for weeks now and seemed perfectly content to remain on land.

As Jason was taking her back to her house that afternoon, Joy said, "You know Mother is going to be madder than an ol' wet hen, don't you, Jason?"

"I can't help that, Joy. Her daughters moved away when they married so she shouldn't expect that her son wouldn't wish to do the same. My wife deserves her own home. So as soon as Stormy is able, we'll be moving. Father will understand my feelings so he'll be able to soothe mother's ruffled feathers."

Joy smiled. "He's always seemed to be able to do that, hasn't he?"

Jason's instincts had been right about his firstborn child. Stormy had a darling little eight-pound cherub of a daughter the first week of July. Doctor Winston had never seen a more enthusiastic family gathering as there was when he made the announcement in the parlor.

Jason quickly dashed up the stairs to see his wife

and daughter. He swore she was the most beautiful ever born. She looked like a doll lying in Stormy's arms. With a teasing look, Stormy said, "Jason Hamilton, you couldn't deny this child even if you wanted to. She's the image of you."

It was wonderful to see his lovely Stormy feeling so full of spice and ginger after delivering such a big baby. He bent down to kiss her tenderly and murmur words of endearment. "I don't know how to tell you how I'm feeling. This is a moment that will never come again, a special moment for me."

Stormy was right—his little daughter had ringlets of black hair like his and her eyes would surely turn as black. Those little eyes were open and looking directly at him with that same piercing look he had. Jason let his long, slender finger rub his daughter's tiny hand and her fingers curled around it. The feel of that tiny hand made him lose his heart instantly. He knew he was going to spoil and pamper her—Stormy knew it, too—she had only to look at his face as he gazed down at his daughter.

They named her Sheila Marceline to honor his mother and Stormy's beloved Marcie. But one Sheila and one Marcie in the family was enough so they both agreed their daughter would be called Marceline. Jason thought it was a beautiful name befitting his beautiful daughter.

Since Marceline was the first grandchild of the Hamilton family, her arrival stirred quite a wave of excitement. Addison and Sheila strutted around like proud peacocks.

Stormy made a quick recovery and it was wonderful to be trim and slim again. Only one thing was marring her happiness—she was concerned about her family back in the Carolinas, having heard Jason's and Addison's recent conversations. They spoke of things

Stormy didn't understand, but she knew that her pa and Marcie could be in danger.

She'd heard Lord Addison tell his son, "It's not about abolition, Jason. Young men are going to die on the battlefields for a cause that has nothing to do with freeing slaves. The French support the South—they sympathize with their feelings and understand their genteel ways. The English are supporting the North because with their practical way of thinking, the North's factories are where the future is, not the farmlands of the South. I've heard a lot of talk at my club."

"So it's for money and power that blood will be shed," Jason remarked.

"A bloody lot. The South will be ravaged and the North will be the victor," Addison projected.

Neither of them was aware of how intensely Stormy was listening to every word. It wasn't until they retired to their bedroom that he realized how upset she was. He also realized she had a right to be—Kip and Marcie could indeed be victims of a bloody war between the North and the South.

He spent little time at the shipping lines the next day. He'd hired a couple to be his caretaker and housekeeper. He checked to see that Peter Emery and his wife, Wilhelmina, had moved into the quarters above the carriage house as they'd planned.

He'd felt they would be the perfect pair to work for him. Peter was an old seafaring man who would no longer go to sea. He anxiously accepted Jason's offer to tend to the grounds and run errands for him while he was busy at the shipping lines. Wilhelmina was to be their housekeeper and cook, as well as helping Stormy with the baby.

When he found the two of them getting settled into the carriage house, Jason was ready to go back into London. He went to search for Davy Dawson, a bold, dashing sea captain. He'd known Davy for almost five years and he'd heard rumors lately that he was running guns and ammunition to the South. Jason figured if he offered Davy a handsome sum he'd be willing to slip into Cape Fear and bring Kip and Marcie out.

Like Davy, Jason's sympathy was with the South. But more important was getting Kip and Marcie out of there. Luck was with Jason, for Davy was leaving the next morning for Georgia. The cocky Dawson knew once he'd slipped the blockade, getting to Cape Fear would be no problem.

So he and Jason made a deal. He gave Dawson half of his fee and a letter to present to Kip. But he said nothing to Stormy—he didn't want her to be devastated if the plan didn't work.

While Jason was busy with all his activities, Stormy was taking full charge of her life. Each day she became stronger and more vigorously able to tend to her baby. In a most gracious way she let Lady Sheila know she could care for her little Marceline, so Sheila found she had time on her hands.

Jason constantly scrutinized Stormy. He was amazed that she was strong enough to take charge of Marcelina by the first of August. Each night she came downstairs to dine with the family.

So he announced that he was telling his parents that they'd be moving to their new home in two weeks. "It's time, Stormy. Everything is ready for us over there and I can tell you're ready."

"Oh, Jason—I'm definitely ready. I don't need help taking care of Marceline," she assured him.

Needless to say, Lady Sheila was not as prepared for Jason's announcement as Lord Addison was. He knew Jason would want his own place.

It took every ounce of her strong Irish will for Sheila not to get emotional about her son's announcement that evening. Addison's calm influence on her later in their bedroom made her admit that she had been thinking foolishly. Of course they would want their own home now that they were a family, she realized.

"Well, I have a lot of nursery furnishings on my hands," she declared.

"Sheila, dear—you've always been so impatient! You've got Joy, Jane, and Angela who will sooner or later have a need for it."

"Oh, I don't know, Addison. But at least I finally became a grandmother!"

"Sheila—I think I know why I fell in love with you. You're all the things I'm not. We're so different it's no wonder that no one thought our marriage would last. But we fooled them didn't we?"

A slow smile lit her face. "Only because you're a saint, Addison, to put up with me."

Davy Dawson ran the blockade, hitting the Georgia coast, and he had no problems as he moved to Cape Fear under the cover of darkness. He presented the letter to Kip. Kip was ready to leave—he hadn't been able to make his runs on the *East Wind* and he'd lost Paddy, who had died three weeks after Stormy and Jason left. Marcie had seen how devastated Kip was—he was living in utter frustration.

So they gathered up their belongings and left Kip's cottage at midnight to board Davy's *Southern Belle*. Kip admired the clever English sea captain as he maneuvered to get through the blockades. He had done this many times, and as Kip got to know Dawson, he came to like this arrogant, reckless Englishman very much.

It was smooth sailing aboard the *Southern Belle*. Kip, who had been a boatman all his life, had never crossed an ocean—nor had Marcie—so the voyage was exciting for both of them.

Arriving in London and being reunited with their daughter and Jason was the most wonderful thing that had happened to them since they'd spent so much time with her and Jason back in the early spring. Seeing their granddaughter for the first time was a moment they'd never forget.

The calm English countryside was like a tonic to Kip and Marcie. Jason offered Kip a job at the shipping lines which he gratefully accepted—he had no idea how long they'd remain in England.

Three weeks after their arrival, Kip found himself working with his son-in-law. He and Marcie settled in their own cottage not far from Stormy. Marcie quickly adjusted to her new life in the English countryside.

It was wonderful for them to see Stormy so often. And for Kip, it was satisfying to be working daily. He hadn't been able to make his usual runs back home for many weeks. Like a lot of people in Southport, he and Marcie were apprehensive now about what the future held. It was a far more relaxed atmosphere here in Stormy's new country.

One afternoon Marcie went over to visit Stormy, who always welcomed her company. She was happy to see that Marcie seemed so content. "You like it here, don't you, Marcie?"

"My nerves have finally settled down, Stormy. Being idle was also telling on your pa, too. But his hands were tied, so time hung heavily. Of course, Paddy's death hit him hard, as I'm sure you know."

"I want you to stay here in England," Stormy declared.

"That will depend on your pa, honey. I'm happy wherever Kip is. And being with you has been so wonderful for me, Stormy. It was lonely in that cottage without you around," Marcie confessed.

"Persuade Pa to stay, Marcie, and he'll get to see his second grandchild arrive. I haven't even told Jason yet, but I'm sure I'm expecting again," she said happily.

"Oh, Stormy—how wonderful! I must say that could be enough to make Kip want to remain here," she said with a smile.

"Caution him to say nothing to Jason just yet, Marcie."

Marcie promised—and then she prepared to leave for her own cottage.

Jason and Kip left the shipping offices at the same time and Jason dropped him by his cottage before he traveled on to his place.

Jason already suspected his beautiful, green-eyed wife might be expecting again—she had that special glow about her. He knew every soft curve of her body so well—for the last two weeks he was sure he felt a slight change in her.

He'd seen certain changes in the little stowaway he'd first met back in Carolina and yet, some things about Stormy had never changed. She was still the honest, unpretentious girl that he'd fallen in love with. He never wanted his beautiful lady to change.

Lord Addison and Lady Sheila were delighted at the miraculous changes in Jason. He was doing a fine job running the shipping lines. Addison had no reason to make the trip into London as Jason had taken full charge.

Lady Sheila swelled with pride when she saw what a doting father he was with little Marceline. She knew it was a glorious marriage—he and Stormy still had the look of love about them.

Jason's passion was now the girl he first called Princess—no longer the sea or his schooner!

His instincts told him this baby would be a son. Stormy had named their daughter so he intended to name this baby—he was certain Stormy would grant him that wish.

The baby would be named Addison Monihan Hamilton and Jason would call him Andy.

Eight months later, the baby made its arrival on a bitter winter's night. London was having the worst ice storm it had had for years. Jason was forced to deliver his son because the doctor wasn't able to travel.

Jason recalled saying on the night Marceline was born that he'd never have a moment as special as that one. How wrong he had been!!

Bringing young Andy into the world gave him a feeling of exaltation he would not have believed possible. Stormy had felt no fear because the doctor wasn't there since Jason was tending to her.

As always, she'd felt safe and secure in Jason's tender and devoted love!